Maisey Yates is a *New York Times* bestselling author of over one hundred romance novels. Whether she's writing stories about strong, hard-working cowboys, dissolute princes or multigenerational families, she loves getting lost in fictional worlds. An avid knitter, with a dangerous yarn addiction and an aversion to housework, Maisey lives with her husband and three kids in rural Oregon. Check out her website: maiseyyates.com

Reese Ryan writes sexy, emotional love stories with family drama, career dilemmas, and a cast of complicated characters. Connect with Reese, award-winning author of the fan-favourite Bourbon Brothers series, @ReeseRyanWrites via Facebook, Twitter, Instagram or TikTok, or at ReeseRyan.com. Join her VIP Readers Lounge at bit.ly/VIPReadersLounge. Check out her YouTube show where she chats with fellow authors at bit.ly/ReeseRyanChannel

D1439700

ONE NIGHT RANCHER

MAISEY YATES

A COWBOY KIND OF THING

REESE RYAN

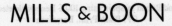

ISBN 978-0-263-31751-0

0123

MIX
Paper | Supporting
responsible forestry
FSC C007454

This book is produced from independently certified FSC™ paper
to ensure responsible forest management.

For more information visit www.harpercollins.co.uk/green

MILLS & BOON

First Published in Great Britain 2023
by Mills & Boon, an imprint of HarperCollins*Publishers* Ltd
1 London Bridge Street, London, SE1 9GF

www.harpercollins.co.uk

HarperCollins*Publishers*
Macken House, 39/40 Mayor Street Upper,
Dublin 1, D01 C9W8, Ireland

One Night Rancher © 2023 Maisey Yates
A Cowboy Kind of Thing © 2023 Harlequin Enterprises ULC.

Special thanks and acknowledgement are given to Reese Ryan for her contribution to the *Texas Cattleman's Club: The Wedding* series.

ONE NIGHT RANCHER

MAISEY YATES

To Nicole Helm, who is always here for my 11:11 texts and stories of visits I've had with birds. There is infinite value in having a friend who just gets you.

One

"You have to spend the night in the hotel if you want to buy it. Because they had too many people back out. Isn't that completely wild, Grandpa? I mean, I'm sure that it is haunted. Nothing can be around that long and not be."

Cara Summers looked up at her grandfather. He was sitting on the shelf behind the bar. In an old Jack Daniel's bottle.

Just as he had asked.

Cara had done her very best to fulfill his last wishes. Cremated and then placed on that shelf behind the bar so he could see everything.

He didn't answer her question.

At least not audibly. She didn't expect him to. Though she often felt his presence. It wasn't anything she could really describe. But she knew he was there. It was why she talked to him. Almost as easily as she had when he was here. Hell, maybe it was even easier because he didn't interrupt.

"The bar is empty, scrap. Who are you talking to?"

She knew the voice. She didn't have to turn.

Even if she didn't recognize the tone—and of course she would, after this many years of friendship. It was the way it made her feel. Because that was the thing. Jace Carson was one of six brothers. They all sounded relatively similar. Deep, rich male voices. But not a single one of them made goose bumps break out over her arms or made a suspicious warmth spread all through her body when they spoke. No. That would be way too convenient. Kit Carson liked to flirt with her, or at least he had before he had married Shelby Sohappy. And Flint enjoyed flirting with her to rile Jace up. But she knew that none of it was serious. Well. She had a feeling that any number of the Carson brothers would've happily had a dalliance with her if she was of a mind. They weren't exactly known for their discernment when it came to women. Every one of them except for Jace. Oh, Jace wasn't discerning either. But Jace was…

He was not interested in her that way. And just the mere suggestion of it made him growl.

They were friends. Best friends. Had been since middle school. It was a funny friendship. He was protective of her. And sometimes a little bit paternalistic. Or brotherly. But that was the thing. He saw her as a younger sister. The younger sister he no longer had, she knew.

And in some ways, she was an emotional surrogate for what he had lost when he had lost Sophia. She knew that. She'd always known it.

Every so often these days it made her feel bristly and annoyed.

Because the problem with Jace was that she wanted him.

And he didn't want her.

"Just telling Grandpa about my next move."

"Right," he said looking around the bar. "Is he here now?"

"He's always here," she said, gesturing to the make-shift urn.

"Cara…"

"I know you don't believe in any of this. But I do. I believe that I can talk to him. And that he hears me."

"I'm sure that's comforting."

"I think that sounds more condescending and less accepting than you think."

"I don't mean to be condescending. But I don't really mean to be accepting either. Just… I can understand why you need to think it, I guess."

That was Jace. He just didn't have a fantastical bone in his body.

He himself was a wonder. A masculine wonder. Over six foot but with broad shoulders, a well- muscled chest and not a spare ounce of fat over his six-pack abs.

He had a square jaw and compelling mouth with the thin white scar that ran through his upper lip. His nose was straight, his eyes the color of denim. Each Carson brother was sort of the same man in a different font, a remix of very similar and very attractive features.

It seemed kind of unfair that all six of them were just there. Exposing the female populace to their overwhelming male beauty. But there they were.

The really unfair thing was that none of their particular beauty called to her the way that Jace's did.

When she had been a kid, the first time she'd met him, it was like the hollow space had opened up inside of her chest, just to make room for the sheer enormity of the feelings that he created within her.

She could still remember that moment.

She'd been so angry. And so hurt. Wearing one of her oversize T-shirts to school, her grandfather's wristwatch, a pair of secondhand sneakers and jeans with holes in the knees. She had a brand-new pink binder that her grandfather had gotten her, and she knew that it had been a big deal. There were so many years where the bar that her grandpa owned—The Thirsty Mule—barely made ends meet, particularly back then. The downtown of Lone Rock had been functionally dead in the early 2000s. All the way up until the 2010s, and there just hadn't been a whole lot of money to go around.

Most of the shops back then had signs in the window that they were for sale or rent, while they sat empty.

Not only that, her grandpa just hadn't known what to do with a young granddaughter that he had taken in a few years earlier.

He loved her. Fiercely. But he had all sons, and his wife was long gone. And the gesture of buying her the pink Trapper Keeper that she had wanted so much had been… It had meant the world to her.

But there was a group of girls at the school who lived to terrorize her. For being tall and skinny and flat chested. For not being cool at all. For the fact that half of her clothes were men's, and certainly weren't in fashion. For her long blond hair, her freckles, her horse teeth…

She was occasionally amused by those memories. Because suddenly at age sixteen her boobs had come in, and when they had come in, it had been a real boon. She was stacked now, thank you very much. And it turned her a pretty impressive amount in tips on a nightly basis at the bar.

Whatever.

She thought maybe she should feel a little bit guilty that sometimes she wore a low-cut top to collect a bit more cash. But then she thought of the girl that she had been in seventh grade. The one who'd had *president of the itty-bitty titty committee* written on the outside of her locker door. And then she pulled the tank top lower and leaned toward the patron with a big smile. Everybody had their childhood trauma.

But, her breast boon notwithstanding, she could clearly remember when that same group of girls had taken that light Trapper Keeper with its beautiful white butterflies and tossed it into the dirt.

And one of the boys on the football team had held her back while they'd made sure that it was irreparably torn and stained.

She hadn't let them see her cry. No, she turned around and punched the boy right in his face. And then she got sent to the principal's office. For fighting.

"What was I supposed to do? He was holding on to me."

"You're supposed to go and get a teacher," the principal had said, maddeningly calm.

"Why wasn't a teacher there to help?"

"They can't be everywhere at once. You can't retaliate. You have to get help."

She had decided that was bullshit. Then and there. She had burned with anger.

And in fact, had said as much to the principal. "That's bullshit."

"Young lady, we can't tolerate that language."

And that was how she had found herself suspended, because she had thrown even more language in the principal's direction. And the funny thing was, she had just been channeling her grandpa and the way he talked on any given Sunday.

But then, that was the root of the problem. Everything about her was wrong. Wrong on some level. She said the wrong words, and more, the wrong things. She didn't know how to be a girl. Whatever that meant. Except that she knew that she wasn't even in the same species as those other girls. And not just because she wasn't a bitch. They had really been bitches. They were *still* bitches.

But she had ended up crying down by the river behind the school. Not sure how she was going to go home and tell her grandfather that she was suspended for a week.

And she was trying to wash the dirt off the binder, scrubbing at it in the water, trying to find a way out of her misery.

And that was when he'd appeared.

He'd been in eighth grade. Tall and lanky at the time, with shaggy blond hair. His family had only come to town a couple of years before, and any other family would have still been considered new. But while the Carsons hadn't lived in Lone Rock for a few years, they owned land there and were part of the original founding families, so they were considered foundational, not new.

"*Hey,*" he said. "*What's the matter?*"

"*Nothing,*" she said. "*Well. Everything. First of all, middle school is bullshit.*"

"*Right,*" he said. "*No argument from me. Why are you crying?*"

"*I got suspended. Because these girls ruined my*

binder. And this boy was holding on to me so that I couldn't stop them. So I punched him in the face."

"Good," he said, nodding decisively.

"Then I told the principal that I thought middle school was bullshit."

"And that's why you're suspended?"

"Yes."

"It all sounds reasonable to me. Not the suspension. Everything you did. The question is, why didn't it seem reasonable to the principal?"

"I can't answer that."

"I'm Jace Carson. What's your name?"

And she suddenly felt shy and self-conscious. Because he was an older boy. And he was just so... Cute. And older boys, or boys her age, or really any boys, never talked to her.

"I'm Cara Summers. But I warn you. I'm not cool. And they call me horse teeth. And if you talk to me, they probably won't think you're cool either."

"Seventh graders? I'm fine with that."

He had walked her home. He had helped her explain the situation to her grandpa. And then he had helped with some chores around the property.

He told her a couple days later, after he came by to visit and finish some of the work, she reminded him of his sister.

He hadn't explained any of that then.

But later, about six months into their friendship, he told her that he had a sister who would be her age now. One who had died when she was a little girl. "You remind me of her. Makes me want to look out for you. The way that I looked out for her."

And that was it. They had really been best friends ever since then. Through a whole lot of things.

She'd admired him, for years. Just looked up to him like he was a god.

And she felt weird and possessive, and hadn't particularly liked it when he had girlfriends.

Not that he ever had them for all that long.

And she knew that when he was out riding in the rodeo he did a lot of casual hooking up. But she just did her best not to think about that.

It wasn't until one night at the bar, when she had been back there helping her grandpa, that she had really watched him putting the moves on a woman. He had his hand on her hip, and then he'd let it drift slowly up to her waist, and Cara had felt a physical, visceral response to it.

And that was when she'd realized.

It was when she'd realized that she wasn't just possessive. She didn't just admire him.

She was attracted to him.

She wanted him to touch her like that.

And she thought about saying something. About asking him if he would be her… It was so embarrassing. If he would be her first. Because she trusted Jace, so, it seemed like a pretty reasonable idea.

But then her grandpa had died. And that had been one of the single most devastating, destabilizing things that had ever happened. And in the four years since, she had done her level best to build herself back up. To take the bar and build it up. And handily, Lone Rock was having a bit of a boom, a resurgence. People were enjoying traveling locally, taking road trips, spending time in small towns.

There were all these posts that went up on the internet. These most charming small town posts, and Lone Rock was almost always there, as an 1800s gold rush town that still had original Western facades on a bunch of the buildings. With outlaw lore deeply embedded into the dirt all around, it was an attractive place for people to come and visit. Which was why she was now ready to invest in the hotel property. She wanted to reopen it. She wanted to get it online. It was haunted, that was the thing. And ghost stays were incredibly popular.

It was just that there had been three buyers that had backed out, and now the seller—who didn't live in Lone Rock—was demanding that potential buyers spend at least one night there to prove that they could handle it. To prove that they knew what they were getting into.

She wasn't afraid. In fact, she loved that stuff. It was just the idea of spending the night there alone…

It didn't really appeal.

But that was future Cara's problem. Right now, she had a bar to run, and Jace was here.

"What brings you in?" she asked.

"Beer. And a burger. I figured I would try to miss the evening rush. It's too hard to talk to you when you've got all those bros crowded around the bar drooling on you."

She rolled her eyes. It was the funny thing about her relationship with Jace. It wasn't like they didn't acknowledge those kinds of things. He talked about men panting after her all the time and was often growling at his brothers when they made commentary that was specifically designed to rile him up.

And she often talked about the way women acted like fools around him.

But they didn't make it personal. It wasn't about what he thought about her. But what other men thought.

And of course she never shared any actual details about her love life.

Well. Probably because she didn't have one.

That was irrelevant.

"Nobody drools," she said. "And even if they did, I don't mind if they leave tips."

"Yeah. Well, the place has become awfully popular."

"It's definitely different than it used to be."

"Too bad Mitch never got to see it."

"Of course he sees it," she said. "Like I said. He's here all the time."

"So you're telling me that his spirit lives on, and he's still hanging out in the shitty bar?"

"That's back to what I'm telling you. Anyway, I was just telling him about the hotel."

"You still fixating on that?"

"Yes. I'm going to until I get to buy it. There's just one weird little hoop to jump through. There were a couple of other offers in, but they fell through, because when they were looking around the place, there was some stuff that was... A little disconcerting. So now the owner is demanding that somebody spend the night there before they put in an offer. So... I'm gonna spend the night."

"You're gonna spend the night in the hotel? Why?"

"Because it's haunted. That's what I mean, people keep backing out because there's all this haunting stuff. I guess he's come close to selling it twice, and they were about to sign the papers when something spooky happened. So..."

"So you have to spend the night in the place to prove that you're not going to back out on the sale?"

"Yep."

"That's the dumbest thing I've ever heard. Why is he letting people with overactive imaginations cause so much grief? And why give any credence to it?"

"It works in my favor—it gave me enough time to get all my finances together. Anyway, I *want* it to be haunted," she said. "I can get it on the national list of most haunted places in the United States. People come from all over to stay in haunted hotels. It's something they're fascinated by."

"I don't want to stay in a haunted hotel. Because that's how I know the owner is a pancake short of a full stack."

"So you think I am not playing with a full deck?"

"I think that you are a bull short of a herd."

"Rude."

He shrugged. "Sorry if you don't like it."

"I don't think you are. I think you're always far too happy to give out your opinion."

"Oh well. You keep me around. Did you put my order in with the kitchen?"

She groused, but punched his burger order in at the register, then went over to the tap to pull a draft beer for him. She knew what he liked. She didn't have to ask. She had it in the glass, and he took a seat at the bar. There were only three other patrons inside, and they were in the corner next to the jukebox, not listening to anything that was happening over at the bar, from her conversation with Jace to her earlier conversation with her grandpa.

"It would be nice not have to be at the bar all day every day. If I make some money with the hotel, I can hire more people."

"Except, it's a huge additional expense."

"I know that. I've saved up for it. I can afford it. Especially if I can get it to a certain capacity during the high tourist times. But there's just not much in the way of lodging around here. Yeah, there's vacation rentals, but the only other hotels are thirty to forty minutes away. Hotel right downtown would really be something."

"You know, if you need money…"

"I'm not taking your money. I've basically been taking your charity since eighth grade, and I have no interest in continuing to do it," Cara said.

"It's not charity. It's friendship. Anyway. When are you fixing to spend the night in the hotel?"

"Tomorrow night. I'd… I don't know. There's no real furnishings in there. It's going to be a little bit… Bracing." She wrinkled her nose.

"I don't really like the idea of you staying in a big empty insecure place by yourself. Especially not when some people might know that you're staying there," Jace said.

"I stay at the place I *live* by myself all the time."

"I don't know. This just feels different to me. I'm not comfortable with it. I should stay there with you."

"That's fine," she said, ignoring the slight jumping in her stomach when he offered that.

She had spent the night with Jace any number of times. Mostly camping. But, what would this be if not camping? They would end up bringing sleeping bags and probably a space heater.

It would just be like all the things they'd done when they were kids.

"Yeah, all right. That sounds good. In fact, now the burger's on the house."

"Why? You don't have to pay me to stay with you. I want to keep you safe."

"You get a free burger because you're submitting yourself to going on a ghost journey with me. And I know how much you hate that stuff."

"Please don't tell me you actually think that it's haunted."

"I think it might be. It stands to reason. It's historic. There were so many gunfights in this town back in the day…"

"Why are you talking to me about ghosts like there's anything logical about them? Come on. It's ridiculous, Cara, and I think on some level you must know that."

"I do not. It is as reasonable and logical as anything else in this world, Jace. And you know what, you'll see. I think that we will have a haunting."

"I don't think so."

"If we don't, it'll be because he's scared away by all your skeptic energy."

"Well isn't that convenient. An even better reason for you to have me out. Because if you don't see a ghost, you can blame me."

"Don't be silly, Jace. I always blame you."

Two

"She thinks it's haunted," Jace said, looking at his brothers that night as they sat around the table outside at the Carson family ranch.

Their mom had ordered a big spread from the barbecue place on the outskirts of town, and they were all enjoying a meal together. Well, everybody except Buck, who hadn't been home in nearly a decade. But the rest of them were there, including Chance and Kit and their wives. Callie wasn't there, because she lived in Gold Valley with her husband, but that was a different sort of absence than Buck's.

Callie wasn't home because she had a life. A happy, functional life. Buck wasn't home because he was a mess.

And what they had around the table was like a strange, evenly divided set of teams. Kit and Chance, settled with their wives, done with the rodeo. Flint and Boone, single, happy about it and definitely not done punishing their bodies on the circuit.

They were all very certain in those things.

And for some reason, more and more, Jace wasn't.

He had never been one to wallow in uncertainty. Or even entertain it. You couldn't do that as a bull rider. You needed a clear eye, a firm grip and some big balls. And he had all three, thanks. It wasn't uncertainty, more a feeling of the world shifting, and it being harder to plant one foot in Lone Rock and one in the rodeo.

A sense that he was going to have to pick.

Maybe it had to do with Cara buying the hotel. Watching her commit to this life so deeply.

"And you're spending the night with her?" Boone asked, a sly smile curving his lips.

"I spend the night with Cara all the time."

He ignored the looks that he got from all of his brothers. And he ignored the fact that it was a lie. He and Cara had camped occasionally together when they were kids and hadn't really done that as adults, but, whatever.

She was his friend.

And really, more like a sister.

He could still remember the first time he'd ever met her. Crying but angry. So angry. And he had just loved that spirit. That great fighting spirit that she had.

It had drawn him to her right away.

And it had just made him want to… Protect her. Protect her in a way that he had never been able to protect Sophia…

"Oh yeah. Adult sleepovers?" That question came from Kit, who got an elbow in the chest from his wife.

"No," he said. "Because we're friends. And unlike

you assholes, I actually don't see it as a conflicting thing to have a platonic friendship with a woman. Because I see her as a whole human being and not a sex object." His sisters-in-law, Juniper and Shelby looked at each other, and then they applauded.

"Thank you," he said to them.

"Our husbands are animals," said Shelby.

"And jackasses," said Juniper.

"I know that," said Jace. "I really don't know how the two of you put up with them."

"They're hot," said Shelby.

"Well," said Jace, frowning. "That kind of bums me out. Next time, don't take it there."

"Sorry," said Shelby, grinning.

"The point of the story," said Jace, "is that she thinks the place is haunted."

"And you don't?" Flint asked.

"I don't believe in that shit. You can't tell me that… I mean, come on."

"There's a lot of things in the world that can't be explained," said Kit. "I would never presume to know whether or not there were ghosts."

"I would," said Jace. "I presume it. You can't see it, you can't measure it, you can't prove it."

"You can't disprove it," Boone pointed out.

"Oh, shut the hell up, Boone," said Jace. "That's not a valid point and you know that."

"Seems valid enough to me."

"I don't see why you're all so invested in harassing me about Cara, anyway. She's been my best friend since middle school."

"It's because it makes you mad," said Boone. "It's that

simple. And you fall for it every time, little brother. It's one of my favorite things about you."

He scowled. It really was a bitch being the youngest out of these jackasses. Well, the youngest except for Callie.

Callie had come much later, her parents hoping for another girl after the loss of Sophia.

But he was the youngest boy, and often the subject of quite a bit of harassment. Which was fine. It was just that he wished he wasn't such a chronic youngest that he fell for it.

But maybe that was one reason that Cara had felt so important to him when they had first met.

She filled the gap in the family. A gap in his life.

He had that other person, right there. He loved his sister Callie. But she was a *baby* sister.

Sophia had been close in age, and Cara was more like that.

He had just... He had just missed Sophie so damn much. That dynamic they had. Then he'd met Cara.

"Well, alternatively, you could all grow up."

Boone grinned. A big, broad smile that made Jace want to punch him. "I know you are but what am I?"

So he did punch him. Just in the shoulder.

"You're the worst."

"I know," said Boone.

And the thing was, maybe nobody would ever understand his relationship with Cara. He needed it. She was maybe the single most important person in his life, as much as he loved his family.

She had needed him, and that mattered to him.

Because the rest of his family... It wasn't the same.

His parents needed Callie in a particular kind of way, because she had healed them.

They had needed Buck, who would then abandon them. And their older sons had taken on a lot of the burden.

Their father was so into the rodeo, and they all rode in the rodeo. It was just there was an excess of them.

So one of them wasn't particularly more important than the other in all of that.

But as far as Cara went? She needed him.

He looked out across the table, at the barn, and saw a bright white butterfly land on the bright red wood. It fluttered its wings for a second before it lifted off again and continued on his way. That moment sort of reset his thoughts, cleared them out.

He wanted to help her and he… Dammit, he worried about her making a big business move like this without him around. There would be repairs needing done, and systems to set up…

She needed him, and he guessed on some level he needed to be needed. Which was why he was submitting himself to the ridiculous ghost thing—even though all of that made him irrationally angry—and why he wasn't going to let his brothers make him too angry with all their nonsense.

As far as they went, their nonsense didn't matter.

What mattered was Cara.

And making sure she was taken care of. So that was exactly what he would do.

The old hotel building was beautiful. It was at the very end of Main Street. A three-story building with balconies and wooden porch rails. Old Western lettering that said Lone Rock Hotel. She could imagine it repainted. The gold around the border of the letters brightened.

She could imagine it lit up bright in the night. Filled with guests.

It would be like…

Almost like a family.

She shook that intrusive thought off. She hadn't expected it. And it wasn't particularly welcome.

Then she heard the sound of an old truck pulling up to the place and she turned and saw Jace.

"Hi," she said, even though he was still in the truck. She waved, so that he knew that she had greeted him.

She immediately felt kind of silly.

She cleared her throat and tucked her hair behind her ear.

She still felt like a lanky, gangly teenage girl around Jace sometimes. And that was silly. But then… The whole thing with him was often silly. She was comfortable with him. More comfortable than any other living human being. But at the same time, there were moments of intense awkwardness. Moments where she was so deeply aware of what she felt.

And in those moments she became unbearably self-conscious. In a way she just… Never was around other men. She thought it was funny that she tended to make them self-conscious. She wasn't overly concerned with her appearance, and she didn't spend a ton of time on it. But, she liked to put on a little bit of makeup and enjoyed a little bit of cowgirl bling. Studded belts and tank tops with a little bit of rhinestone energy.

She liked the attention that got her.

She never worried one way or another if random men

thought she was pretty. If they did, great. If not, she didn't care.

And yet, all that insecurity came back to her sometimes when she stood there looking at Jace. And she could never really quite reconcile all of those things. The fact that in general she was more confident than she had ever been and the fact that she was often the most comfortable around him. Then also the least.

He got out of the truck, and she shoved all of those things off to the side.

"I hope you brought a sleeping bag," she said.

"Yeah I did," he said.

"I brought a space heater too," she responded. "You know ghosts can really bring down the temperature."

She watched his facial expression as he made the clear, deliberate decision to ignore her ghost comment. "Are we meeting anybody?"

"Other than ghosts?"

"Cara."

She smiled. "No. We got sent a code to open up a lockbox on the back door. So let's go hunting for it."

She went around back and she could hear his footsteps as he followed her.

She felt unbearably self-conscious of the fact that he might be watching her.

She banished that. It was Jace. They were friends. Maybe it was the strangeness of spending the night with him, but it wasn't like they had never done that before. Of course they had.

It had just been a long time, because they were grown-ass people, and they didn't tend to have sleepovers anymore. Or camping trips.

But they had. This was hardly singular.

"How did the rest of the night go last night?" he asked.

"Just fine. Like always. I know it's a shock to you, Jace, but my world turns just fine when you aren't there."

He looked at her. And it was far too clear a look.

For some reason, her stomach went tight, and she had the vague impression that maybe he could see into what had happened last night after she had gone home. No. She refused to think that. She refused to even entertain that thought. Because, if at three in the morning she had finally stumbled home and gotten into the shower, and if, when she had started to run her hands over her body as the water had cascaded over her curves, she had had a few moments where she had let herself imagine that they were Jace's hands skimming over her skin, and then maybe she had some trouble falling asleep, and she had taken those erotic thoughts to her bed with her and let them carry her off to a natural conclusion...

She really did try not to think of him that way. Yeah, it was one thing to think that he was hot; it was quite another to have actual, full-blown sexual fantasies about him, which just felt intrusive and wrong, and she always felt quite guilty after.

And she only ever did it on nights when she was really exhausted, and good sense had deserted her and...

Whatever... She supposed that she could justify that all she wanted, and the end result would still be the same. It was sort of shitty to think about your best friend like that.

And here she was, thinking about her best friend like that. Again. While he was standing right there. She cleared her throat and aggressively undid the padlock that contained the key, typing the code in with a lot more force than was strictly necessary. And then she pushed the door open and exhaled.

It was beautiful in here. She had come inside one time when she was a kid, and her grandfather had been looking at the property. It had been a pipe dream to buy it then. There had been absolutely no way. There wasn't enough tourism in town to make it worth it, and they had been financially strapped as it was.

But it had been his dream. And ever since then, it had been hers. Other than the one time they had gone inside to look at the place, she had only ever seen it from the outside looking in, and in pictures. But even now, dusty and in a bit of disrepair, it was the most beautiful place she had ever seen.

The floors were real wood, the drapes might be full of dust and mites and God knew what else, but they were beautiful.

They would just need some cleaning.

A deep rich red, with velvet damask. The wallpaper was lovely, but would definitely need to be replaced with something authentic. It was too water-stained to be restored, she had a feeling, and anyway, it would be less expensive to simply replace it all. But the original front desk was still there, a beautiful oak that needed to be oiled—she knew all about that, because the original bar from the 1800s was still in The Thirsty Mule, and she had ample experience at taking care of it.

There was a big crystal chandelier that hung in the center of the room, and it was the thing that gave her the biggest thrill.

The entire hotel had been outfitted with electricity and indoor plumbing by the 1920s, and it was currently such a glorious mix of all the errors that had come after and the original foundation. She loved each and every layer of history.

Enough that for a moment, it had knocked her out of her Jace haze. But only for a moment.

She turned and realized that he hadn't followed her inside. And then a moment later, there he was, holding both sleeping bags, the space heater and the bag of groceries that she had brought, so that they would be able to eat something tonight.

"I like it," he said, looking inside. "Slumber party snacks."

They weren't just snacks—she had a whole charcuterie situation in there, but she couldn't find any wit rolling around in her head right now.

For some reason the words *slumber party* made her fidgety.

"You know me. I don't like to be hungry."

"Who does?"

"Well, no one I assume, but not everybody will launch a feudal war over hunger pangs. But you know I will."

"That is true."

"Anyway. This is it. Isn't it great?"

"It is a lot of space. Just this room is a lot of space. Empty space."

"I'm not destitute, Jace. I pretty obsessively squirrel money away, actually. Anyway, Grandpa had a life insurance policy, and I've got that socked away in savings too. I've been living with my belt tightened so that I can get this place. But I have it all planned."

"Yeah, and you're secretive too."

"I haven't talked to you about it because I knew that you would be… This," she said, gesturing toward him.

And then he did something that shocked her. He

reached out, wrapped his hand around her wrist and made that same gesture but practically up against his chest, all over again. "What is… All this?"

The way that his calloused fingers felt against her wrists sucked all the air out of her body. She felt like she was gasping. She felt like she was losing her mind. And she couldn't remember what she had been about to say. Because he had touched her, and she hadn't been expecting it. It wasn't that they didn't touch. They did, casually enough on occasion. But there was usually a flow to it, or something that felt slightly mutual. This was combined with her fantasies last night, and the fact that they were in the hotel now…

"You're a skeptic," she said quickly, suddenly finding the words and retrieving them from deep inside of her brain. "About everything. And I needed to be able to dream about this. If I wanted skepticism, I would ask for skepticism. But I don't want skepticism. I wanted to be able to believe that something magical could happen. That I could fulfill this long-held wish that my grandfather had… And you know what, I needed to be able to believe wholly in it and in myself in order to make it happen."

"You are perilously close to sounding like one of those self-help gurus that I hate. You were practical. You worked hard. It's hardly manifesting."

"You know what, I don't see what harm manifesting does?" She was getting irritated at him, and that felt welcome. Necessary even. "You're so skeptical about everything—this is my point. There is no way that thinking negative thoughts is actually better than thinking positive ones. And I didn't need any doubt to creep in. Yes, I did have to do the work, and I acknowledged that. But

I also needed to believe in order to stay motivated to do it. And you…" She decided that since he had touched her, touching him was fair game. She put her fingertips on his chest and gave him a slight shove. "You are nothing more than a Debbie Downer."

Her fingertips felt like they were burning from where they had made contact with his well-muscled chest, and she realized that it was something that had definitely punished her more than it punished him.

She folded her fingers in and rubbed them against her palm. It wasn't really a punishment, if she were honest. Touching him felt good. It was just that it led to all sorts of other thoughts that didn't have a place to go, and that was what made it all feel like torture. That was the problem.

"Right. Well. I'm sorry that you feel that way. I would've supported you, though. I do support you. And if I try to provide a…counterweight to your buoyancy, it's only because everybody needs a ballast, right?"

"I guess," she said. "I get it. I do. But the thing is, you treat me like I'm a kid. We are like a year and a half apart, Jace. There is no call to treat me like that."

"Yeah, there is," he said, his voice suddenly going gruff. "Where should I put the stuff?"

She knew what he was thinking. She knew what he was going to say. She wasn't going to give him a chance to say it. "Well, I don't know. We have to find a bedroom. We might as well find the best one." They started to walk up the stairs. One of them creaked, but it wasn't so bad.

The carpet on the stairs was somewhat threadbare, and she wondered if it would just be the better part of valor to get rid of all of it and reveal the honey oak beneath.

But there would be a lot of expense involved in re-furbishing the place. Still, it would be worth it. And she could afford it. Really, for the first time in her life, she could afford a dream, and it was brilliant and amazing.

She was not a kid.

And she was definitely not Jace's baby sister. No mat-ter how he acted.

The hallway was long, with numbered doors facing opposite each other. Ten in total. "All right. Let's see what we have."

The first room was entirely barren, with lace cur-tains that barely covered the window, and she decided that unless they had to, that wasn't going to be the room.

The next room was filled with nightstands and ward-robes and other miscellaneous furniture—a dining table and some chairs, all stacked up and filled from back to front. "Well, I guess it's good to know there's some fur-niture left in here. Some of it is probably salvageable. Or at least, we can use the wood for something. There's probably some local artisans that could make something great with it."

"Yeah," he said.

And she could tell that he was biting his tongue. Damn him.

He was trying—that wasn't fair.

"Let's go, so that you don't pull a muscle," she said, carrying on down the hall and opening two more doors, before deciding to open another.

And in that room, there was a bed.

A big bed that was likely full of dust and had a rich brocade bedspread on it. There were canopy curtains and matching velvet curtains over the window. It was set as if it was exactly prepared for guests. A nightstand, wardrobe, a small vanity with a bowl and a picture, which she knew would have been used as a washbasin.

"Well, here we go," she said.

"Look," he said. "I don't even believe in this haunting business, and even I know that if one of the rooms is going to have a ghost in it, it's going to be this one."

"But you don't believe in ghosts," she said. "And I want to see one, so that declaration is hardly a deterrent." She grabbed a sleeping bag out of his hand and looked around the room. "I hope you don't have allergies."

"No. Thankfully. Otherwise living on a ranch would be rough. I can deal with a little bit of dust."

"You can sleep in the bed if you want," she said, grinning at him.

"Yeah. I'll skip it."

Then suddenly, it was way too easy to imagine the two of them in a bed, and she wondered if she had miscalculated by choosing this room.

It was one thing to think about sleeping on the floor with sleeping bags—which they were still going to do—it was just that the fact that they were in a room with a big bed…

She was starting to feel a little bit sweaty. She was starting to feel a little bit shaky. Jittery. And she just didn't have the presence of mind to figure out how to not feel that way.

It's Jace.

This was the problem. It wasn't like this all the time. It was just like this sometimes, and usually for set periods of time. Like, something would happen, there would be a touch, a little bit of something that felt out of the ordinary that brushed up against her hormones, and then she would have a fantasy about him, and then things would feel awkward, but then they didn't usually spend the night in the same bedroom.

"Okay," she said, desperate for a reprieve. "You lay out the sleeping bags and get the space heater going, I'm going to go downstairs and see what I can find in the way of utensils and get some snacks prepared. And, I also brought a bunch of downloaded movies."

"Awesome. See, we don't need ghosts for entertainment. We can entertain ourselves."

Three

He stood there in the middle of the room, completely motionless for a good thirty seconds after Cara left. He could not quite figure out why there was something about his own words that hit him wrong. They could *entertain themselves*.

He also couldn't figure out why his chest still felt electrified where she had put her fingertips.

Things were a little bit weird. And he wasn't quite sure what to make of that. But he did as he was asked. He laid out the sleeping bags at the foot of the bed, then plugged in the space heater between them.

This kind of amused him. It was a little bit like a campfire.

He looked over at the bed. And he ignored the rising tension in his gut. There was no reason to be tense. His idiot brothers had gotten in his head was the thing.

They specialized in that. That was what older brothers did, after all, but what they did not do was understand that Cara was a sacred object.

And Jace was not a man who fucked around with the divine.

No. He knew that he had no call ever taking her out of the category that he'd put her in all those years ago. His best friend. And the woman he wanted to protect more than anything in the whole world.

She'd had it so hard, and he just wanted to shield her from ever having another hard thing happen to her.

She wasn't a woman to him. Not really. She never had been.

Yeah. There had been the unfortunate moment in high school when she… Filled out a little bit and he'd been seventeen—nearly eighteen—and not as experienced as he was now, and it had been a little bit difficult to keep from marveling at the changes that had occurred. But that was teenage boy shit. Dumb shit.

He was a grown man.

He had been riding out on the rodeo circuit since then, and he had a hell of an education in the female form during those years.

He'd also learned a lot about himself.

There was something about having the miraculous beaten out of you at an early age that made it impossible to believe in lasting love and connections. Well, it did him.

His parents had clung together after Sophie had died. They'd had Callie. They'd kept on hoping. He supposed.

Callie, well, she hadn't been alive when Sophia had died, so while she knew, she didn't really know.

Chance and Kit, their love stories were gritty. More

than they were miraculous, he supposed. They had both fallen for incredibly tough women, women who took every opportunity to take them to task when they needed it, and Jace found it amusing as hell.

He was happy that they could do that thing.

But then there was Buck, who had left town under a cloud when he was still in his early twenties. Buck, who clearly couldn't find anything miraculous to hold on to.

And Flint and Boone were as noncommittal as he was in the relationship department. Meaning, they didn't have them. Flint had quite famously broken up with the woman who'd gone on to be a famous country singer. And the song that she'd written about him—when it had hit the airwaves a couple of months ago it had caused a slight explosion.

Granted, she didn't use his name, but everybody knew it was about him. Everybody.

People around Lone Rock were too smart to mention it. But… Yeah, occasionally he and Boone would trawl the online forums looking for things to interrogate their brother about.

"Where is the scarf, Flint?"

"Yeah. Where is it?"

"I don't know what the hell you're talking about," he would growl.

"She claims you kept her scarf."

"Fuck you."

"That reminds me, there was a key chain…"

"There is no key chain," said Flint. *"It's not about me."*

Point being, he was the only one of them that had tried a relationship, and it hadn't gone well. Boone sure as hell wasn't stupid enough to even try.

He just didn't have it in him. He thought you had to be some kind of crazy to invest in a relationship like that. You had to be some kind of starry-eyed, and a hell of a lot of things he just wasn't.

He would never drag a woman through that.

He had never wanted to. He had his family, he had Cara, and that was enough.

A moment later, she returned. "Well, I managed to get this all set up." She had a tray of meat and cheese, and two wineglasses, plus a bottle of…

"Rosé?"

"You got a problem with that?"

"A prissy meat and cheese tray and a bottle of girls' night out wine?"

She stared at him blandly. "Not when there's no one else here."

She sniffed as she settled onto her sleeping bag and set the tray out in front of her. "Your toxic masculinity is strangling you to death."

"No." He settled down on his own sleeping bag and reached out and took a wedge of cheese. "It would be if I refused to partake. But here in the sacred space…"

"You're an idiot," she said.

"Yeah. Probably."

"Are you going back out to the rodeo?"

He had been avoiding that direct question. Not even his brothers had asked. Boone and Flint were still at it, but Buck had left a long time ago, with Kit and Chance retiring recently.

Jace was younger than Boone and Flint, but he knew he was getting to about the age where you had to start considering how many permanent injuries you wanted to walk around with for the rest of your life all for the sake of chasing continued glory.

He liked a little glory, it was true, but he also valued the fact that he didn't walk with a limp, and the longer you stayed in the game the less likely that was to continue to be a thing.

Their father was on the verge of retirement, and he didn't know that any of them were chomping at the bit to become the next Rodeo Commissioner. Or maybe they were; they hadn't really talked about it. Jace wasn't, that was all he knew. The family was more and more settled in Lone Rock. And maybe that wasn't such a bad thing.

"Don't know," he said.

"You really don't know?"

"I really don't."

"That doesn't seem like you."

"Maybe not," he said, shoving some of his discomfort aside. "I don't know. Stuff is changing. It kind of started with Callie getting married a couple years ago, and now… I don't know. The family's more settled here. For a long time it seemed like my dad was just running. Running from everything. Running from his grief and all of that… But they've expanded the ranch here so much, and I think he's finally ready to quit moving around all the time. At his age, he probably should've done it a long time ago, but given that he's him… I think it might be kind of a big deal."

"That makes you think about change."

"It just makes me wonder what I'm doing. The thing is, we've all won the top tier of all the events that we've ever competed in. There's a point where the only way you can go is down. So then you ask yourself why you're doing it."

"Do you love it?"

It was a strange question. He never really thought about it. Rodeo was the family business. He knew there were spare few people for whom that was true. But since he was a kid, his father had been the Commissioner of the Pro Rodeo Association, and it had been a given that they would all grow up and compete. Callie had competed in saddle bronc events for a couple of years; she was taking a break to have a baby, which was great. That had meant a lot to her, breaking that barrier as a woman, and she had paved the way for a whole lot of other women who wanted to do the same thing.

She had a reason for being there.

Kit and Chance were top in their field. He had done bareback broncos for a number of years; he'd ridden bulls. That was all after he and his brothers had done a little bit of tie-down roping in their early years. He didn't know that he loved it so much as that he wore it comfortably like a pair of battered old jeans. And he didn't know what else fit. Ranching. They had a big family ranch.

But it was an interesting thing to grow up in a family where you didn't wonder what you would be when you grew up. There was a legacy that you inherited, and you stepped into that. But then, Cara knew about that. He doubted she owned the bar because she loved it the most. He could see that this hotel thing meant a lot to her but he had to wonder…

He gestured to the room around them.

"Is this actually something that you want, or is this just what Mitch wanted to do?"

"I actually do want it," she said. "I've loved this place since I was a kid. And yeah, some of it is that it makes me feel good to fulfill his dreams. Because he couldn't.

And he was there for me. He was there for me when no one else in my family was. My dad was… I still don't know where. My mom was where she is now. Drugged out of her mind in a trailer park somewhere making bad decision after bad decision with men. And… I had Grandpa. I don't think I'm doing it just because I want them to be proud or anything like that. I'm doing it because the things that were important to him became important to me. This town became important."

"Yeah."

"I guess I have to ask you the same question. Are you in the rodeo just because it's what your dad wants you to do?"

"No. To be honest, I don't think my dad cares what we do. In fact, I think he would've been perfectly happy if we had never risked life and limb out on the circuit. He loves it, but he's realistic about the risks. Especially after that kid died a couple of years ago… He was never really the same after that. Never looked at the rodeo the same."

And that was a shame. Because the rodeo had been his dad's escape from his grief. Jace knew that, because he understood it. He moved around, and he moved around a lot. Motion kept you from thinking too deep.

But it felt like he was at a critical point. He didn't want to just keep moving. But staying felt like an invitation to settle into pain.

Of course the alternative to that was processing it, but he'd spent years avoiding that.

Years using Cara as a surrogate.

But watching her now, watching her actually take control of her life and get what she wanted shamed him a bit.

"I'm sorry. I know it was your dream…"

"It wasn't," he said. "The rodeo was easily available to us. And we had to do something. But I think it was more than that. It was easy for us to pivot into it because we knew all about it. It must be different when it's your dream. When you have to chase it. It was more like that for Callie, because Dad sure as hell didn't want her out on the horses. Drove him nuts. Still does, to be honest, but he's accepted that is something he's not gonna win with her. He's accepted that is something she's going to do, and she's a grown woman, so you can't stop her. I mean, she married Jake Daniels just to get access to her money."

He'd never anticipated the money. Didn't care about it. Didn't need it.

That shamed him a bit too.

"I never asked, do you all have trust funds like that?"

"Yeah. But we get it when we turn thirty."

"So you're getting yours soon."

He really hadn't thought much about it. He had whatever he needed. He turned quite a lot of money on the circuit; he got in a fair amount of endorsements. He had it pretty easy, honestly.

"Yeah."

"You don't know what you want to do with it?"

"I guess not."

He didn't like that. But then, thinking about the future wasn't his thing. It was that whole… Well, he guessed it was a lot like what she had accused him of. She hadn't wanted to tell him about her dreams because he had the unfortunate inclination to bring reality down on them. And as for himself… He didn't really dream.

"I don't like to think ahead. I live in the moment. I like to work. It's clarifying. In that sense, I guess I do love to ride in the rodeo. You get a surge of adrenaline not like much else. Not really like anything but sex, to be honest."

And then she blushed. All the way up her neck to the roots of her hair. Then it surprised him, because it wasn't like Cara was a prude. She worked in a bar. She heard rough talk all the time. Hell, she wandered around the place looking like *Coyote Ugly* half the time, which she could do without, and men checked her out all evening. She seemed to get a kick out of it. Because she was in control of that interaction, and could bounce their asses out of the bar if they got unruly.

He hadn't expected her to blush just because he mentioned sex. But then he looked behind her and saw the bed, and the earlier tension returned.

"Anyway," he said, clearing his throat. "I didn't really think about what I would do with it. I didn't really think about what I would do when I was done with the rodeo. And anyway, I could coast on that for a few more years if I wanted to."

"You don't want to, though," she said, reaching out and taking a piece of cheese. She seemed to recover slightly from the earlier incident.

But he had to wonder why it had been an incident at all.

"How do you know that?"

"I know that," she said, "because it's not like you to have doubts, and you do. If you're uncertain, and you're pausing, then there's something else going on."

He didn't like that. Didn't like that shifting sand feeling underneath his feet.

It probably had to do with his brothers getting married. It was just a change.

Made him contemplate what things would look like for him, because they wouldn't look like that.

He also didn't love that she could read him so well. He needed to be able to read her. It was important. He had to protect her. Take care of her. Make sure that she was doing all right. The thing was, he had his whole big family. And since her grandfather's death, Cara had nobody. She'd always had fewer people than him. And it made him really important. It made what he did for her really important.

So yeah, he kind of prided himself on knowing what was going on with her, on keeping track of her. On making sure that everything was all right.

But the fact that she seemed to be able to read him... He wasn't sure how he felt about that.

"You know, there are some other shops on Main Street that are being sold. The businesses are still going to be there, but the buildings are up for sale..."

"Are you suggesting that I invest in real estate?"

"It's an idea."

It was. It was also... Roots. Ties. It wasn't like he was planning on leaving Little Rock. No, that didn't really factor into his plans. But he also didn't own land for a reason.

And what exactly is that reason?

He shoved that thought to the side.

"What movie are we opening with?"

"Oh," she said. "You're going to love this." She settled onto her sleeping bag, grabbing her tablet and setting it up on the floor. She rested her elbows on the sleeping bag, and her chin on her knuckles. "I thought that we needed some nostalgia."

"Oh no," he said.

"Do you remember when we skipped school and we drove down to Bend and we went to see our favorite buddy cop movie?"

"No way."

"Yes way."

"You can quote that movie in its entirety. Do you actually need to watch it again?"

"Yes I do. Because you know that if I were a lion and you were a tuna…"

"You're ridiculous," he said. But he did find it endearing. He liked that she enjoyed a raunchy comedy, just as much as he did. Though, this was not his favorite.

"Don't worry," she said. "I also have the terrible dream movie you love so much."

"Thank you."

"And you know, an array of teen movies. From *Mean Girls* to *Easy A*."

"I don't like those movies."

"I know you don't. I don't care. But we'll probably fall asleep before then, because we are not eighteen—we're old."

"Speak for yourself."

"I'm younger than you," she said.

"Yeah," he said, nudging her with his elbow.

She looked at him and wrinkled her nose, and for some reason, he found his eyes drawn to the freckles there.

They were cute. Just a little sprinkling of them that went from her cheeks over the bridge of her nose. They highlighted her green eyes somehow. Beautiful eyes. Slightly feline. She wasn't wearing makeup tonight, so her lashes were pale. Often, she wore a real dark mascara that made her eyes feel like a punch in the gut.

This was more like a slow, spring sunrise. A whole lot of green and gold.

That tension had returned.

"All right. Get the movie going," he said.

"Gladly," she said, pouring a glass of wine and handing it to him, before pouring herself one. He lay back on his sleeping bag and decided to pay attention to the movie, instead of the color of her eyes.

Four

She was just so aware of him. Of every inch of him. The way that he was lying on the sleeping bag, the way that his arm shifted, the way his whole body shifted when he went to take a drink of his wine.

When he grabbed some cheese off the cheese board.

She was starting to feel light-headed, and she had a feeling she needed to go get some more food, so she wasn't off on her alcohol-to-protein ratio. But she found herself drinking a little bit faster the more her nerves flared up in her gut.

This was ridiculous.

But the problem with choosing movies that they had gone to see together in high school was that it reminded her of being in high school with him. That was when her little crush had started acting up. Oh, it wasn't when she had realized that she wanted to sleep with him——

that was a more mature realization. But the butterflies over his arm brushing hers when they sat together in the movie theater… Yeah. That had been pure high school.

And she really wasn't nostalgic for it. And here she was, alone with the man in an empty house—unless there were ghosts, there could be ghosts—as an adult, having those same feelings.

It was almost funny.

It was *almost funny*, that now they were adults, absolutely alone and unsupervised, adjacent to a bed, and she was *still* in no danger of Jace Carson trying to pressure her into sex. No. She was much more likely to try to pressure him into it.

The idea made her feel lit up from the inside out. Entirely too warm. She did her level best to look back at the movie.

The next one was not her favorite. It was too mind-bending and she didn't like it. She liked things that had resolved endings, at least. She would prefer a happy ending. But the ambiguity of it all made her itchy, and she started to get restless.

"I'm going to go downstairs and get another bottle of wine," she said.

"Another bottle of wine?"

"Yes. I think that sounds like a pretty good idea, don't you?"

"Yeah. All right."

She knew it wasn't a great idea. She was already feeling a little bit wobbly and loose, and she was in such a weird precarious place with him it…

Well, she had been friends with the man for thirteen years. It wasn't like she was just suddenly going to break it.

She pondered that when she went to get the package of cupcakes, and the new bottle of wine.

Something crashed to her left and she whipped her head toward the sound and she stopped.

She waited to see if she heard another noise, waited to see if anything else shifted, but all she could hear was her own breathing. Ragged. Too fast.

"For heaven's sake," she muttered to herself.

She was such a mess.

She was being ridiculous because she was tipsy and anticipating ghosts and strung out on Jace. And maybe more wine was the wrong thing, but maybe it was the right thing because she needed to calm down. Maybe if she could loosen up, she'd get her equilibrium back.

She waited a few breaths more and didn't hear anything else, so she took the cake and wine back upstairs.

Jace was sprawled out on the sleeping bag on his back, his arm thrown over his face, his shirt lifted an inch or so, so she could see his flat, toned stomach.

Dear sweet Lord, she needed an intervention. A miracle.

Or maybe just wine.

"I'm back with more," she said, standing over him.

His mouth curved into a smile, his arm still thrown over his face, and she was so fixated on that she never saw his other hand coming.

Suddenly she found herself grabbed at the back of the knee and she shrieked, going down fast. And it was only his muscles that stopped her from crashing to the ground, as he somehow managed to guide her down to the sleeping bag slowly with *one arm*.

"Jace!" she shouted, folding down over the top of him.

He was warm under her.

And hard.

And *oh no*.

She was lying across him, folded at the waist over his chest. She scrambled hard to get off him but not before her hand made contact with his *very firm* ass.

She rolled the rest of the way off him, then scrabbled back for her wine and cake. "Why are you such a child?"

He was reclining, looking at her like...

She had to look away.

"I'm definitely not a child."

"You're immature. I heard a noise downstairs," she said, desperate to not think about the fact he was so very not a child, but clearly a man. "Maybe it was a ghost."

"Well, it wasn't. Because ghosts aren't real. But that cake looks real and I want some."

She still hadn't quite recovered from the full body Jace contact. "I don't know if you can have any because you're being mean."

"I'll take it from you."

He would too. And if there was one thing she could not handle now it was a wrestling match over cake, so she surrendered it, but she did not do it graciously.

And then she poured herself more wine.

They finished his favorite movie and then went on to hers. And she was definitely more than a little tipsy by the time they decided to put in their final comedy about a bunch of high school seniors' quest to lose their virginity.

They'd seen it a hundred times. She had no idea how they'd ever watched it before without her feeling immeasureably uncomfortable.

"Man, I don't miss high school," he said, tipping back his glass of wine. She watched his throat work, watched his Adam's apple bob up and down, and it made her feel a little bit giddy. She looked away.

"Yeah. Wasn't exactly the greatest time of my life either."

It was a lot of feeling weird and awkward. First with a flat chest, then with curves. But weird and awkward all the same.

"It's just the ridiculousness of it all. All the kids who think they're kings and queens. Of what? The cafeteria. It's ridiculous… All the hormones. Maybe back then I should've decided what I wanted to do. But I was too busy worrying about things like that. Granted, I was a senior when I lost my virginity."

She blinked. "*No.*"

Was he about to confess to her that he was an awkward, college virgin? She didn't know what to think about that.

"No. More like a junior."

In *college*? No. That was when she realized he meant…high school. When they'd been friends.

"Why didn't I know that?" she asked, her tongue feeling loose and lazy. And she was annoyed that she had asked that. But she was annoyed that he had mentioned it.

"Did you want me to tell you that I got a fake ID and went to the next town and hooked up with some woman in a bar?"

"You didn't," she said.

"No. Not kidding. That's what I did. I didn't figure that an inexperienced virgin should inflict their inexperience on another virgin, you know what I mean?"

She frowned and wrinkled her nose. "Yeah. Sure."

"I don't know. It just never seemed like the thing to

me. I'm still like that. I don't like to have a fling with
women too close to home."

She frowned. "Right."

They should not be having this weird, wine addled
conversation because she was already in a strange space,
and now she was grumpy with it.

And they were supposed to be watching a comedy.
Granted, one they had watched multiple times before,
but still.

"I've never had sex with a virgin, actually," he said.

And that did something weird to her. To her body.
Her soul.

And she knew, she knew that she needed to stop herself from saying something. She knew that she needed
to get a grip. She knew that none of this whole conversation was about her. Or maybe it was. Maybe it was
about their friendship. The fact that they were now, and
had always ever been friends. So while maybe he hadn't
confessed to his sexual shenanigans when they were
in high school, he didn't think anything of telling her
now. Which… Hurt, actually. He should be a little bit
uncomfortable talking to her about sex. It should make
him imagine having sex with her. She had *great* boobs.

And he was a straight man. Why wasn't he into her
boobs? It wasn't fair. There were all kinds of random
men at the bar who would love to see them. And Jace
just seemed immune. And he was sitting there talking
about sex. Like it was nothing.

"Well," she said, "I guess you're not half the stud that
I thought you were," she said.

"I'm not?"

"Yeah," she said. "I would've thought that you had

sex with all kinds of virgins. Corrupter of innocents and whatever."

"No," he said. "One of the few things I haven't done."

"Well," and she could hear it in her head before it came out of her mouth, and there was some reasonable rational part of her that was crouched in the corner shouting: don't say it, Cara. But that rational, reasonable part of her was drowned out by Wine Cara, who had some opinions and wanted to express them. Wine Cara was a bitch, and later, she and Wine Cara were going to have a stern conversation. But she was just on the ride right now. "If you wanted to have sex with a virgin, I can help you with that."

"Excuse me? Are you offering to find me a virgin through your bar contacts?"

He didn't understand.

She could turn back now.

She didn't.

"No," she said, pushing his shoulder. "If you wanted to have sex with a virgin, just have sex with me."

Five

Jace was frozen. And for a full ten seconds you could've heard a pin drop. Except then suddenly there was a huge crash, and Cara scampered across the distance between them and pressed herself against his chest, her eyes wide. "What the hell was that?"

"I don't know," he said, and he didn't know if he was answering her question about the noise, or if it was about the fact that she had just told him she was a virgin and essentially offered to have sex with him.

His heart was thundering hard, and he told himself it was because of the crash, because it had startled him. And not because Cara was pressed up against him.

Which he told himself was because of the wine. Everything that had just happened was because of the wine. And there was no call getting all worked up about that.

No call getting angry. Or reading too much into it or anything like that.

Except, they probably needed to figure out what that noise was.

"Where did it come from?" she asked.

"I don't know," he said, peeling himself away from her. But the heat from her body remained, and he felt somewhat branded by it all.

"It's probably your ghost," he said. "Didn't you want there to be a ghost?"

"I didn't want it *to scare me*," she said.

Then she looked up at him, her expression dazed. "Oh," she said.

"What?"

"I just told you I was a virgin."

"Let's put a pin in that," he said. "By which I mean let's not talk about it again."

He hadn't really meant to say the last part out loud. But he was a little bit tipsy, and even though the noise had done something to sober them up a bit, it wasn't fully complete.

"Fine then. But let's go see what it is."

She got up and started to pull on his shirt. He pushed himself up, and grabbed hold of her arm. "Whoa. Did it ever occur to you that it might actually be an intruder?"

"No," she said, her eyes wide. "I just thought it was a good old-fashioned haunting."

"What if it isn't?" he said. "That's something to keep in mind. That's why I'm staying with you. What if one of those perverts from the bar knew that you were staying here?"

"That's creepy, Jace," she said. "If I thought that the bar patrons were like that that I wouldn't let them in."

"I don't trust anybody. Bottom line. So stay with me, and we'll go see what it is."

"I can't even tell where it's coming from." Suddenly, there was another crash, and she pressed herself against him, and he became extremely aware of the way her breasts felt against his arm. Firm and full and high. And more than a little bit enticing.

A virgin.

What the hell?

What the hell?

He did not have time to focus on that, because he needed to see what was happening down the hall. Or maybe… He stopped and listened. Maybe down the stairs.

"Did you leave anything open when you went downstairs?"

"No. I didn't open anything."

"Did you hear anything when you went down there?"

"Again," she said, "no. I didn't."

"Come on."

The sound was consistent. And raucous.

"I doubt that's a ghost," she said.

"Oh, because they aren't real?"

"No," she said. "Because it's an easy sound to follow, and anybody who had spent the night here previously could've followed it themselves. I would think that the haunting was a lot more…you know, ambiguous."

"Oh. Ambiguous haunting. As opposed to one of those big, obvious hauntings."

"*Clearly*," she said.

"Come on."

"Do you have like a gun or anything?"

"In a lockbox in my truck, yes. But not in the house."

"But it's where you can get to. If you need to."

"We won't need it. Whatever's going on, I'll finish it hand to hand."

He felt her relax.

"I'll take care of you," he said. "I always take care of you."

And that was when he realized he didn't want her coming toward the noise with him. "I want you to stay here," he said.

And then he turned to face her and felt like he'd been punched in the stomach. She was looking up at him, those pale lashes all spiky, her green eyes searching.

And he couldn't get their previous conversation out of his head.

Except over the top of that he felt a surge of protectiveness.

And without thinking, he reached up and touched her cheek. "Stay here."

Her eyes fluttered closed, and she swayed toward him, just slightly. And everything in him went tight. He took a step back. "I'll be right back."

He went down the stairs and toward the kitchen. The noise was definitely coming from the kitchen. From the pantry.

He heard footsteps behind him and turned sharply. "I told you to wait upstairs," he said.

"I didn't want to," she said.

"I didn't ask what you wanted, Cara. I'm protecting you."

"Well now whatever it is knows we're here," she said. "Because you're being loud."

"You're being loud," he said.

"It's coming from the pantry," she said.

"Yeah. I got that."

He reached out and opened up the pantry door, quickly. And there, inside a flour sack, he saw a big fat ring tail. There was a movement, followed by a cloud of pale white dust, and then a small masked face and two spindly claws appeared over the edge of the bag.

"What the ever-loving hell?"

"It's a raccoon," she said, sounding charmed.

"Those fucking things will eat your face off," he said.

"They're adorable," she said.

"They're menaces," he said. "All right, you little bandit, get out of there."

He was not about to call animal control over one small ring-tailed menace. Hell no. And he didn't think that was just the wine talking. He was going to be able to get it out of there.

"I hope you're happy by the way," he said. "Because I knew there was a very reasonable explanation for why people were hearing noises in the house."

"It's a raccoon," she said. "And a raccoon is not a ghost."

"That is my point."

"No," she said, shaking her head. She wobbled, and he realized that Cara was still a lot more tipsy than he was. "I mean, if it had been a raccoon the whole time, then they would've seen it. But it wasn't a raccoon the whole time. It was a ghost the rest of the time. And it's just a raccoon now."

"Whatever. I would've preferred a ghost, because then we could just have an exorcism or some shit, but it's a raccoon, and now I need to chase it out."

"I want it to be my pet."

"It can't be your pet. Don't be ridiculous." He kept

watch on the creature, which was staring at him with beady eyes, and he reached into the corner of the pantry and picked up her broom. "I will use this on you," he said.

"Are you cleaning up the town, Sheriff?" Cara asked.

"You're drunk. Get out of here."

He supposed that he should feel better knowing that she was drunk. Maybe she had been teasing. About the whole virgin thing. That couldn't be true. She worked at a bar. She looked like... Like that.

And she sure as hell had to have been teasing about... Him.

"All right," he said, talking to the raccoon again as he extended the broom. "Get outta here."

It snarled and leaned forward, chewing on the bristles.

"Get out," he said, brushing at its face.

It growled again, but leaped out of the flour sack, shaking itself off like a dog after a bath, and sending white dust everywhere.

It started to come toward the door of the pantry, and he put his arm out over Cara, moving her to the side as the snarling beast loped out of the pantry and through the kitchen.

"And open the door," he said.

"I mean, the question is, how did it get in?"

"That's a good question, but we need to get it out first."

"He's just going to come back."

"Fine. We'll work on raccoon prevention once we've done raccoon eradication."

He went to the side door off the kitchen and propped it open with the doorstop, then took the broom and pushed it against the raccoon's rear.

It growled again, but picked up the pace, scampering out the door and disappearing into the night.

"For God's sake." He lifted up the doorstop and shut the door. "I was not expecting that."

"No. That was ridiculous."

"Really, really ridiculous," he said.

"But cute."

"It was *not* cute."

"I disagree."

"So, you might not have a ghost in the hotel, but you might have raccoons. And, we don't know how they're getting in, which is going to require some kind of a fix. This place is a death trap," he said.

"It is not a death trap. I just wish that I had evidence that it's haunted."

"You're not going to get that, because it is not haunted."

"You don't know that," she said.

"Well, the problem is, I fucking do. Because ghosts don't exist."

He was just glad to be having this argument with her, because at least he was on stable ground.

And it wasn't about… Any of the things that had happened before.

"Let's go back upstairs," he said. "We'll look for raccoon entries in the morning."

"Okay."

They had kept the movie playing, but it didn't matter, since they'd both seen it a whole bunch of times. She drank another glass of wine, and he didn't say anything, because he was actually hoping that they might just get past all that. That she might forget it had happened. And she seemed to have.

When the movie ran out, she fell asleep on the sleeping bag. And he lay back on his own. He was lying on his side, and he could see her, in the moonlight coming through the window. The gentle swells of her breasts rising and falling with each breath.

And he couldn't take his eyes off her.

She was beautiful, and he'd always known that. But…

It was like a cascade of things he had held back for any number of years were suddenly rolling through him.

He had kept any thought of her as being a woman— a woman who was available to him— entirely subdued for all these years.

And she had undone it all with that tipsy offer. Because suddenly, he couldn't stop making it real. Couldn't stop seeing it as something vivid and specific and possible. Pushing his hands up underneath her shirt and revealing her skin. Had no one ever done that? Would his hands really be the first hands to…

No. He protected her. That was what he did.

He shielded her. From hard emotions, and held her when it was all unavoidable.

And there was no way in the damned world that he could protect her if he was…

He turned over onto his side and faced away from her, desperate to do something to find a way to get his mind out of the damned gutter.

And then she made a little whimpering noise, and he sat up. He couldn't take it. He crossed the room and got up on the bed and lay down on his back. He didn't care how dusty it was.

He needed some space. He just needed some space.

Cara felt dizzy when she woke up. And she couldn't figure out why she woke up, because it was still the middle of the night.

And then suddenly, she saw what looked like a light.

A floating orb in the middle of the room. It was low, at eye level with her on the ground. She sat up and looked around, and she saw that Jace wasn't on his sleeping bag. She scrambled up, her heart thundering. And then she noticed him on the bed, sleeping.

She scrambled up on the bed beside him, but he didn't move. He was snoring. "Go away," she said to the floating light. It zigzagged in the room. "Please go away. You're scaring me."

The light seemed to respond. It stopped, and then she swore she saw…that it wasn't an orb or just a light, but it was a butterfly. A bright white butterfly.

And she sat there blinking, completely uncertain of what she had seen. Maybe she just had something in front of her eyes because she was a little bit hungover or whatever from just having drunk too much wine. All she knew was that it creeped her out. She grabbed the ties on the curtains, and let them fall around the bed. She and Jace were completely boxed in there in the canopy.

She curled up in a ball and lay beside him, trying not to breathe too hard.

She just wanted to go back to sleep. And she wanted to hear nothing. So she focused on the sound of her breathing. His breathing. Tried to make it loud so that she wouldn't hear anything unnerving.

Hoped that orbs couldn't come through curtains.

She swallowed hard, trying to get a hold of herself.

And finally, she drifted off into a fitful sleep.

Six

When Cara woke up, it was dim. She squinted and realized that she was sleeping on a canopy bed. And she could see little shafts of sunlight coming through the cracks in the curtain.

Oh right. She had woken up and thought she'd seen… A ghost last night. An orb. A glowing butterfly? She had read a lot of things written by ghost hunters, and enough to know that orbs usually indicated some kind of paranormal activity. Glowing butterflies, she had no idea.

She immediately questioned that, because the fact that she knew it meant that it was something that had been suggested to her prior to being here. Which meant she could easily have dreamed it, freaked out and…

She turned to look at Jace, who was asleep in bed beside her.

And everything in her stopped. Stopped thinking about ghosts. Stopped thinking about anything.

All she could do was stare at him. He looked a lot more relaxed sleeping. Way more relaxed than he ever did in person. In person he always looked like he was ready to leap into action. At any moment. To vanquish a raccoon or...

Oh no. There was a raccoon.

Last night had gotten very strange, and it was all a little bit fuzzy, because she had been drunk. She'd had way too much wine because she was nervous. But yes, they heard a noise and it had turned out that it was a raccoon. They'd gone downstairs, Jace had vanquished the raccoon...well, he had scuttled out of the room...

But something had happened before that.

But she was stopped again by the sight of him. His profile.

By everything. Just everything.

She took a deep breath. And the scent of him was almost overwhelming. Then she suddenly felt a little bit creepy, sitting there and staring at him like that. Checking him out. She sat up, pulling her knees up to her chest, and her head gave a decisive, definitive dull thud.

Great. And she had a hangover.

If you wanted to have sex with a virgin, you could have sex with me.

She slapped her hand over her mouth.

No.

She had not said that. She really needed that to be a dream, or just something she had thought, or just...

If she could see it clearly. Play back that whole conversation. Everything that had happened right before the raccoon... The raccoon had interrupted the conversation. She had literally *propositioned* Jace and had told him that she *was a virgin*.

She squeezed her hands even more tightly over her mouth to keep from whimpering out loud.

No. And now she was up here in bed with him, and he was going to think that she was… That she had lost her mind.

I promise I'm not trying to hit on you. It's just that I saw a ghost. And I freaked out.

Yeah. That would go well. Just great.

Her heart was thundering out of control. Was he going to say something? Was he going to call her out for hitting on him? Was he going to ask about her virginity? Oh, she could think of nothing more embarrassing. It was a literal horror. The idea that he knew… No.

She couldn't bear it. She really couldn't bear it.

But maybe he wouldn't remember. He had a little bit of wine himself. And they'd made it through the night in the haunted house. Which was… Pretty haunted. Except maybe that it had been a dream. Because she'd been drunk.

She really didn't know what to think. She didn't know what to hope for.

And suddenly, he made a very masculine noise and stirred in his sleep. And then he turned over and looked at her, and she felt like the whole world lit up.

He was the most beautiful thing she'd ever seen. It hurt to look at him.

You love him.

No. She really didn't need to think that. She tried not to think it. She tried to never, ever think it. Yes, she loved him. As a friend, almost a brother, really. But the feelings…the attraction feelings… Those things she tried to keep separate and in their own box. Desire didn't have to be anything deeper.

But right now, lying next to him in bed, it was hard to keep it separate. They seemed to wrap around her completely, like invisible vines. Jace. And everything he was to her, along with how much she wanted to lean in and...

She rolled in the opposite direction. Fast. And went right off the edge of the mattress, down to the floor.

"Ow!"

She looked around the room, all lit up with daylight and felt...silly. About the whole ghost thing. About getting into bed with Jace...

"What happened?" She could hear him moving behind the curtain.

"I fell. I..."

"Were you up here?" he asked, and she was thankful he was behind the curtain and she was on the floor.

"Yeah I...something freaked me out last night." She winced. "So I got in bed and closed the curtains. Sorry."

"No need to apologize."

She heard his feet hit the floor on the other side of the bed, and she stood up quickly because she didn't need for him to see her on the floor in an undignified heap when she was sure she already sounded like an undignified heap. He didn't need visual confirmation.

She smoothed her hair and tried to lean casually against the bedpost. He came around the corner of the bed and she ignored the way her heart throbbed. "Morning," she said.

"You made it. The hotel is yours. Assuming you still want to buy it after Raccoonageddon."

"Oh, if anything I want it more."

"This is why you need a full-time babysitter, Cara."

"Don't worry. I'm bringing Grandpa's whiskey bottle over."

"Cara… That's not what I mean. Let's go out to the diner and get some breakfast."

And she was grateful for that. Because she needed to get back somewhere more familiar with him. On regular old footing. He was acting normal. Unaffected. Standing there in the same jeans and Henley he'd been wearing yesterday, he almost looked like last night hadn't happened. And maybe… Maybe he didn't remember. It wasn't like they'd done anything. It was just that she'd… Told him one of her more embarrassing secrets, and… Really, it wasn't so much like she had propositioned him. She could play it off like it was a joke.

It was just… It had not been a joke. And it hurt her to know that at the very first moment, she had exposed herself like that. Why had she done that to herself? He didn't want her. If he did, there had been ample opportunity for him to let her know along the way. Not that she had really ever let him know. But… There also hadn't been anyone else.

She ignored the ache in her chest that was still there from moments ago. From that terrible, ridiculous thought about love.

She didn't need to go thinking things like that.

And she didn't need to go marinating in all these feelings. They were just Jace and Cara, the same as they'd always been. One weird moment wasn't going to change that.

They packed up their things and went back out to Jace's truck.

"If you want, I can drive us over to the diner, then swing us back by here."

"Sure," she said.

The diner was packed. It was Sunday morning, and a whole lot of people were there for free church bacon and eggs. And a lot of other people were there for a hangover cure. The diner was where every kind of person in Lone Rock met.

"Good morning," said Rosemary, who had been hostess at the diner ever since they had graduated from high school.

"Morning," said Cara.

"Two," said Jace.

Rosemary gave them a sidelong glance.

All right, they had shown up at the diner for breakfast together. But hey, they had spent the night together. It was just it wasn't like that.

It was frustrating. Knowing that everyone in town basically assumed that she and Jace were sleeping together, when they absolutely weren't.

She wanted the diner to be a normalizing moment, and in many ways, she supposed that it was, since these kinds of speculative looks were normal for them. It was just that… She wanted to not think about him that way. And there was a strange kind of intimacy that seemed to linger between them after last night.

They sat down at the booth, and Rosemary handed them the menus. "Coffee?"

"Yes," they both said at the same time.

"I have a bastard of a headache," said Jace.

"You weren't even that drunk," she pointed out.

"It's that sugary girlie wine," he said. "I can drink Jack Daniel's and feel nothing the next day."

"So what you're telling me, is that you're not man enough for girls' night."

"I am not," he said.

"Maybe your toxic masculinity is protecting you."

"I would maintain that," he said.

A few moments later, their coffee arrived.

"Do you need a minute?" Rosemary asked.

"No," said Jace. "Bacon and eggs. Over medium. Hash browns, sourdough toast."

"Same."

Rosemary nodded, then left, and both she and Jace lifted their coffee mugs up and took long drinks.

As soon as that first hit of caffeine touched her soul, she started to feel slightly more human.

"I want to invest in the hotel."

"What?"

"I was thinking. After we talked last night, about the trust fund, and all of that... I want to invest in the hotel."

"You want to invest in the hotel. And when you say that, you mean you actually want to do this, and this isn't you doing some kind of misguided older brother thing?"

She was trying to sort through the tangle of feelings that this offer brought up. There was a certain measure of relief, because having some extra financial support—especially considering that there was clearly a raccoon porthole somewhere—was great. And certainly offered her a little bit of reassurance. But then also, if he remembered that conversation from last night...

Of course, that conversation had only been a couple sips of wine in, and it had come before all the raccoon stuff, way before, meaning she hoped that what had come right before the raccoon stuff, had been swallowed up by both that and the wind.

"So you want to... You want to throw backing behind this?"

"Yeah," he said. "I do need something that I believe in. That I want to invest in. Why not the town?"

"I just can't escape the feeling that actually what you're doing is acting like a mother hen."

"I prefer older brother."

Oh well. He might as well have just taken the butter knife next to his right hand and stabbed her in the heart. Done a little dance around her body as she bled out for good measure.

"I don't need an older brother," she said, her tone crisp. "Thank you. A friend, who sees me as an equal, sure."

"Me feeling like an older brother doesn't preclude me seeing you as an equal."

But it definitely precluded him seeing her as a woman. Great. Maybe it was even worse than she was thinking. Maybe he did remember what she had said last night, and he was not surprised that she was a virgin, and also didn't take seriously her offer for him to relieve her of it at all, because why would he, because she would've had to be kidding, because obviously they weren't attracted to each other.

She was rescued by the arrival of her breakfast, and she tucked into her eggs fiercely, mixing the yolks up in her hash browns and dipping her toast in the rest.

"You okay?"

"Starving," she said.

"Yeah. All right. Anyway, I figure if you're going to go over to the bank today, maybe I can go with you. And we can maybe have me cosign the paperwork."

"I don't need you to cosign, Jace. And if you're thinking that's a way to help keep me safe or bail me out or whatever…"

"Hey, all right. If you don't want my name on the paperwork, that's fine. I really was just trying to be helpful. I promise that I'm not… Doubting you."

"Whatever your crisis is, it doesn't have anything to do with me."

"Not a crisis," he said. "I've basically lived my life this way on purpose. I don't have a lot of connections. Other than my family, and I love them. And I've got you. But I don't own property, I don't do a job where I am doing any one thing for any length of time. I got all this money that I earned riding bulls, and you tell me what's…meaningful about that? Now I'm going to get a whole bunch of money that I didn't even earn. I don't know. Part of me wants to live that way, but… At this point… It's also starting to seem a little bit pointless. And useless. You want things, and I admire that. You're right. I don't put a lot of stock in dreams. And I'm still not in a place where I want to put any in my own. Or even have any of my own. But I'm happy to invest in yours. Don't see it as anything other than that. Your dreams feel valuable to me. So…"

"Yeah," she said, her heart seizing up. "Okay."

Why was it like this? Why was he like this? It really… It really got her. Right square at the center of her chest. He was doing this for her. And not to be condescending or anything like that, just because he cared.

And she didn't know why in the hell that made him feel like he was sitting further away from her than he had been a moment before. Because it should feel like they were closer.

But there was just something… There was something. Something that was there for her that was missing for him.

And she would never be able to talk to him about it. She would never be able to bridge that gap, because he was all she had. She had made an idiot out of herself last night. But there were a ton of handsome men. A ton of them. She saw them every night at the bar. Little Rock was lousy with hot cowboys. If that was her thing, then there was ample opportunity for her to pursue that. The one thing she would never be able to replicate or re-create was this relationship with him. The one thing she would never be able to have again, with anyone else, was what she had with Jace. This long-standing, completely trusting friendship. Something that was kind of more like family, if she were honest.

And he was the only family she had left, really.

He was important to her. In ways that were so complicated and imperative, there was no untangling it all. "Okay," she said again. "I'll take your help. You can invest, but I'm going to sign the paperwork on my own."

"Fair enough. What I'd like to do is help finance the remodels then."

"All right," she said.

"Then you have yourself a partner."

"A haunted house partner," she said.

"It's not haunted by anything but raccoons."

"Still. That's pretty haunted."

She reached across the table and stuck her hand out. And only when his large, warm, calloused hand wrapped around hers completely, did she recognize the error of her ways. Yeah, maybe that wasn't the smartest thing to have done. But he was her friend; she wasn't going to just not touch him. To not shake his hand.

So she did, firmly. And then brought her hand back

over to her side of the table and started shoveling more eggs into her mouth.

"I'm going to make my offer right after breakfast," she said, around her eggs. "Then I'll sign the paperwork, and then... We can make a meeting with the contractor."

"All right. Sounds good."

By the time he got back to the ranch, he almost wasn't thinking about that moment last night, over and over again. Almost.

He thought that he had done a pretty good job playing it cool this morning. But when he'd woken up, it hadn't been the raccoon that he thought of. It had been that moment when she looked at him, all glossy eyed, and told him that she was a virgin.

And that if he wanted to have sex with one...

Holy shit.

He had no idea what he was supposed to do with that.

Because he hadn't been able to get it out of his mind, and he was...

His body stirred.

Hell. And damn.

But he was resolved in his decisions to invest in the hotel. Even more so after last night. She needed him. If he didn't help, she was going to end up neck-deep in debt.

And maybe... Okay, maybe he needed her too.

Maybe he was ready to admit it was time to make something of his own.

But this was the thing. Whatever had happened last night, it was an anomaly. He wasn't going to let that dictate his actions, but it might also be telling him that he needed to stop and make a choice.

He was all thrown off because he was indecisive. So he was indecisive no more.

He was investing in the hotel. He was staying.

He'd realized this morning at breakfast that he couldn't afford to be wishy-washy. Not now. This was the time to make a decision.

He put his truck in Park and got out, stepping toward the barn. There had to be something to do. It was a ranch. There had to be something physical that he could pour himself into.

He was just about to go grab a rake, because God knew he could probably always muck a stall, when his brother Boone appeared from one of the stalls. "Howdy," he said. He looked him over. "You look... Not particularly well rested."

"What's your problem, Boone?"

"I don't have a problem. You seem to."

"No problem. Just thinking about some things."

"Oh yeah?" Boone crossed his arms over his chest and leaned against the stall door. "What kind of things?"

"I decided to invest in Cara's hotel thing."

"Her hotel thing?"

"Yes. You know, she's going to buy the Little Rock hotel. I thought that I would throw some money behind it. What she wants to do is pretty ambitious and... Anyway, I get the trust fund money next week."

"Wow. Well. Good for you. And here I thought you were just going to use it the way that I did."

"Hookers and blow?"

Boone laughed. "I mean, basically."

"I think we both know that isn't true," said Jace.

"Hey. You don't know."

"I think you pretend there's nothing more to you than that, but we all know there is."

"There maybe used to be," he said. "But there's not now." He got a slightly distant look to his eye.

It was impossible to know what Boone thought about anything. And yet, sometimes, Jace thought there was something in his brother that was just plain sad, and it wasn't the same kind of sad the rest of them were—they shared a common grief, so there was a bit of it that was inevitable. But there was something else to Boone, he just couldn't quite say what it was.

"Have you ever thought about investing in property?"

"Sounds dangerously like settling down," said Boone. "And that is also not in the cards for me."

"So you just going to… What? And I'm serious, because I'm trying to figure this out too. You just going to have all this money, and nothing to invest it in. Nothing to make your own."

Boone shrugged. "I have to find something that was worth making my own. Something that didn't belong to someone else, that is."

"Do you want something that does belong to someone else?"

"Story time's over," said Boone. And he knew that he'd hit a nerve.

"What's going on?"

"Nothing. And anyway, none of your business. But there's nothing wrong with just living life. Nothing wrong with… Hell, I mean, we've all accomplished things in the rodeo."

"Yeah. We got a bunch of belt buckles. And a bunch of money. It's just… Sometimes I ask what it's all for."

"What do you mean? It's our family legacy?"

"It's Dad's legacy," Jace said. "It's not mine. I never sat down and decided that it was something I wanted to do. I just did it. And now I guess sometimes I want something that's a little bit more… Mine."

"So that's where this hotel thing comes in?"

"I guess so."

"Well good luck to you. It still sounds an awful lot like an entanglement to me. And honestly, another thing that makes you and Cara basically married. Now you're business partners too? I don't know about that."

"Good thing is I didn't ask you," he said. "Didn't even start to. You're the one who asked. I'm just letting you know."

"Right. Well. I wish you the best of luck with that endeavor. And hopefully whatever else has you tensed up. Because something tells me it's not just that."

And then his brother left, but Jace still felt irritated. Because damn him, he was right. He was right about the fact that there was something else bothering him.

It was the fact that his body seemed to have developed an irrepressible interest in Cara.

He couldn't claim that it was sudden. It felt sudden. But it was just… He knew that she was beautiful. It was just that he had never let that matter. Because what did beauty matter? There were a lot of beautiful women. But there were very few people in his life that he cared for like he cared for her. And there was no one exactly like her. So he let all that fade to the background, and he never let it become attraction.

But there it was. Just suddenly. He was… He couldn't stop thinking about the way that she'd said that, and the inevitable thoughts that had followed.

How much he wanted…

Hell.

He wanted her.

No. He didn't have to let it go that far. He had a little bit of an interest there, but that was it. That didn't mean that he wanted her. And it didn't have to be anything too deep.

He wouldn't let it be.

In fact, tonight he would go to the bar, meet with her and talk her plans over with her. He wasn't going to let it be weird. He was just going to keep it the same. It was entirely possible Cara didn't even remember saying that to him. She hadn't acknowledged it all day. Not at all. Maybe she had even been kidding. Because he just couldn't imagine…

Except what was becoming easier and easier to imagine was his own hands skimming over her curves.

He could remember when he had pulled her down on top of them last night. How soft she'd been.

It had been a juvenile thing to do, but the feelings that had resulted had been anything but.

And then after that…

You've been tempting it. Teasing it.

He would've said no. That he'd never done that. Not with her. But the way that he had teased her last night, even before she'd said that to him about her virginity… It made him wonder. It made him wonder what he was actually thinking.

He needed to get back on the road, maybe. Maybe that was the issue. He'd been home a long time. And after school, for most of their friendship, they had gotten some decent-sized breaks from one another while he went out on the rodeo. And he usually hooked up when he went out on the rodeo. Quite a bit.

He didn't like the way that thought made him feel. Like it was only having sex with other women that kept him from being attracted to her.

That it was only some weird dry spell now that made him feel different.

He felt like it cheapened what they had between them, and like it cheapened her a bit, and nothing about Cara was cheap. He gritted his teeth and tried to get a grip.

Yeah. Tonight he would make sure that things got back to normal. And pretty soon that little snippet of conversation would fade into the background. It would just become one of the many conversations they'd had, and it wouldn't stand out as being anything more than what had gone on before it.

Just a snippet of things they'd said to each other.

It didn't have to echo in his mind. It didn't have to echo in his body. It really didn't.

So he took one more shovelful of manure and relished the ache in his arms.

He was going to work until he was busted. Then he was going to go have a drink with his best friend. And make some plans for the new business venture.

It wasn't like being married. Because being married wasn't in the cards for him. Not ever.

But this? This felt better. This felt right. This felt like he was getting close to doing the thing that he needed to do. Because something had to change. He wasn't going to turn thirty and just stay the same old way. Boone might be comfortable with that, but Jace wasn't.

And this was the right step forward. He knew it.

So he banished anything that felt wrong and kept on shoveling.

Seven

By the time Jace stumbled into The Thirsty Mule with two of his brothers, he was pretty damned tired. Which was exactly what he wanted. He wanted to be bone-tired by the time he hit his bed tonight. And he definitely didn't want to think. He saw Cara standing behind the bar, glowing. She was lit up like a firecracker. Laughing and talking to two men sitting in front of her who were… Looking down her top.

And suddenly, Jace couldn't look away. Not from down her top, though his eyes definitely drifted there. But just from her. Altogether.

Her blond hair was lit up like a halo, and she looked so damned happy. She had on makeup tonight. Dark mascara and glossy pink lipstick. There was a glow about her cheeks, and he had a feeling she dusted some kind of sparkling powder on there. And yeah… If he wasn't mistaken, she had put a bit of it on her breasts…

"Damn. She is pretty."

That came from Flint.

Jace scowled. "Shut the fuck up."

"Down boy," said Boone.

"Well. If you guys could stop being perverts about my best friend for five minutes, that would really help. You treat her like an object, and I'm sick of it."

"To be clear, when we tease you about her," said Boone, "it has nothing to do with her, and everything to do with you. Right now has a bit to do with her. Because damn."

The problem was, he couldn't even disagree. But it didn't feel like objectifying her. Not really. It felt like something else. Something different. It felt like something singular, like something had reached up and grabbed him by the throat and shaken him hard. And he didn't like it. No, he really didn't. Worst of all, his brothers were there. Worst of all, there was a bar full of people. If there wasn't…

He could see it clearly. Going over to the bar and leaning over, hooking his arm around her waist and…

No. What the hell? She was supposed to be like a sister to him. She was…

There was something unraveling here, and he couldn't quite put a finger on it. And maybe it had to do with all this need to reframe his life. With all these thoughts he had about what he wanted to do with his life and himself. Maybe he was looking for something to hold on to, and there she was.

Hell. She'd always been the thing he'd held on to.

Maybe that was what he was doing now. Just so desperate to find something that he…

He gritted his teeth and went to the empty barstool and sat down. Boone and Flint sat on either side of him.

Cara whipped her head to the side, and the moment that she saw him… There was something on her face, and he couldn't quite read it. But it reminded him of the sun coming up from behind the mountains. It reminded him of some kind of beauty he never considered before. Something that had never been spoken about or written about or even sung about. And he was not a poet by nature. But there was something that stirred inside of his soul that defied words and poetry. Something that made him feel unworthy. Of standing there. Of looking at her.

Of being in this spot.

He looked up behind her, at the Jack Daniel's bottle there that contained Mitch.

And he didn't believe in that sort of thing, but he had to wonder if the old man knew somehow. Maybe he'd just put a hex on him. Left a spell behind here in the bar that would affect any man that ever looked at Cara.

Why was that less insane than thinking he might be here now? He couldn't say.

Except he'd always been pretty clear within himself that… That the end was the end.

But hoping for anything else was just trying to put a Band-Aid on the pain that life brought.

He was resistant to Band-Aids. He preferred to rub a little dirt in it and get on with things.

Yeah. You get on with things so well. You're thirty years old and have no idea what you want.

"Can we get a drink?"

His voice came out harsh, and he felt bad, because

he sure as hell didn't need to talk to her that way. Especially not when she just looked at him like that. Her expression fell, and he felt like a dick.

"Yeah." She had recovered quickly, grinning like he was just another bar patron. She often did that. It was part of the show, after all. She didn't break character when she was behind the bar.

She moved over and put her hand on her hip. "Boone? Flint? What can I get for you?"

"Something strong," said Flint.

"I drew the short straw," said Boone. "I'm driving. So I'll just have a beer."

"I know what you like," she said to Jace.

And the words felt like a swipe of her tongue, straight down the center of his chest.

And that was a weird and graphic metaphor that he'd certainly never thought before. Not about her.

"She knows what you like," said Boone.

"I could know what you like too, Boone. If you'd let me."

"Shit," Jace said. "It's bad enough that they pull this kind of stuff to make me mad. Now you're in on it?" he asked.

Cara looked at him blandly, then shrugged. "What's the harm in it?"

"God Almighty," said Jace. "You're all going to be the death of me."

She winked at Boone. *Winked* at him.

"Well," said Boone. "Never mind. I take back everything I said about you practically being married to her. She's obviously single."

"Really, are you just trying to make me mad?"

"Why are you so mad?" Flint asked.

And the problem was, he didn't have an answer. Not a good one. Not a good one at all.

"I want a burger," he said. "If you're done flirting with my brother."

"Yeah, I'm done," Cara said. "For now."

She walked back down the bar, and he couldn't help but watch the wiggle of her hips, the way her ass looked in those jeans.

It was like the floodgates had opened, and now that he had noticed, he couldn't stop.

If you want to have sex with a virgin...

She couldn't be a virgin. She just couldn't be. And it wasn't because he didn't believe she was capable of making that choice, he just didn't... She exuded sex appeal. She was so comfortable with herself. With her body. The way that she handled the men in the room was... She had them all eating out of the palm of her hand. She just seemed like a woman who was *experienced.* He had accepted that. He didn't really ever think about it. They didn't talk about that sort of thing. That was fine. It wasn't part of their friendship. They were sort of open...

And now that he thought about it, he couldn't remember her ever dating anybody, but the thing was, he was gone sometimes. And anyway, he figured that she probably had her share of hookups working at the bar and...

He looked at all the men sitting around the bar. The thought of any of them putting their hands on her made him so angry he couldn't even see straight.

She leaned forward and started talking to two men down at the other end. They were getting an eyeful down her tank top, and the thing was, he knew that she knew it. And that if she didn't want them to, she wouldn't hold herself in that position. She was a woman in total control of herself. She knew exactly the effect that she had on men, and she was happy to have it.

He just couldn't see…

But maybe that was his own wrongheaded thinking. Maybe it showed what he knew about anything.

It was almost funny. That there was something he didn't know about Cara Summers. That there was maybe something he didn't understand about women.

And hell, sitting there looking at her like he was, he wondered if there were some things he maybe didn't understand about himself. And that was a whole other Pandora's box of freaky-ass shit he didn't want to open.

His brothers and his burgers arrived a few moments later, along with their drinks, and he did his best to listen to Boone talk about his plans for the next rodeo season.

His plans to get on the road.

Flint had similar plans. And he realized just none of it… Resonated in him. Not anymore.

He shoved down his french fries.

"I think I'm going to stay here," he said.

"Really?" Boone asked. "You're not going back out there?"

"I want everything. I've made tons of money. It's time for me to figure out the next thing. I need something that's… I need something that's mine."

Right when he said that, he looked back behind the bar, and his eyes connected with Cara's and, on God, he had not meant for that to happen. But it had, and it resonated down deep inside of him. Made him feel something he really wished he hadn't.

"I mean, more power to you," said Boone. "But I'm not done with the glory."

"I mean, I could do with a little bit less infamy," Flint mused.

Boone snorted. "It'll pass," he said. "Nobody's going to remember that Tansey Martin wrote a song for you in another year."

"It's not about me," said Flint, practically growling.

"It's not? Because I seem to recall…"

"She didn't love me," said Flint. "If she had, I would've known."

"You think so?" Boone asked.

"Yeah," said Flint. "I think so. It was nothing."

And Jace didn't quite believe that. And maybe it was asinine of him, but he kind of liked the fact that his brother wasn't really as certain about things as he tended to pretend.

Boone and Flint were not as gloriously unattached as they pretended. Commentary from the last couple of days had shown him that.

Of course, that didn't really help much. It only made him wonder if he'd ever been as detached as he pretended. If he'd been lying to himself as well as he ever had to anyone else.

They finished their burgers, and Boone downed another shot, simply because he could.

"Let's go," Flint said. "I'm bored of sitting here sober."

"See you later," said Jace. "I'm going to hang out for a bit."

It was getting crowded in the bar, and he didn't like the idea of leaving. Not with Cara looking like that. Not with all these men here staring at her.

You just want to keep staring at her.

She was his friend. It was more than that. It would always be more than that.

His brothers left, and he kept his position at the bar. Kept it until things started to fade out. Until Cara rang the bell for last call.

Until the very last patron exited the bar, and they were the only two people left inside.

"I'm going to need a ride home," he said.

He wasn't drunk. All the whiskey had left his system a couple hours earlier. He wished he were a little drunk.

"Weird," she said. "I don't seem to recall agreeing to that."

"I figured you probably wouldn't leave me here."

"Well, that's where maybe you don't know everything about me."

It was on the tip of his tongue to say that he knew more about her than he had a week ago. That he knew more about her than he wished he did.

But he was trying to get them back on equal footing.

It was tough. It was damn tough when she was standing there looking like she did. When she was looking like the embodiment of...

He cut that thought off.

He was about to think that his best friend looked like the embodiment of sex.

And that was not what he wanted to be thinking. Not now. Not ever.

"I figured we would talk a little more. About the hotel."

"Oh great," she said, leaning back against the bar. She arched her back slightly, and he couldn't help but notice the way that her breasts thrust upward.

He looked away.

"What are your plans."

"Well. That kind of all depends. On how deep of an investment you're talking about here."

He looked back at her, because even though he was feeling off-kilter at the moment, he would damn sure make eye contact with Cara when he was talking about business. When he was talking about things that mattered. "The thing is, I have more than enough. I've never been one to sit around and be idle. The rodeo might not have been my dream, but if I was going to do something, that I was going to be the best at it."

He cleared his throat. "When you have brothers who are determined to be the best at all the same things... Well, it gets a little bit competitive. And on the youngest. So I came after them. And everything they did, I wanted to have done, done better. Every record they had broken, I wanted to come up behind them and break it too. As you pointed out, I'm not a big visualizer. I'm not a dreamer."

He looked down at his hands. It was high time he did something with those hands. Built something. Made something. And doing it for Cara...that just made sense. "I just put one foot in front of the other. I live in the moment. Because of that... I went. There's no room for nerves to creep in. No room for anxiety. No room for what-ifs. And the point of all that is, I made a lot of money doing that. I'm proud of that money. Because it's mine. The money that I'm getting from the trust fund? It isn't. It's not mine. That comes from my dad. It comes from everything that he built. And the more I think about it, the more I want to invest in something permanent with it. Because I have it, whether I feel like

I have a right to it or not. So. The budget's big. Did you want an in-ground pool?"

She laughed. "No. I don't think I need a pool. But… I don't really know what to do with this offer. I don't… We're friends, and I know that you care about me. You always have. But this…"

"It's a business decision. I mean, I expect a cut of it. But at least then I'm working for it. No?"

"For a man who claims he doesn't think ahead… You sure have a plan."

"Look. I just don't…" He looked at her, at the hopeful expression on her face. The glitter in her eyes. "Forget about it," he said.

"Forget about what?"

"Forget I was gonna say anything. It's not anything that we need to talk about."

"I want to talk about it. Tell me. Tell me what's going on."

"All right. You know, when somebody that you love is dying, thinking ahead just means thinking to a future without them. And I never could muster up a belief in miracles. So I just knew that if I imagined what I wanted to be when I grew up… I would be imagining a world without Sophia in it. It's a habit. All right. It's a habit that I never got around to breaking."

It was one reason he was all or nothing. In the moment and never in the future. Black-and-white was easy, and he'd lived a black-and-white life. He'd known there would be a before and an after. Sophia here. Sophia gone. There were no shades of gray in loss.

He found there weren't really any shades of gray in life.

Those glittering eyes went liquid.

"Jace…"

"It's been a long time. I don't live in the past. That's the other thing. You learn to live in the present, and she can't… You can't go back there either."

"Well that's pretty sad. Because even though she's gone, she is your sister. And maybe it would be nice if you could revisit her."

"She's gone."

"I don't believe that the people we love are ever really gone, Jace," she said. She looked back at the bar, up at the bottle that held her grandfather's ashes. "You know I talked to Grandpa every day. He's with me. I believe that."

"Well. Sophia's not with me. She's gone. One day, she just died. And she was never with me again. That's all I know."

And he didn't know why he had always felt so hard-line about that. So rigid. Maybe because if there were miracles to be had in the world, if divine power existed at all, and it had not extended its hand to keep Sophia with him, physically with him, then he didn't see the point of it anyway. And frankly it was a bigger comfort to believe there was just nothing there. That was all.

Maybe some people preferred the comfort of faith. He didn't find it comforting. He didn't find it comforting to think that there was someone who could've lifted a finger to save her, and hadn't.

He didn't find it comforting to think that somebody might be there in spirit when he couldn't actually talk to them.

And he didn't like to think about any of this. Because there was no damned point to it. None whatsoever. It didn't accomplish anything. Didn't fix anything.

He didn't know why she was pushing.

"I'm sorry that I never met her," she said.

He thought back to the boy he'd been when he had met Cara. "Well, you and I never would've met when she was alive. Because we had to live in Portland as long as she was sick. Make sure she was near the hospital."

"I know. I'm just talking about what-ifs."

"I don't get the point of those."

"Not even a little? Like you never ask yourself... What might happen if you set your foot on a different path? This one or that one?" She looked up at him, and her blush pink lips parted. She drew in a breath, and her breasts lifted.

Fuck. Right then, he wanted to ask what if. Wanted to ask what would happen if he stepped on a different path. But to what end?

Since when do you care about the end?

One foot in front of the other. Just as far as the eye could see. And no farther.

If a man was meant to see beyond the horizon, there wouldn't be a line.

But there was. Firmly drawn. You weren't meant to look ahead too far.

And right now, it was easy to believe that there was nothing outside of this bar. The thing outside of this moment. It was how he felt when he got on the back of a bull.

There was nothing but that. But his thighs pressed against the bull's flanks. The breathing of the animal as he prepared for the chute to open. For the fight to begin. The rush of adrenaline in his own body as he prepared for the fight of his life.

Those were the moments in life he loved, because

they narrowed down to fractions of a second. To a single moment.

To everything.

Everything being within reach. Everything being within sight.

There was simply his hand wrapped around the leather strap, the sensation of that pressure pushing the glove more deeply into his palm. The smell of the dust and the animal. The sound of Garth Brooks and the crowd.

This moment was like that. Suddenly, there was nothing. Nothing but her. Nothing but him. Even the edges of the room had gone dark and fuzzy.

The jukebox was playing Luke Bryan. The room smelled like alcohol, fry oil and tobacco. And she looked like heaven. Something bright and glowing against the darkened backdrop.

And there was no moment beyond this one. Nothing beyond the next breath.

And nothing, nothing beyond the last breath.

And so it seemed the easiest thing in the world to take a step toward her. And then another. The easiest thing in the world to square his body right in front of hers, and watch as she pressed herself just slightly against the bar. Away from him, but her eyes told him that she didn't actually want to move farther away.

And then her eyes dropped to his mouth, back up to his eyes. And if he were to ask what they were doing, he wouldn't have an answer. If he were to ask himself why the hell he was about to do this, he wouldn't have an answer.

But he just didn't need an answer. He didn't need a fucking answer. Because that meant that there was something beyond this. And right now he wasn't acknowledging that. Not even a little bit.

It was only this. Only this.

And that was when he planted his hands on the edge of the bar, on either side of her body, and looked at her like he might be able to find some answers at the very bottom of that green gaze.

She lifted one hand and placed it on his chest. Warm fingertips flexing there, shifting the fabric of his shirt over his skin. His heart rate kicked up, like he was about to ride, and the world narrowed even further. Pink cheeks, pink lips, green eyes.

She looked up at him from beneath her lashes and leaned in. He felt her breath against his skin. Then she moved her hand to the back of his neck. Her fingertips were so soft. Impossibly.

Cara shifted, leaned in, stretched up on her toes.

And she kissed him.

Eight

Oh, she was doing it. She was kissing him. Her mouth brushed his, and a streak of heat went through her that she couldn't deny. She pulled away, almost the instant their mouths touched. "I'm sorry," she said. She turned away. "Shit. I'm sorry," she said again.

He grabbed her arm and turned her to face him, his hands curved around her forearms, and gripping the edge of the bar, pinning her there. "You just kissed me."

"I did," she said.

And suddenly, she found herself being hauled toward him, and he wrapped his arm around her waist, pushing her body against his, and when he kissed her, he did not move away.

No. His kiss was deep, hard. Hot.

And it was Jace.

She wanted to pull away and scream with the hysteria of it.

Jace.

It was Jace.

And he was kissing her. His lips were firm and expert, and then he angled his head, and she opened her mouth to him. And his tongue slid against hers. Jace's tongue.

And she was trembling. Immediately wet between her legs. Because her fantasies had primed her for this moment over the course of years, and yet it was so much better than she had ever imagined that it could be.

This kiss was beyond anything that she had ever fathomed a kiss might be. He was everything. And too much all at once. So tall and strong and hot. All-knowing. Like he was demanding a response from her. Like he was willing it from the depths of her soul.

And she couldn't doubt. Because how could she, when she was being kissed by a man who so clearly knew exactly what he was doing. A man who didn't seem to have doubt anywhere in his body, anywhere at all. And she would know, since she was currently plastered against his body.

He pulled her away from him, and looked down at her. "Are you really a virgin?"

"Well. I thought we weren't talking about that."

"You *kissed* me, Cara."

"You also kissed me. So I think we're even."

"Not even a little bit. Were you serious?"

"Was I serious?" She squinted, and tried to look confused.

"You are not fucking confused. You know exactly what I mean. Were you serious?"

"Yeah," she said, realizing that it was all futile now. And if she got weird about it, it was only going to be weirder. If she pretended, after kissing him like that and then returning his kiss like he was oxygen and she was suffocating to death, it was only going to look more extreme. More ridiculous.

So there was just a point where she was going to have to exhibit some honesty. "I was serious. Yes. I haven't ever been with anyone. And you know, it's one of those things... That at this point it's kind of weird and left undone, and if you would like to be the one to help me out with it, then I am okay with it. It just has to be the one... the once. I appreciate the fact that you're already helping me with my hotel. And it might be a little bit much to ask you to pay for renovation and also have sex with me."

Well. She wanted to crawl under the bar. She had just said all those words to Jace, and she wasn't even drunk. She couldn't blame them on anything like that. Couldn't take refuge in the fact that she was maybe being an idiot.

"You're a virgin?"

"Yes."

"And you would like to not be." He said it not so much as a question, but as a clarifying statement.

Though in general, that wasn't true. If she had actually wanted to lose her virginity, if it were even a thing to her, then she would've done it. It was just that she... She was stuck in some kind of weird limbo with Jace.

Weird limbo. Weird way to say: you're in love with him.

Hell. She didn't want to think about being in love with Jace. The very thought made her want to cry. She didn't want to be in love with Jace. It was fucking stupid. She did not want to be in love with Jace.

But as she stood there, looking at him, at that precious, dear, familiar, wonderful face, she knew it was true. And it was why she had never been with anyone else. Because there was just nobody that made her feel even a fraction of what he did. Because being with somebody else would be a mockery of what they had. Because it wouldn't come close to what she actually wanted it to.

"I want you," she whispered.

She wished her voice was stronger. She wished it wasn't so small.

And it was so far from the whole truth that it made her want to laugh. And it was so desperately inadequate that it made her want to cry. And so exposing that she wanted to cover herself. But looking at him, she could see the promise of something. Like the sun rising, flooding the moment with hope. With light.

And what if… What if she could have everything with him?

It was a bright, brilliant moment, but she let herself have it. Even though she didn't think it was realistic. Even though she didn't think it would ever… Ever amount to anything… She let herself dream. If only for a second. She let herself dream, because it felt right. She let herself dream, because sometimes dreams were all you had. And they were beautiful, and magical, and you should hang on to them when you could.

And who knew if she could actually have everything with Jace. She'd never been all that special.

Except to him.

But then, she also knew that he was a difficult bastard. Who didn't have a romantic bone in his body.

He didn't do long term, or even an exclusive kind of short term. Yeah, she also knew that.

"You want me?" His voice was rough and she felt it between her legs.

What was she doing? What was happening right now? He was her friend. Her best friend. Hers. And she was just telling him, and he was looking at her like he might want her too, and she wanted to run. From him and to him.

She cleared her throat. "Is that not apparent?"

He cut her off by pressing his mouth to hers, and a rush of warmth overtook her. He wrapped his arm around her waist and brought her close. And when he kissed her… It was deep. It was real, and it was the most full-on, intense moment of its kind that she imagined anyone had ever experienced. She didn't want to talk. She didn't want to think. She didn't want to do anything but feel. She just wanted to feel. Feel this. Feel him.

She wanted it more than anything.

And she had to laugh, because she sort of wondered if they were being utterly themselves in this moment. If she was trying to manifest forever while he deeply denied any sort of future.

But maybe it didn't matter, because their truth and their beliefs were coming together right in this moment, and it was resulting in a kiss, so… She supposed that was all perfect.

And maybe she would take a page out of his book. Just this once. Because the scrape of his stubble against her cheek was magic, and the slick friction of his tongue against hers was doing wild and reckless things to her insides. Because the feel of his big hands, gripping her waist, smoothing down her hip. Oh, it was her fantasy. Her moment. It was the thing… It was everything.

She started to shake.

And he was Jace, so he noticed.

"You okay?" he asked, brushing his hand over her cheek.

"I'm okay," she said. "I just… I watched you once. Pick up a woman in the bar. The way that you put your hand on her body… I went home and I fantasized about it."

"Fuck," he said. "Don't tell me things like that."

"Why? We're already here."

He huffed a laugh, soft and sexy, and then he smiled. Just a little. "Well. Damned if that isn't true."

And then he kissed her again, and she was drowning.

She pushed her hands up underneath his T-shirt and groaned when she made contact with his hot skin. With his hard-packed muscle.

She started to pull off his shirt.

"Look, as much as I think it would be fun to do this on the bar, I think that we need to bed."

"What?"

"Seriously. You've really never been with anybody?"

"Yes." She moved her hands over his chest. "I've never been with anybody, and I want to be with you, and I'm feeling a little bit desperate."

"And there will be time for hard and fast, I can assure you. I'm all for it. But, we need to do slow and thorough first. Because I take care of you. Bottom line. You're mine, Cara. Mine to protect. And I'm gonna make this good for you. And that means we need to bed. And we need time."

"I'm a virgin," she said. "But I am not an *untouched* virgin. I have a vibrator."

"Praise the Lord, and hallelujah. But, I still want to take my time."

"I just mean… I actually know when I'm about to come. And believe me when I tell you…"

"Save the dirty talk," he said, pressing his thumb against her lips. "We're gonna have me coming a whole lot earlier than either of us want."

It was the fact that he made eye contact with her when he said that that nearly sent her over the edge. The fact that it was Jace.

Her Jace.

The fact that she had looked up and seen him down by the riverbed when she'd been crying when she was just in middle school, and he looked at her with those same eyes. And now he was looking at her like this, talking to her like that.

It was enough to send her straight over the edge.

Jace. This was *Jace.* And she didn't even have to tell herself that to cement it in her mind, because it could only ever be him.

She had been waiting for this. All this time.

"Well. We can go back to… To the house."

The house that she had inherited from her grandfather wasn't that far out of town.

"Yeah we can."

"It's convenient, since you don't even have your truck here."

"Yeah," he said, his voice ragged. "If I were a different man, I'd be tempted to say that I planned it this way. But you're you, so I definitely shouldn't of done that. And I'm me, so I'm not supposed to… Plan."

"Did you?"

"I'm not going to lie to you. What you said about that got to me. I try to not think of you that way. And when

I say try, I mean I decided not to, so I didn't. You must know that you're beautiful."

"I know that men respond to me a certain way. I don't know that I think that is beautiful."

"Well you are. You're basically a damn sunrise. All right? I'm not good at that."

"That's a lie. You pick up women all the time. You must be very good at flattering them."

"I'm good at empty flattery. I'm good at letting those words roll off my lips without even thinking about what they mean. Hey gorgeous. Hey baby. You look beautiful. Like a dress. But it would look better on my bedroom floor."

She blanched. "Please tell me you've never said that."

"I probably have. I probably didn't even pay attention to what it really sounded like. But I guarantee you that neither did she. Because we were both there for one reason, and it didn't matter if we liked each other. It didn't matter. It's the perfect kind of hookup for a man like me. Who doesn't think about tomorrow." His voice pitched lower, and she shivered. "And you know, even though I don't think about my tomorrows, Cara, I know one thing about them. You'll be there. And that matters to me. It matters a hell of a lot."

Her throat went so tight she could hardly speak. "It matters to me too."

"So what I say to you matters. I'm not to give you empty compliments. And maybe that wasn't a great one, but I meant it. I meant it all away from my soul. I promise you that. You're beautiful, and I had to put blinders on to not notice. I did a pretty bad job of it when you first… Filled out."

She laughed, which felt good. "Diplomatic," she said.

"Tonight, I was watching those men look at you… And seeing you the way that they did… Well, it made me want to strangle them, but it also made it impossible to look away from you. But I want to make it very clear it's not like I didn't notice. You don't have the kind of beauty a man doesn't notice."

"Thank you," she said. "But we don't need to talk."

Because it they kept talking, then maybe she would have to share more about what she felt. Maybe she would have to share more about the way that she felt about him. The way that she had always felt about him.

"Take me home and make me feel good." And it wasn't the smoothest thing, but it was real. It was raw and it was honest. And he seemed to find it undeniable. Because that was when he grabbed her arm and led her out the back door of the bar.

And it was her truck that they needed to take, but she fumbled around looking for the keys, and finally he took pity on her and fished them out of her purse for her and got into the driver's seat.

Her house was a modest one, on one of the streets just a couple of blocks from the bar. All the houses on the street had been built in 1974. All of them the same sort of small and nondescript, or at least they had been originally. Some had been added onto over the years. Made a little bit more fancy a little bit more spacious. But not hers.

It was still the same as when she had lived here with her grandpa. The same green shag carpet. The same daisy pattern countertop in the bathroom.

She loved it because it reminded her of him. Because it reminded her of home.

Jace was a lot like home too, and somehow, right

now the combination of the two didn't feel comforting. It simply felt dangerous.

They had spent the night together, shared a bed back at the motel, but this was different. It was different, and so were they.

And she fought against the thought that argued with that. That told her they were just the same. And doing this was risky. As risky as it ever had been. And she needed to be careful. So goddamned careful. And she was taking a risk because she wanted to touch him so badly.

But the fact of the matter was, the horse had bolted. They could turn back now, and things would still be different forever.

Because the acknowledgment of the feelings was the horse in the room. And the sex didn't have to actually happen for it to have been spoken of. And they'd already kissed. So there was no point turning back. Because if it was going to break something, then they'd broken it back at the bar. Maybe they'd broken it back at the hotel.

Maybe they'd broken it at some other point along the path that she couldn't even identify.

Maybe it had shattered for her the moment she had seen him put his hand on that woman's hip and envied her. Maybe that was the point from which she had been too far gone to go back.

And so she really had to be like Jace this moment. And just go forward.

But not look too far ahead.

He got out of the truck and took her keys and unlocked the front door.

She walked in first, and the very familiar room suddenly didn't look so familiar. It looked foreign and a little bit frightening, or maybe that was just her own body right now.

Foreign and a little bit frightening. Not at all what she was used to. Not at all what she expected.

And then he closed the door behind them and locked it, and suddenly it all felt so real.

She was hyperaware of everything. The sound of her breathing. The sound of the forced air coming through the vents as the heater came on. The sound of his footsteps as he walked toward her.

"Jace," she whispered.

"Cara."

It was in affirmation. That he was well aware of who she was. That he saw her. That he wanted her too.

And that was what she really needed to know. More than anything.

"This isn't just the virginity thing, is it? It's not just a novelty for you?"

"I've never found anything about virginity novel. I don't care about it. But I do care about you. I care about what you want. And you waited a long time to do this and... I want it to be good for you. So no. I don't care about that. What I care about is you. That's it. Beginning and end of story. It's you, Cara. You're what matters."

She felt like her heart was being peeled, layer by layer, like all the resistance that she had left was being stripped away. And she really didn't have much. And yet it was brutal. Utterly brutal. She hadn't expected this. That a moment so deeply desired. So anticipated, could be quite so uncomfortable.

But it was like he knew. Right then. Like he knew just what to do. He leaned in and kissed her. And he made it impossible for her to think. And that was just exactly what she needed. A reprieve. And that was what he excelled at. She could see the appeal. Why he lived the way that he did. She could see why it felt great to block out everything but the moment. Absolutely everything.

And so she let his kiss carry her away. Or maybe keep her grounded. To the spot instead of the moments that would follow. The moments where he would see her. Touch her. Tease her in a way that no other man ever had.

Yes. She kept herself in this moment, so she wasn't quite up ahead to those.

His hands were strong and certain as he gripped her waist, rooted her to the spot, to the moment.

Her heart began to throb, her body aching with need.

It was just so good. And it surpassed everything. Every single one of her fantasies. Every single one of those illicit evenings she'd spent thinking about his hands on her body. The reality was so much sweeter. So much better.

And then suddenly, she wanted to see him. Because after all, it was her fantasy. Because after all, she was the virgin.

She pushed her hands up beneath his shirt, and he took the hint, reaching behind his head and gripping the back of his T-shirt, pulling it up over his head in a way that left her mouth ajar.

"How do men do that?"

"What?"

"I dunno. It was just the sexiest thing I've ever seen." At least, it was. It was the sexiest thing she had ever seen until she saw his body. His broad shoulders, his pectoral muscles, with just the right amount of hair sprinkled over them, his lean waist, his corrugated abs.

She licked her lips. She had seen him shirtless any

number of times, but this was the first time that it had been okay for her to touch. She could touch him now.

It wasn't inappropriate for her to do that. Because he wanted this. He wanted her.

She reached out and pressed her hand against his chest. It was so hot, and she could feel his heartbeat raging there.

She was actually touching him. His skin. His body.

She hadn't done that, because they were friends. And you didn't do that to your friend. Except she was. And he was still her friend. Every bit as much as he had been before. Before she had touched him. Before everything.

He was still her friend.

She looked at him, searching his face, and suddenly, she couldn't find that assurance there. Because he looked like a stranger just then. There was something about the tension in his expression, the sharpness in his eyes. She had never seen that look on his face before. She wondered how many other women had.

But you have this other part of him. And no one else has that.

It was true. And she knew it. They had a connection, and it was bigger than this. Right then, she needed to expand the moment. To include their past.

It made her heartbeat settle just a little bit.

She continued to move her hands over his muscles, slowly, between his pecs, down to his abs, where she let her fingers drift over the ridges there. She swallowed hard. And she looked back up at him.

"What should I do?"

"Whatever you want."

"Well... I don't know what I want. Could you... Can you take control, please?"

And it was like a blue spark flashed in his eyes. It was like everything shot off like a rocket. An explosion between them.

She had felt safe with Jace, all this time, for all these years, and just now, it was like she was poised on the knife's edge of danger. Like she could see there were vast dimensions to this man that she didn't know, had never known. It was more than just tension in his face. She had opened the door and discovered vast rooms of Jace that she had never realized were there.

And he was the key to her opening the door to those rooms inside of herself too.

She just knew.

But it wasn't only that she was discovering all this about him, she was about to learn a whole lot about herself.

This was terrifying. It really was.

And wonderful too. Amazing. Something more than she had ever imagined possible. Something different.

And her fantasies about Jace hadn't prepared her. Because those were her fantasies. It was her hand on her body. Directing the tempo, directing the speed. Deciding exactly what happened when.

She had just turned the control over to him, and that meant to surrender.

On a level she had never quite dreamed.

"Are you sure?" he asked, his voice rough.

"Yes."

"If there's something I do, and you don't like it, you need to tell me to stop."

"I will." But she couldn't imagine him doing anything she didn't like. That was actually what scared her. That she wasn't sure there were going to be easy limits to this. Because discovering that he wanted her, and further, discovering that she wanted badly to surrender to whatever that meant…

It was like being tossed into the deep endlessness of the sea.

She wasn't sure it had an end.

"I want this," she said. "I want… I want you."

He growled, closed the distance between them and gripped her hands in one of his, effortlessly pinning her wrists behind her back, low, pressed against the dip in her spine right above her rear.

"Good."

The word was hard.

Final. Firm.

She loved it.

And what she loved even more was that taking care of her didn't look like being easy on her.

She didn't want easy. Because nothing had been easy to get to this point. So why should it be easy now? She just wanted to revel in this. In him.

Jace.

Her best friend with the stranger's eyes.

He kissed her, deep and fierce and hard. And then he trailed the line of kisses down her neck, to her collarbone, on down farther.

Her tank top was low, and when his lips made contact with the plump skin of her breast, she froze. It felt so good. So good. His mouth was hot, and everything in her was blooming with desire.

She had been ready to come from his kiss back at the bar, and this was… This was more extreme. More intense.

He reached down and grabbed the hem of her tank

top, pulled it up over her head, leaving her standing there in her black lacy push-up bra.

"Holy hell, Cara. You are really something else."

His eyes were appreciative, hungry, and there was no amount of male appreciation, or compliments, that would ever equal this moment. This moment when Jace Carson looked at her with lust in his eyes.

She had the sudden, ridiculous thought, that this was the highest purpose her breasts had ever had.

And it made her eager for what came next. Not nervous. But before she could unhook her bra, he reached behind her and did it, releasing it and casting it onto the ground. Her nipples went tight underneath his intense scrutiny.

She shivered.

"You are so fucking beautiful," he said, pressing a kiss to her collarbone, down farther, capturing one nipple between his teeth and tugging hard.

"Jace," she said, pushing her fingers through his hair, holding him to her breast as he sucked her, the sensation going deep between her thighs.

"You like that?"

"Yes," she said. "Basically, whatever you do, assume I like it." Her voice sounded desperate. Panting. She loved every minute of the moment. Of his touch.

He moved his hands up then, cupped her breasts as he took his attention back to her mouth. As he kissed her, deep and thorough while his thumbs skimmed over her breasts.

"Please," she begged.

He unsnapped her jeans, undid the zipper, and she began to kick her shoes off while he pushed her pants and underwear down her legs.

And then she was just naked. In front of him. In front of Jace. And it felt right. It felt good.

The way that he looked at her… Like he wanted to devour her. And she was ready. Ready for it to be more than just a dangerous glint in his eye, a hint, a promise. She was ready for it to be real.

He put his hands around her waist, smoothed them down her hips and back up, skimming the undersides of her breasts, before traversing a path down her body again, and all the while, his eyes were locked onto hers. His gaze intense. She shivered, and she wanted to look away, but she found that she couldn't. All she could do was stand there, trembling beneath his hands.

"So beautiful," he said.

And then he picked her up, like she weighed nothing, held her in his arms as he carried her to her bedroom. Of course he knew exactly where it was. He had been in it any number of times, but not with these dangerous eyes. Not with her naked and him halfway there.

But that he knew where he was spoke again to the familiarity of what they were.

He set her down at the center of the bed and stood back, kicking his boots off, his hands going to his belt.

And she froze. She wanted to see him. Jace. She had never seen him naked. Of course she hadn't. She had never seen a naked man before. She could see the outline of his arousal through the faded denim of his jeans.

He was big. Not that she had any comparison or anything like that. But she could still tell he was big.

She licked her lips as he began to undo the belt buckle. As he began to pull the leather and slide it through the belt loops slowly.

"Yes," she whispered.

"You looking forward to this?" he asked, his voice husky.

"Yes," she confirmed, her own voice sounding scratchy.

"Good. Because it's for you, baby. This is definitely for you."

"Don't call me that," she said.

"Don't call you what?"

"Don't call me 'baby,' please. Call me Cara."

"Cara," he said, his voice coming out a growl.

He pushed his jeans and underwear off and revealed the extent of his arousal.

"Oh my," she said.

"Now that's not like you at all," he said.

He was confident, no nerves at all, and he didn't need them. He was gorgeous. Every inch of him sculpted and lean and glorious.

His manhood was thick and just plain beautiful. She wouldn't have expected she'd think that about male anatomy, but she damn sure did. About Jace.

He moved over to the bed and pushed one knee down into the mattress, looking at her. Then he put his hands on her knees, smoothed them up her thighs, before forcing her legs apart.

"Jace," she said, the word a protest.

"Don't hide from me," he said, the command so firm she had no choice but to obey. She relaxed her thighs, let her legs fall open.

"That's right," he said. "Show me everything, baby. Show me."

She relaxed even further, and she felt herself getting more and more aroused beneath the sharpness of his gaze. Then he pushed his fingers right between her slick folds, finding her wet with desire for him.

Heat flared in his eyes. "You're so perfect, Cara. So perfect. And I need to taste you now."

She was about to protest, she really was, but then he lowered his head, buried his face between her thighs, and his tongue was so perfect and unerring that she couldn't breathe. Couldn't think.

She looked down, and immediately, her arousal inched its way up higher. Impossibly so. But it was undeniably Jace's head there. Between her legs. Undeniably her best friend licking her, tasting her.

She gasped, the beginnings of her orgasm pulsing from deep within her. And then he pushed a finger inside of her, and she lost it completely. She pulsed around him, arching her hips upward as her release slammed into her.

"You're so hot," he growled, moving up her body and capturing her mouth with a kiss. She could taste her own desire on his lips, and she found herself right back where she had been only moments ago. Turned on and ready to go.

He kissed her as he worked a second finger inside of her, and she moaned, letting her head relax against the pillow. There was so much that she wanted to do. She wanted to pleasure him with her mouth. She wanted to kiss him all over. She wanted… Him. All of him. But she didn't have the words to say that, because she was simply lost. Lost in the moment, lost in him.

He pushed a third finger inside of her and she arched her hips into the stinging discomfort.

"I know you said you had a vibrator. But I still want to make sure you're ready."

"Believe me," she whispered. "I'm ready."

And it was absurd. These impossibly intimate things they were doing. That they could go from being platonic all their whole relationship, to this, in the space of only an hour didn't seem real.

And somehow it seemed right all the same.

Because it had been there. Beneath the surface. Because it wasn't random. Because it hadn't come from nothing. Because it was the truth, was the thing. The truth of how she felt about him.

And she supposed the truth of how he felt about her, even if it was limited to the physical and didn't extend to anything emotional.

Because you couldn't take this. Couldn't manufacture it, and she wasn't even tempted to ask if he was just doing her a favor. Because he was different in this moment. Because it wasn't brotherly Jace who had helped her out of any number of scrapes or taught her how to shoot or anything like that.

She would know if that's what he was doing, because she knew him.

"I hope you have... Condoms," she said.

"Yeah. I do."

The words were strange, the tendons in his neck standing out.

He withdrew from her and went to where he had discarded his jeans, grabbed his wallet and took out a condom packet. He tore it open, then positioned the protection over the head of his arousal, rolling it down slowly, gritting his teeth as he did. It was so erotic to see that. She shivered. And her teeth were still chattering when he came back to the bed, when he steadied her with a kiss, settling between her thighs, and the blunt head of his arousal pressed against the soft, slick entrance of her body, and she held her breath as he filled her.

Yeah, she had penetrated herself with a vibrator before. But that was different. It was hard, and it hadn't been this big.

She could feel him, pulsing inside of her. She could feel how this was different.

And it was… Him.

She looked up at him, and their eyes met. She fought against a strange swell of emotion in her chest. Jace. Jace was inside of her, and she didn't think anything could have prepared her for that. For the enormity of it. For what it meant. And suddenly, it did feel like too much. It felt like too much too fast. Too much for forever. Because one thing she couldn't deny was how deep her feelings ran for him when he pushed himself all the way inside of her and she felt whole. Complete. Felt like she had never wanted anything quite so badly.

Jace.

She didn't know if she said it out loud, screamed it, whispered it, or if it just resonated in her soul. All she knew was that he was there. And she wanted him.

All she knew was that it was too late to turn away. All she knew was that there would be no going back to the way things were before. Because it was too profound. Too real. Too utterly and completely earth-shattering.

And then he began to move, and each thrust of his body within hers pushed her closer and closer to that inevitable peak. She would've thought that it had been too much. Too intense that last time for her to be able to achieve it again, but here she was. His movements became sharp, hard. And that was when it was like being lit on fire. When there was no more control. No more tenderness because he was trying to take her innocence into account. This was hard and rough and primal. It was what she had asked for. She wrapped her legs around his waist, and it made him go deeper. She gasped at the impossibility of it. And how glorious it was.

"Jace…"

"Cara," he ground out, thrusting hard and fast until his control unraveled completely. Until it was like a desperate race to the finish line. She screamed out her pleasure before she even realized her orgasm had crashed over her. And then she was lost. Swept out to sea. Couldn't find a foothold. Couldn't get purchase.

"Jace." She said his name again. It was her battle cry. Her prayer. Her sanctuary and her tempest all at once.

And then his own release took him. He lowered his head, pressing his forehead hard against hers and pumping into her wildly, before going still, and she could feel him pulse deep inside of her. He growled, something feral and uncivilized as his release took hold. And then they lay there together. Sweat slicked and breathing hard.

And she tried to remember the before moment. When they had been the way they'd always been. When they hadn't seen each other naked. When he hadn't been inside of her. And she realized that moment would never be able to stand on its own ever again.

Because they would've always done this.

Because every memory she had of him now would be colored with knowledge.

Of who he was when he made love. What he looked like beneath his clothes. How it felt to have him buried deep within her.

It wasn't just the after that was changed. It was the before.

And she really hadn't taken that into account. But here they were. Inglorious and changed.

Reduced to the very essence of who human beings ever were. Horny, sweaty messes, who had reveled in improbable things only a moment before.

And there was not another person in the world she could have ever done it with. She knew that much. It was clear as could be.

She didn't want him to say anything. Because she didn't want to move from this space into the next one. She didn't think she could handle it. She just needed to sit in the quiet for another second, try to find her breath.

She wasn't sure that was possible. So she just kept on trying until her eyelids got heavy, and the last thing she saw before she drifted off to sleep was him lying beside her.

Nine

He couldn't remember the last time he'd had a cigarette, but thankfully, along with condoms, they were
always in his pocket.

Because sometimes, after a night of heavy drinking,
only a little nicotine would do. He hadn't been drunk
on alcohol tonight, though. It was her.

The night was still and cold, and he sat out there on
her back porch, staring off into the darkness. He didn't
have his truck, so he couldn't leave. Anyway, leaving
after he had just...

After he'd just screwed his best friend's brains out,
was maybe not the best way to go. But then, was he
screwing her brains out, or had she done it to him? It
was hard to say.

It never felt anything like that before. Their connection, combined with the chemistry... It was unreal.

He flicked the switch on the lighter until it started up, lit the cigarette and took a deep drag off of it, then watched the glowing red end and the smoke curl up into the night.

"What are you doing out there?"

He turned around and saw Cara looking at him through her partially opened window.

"Sorry. Didn't realize the window was open."

"I woke up before I smelled the cigarette smoke."

She shut the window, and a moment later, the glass door slid open, and she stepped outside. "What's this?"

"Nothing. Just… Cigarette break."

"You don't smoke."

"Not usually. But, sometimes."

"Is this when I find out a whole bunch of things about you I didn't know?"

"It wasn't a secret."

"I guess."

She sat in the chair next to him. There was the space of a small, round table between them. She was dressed in an oversize T-shirt and nothing more. Her blond hair was a wreck. And he knew why.

A knot of guilt formed in his chest.

Was it guilt? He didn't think it was. It was something else entirely.

He wanted to call it uncertainty. But the fact of the matter was… It was a resistance of certainty.

He'd taken care of her. It was what he had purposed to do. He had a great time having sex with her. It had been great. They'd both enjoyed it. So there was nothing to feel guilty about. She'd consented enthusiastically, as had he.

It was what he felt like required doing in the aftermath.

"So why don't you tell me why you've never been with anybody before."

"Really?"

"Well. I have licked you between your legs, Cara Summers. So I think that maybe we don't need to have barriers up between us."

"Tell me about the cigarette, first."

"Sometimes I smoke after sex. There. It's that basic. Or when I'm really drunk. Sometimes both of those things are happening at the same time."

"Oh. It's just..."

"It's relaxing," he said. "That's all."

"I see."

And hell, because he had had his face between her legs, he didn't really see the point in holding back the truth of it. "I was never really all that into hard drugs. And let me tell you, there's opportunity for all of that out on the rodeo. I've tried just about everything. But mostly, what I learned was how to smooth out the rough edges incrementally. Little whiskey here and there, an orgasm is a great sleeping pill. A cigarette will finish you off. That's it. When I don't want to think anymore, those are the things that I do. I'm a high-functioning self-medicator."

"Oh. I guess I just... I see you as someone who's amazing and strong and doing really well. I guess sometimes I don't see how much pain you're still in."

"No, didn't you hear what I just said? I'm not in pain, because I know how to keep all that going. An unbroken chain."

"Sure. So it's not really because of me specifically. This is just a thing you do."

"I needed to think."

"Did you… I mean… Was the sex good for you?"

He sat up straight. "You can be in any doubt of that?"

"Yes. I can. Because I'm just a person. A person who is very… Vulnerable, when it comes right down to it. There's a reason that I haven't been with anybody. And that is what you wanted to know. I grew up so isolated in a lot of ways. Everybody here was mean to me. I wasn't cool. I was this poor, very unfashionable girl, who lived with her grandpa. White trash. My mom was a drug addict and everybody knew it. And I never knew who my dad was, and everybody knew that too. I was one of those kids. The ones that nobody wanted to touch. And it was my grandpa, and the bar and the town that ended up grounding me here. And yeah, I like to flirt at the bar. But can you imagine if I actually let any one of those guys sleep with me? Then they would all think that they could. It's all fun and games when it's flirting." She looked away. "And anyway, what I said is true. I saw you touch this woman one time… All I could think about was what that must be like. And I swear to you, Jace, you are my friend, and you always have been. And I feel guilty about this. I do. But I've thought about sleeping with you. A lot."

He took another drag on the cigarette. "Tell me," he said, blowing the smoke out into the air.

"The night before the hotel… The night before I… I told you that I was a virgin… I couldn't sleep. I started thinking about you and… Then it seemed like the easiest thing in the world to touch myself."

He flicked the cigarette down onto the ground and twisted his boot over the top of it. "What are you telling me exactly?"

"I touch myself sometimes and think about you.

About you being the one to touch me. About us… In bed together."

"You know, it's a good thing I never knew about that before now. Because you would not have been untouched all this time."

"You don't feel violated by that?"

"Did you really think I would?"

"I don't know. Sometimes I felt really guilty about it. Like it was an invasion of your privacy. But…"

"But, you were too horny to care?"

She laughed, and he could see that her cheeks had been stained dark pink with just a little bit of charming embarrassment. "I guess. Isn't that kind of the human condition?"

"Yeah. Often. I guess tonight is a good example of that. Look, Cara, for me… I decided a long time ago that I wasn't going to look at you that way. I wasn't going to let myself think about you that way because I had to protect you. For all the people that were mean to you, from anything that they might say. Because you're right. There was stuff. About your parents. And I didn't want anybody to think that I was using you like that, and say the kinds of things about you that they said about your mom."

"Oh."

"So that's one reason. The other is just that I wanted to take care of you the way that I would've taken care of Sophia. And so I put you hard in that category. Sister. I wanted to treat you like my sister. But you weren't my sister. That's the thing. And it's funny, because I fancy myself a realist. I don't talk to ash bottles on the shelf in the back of a bar. But I sure as hell have spent my life trying to compensate for her not being here like she could see it. Like she can see what I'm doing. Like it might mean something to her. Shit. I never really realized that about myself. It's a hell of a thing. It really is. I like to tell myself that I'm too... Logical. Realistic. But I'm just living as a tribute for a ghost I claim I don't even believe in. So, what am I supposed to do with that?"

"But not tonight," she said softly, looking down at her hands.

"No. Not tonight. That was about you and me."

And yet again, that feeling rose up inside of his chest. That booming need to do something.

He'd been telling himself that he didn't know what he wanted for the last couple of months, and yet at the end of the day, he was pretty sure he knew what he had to do.

"Will you come back to bed?"

"Yeah," he said. "Just a minute."

"Will you brush your teeth first?"

"Only because you asked nicely," he said.

She stood up, and walked back toward the house and turned and looked at him just one last time before she slipped into the glass door.

And he sat out there for just a few moments longer, until everything inside of him went still. Until all his certainty crystallized.

Then he stood up and went back toward her bedroom. But not before he stopped and brushed his teeth.

He had kissed her goodbye this morning around five o'clock, and she had a feeling that had been on purpose, because they hadn't had a chance to talk.

The kiss hadn't been on her mouth. It had just been on her cheek.

They hadn't had sex again. He pulled her up against

him and said something about her being sore, and told her to go to sleep. She didn't know how he got home—if he called one of his brothers or if he'd taken a cab…

She felt a little bit melancholy, and she carried that all through her day. Her offer was accepted on the hotel, and she made an appointment to go and sign papers. It also happened to work out that the contractor she wanted to use was free to meet with her at the property that afternoon. And all of that should've been great and exciting and more than enough of a distraction to stop thinking about Jace.

It was perfectly normal for them to not have communicated on a random Thursday.

It was just that they had never not communicated on a random Thursday the night after they'd had sex.

They'd had sex.

She wasn't a virgin anymore.

Sex sounded so clinical, even in her head.

She would call it making love, but it hadn't been especially sweet either. It had been… Wrenching. A rending.

It had been something else entirely.

And now so was she. And maybe so were they.

She couldn't shake that image of him, sitting with his elbows on his knees in that chair on her back patio, the cigarette between his fingers. His cowboy hat on like he was fixing to leave in the middle of the night.

She had to say something to him. Because he was her friend.

Because she didn't want him to go.

She sighed and pulled her truck up to the front of the hotel. It was almost hers. Just a few signature pages away.

The contractor was already there, his big white truck

parked out front. She got out and tried to smile. She'd been trying to smile all day.

"Hey," she said. "Glad you could make it by today."

"Good to see you, Cara."

Mike Colton was a regular at the bar, and they had a pretty good rapport. He was never flirtatious and didn't flirt with any other women in the bar, which was good, considering he was married. So she had a pretty high opinion of him right off the bat. Plus, she knew he did good work.

"Let's take a walk through the place."

She heard the sound of an engine, and turned around. Just as Jace pulled right into the driveway.

"Oh," she said.

Her mind went blank. Jace put the truck in Park and got out, and her tongue was suddenly as dry as a patch of scrub brush. "I didn't… I didn't realize that you were coming," she said.

"Of course. I just figured… You know, it's my investment. I thought I'd come by and look."

Except he hadn't known that she was meeting with the contractor today, because they hadn't talked. So she wondered what had really compelled him to come by here.

Yeah. She really did.

"Good to have you," said Mike. Who, to his credit, did not immediately start deferring to Jace, which made her feel even better about choosing him to be the contractor.

Except suddenly she was resentful. Resentful that she was in the middle of the contractor meeting. Because she wondered why Jace had come to find her. She wondered why he was really here. And she wondered what he was thinking.

She went around to the back, where the lockbox was, and popped it open, taking the key out from the inside. "Here," she said. "I'll show you the inside."

They walked in, and Mike started explaining about the good bones and all kinds of other things that construction types said.

"It's nice," she said. "It just needs some updating."

"Yeah. If you don't mind, I'll take a walk through, and I'll let you know what I think."

"Yeah. Just, you let me know what you think homeowners are always asking you for. I need to make sure that I have all the amenities that I could possibly want for guests."

"I'm betting it's going to focus a lot on the bathrooms," he said. "That can get expensive. But believe me, it's always worth the investment."

"She can afford it," said Jace.

Mike smiled, then started to walk through the room, clipboard in hand, making notes.

She turned to face Jace, the minute they were alone. "How did you know that I would be here?"

"I didn't. I happened to be driving to the bar. I saw your truck parked out front."

"Oh."

"I was looking for you."

"You were?"

"Yeah. I wanted to talk to you. Because…" He stopped talking. He wrapped his arm around her waist and pulled her up against his body, full-length, and then he kissed her. Kissed her the way she wished he would've done this morning. Kissed her the way she wanted so desperately to be kissed.

"Oh," she breathed.

"Cara…"

"Sorry," said Mike, clearing his throat. "I just wanted to show you something concerning."

"It's already concerning," said Jace.

"Is it a hole where raccoons could get in?" Cara asked.

Mike frowned. "No. Am I looking for one of those?"

"Yes," said Jace and Cara at the same time.

Mike's eyebrows shot up. "Look, as long as you're realistic about the place."

"I think we're pretty realistic," she said.

Mike led them back to the pantry area where there was some rotted wood in the back. "I'm just worried I'm going to find more things like this," said Mike.

"Like I said," Jace said. "We really do have the budget. We don't want to cut any corners. This needs to be a luxury escape. Affordable, but the kind of people that want to travel here and stay in a historic place, want it to be charming without being uncomfortable. We don't want them thinking it just feels old and outdated. We definitely don't need soft floorboards."

"Of course not," she said.

Mike looked between the two of them, and she knew that they were now in an uphill battle with gossip. Because he had definitely seen them kiss.

"I'll keep looking around," said Mike.

"Well," she said, when they were alone in the pantry. "He saw that."

"Fine with me," said Jace.

"I mean, the argument could definitely be made that most people will think that we were already sleeping together, but…"

"I wanted to talk to you about that. I'm staying here. I'm not going back to the rodeo. I'm investing in the hotel. It isn't that I don't know what I want, it's that I was resisting what I want. You know I don't like dreams. And you know I like everything locked in place. I like it sure, I like it certain. The hotel's a little bit of a gamble, but I don't mind gambling with money. As for the rest... Nothing in my life is mine. And that's by design. Whatever I don't have, I don't have because I didn't want it. I love my family, but I recognized pretty early that loving people is painful. I've been riding the rodeo because it was there. Because it was something to do. But that's not enough for me anymore. I need something that's mine. I'm going to stay in Lone Rock—that's what I'm trying to tell you."

Her heart started to throb. "And?"

"And I want you. I want you, Cara."

"You... You want me?"

It wasn't really a declaration of love... Did she even want a declaration of love? The very idea was sort of terrifying. She hadn't fully let herself process her feelings for him. And he was... Well, he wasn't a romantic. That much was sure and certain.

"Yes. I want..."

They heard footsteps again. "Hold that thought."

Mike returned. "Sorry," he said. "Just wanted you to look at some things in the bathroom."

"Rain check," he said.

Her heart was thundering so hard, she didn't think she could take a rain check. But they did decide that they would just go ahead and follow Mike while he looked around. "I'll write up a bid," he said an hour later. "One that's based primarily around modernizing the bathrooms, making sure you have new plumbing, good hot water heaters and modern fixtures in the kitchen, which

I know won't really have anything to do with the guests, but if you're going to hire anybody to do some cooking... It'll make things easier."

She really didn't care about cooking. Or plumbing. Or anything but what Jace had been about to tell her, but she knew she couldn't completely abandon the point of all of this, not right now. Not when the point of this was business, and not for her to kiss Jace. But she really wanted to kiss Jace.

And find out exactly what he had been about to tell her.

"It all sounds great," she said. "Thanks, Mike."

And she smiled, hoping that he would get the idea that her smile was the period at the end of this sentence. And he did, giving them a half wave and heading out the door.

She looked up at Jace. "I would really like to hear what you were going to tell me."

"Well. You're my best friend. And I want to be part of this venture with you... And you know, I just don't like halfway shit. I think we should get married."

Ten

He'd thought about it. He was confident in it. And he knew that there were a whole lot of people who wouldn't understand how he had gone from friends, to sex once, to wanting to get married, but he wasn't a man who operated in halfway zones. He was a man of absolutes. He hadn't committed to anything, not for all of his life. And if he was going to commit to any one thing, then it was going to be Cara. There was no way he was going to have sex with her, then pretend that it hadn't happened. There was no way that he was going to…

No. There was no way on earth that he was going to be cool with her moving on and being with other people. And that meant that there was only one option available to him. Locking that shit down.

That was it.

He was in on the hotel. He was in on everything.

Whatever she wanted, whatever she needed. He wanted to buy land. And he wanted to build a house on it. And he was going to… He was going to do what he had always promised that he would do. He was going to take care of this woman.

That feels perilously close to a dream.

It wasn't a dream. It was action. It was a plan. It was what needed to happen.

"I… I don't understand."

"The way I see it, it's about the only option we have. Do you want me to sleep with someone else?"

"Hell no," she said.

"I don't want you to sleep with anyone else. Do you want to sleep together a couple more times and see where it goes, take the chance that it might burn out?"

"I…"

"No. Because do you think we can possibly go back? Do you think that we can pretend that never happened?"

"No. And it's why it never did before. And it's why it was… Well, I guess it was a bad idea."

"But it wasn't an idea, was it? It was a thing, and it happened. And I think it was undeniable. Neither of us decided to do it. We didn't just think… Well let's see what happens. We didn't think at all. And listen, when it comes to life, one thing I know is that I'm committed to you. I'm committed to you in a way that I never have been to anyone I'm not related to. So one thing I know for sure is that I've always wanted you to be in my life for all my life. I was never planning on having it be any different. So if I'm going to put down roots, those roots are going to tangle up with yours, Cara. That's just a fact."

"I don't know what to say, Jace. I… I really didn't

expect for you to be proposing after one time of being together."

"Think about it. How would it have ever ended in another way?"

It couldn't. That was the thing. And yes, they were different. She was sparkly and fantastical, and he was him. But there had never been another person that he had ever known needed to be by his side for the rest of forever.

"The thing is," said Cara. "You usually travel for half the year. And… You're one of my favorite people on earth. Hell, I think you might be my favorite person on earth, but living together and… And we had sex once."

"What do you want from your life? I mean, do you want to work at the bar every night until two thirty in the morning?"

"No. It's why I'm expanding. It's why I'm buying the hotel."

"Did you want to get married? Start a family?"

"Do you?"

It was a good question, because he'd never given much thought to it. It was part and parcel of the whole not thinking ahead thing. "If you want kids, then yeah."

He would give her whatever she wanted. He realized that. Whatever was in his power to give, he was going to. Because she was Cara, and she had been essential to him from the time they were kids. And he never dreamed of a wife and a family, but… He'd have kids. For her.

"But you don't want them."

"No. I think you're misunderstanding. It doesn't matter what I want. Or maybe better put, what I want is tangled up with what you want. With what makes you happy." What he knew, the conclusion he'd come to, after he'd gotten up at the butt crack of dawn and gone out to work himself to death, because it was the only way to get any kind of mental clarity was that he couldn't imagine letting another man take that position in her life. It wouldn't do. There would be no burning out his attraction for her. There would be no forgetting that those things had passed between them.

And that meant making it permanent. Whatever that looked like for her.

He had done his level best to be whatever she needed over all these years, and he would keep on doing it.

"Can I... Take a rain check on that question?"

"You're the one who asked it."

"Yeah. Kind of. I asked what you wanted, and... Never mind." He could see that something was bothering her.

"I want this," he said, something intense tugging at his chest. Undeniable. "Because there's no other way that I can imagine us getting all the things that we want. You and me. Together. And together like we were last night."

"I... You know, half of what bothers me about this is everybody's just going to think they were right all along."

He couldn't help it. He laughed. Because of course of all the things that would bother Cara, what other people thought—not in terms of appearances, but just in terms of her being proved wrong in any kind of way—was high on her list.

"Yeah. We are going to get mercilessly harassed by my brothers."

"I'm not sure anything is worth it," said Cara.

"You know it is," he said. "Come on. Remember last night?"

And she turned pink. From the roots of her blond hair, all the way down to her breasts. At least, the part that he could see.

"Cara. Don't you want that?"

"Yes," she whispered. "I do. But marriage is a big step and I just don't…"

"Remember what I said, about the ride. About the certainty. I don't do halfway. I don't and I won't. The only reason that I felt uncertain these last few months is because I knew I needed to make a decision. It was either go back all the way, or be here all the way. I felt all this time like I didn't have anything that was mine. Like I didn't have anything to claim. While I do now."

"Are you… Claiming me?"

"Yes. I sure as hell am claiming you. As mine. My best friend. My lover. I hope my wife."

"It's just… It's a lot. And it's like a complete one-eighty from where we were just a couple of days ago? I don't…"

"It's not a one-eighty. It was just a step closer to each other. There's not another person that I can think about living in a house with. Building a life with. You know, it really pains me to say that Boone was right. We're in each other's lives, and now we're in business together. We are enmeshed in each other's lives in every single way. It feels right. It feels like time."

And he had never meant anything half so much as he meant this.

"You're really not going to let me even think about this?"

"Do you need to?"

Her eyebrows shot up. "You really are kind of an arrogant son of a bitch."

"Yeah, but you knew that about me. You knew that the whole time."

"I did, but I guess I've never been in a position where it was directed at me."

"Oh it has. It's just that I dial it up in increments, and eventually, you get kind of dead to it."

She laughed. "Apparently not."

He leaned in, and right then, he couldn't take it anymore. He wanted her. He needed her. He hadn't realized how much until he had showed up at the house and seen her.

That was the thing—this wasn't going away. And he was a man who made decisions. A man who went with the moment.

And the moment had dictated that they kiss. It had demanded that they go to bed together. And that turn of events demanded this. And nothing less.

That was the simple truth of it all. And so he kissed her. On an indrawn breath. Captured it with his lips and turned it into a sigh of desire.

"Please," he said.

"Oh shit. Now you even said please? That really is a miracle."

He smiled against her mouth, and he felt her smile back.

He kissed her, and he was overwhelmed by the reality of it all. That it was her.

And the rightness of it too. Now that he'd made the decision… It was right. It was just right.

The decisiveness roared through him. And suddenly, it was like every piece of his life was locked into place, in perfect alignment. For the first time in maybe ever.

This was right. This was what he was supposed to

be, where he was supposed to be, with who he was supposed to be with.

So he kissed her. Right there in the ghost hotel, right there, where all this had started. Or maybe it had started long before. Before she had ever looked up at him with those starry green eyes and told him that she was still a virgin.

She wasn't anymore. He'd seen to that. Now she was his.

He picked her up, because he liked to do that, and carried her toward the stairs. She wrapped her arms around his neck and kept on kissing him, and they went down the hall, to that room, where they had shared a bed, because this time, he aimed to share it with her properly.

The curtains were still drawn around it, and he pushed them aside and set her down on the blankets.

"You know," she said. "None of it's actually dusty."

"You know, I wouldn't have cared if it was. Because all I can think about is being inside of you again."

"I might've thought about the dust. But I appreciate that as a ringing endorsement of my sexual prowess."

"You wouldn't have been thinking about dust." He kissed her lips, her cheek, her neck. "I would've made sure of that."

He laid her back on the bed and let the curtain swing shut. It was dim behind the curtains, but he liked the intimacy that it gave. He stripped her shirt slowly from her body, and even in the dim light, he could see her shape just fine.

He unhooked her bra and threw it to the side. And he was in awe. Of the fact that he could do this with her now. That she was his, and he could just look his fill when he wanted to. No more restraint. No more pretending she wasn't the most beautiful woman he'd ever seen.

He moved to her jeans next, stripped her completely of her clothes and admired all of her. Her stomach, the curves, the dips, her belly button. That downy patch of pale curls at the apex of her thighs. Her legs.

All of her.

She had always been the strongest, funniest woman he'd ever known, and on some level, he'd known she was the sexiest, but he'd tried to keep himself from living in that space. And now he'd moved in permanently.

She was everything.

Absolutely everything.

He kissed her neck, her breasts. Kissed her until she was shivering. Teased them both.

And then suddenly, he felt her hand pressed against the center of his chest, pushing him away. She sat up, grabbing hold of the hem of his shirt and pulling it up over his head. It was like she had come alive with need. She explored his body, kissed his chest, went down his abs and started to undo his belt. And he knew where this was going next, and he did not have the fortitude to stop it. She unzipped his jeans and wrapped her hand around his arousal, exposing him. She pushed his pants and underwear down, and with her hand wrapped firmly around the base of him, leaned in and took him into her mouth.

"Shit," he said, grabbing hold of her ponytail and holding tight.

"I've never done this before," she said.

And hell. That just about took him out. Then and there.

It was nearly over before it started.

"Damn, woman. You can't just say things like that."

"But I want you. I want this. I want you to know that you're the only one. I want you, with all your marriage proposal, and your certainty to know, that you're the man I fantasized about. You're the man that I wanted. You're the only man I wanted to lick like this." And she made direct eye contact with him while she slid her tongue from the base of his shaft all the way to the tip. "You're the only one I ever wanted to take in deep."

And that was exactly what she did next. And all he could do was hang on. Let her pleasure him. Let her make him his. He wanted her. He wanted this. This was her staking her claim. His had been a marriage proposal, while she was branding him with his own desire. Letting him know that he would never, ever own his own need again. Because it would always be in the palms of Cara Summers's hands.

He let her pleasure him like that until it became too much. Until he got too close to the edge.

"Come on," he said, his voice rough. "I want to be inside you."

"You were inside me," she said, a little grin tugging at the corners of her mouth.

"You know what I mean."

"No, I don't. You're gonna have to tell me."

"I want inside where you're all wet for me. Just for me. You saved that for me too, didn't you?"

And he would never see anything half so beautiful as his best friend blushing over his dirty talk for her.

And if that was his future, and if that was marriage, it made him want to look forward to it just a little bit.

But there was no need to look forward. Because they could just exist in these moments. Every day until the wedding. Because she would say yes. Of course she would. Because how could they ever go back. Which meant it had to be always. They couldn't take a chance on anything else.

He took his wallet out of his back pocket and took a new condom out of there, then kicked his jeans and shoes off the rest of the way, before rolling the protection on quickly. Then he rolled over onto his back, gripped her hips and brought her down over him. "Next lesson. I want you to ride me. So that I can watch you. Give me a show."

He brought her down slowly, positioning her on his aching length. She moaned, grabbing hold of his shoulders as she flexed her hips, taking him in deep. She began to move her hips, gracefully, elegantly. Like dirty poetry. And he had always imagined that his own brand of hedonism and Cara's divinity could never mix, but he was being proven wrong here and now. Because something he would've said was profane, was very definitely not, not here and now. It felt sanctified somehow, and he would never be able to explain that.

And when she reached up and cupped her own breast, squeezed herself, then her nipple, as she continued to flex her hips over him, he just about died, and he'd be hard-pressed to deny the fact that he saw God in that moment.

Her golden hair was wild, and her lips were parted, her eyes closed. As she moved over him, riding them both into a frenzy.

And finally, he lost his patience. He turned her over onto her back, pinning her to the mattress, his thrusts hard and deep. She moaned, arching up against him off the mattress, and her orgasm broke over her, squeezing him tight. "Jace," she said. And when she said his name it was music. When she said his name, it was fuel to the fire.

When she said his name, it was everything.

But it was when she bit her lip and looked up at him, those green eyes staring straight into him, as if she could see all the way down into what he was, that was when he lost it. It was when he looked full in the face of his best friend in all the world, while the wet clasp of her body was tight around his arousal, while her breasts were pressed up against his chest—that was when he lost it.

His orgasm was merciless, grabbing him by the throat and all but tearing it out, the growl that rose up from inside of him a prayer and a curse all in one.

And this seemed right. Sealing their new life together in this place. This place that had triggered it. This place that had been the first step.

He held her close on the bed for a long moment, until their heartbeats calmed down.

"Yes," she said softly. "Yes, Jace, I'll marry you."

"Good," he said, dropping a kiss on the top of her head. Because he could do that now. Because he could kiss her and touch her, and she could do the same to him, because they had erased those barriers between them. And he meant it, that it was good, but he couldn't help but wonder if he'd said the wrong thing, because she didn't look joyously happy, but she buried her face against his shoulder and fell asleep, so he figured it wasn't all bad either.

How could it be?

They were best friends.

Eleven

She really wished that she had a different friend, other than Jace. And she had never really wished that before. She was perfectly fine having all of her friendship eggs in one basket. But the problem was, she had her friendship eggs in his basket, and now her relationship eggs, and she just wished that there was somebody that she could talk to. Somebody that would be able to reassure her that she was making the right choice. It was just that… Jace hadn't said anything about being in love with her. And it was because she knew he wasn't.

The thing with Jace was he was hardheaded, and he was stubborn. And he damn sure thought that his way was the best way. But what she couldn't figure out was exactly why he had decided that he wanted this. She could circle around it. But she didn't think she was quite hitting his motivation on the head, and that worried her a little bit. That she couldn't quite parse it. Yes, she understood that he wanted to put down roots.

Yes, she understood that he could only see this going one of two ways.

That they would eventually take other lovers, or they had to commit to each other. And since Jace was kind of a paperwork, lock, stock, and barrel kind of guy, for him, the answer would be marriage, and not just moving in together. She knew him well enough to understand all of that. But she felt like there was something deeper. And the problem with Jace was he would never admit to that. He would never admit to the deeper. He would never even say it to himself. He was the man who swore up and down there was nothing after this life and he was totally fine with it. He was the man who didn't believe in manifesting your dreams or any of that.

And she was the one who still talked to her grandpa like he was right there with her.

A slight smile lifted the corner of her mouth, and she turned and looked up at the Jack Daniel's bottle. "Well. Jace wants me to marry him. I don't know if you already know that. I kind of hope that you haven't been spying on us. All things considered. But I told him yes and I'm worried. I'm kind of in love with him. Or I'm really in love with him. And I don't think that that's part of this for him. And that scares me."

She waited. For something. For a rush of wisdom.

A glowing butterfly.

She didn't get any of it.

"I think that if I told Jace I loved him he would run away. Because it's like… He wants to do all these external things to take control, but it's the stuff that he can't control that he can't deal with. And I get it. It's because of Sophia."

She took a deep breath. She wasn't getting any answers. Not out of the silent whiskey bottle.

There was a knock at the back door of the bar, and she figured it was probably her delivery from the food services company. She went back into the kitchen, and opened the door. There was a stack of crates filled with various things. Frozen beef patties and other assorted things they needed for the kitchen. And then she heard a sound. A hawk. And she looked up, and saw a bird circling. And it filled her with a strange sort of hope. Sort of resolve.

"Is that you, Grandpa?"

And then it was like she could see his face.

I'm dead. I got better things to do than hang around here.

That's what he would say. And it made her laugh.

Well, maybe that was her answer. Her grandpa had better things to do than hang around here, so maybe she needed to get her life in order. Buy the hotel. Marry Jace. She didn't want anything else. She didn't want anyone else. She wasn't losing anything by marrying him. Yes, the emotions would always be tricky with him. But he cared about her. And it wasn't like she had another man who was desperately in love with her waiting in the wings. It was just… It was just knowing that she maybe cared a little bit more than he did. That was the tough thing. But it would be worth it. It would be worth it to be with him.

Her phone buzzed.

She looked down at the text that she had just gotten.

Dinner with my family tonight?

And she knew that her answer would cement this forever.

Yes.

Yes. She was going to marry Jace. And his family was going to say I told you so, and it would be totally worth it.

Twelve

It was handy that his sister Callie and her husband, Jake, had been planning on coming to spend a few days anyway. They would be here for the announcement, and that meant that he only had to tell everyone in his family one time what he was going to do. That he was leaving the rodeo, that he was getting married. All of that suited him. It suited him right down to the very ground his boots were standing on.

He had it all mapped out in his mind. Yeah, there might've been some merit to giving his mother at least a warning prior to making the announcement, but he just didn't want to get into it. He only wanted to do it once, and he wanted Cara to be there when he did. Because it would make them behave. Maybe.

He had also spent part of the day looking at land.

He wanted something that was near enough to town

that it would be easy for Cara to manage her interests right there on Main Street, but far enough out that they had a good-size plot of land, and opportunity to make it functional.

He was still deciding what exactly he wanted to ranch. Bison, beef or horses. All completely different endeavors.

Roots.

That's what he was doing now. It was the thing he was doing.

What he didn't anticipate, was how Cara would look when she showed up.

He was in his truck, out in front of his parents' palatial country home, all square lines and lots of glass, when Cara rolled up.

He had seen her in a lot of different things. She typically wore blue jeans. She liked her rhinestones, did his girl, and on the evenings that she worked at the bar, she favored a scoop neck, tight tank top all the better to show off her figure. He was used to her in all these things. The casual T-shirt Cara, and sexy nighttime Cara.

But when she got out of the truck and revealed that she was in a soft, floaty sundress, it just about did him in. It had little short sleeves and a rounded neck with a little bow right at the center of her breasts that he desperately wanted to undo immediately. It was short, coming inches above her knees, swinging when she walked. Her blond hair was loose, curling at the ends and blowing in the breeze, and he was suddenly desperate to touch it.

What was this? This shift.

Because somehow, in that moment, it wasn't about being attracted to his friend. It felt bigger somehow. It wasn't just about having permission to find her beautiful—it was about this woman, this relationship, and something deepening.

He had thought of it as adding something on. But now it seemed like it was just all that they had been, but deeper.

"Look at you," he said.

As he got closer, he could see that she had painted her lips with something glossy and nice, that she had just a little bit of mascara and some gold and green eye shadow that highlighted her eyes.

She was sexy and sweet, exactly how you would want a woman to look that you were bringing home to meet your parents and tell them you were going to marry her.

Of course, she had met his parents before.

So it was more about presenting her as his future wife, rather than his friend.

Except when he reached out and took her hand in his, she was still his friend. And when he leaned in and kissed her lips, she was still his friend. And something expanded in his chest all the same.

They walked up the steps together, hand in hand.

"If we walk in like this they're going to know."

"Yeah. I'm committed to presenting this as if it's a thing they should all be aware of."

She laughed. "Okay. I'm sure Flint and Boone won't give you a hard time in that case."

"As long as you stop flirting with them."

"Probably I won't," she said. "Because it bugs you."

And it was his turn to laugh, because she was so committed to being her, and it was one of the things he liked the very most about her.

That she was cantankerous and stubborn and every inch herself. That she wasn't going to change or become softer or bend just because they were sleeping together. Just because she'd agreed to marry him.

"Yeah, well. I might put my foot down about the men at the bar," he said. Because he was testing her. Because he couldn't help himself.

"You're going to put your foot down?"

"I said what I said."

A little smile tugged at the corner of her mouth. "Jace Carson, have we met?"

"Yes we have. Intimately. Naked."

She shoved him against his shoulder. "Sometimes I think you're still the same boy from when we were twelve."

"Close enough."

Except he didn't feel like that boy. He wasn't sure what he felt like. Resolved, so there was that.

He opened up the front door into the house so that she didn't knock—and they walked inside. His whole family was sitting in the broad, expansive living room, on the different couches and chairs in front of the floor to ceiling windows that overlooked the brilliant view. They were missing Buck, who could come back but wouldn't. And Sophia, who was simply gone. And it pained him that those were the first things he thought of, seeing them all together. Just that they weren't all together. And probably never would be.

"Hey," he said. He grabbed hold of Cara's hand and led her into the room. He figured this was as good a time as any. "I'm glad everybody's here tonight."

"It's good to see you," said his sister Callie, popping up from her chair and reaching out to pull him into a hug. She was just a little bit pregnant, her belly starting to round out. He wondered if Sophia would've had kids by now, had she lived.

He wondered if he would have.

If his life would've been different.

If he could've believed in miracles of hope and love for longer.

But Cara felt like an anchor behind him, and he would take that instead.

"It's good to see everyone, but there's something that Cara and I want to tell you."

He looked over at his mother, who was looking at him with an expectation and joy he wondered how she still felt. His mother, who had always been so pretty and perfect. His mother, who had been devastated at Sophia's loss, but seemed to figure out how to keep on going once she had Callie. "We're getting married."

The roar that went through the room was massive.

"Pay up," said Chance.

"Fuck you," said Boone, reaching into his back pocket and pulling out his wallet.

"What?" he asked.

"We have had a bet going for a long time about whether or not you guys were really a couple," said Chance. "And I win. You owe me so much money. Brother, I know you don't have that kind of cash in your wallet, and you're gonna have to write me a check. But we're going to have to make sure that check is good."

"I have more money than you do," said Boone. "I have more endorsements. Because my face is prettier."

"Well, you owe money to me now."

"Are you kidding me?" he asked.

"Not at all," said Flint, shaking his head. "I didn't go

in as hard as Chance did, but Boone owes me money too. But I figure if he wants to work it off…"

"I'm not doing your chores for you," said Boone angrily. He looked over at Jace. "You know, this should confirm that I'm your favorite brother," said Boone. "Because I believed you. You're a liar."

"What are the particulars of the bet?" Cara asked. She went and sat down on the chair facing his family. He supposed this was the very great perk of Cara knowing his family like she did. "Because, depending on if time lines and the like are part of the bet, you might actually not have won any money from Boone."

"Why?" asked Chance.

"Well, tell me the bet."

"That you been secretly sleeping together the whole time."

"Nope. You lose."

"Shit. Really?"

"Really."

"Well, I collect on the part where I said you would end up together."

"Yep," Cara said. "That you can have."

"When did you start sleeping together?" Chance asked. "Because that is probably something I can work out in terms of how much money I'm owed."

"Chance," said their mother, scolding. "Honestly."

"That's very crass," said Boone. "Why don't you just accept that you lost?"

"I didn't, though," said Chance. "Because they're getting married."

"Congratulations," said Kit. "Really."

"Yes," said his mother, standing up and coming over to them. She went to Cara first and took her hand. Cara stood, and something shifted inside of him as he watched his mother embrace Cara. "You're just perfect for him," she whispered. "Exactly what he needs."

That made something strange reverberate inside of his chest.

"Happy for you," his dad said, getting up from his chair and coming over to clap him on the back. "Damn thrilling to have four of you married. Growing the family like this. It's more than we could've ever hoped for."

"Dinner is ready," said his mother. As if she had cooked it. But then, what his mother was great at was catering. And he appreciated that. "Shall we go into the dining room?"

He walked over to where Cara was and took her hand, lingering in the living room for a moment as the rest of the family filtered in.

"You good?"

She looked up at him and she smiled, and that smile just about broke his heart. "Yes. I love your family. And the idea of actually being part of it is… It's amazing."

I love your family.

That did something to him. Echoed through his soul.

Dinner was a pretty damned beautiful roast duck and sides, and there was something about it that pulled him back to happier times with his family. It wasn't that they hadn't had happier times in the last few years—they had. But there was something that just felt bigger and more right. His sister being here with her husband. His brothers and their wives. Him and Cara. "I'm investing in the hotel. Cara just bought it," he said. "She's going to open it up and revamp it and bring more tourism into town."

"That's fantastic," said his sister-in-law Shelby.

"It'd be nice to get some of your beadwork to sell,"

said Cara. "And some art, maybe. I think it would be amazing to have work by indigenous artisans, so that people can get an idea of the real Lone Rock."

"Happy to oblige," said Shelby. "I love the idea of local art being featured."

"You can recommend anybody whose work you love locally."

"Now I'm drunk with power."

"Investing in business," said his dad. "That's unlike you."

"Well. I'm changing some things. I'm done with the rodeo."

His dad nodded slowly. "I thought you might be."

"Done with the rodeo and looking to buy land around here. So that Cara and I can build a house and start a family."

"I'm so happy for you," said Callie, beaming. "This is just great."

But for some reason, his family's joy wasn't quite touching him all the way down, and he couldn't for the life of him figure out why. Cara seemed happy, and he wanted more than anything for her to be happy. No question about that. None at all. He was doing all of the things that he had decided to, and he had announced it, he was certain.

He didn't know why uncertainty was following him. Because there really wasn't any reason for uncertainty. They finished up dinner, and Shelby and Cara had gotten involved in discussing logistics for selling art and featuring art throughout the hotel for sale, and he and his brothers took the opportunity to go into his parents' game room and throw some darts.

Usually, Callie would've joined the boys. But not

today. Chance threw the first dart and hit the bull's-eye. The problem with this was they were all too good.

"Seriously, though," said Chance, when Kit's dart came from behind and hit his, knocking it out of position. "Congratulations. I'm glad that you finally opened your eyes to what you guys had this whole time."

"Same," said Kit.

Flint and Boone exchanged looks with each other. His brother-in-law, Jake, raised his glass of whiskey. "Absolutely. Marriage is the best damn thing."

"It is," Chance agreed.

"Spoken like a man who keeps his balls in his wife's purse," said Flint.

"Spoken like a man who has a diss track about him that's currently number one on the country airwaves," Chance shot back.

"It is not a diss track. And it isn't about me."

"It's about you," said Boone.

"You're a turncoat," said Flint.

"The thing is," said Chance, "I think opening yourself up to all this… It's tough. It's tough to let go of all the shit that you've been through and decide that you want to… Hope."

"Don't go too far," said Jace, picking up a dart and flinging it at the dartboard. He missed the bull's-eye. What the hell was that about?

"It's not about hope or anything like that. It's just… It makes sense. I'm not gonna be in the rodeo forever. Not by a long shot. And I needed to decide what to do. I felt uncertain, but it was only because I was avoiding the most obvious thing. Clearly, going all in on being here is the answer. And then… Cara and I… You know, something happened."

"When exactly?" Chance asked.

"Not your business. But a couple of days ago."

"A couple of days ago?" Three of his brothers asked that at once.

"Yes," he said.

"And you just… Decided to marry her when the first time you've actually ever been with her was a couple of days ago?" Kit asked.

"Are you suggesting that I should be uncertain about what I want from her?"

"Not at all," said Kit. "I just thought maybe you guys were engaged in some kind of serious slow burn and you were just now ready to tell us all. I didn't know that it was like best friends, then you finally hooked up, and you're getting married right away. You didn't even have a chance to find out she's pregnant."

"We don't all have unprotected sex, Kit," said Jace. "You got your wife pregnant the first time you hooked up, but I don't think I got Cara pregnant."

"Whatever. It's how I snared Shelby, so I'm not sorry about it. There was no way she was looking for a relationship after losing her husband. The baby is what clarified some things."

"Again. Good for you. But the way I see it, it just kinda clicked into place, and I'm not a guy that does uncertainty. I care about her. So she needs to be in my life. Forever. Also, I can't have her hooking up with anybody else. Not gonna work. Not after that."

"Are you in love with her?" Chance asked.

The word scraped raw up against the inside of him.

"My feelings for her are stronger than my feelings for anyone else."

"No. That doesn't cut it. Are you in love with her? Are you giving her everything?"

"Everything I had to give," he said. "Look. I'm just not… I'm not into that. I'm not into this kind of impossible to define fantasy shit. I like what's tangible. That's why marriage is so fast. I don't just want to see where things go. I know I want her in my life forever. What more do I need to know?"

"I feel pretty damn strongly," said Chance, "that marriage is a lot about hope. And a whole lot about magic that you can't quite see or touch. Hell. Remember, I had to get amnesia to end up with my wife. Don't tell me there wasn't some kind of… Mystical intervention that happened there. It's not about just being practical. It's not about everything that you can see and touch. It's about something more than that."

He rebelled against that. "Not for me. I don't believe in that kind of thing."

"You better start. Otherwise… I think it's going to be tough for you."

"I've made the decision that I'm gonna make, and I've got everything that I want."

"Right now. But what can happen when she wants more from you."

"I don't know what more there could be. She's important to me. Essential enough that I'm willing to tie myself to her forever. I don't want to be with another woman. That became clear the minute that I touched her. I…"

"Why do you think this isn't love?" Kit asked.

"I don't know," he said. "Who cares what you call it. Maybe it is."

But something in him pushed back at that, and hard.

Like walls he had built around his soul were reinforcing themselves. Reminding him why they were there.

"I'm marrying her," he said. "What difference does it make what we call it?"

"I guess no difference,"

"There you go. Just say congratulations and that you're happy for me."

"I am," said Chance. "But the thing is, being with Juniper healed something inside of me. But you can't go into marriage the same and expect for it to work. Expect for it to heal you."

"I'm not looking to be healed," he said.

"Why not?" Kid asked.

"Because," he said. "Sophia is dead, and there's nothing anyone can do about it. She's gone. She'll always be gone. So the wound should never go away."

He looked down at the whiskey glass he was holding and frowned. It had a butterfly painted on the side.

He looked at the other glasses on the table in the room. Each had something different. It wasn't significant.

They didn't talk about him anymore after that. They just finished playing darts.

Thirteen

Cara felt so surrounded by love and warmth. Her future sisters-in-law fussed over her, and Jace's mother seemed to be just so happy.

And she felt partly like a fraud. She didn't know why. She and Jace were really getting married. They weren't making that up. It was just that… He hadn't said anything about being in love with her. And she couldn't figure out if she was being strange. If she was splitting hairs. Because Jace cared about her. She knew that. She would say it was indisputable even that he loved her. But she just had to wonder if his feelings had actually changed, or if they were just sleeping together.

And then she had to ask herself why it mattered. If it even did.

She had him in her life, the most stable relationship,

and they were going to make it legal. So what did it matter what they called it.

Because you love him.

But what did that matter? Why would it be different if he said he loved her, or if he was in love?

She shoved all of her reservations to the side. And when Jace came back from playing darts with his brothers, he took her hand. "Want to drive over to my place?"

And she did. She really did. She wanted to spend the night with him. She wanted to solidify this whole thing. That their relationship had changed. And also that they were still them. Both felt so important right now. Both felt like it might be everything.

"You can follow me over."

She drove in her car behind him, down the bumpy dirt road that led away from the main house and toward the house he lived in on the property. She pulled up to his place, just behind him.

She got out and walked right to him. "Jace…"

She had been about to ask him where they might live when they were first married. If they would live here, if they would live at her place. But he wrapped his arm around her waist and pulled her to him. And pressed a kiss to her mouth. Fervent, hard and glorious. And maybe it wasn't the time to talk. Maybe it was okay for them to just feel for a while. Maybe it was just fine for them to retreat to this, because it felt right. Because it felt real. Because of all the crazy and uncertain things, this felt like a little bit of something. A little bit of certain. His kiss undid her.

And she wanted… She wanted to project everything that she felt right into him. Wished that she could be emitted to his chest. Wished that she could make him understand.

She wanted that more than anything. To show him. He had taken care of her for the first time, and the second time, he had given her confidence. The second time, he let her ride him, and it had been dirty and glorious and they'd been them. Even as they'd given each other pleasure.

But she wanted something else. Something more and deeper.

She wanted him to know. She wanted to show herself. The difference between love and being in love.

She wanted to see. If she could make it all for herself. If what she felt would be enough to sustain them. Would be enough to keep them together. He lifted her up off the ground, and she wrapped her arms around his neck, and she poured everything that she felt, everything that they were, into that kiss. All the relief that she had felt when he'd first been kind to her down by the creek all those years ago. The need she felt to fill that hole left behind by the sister that he loved so much. The years and years of friendship. Of telling each other things in confidence. Of being there for each other.

Her heart, her soul. Her gratitude for how he had been there when her grandfather had died. For the way that he had effortlessly folded her into his family. And just the way she loved him. Her everything. Her heart.

She kissed him like she might die if she didn't, because she wasn't entirely certain that she wouldn't.

He walked them both back up the porch to his house and through the front door. But they didn't make it down the hall. They just barely made it to the couch. He laid her down on the soft surface, tearing at her clothes. They didn't talk. Didn't joke. Didn't laugh.

It was like a reckoning.

Everything was stripped away but their need. For each other. For this.

And already, she was so aroused by him. And already, she felt like she was lost in him. In this.

She clung to his shoulders and then realized she needed to get those clothes off of him. So she went from clinging to tearing, then her hands went to his belt buckle. Pushing the denim away from his body, as he wrenched her panties down her thighs, her sundress already somewhere on the floor.

His mouth was hungry, his hands demanding, and she loved it.

This man, this man who was desperate for her body—he wasn't a stranger anymore. This was part of them. Part of who they were now. And it was all the more powerful for it.

He put his hand between her thighs and teased her, tested her readiness.

"Now," she said, begging.

He settled himself between her legs and thrust home, establishing a wild rhythm that tested and tormented them both.

It was rough and hard, this coupling. And she loved it. She loved him.

She dug her fingers into the flesh of his shoulders, wrapped her legs around his waist. He said her name. Over and over again. Like a prayer or a curse, she didn't know, but she would take it all. Just as she would take all of him. And that was what he gave.

It was like a storm. The heat generated between them

so bright and intense she thought she might be dying of it. And yet at the same time, it wasn't enough. She wondered if it would ever be enough.

She could feel him begin to tremble, shake. Could feel the edge of his control beginning to reach its end.

And when he found his release, it was on a growl and a shout, and she followed after him, squeezing him tight as he poured into her.

And then she kissed his mouth, his face. Said his name over and over again, because it was all she could think to say. Because he felt like the only thing. This moment felt like the only thing.

But then right at the same time, she looked to the future. To a bright, golden future shining with light, and butterflies. And she wanted that. Hoped for it. Reached for it.

And she knew—she knew that it was time. She knew that she had to say it.

"I love you, Jace."

He felt like he was dying. Really, like someone had ripped his lungs out. Like something in him had been broken, irrevocably. Irreparably.

I love you.

Of course she did. She was his best friend. He loved her too. It wasn't anything revolutionary. But it felt revolutionary, with him lying on top of her on the couch, still buried inside of her. Breathing hard. His mind flown from what had just passed between them, because it was more than pleasure. It always had been.

It was more than sex or release. More than orgasms.

It was something bigger. It was something that had changed them fundamentally. He had that feeling, when he'd seen her walking toward him tonight in that summer dress that he just stripped right off, he had that feeling.

He had this strange, crushing feeling all through the whole night. And he knew himself well enough to know it was when he wasn't acting with integrity. When he wasn't being honest about the things that were going on inside of himself. When his actions weren't matching up with what he knew to be important.

Yeah. That was when he felt these things. When he'd been hesitating to make his move in Lone Rock, to make his move with Cara. Not because he didn't know what to do, but because he hadn't wanted to do it.

And this was another reckoning. Like a gong going off inside of him.

And he didn't know why it felt so different. It was just that it did.

"That was amazing," he said.

And he wanted to cut his own tongue out.

"Yeah. But I said that I love you."

"I know," he said.

She drew away from him, but not all the way. She just sort of wiggled and scooted to the side. "Can you tell me about Sophia? A little bit more."

He nodded slowly. And it wasn't a weird change of subject. Not for him. Not for them.

"She loved butterflies," he said. "Everything had butterflies on it. The canopy on her bed, special hospital gown my parents bought her. Everything." He cleared his throat. "When I saw you that time...with your pink binder thing and it had those butterflies, I... It was like you were supposed to be there."

He heard himself. Heard himself saying all this stuff he wasn't supposed to believe. But he could remember that moment. Like he'd felt led to her. To this other girl who had butterflies.

It hurt to talk about it. It hurt to look back, because there was no good way to look forward. And he didn't like it. But the problem with putting down roots was it demanded a certain level of projecting. And maybe that was all part of the problem. Part of the shift. And maybe it was just that creating the heaviness in his chest.

"Little kids aren't supposed to get cancer," he said, his voice rough. "And a little boy isn't supposed to have to watch his sister die. A mother isn't supposed to have to watch her child die. Just not supposed to happen." And he knew there was no point to this. No point to raging against any of it. There never was. And so he never had. He had just turned everything off. Everything.

But now he felt like raging, for some reason. At what? There was nothing there.

But he wanted to do it all the same.

"She was the brightest, prettiest, most... She was just so fun. And being sick made it so she couldn't be fun. So she couldn't have fun. It wasn't fair. It's not fair. She was just a little girl that loved butterflies. How the hell is it right that she's gone?"

"It isn't. It's one of those big unfair things in the world."

"But how do you believe in miracles, in mysteries? How do you dream and hope and all that shit that you do? How do you do it, Cara? Because I don't get it."

"Because I've accepted that there are things that I'll never know or understand. But I also don't believe that what happens to us here is the end. And so it's a deep tragedy within our understanding, but I just don't think that's where it stops. I can't believe that. Because I look around this world and I see miracles. I see miracles and shafts of sunlight and butterflies. There are always so many butterflies. Around you. Around me. I think she might be with you."

"No. I just… I can't…"

"I get it. It hurts to hope."

"Don't say that. Like you're patronizing me. Like I'm the one who's ridiculous. When you… You're the one that believes in all these things that you can't see."

"But there are so many things that we can't see, Jace. So many things. This, this between us. Don't you see the miracle in that? That you found me? But you found the girl with the pink butterfly Trapper Keeper. That you were there for me, like you were compelled to be. Don't you think there's something magic in that. And here we are, and we were each other's best friends all this time, all this time. And we can be more too. And isn't that a miracle. That not only are you my favorite person to talk to, but when we are together like this… It's so bright and hot and wonderful. What isn't miraculous about that?"

"And why couldn't I have the miracle that I wanted," he said, his words coming out hard. And he could see a brief flash of hurt in her eyes before she dismissed it.

"You know I didn't mean that," he said. "You know I didn't mean I didn't want you."

"I do," she said. "Because I know you. I know you don't want to hurt me. But I think I kind of get that you don't want to love me either."

Her words hit him in the center of his chest. They were quiet. And they weren't angry. They weren't accusing him of anything.

But they cut deep.

And they were true.

"What does that even mean? Between the two of us. What difference would it even make?"

She looked up at him, her eyes sad. "I don't know."

"Well until you know, what's the point of making it an issue?"

"That's fair. Let's go to bed."

"You still want to stay the night?"

"I still want to marry you."

And he would take that. Because he wanted to take care of her. He wanted to be with her. Like they had always been, and like this too. So even though he knew he messed up, he was going to go ahead and accept that.

"All right then. Let's go to bed."

"I just wanted to say… Or I need to make it clear." She said nothing for a moment, and then she looked up at him, her green eyes firm and steely. "I don't need you."

She might as well have shot him directly in the chest. "What?"

"I don't need you. Even when I was a sad, flat-chested middle school girl, I didn't need you. I had been kicking along in my life just fine without you. You were great. You are great. But I would have survived if you weren't in my life."

She stood up then, naked and resolved, and he almost felt like he didn't have the right to look directly at her. "I'm tough. My mom is a drug addict who doesn't want me. Thankfully I don't remember very much from that time of my life. Very, very thankfully. Thankfully, mostly what I remember is my grandfather taking good care of me. I remember you being a good friend. And those things… They matter. But I don't need you. I didn't even need you for the hotel. I had it all worked out by

myself, and I could've waited. I could've waited to re-
model things and patch the raccoon hole. I could have."

"What exactly is your point?" he asked.

"My point is that I don't need you, Jace Carson. I
just want you. So all of these things that you're doing,
all of this stuff that you think makes you indispensable,
that's not what it is. It's watching stupid movies with
you. And it's spending the night in a hotel and fighting
about ghosts. And about whether or not raccoons are
cute or vicious. It's those little things that feel like the
biggest things. The way that we talk about everything
and talk about nothing. The fact that I did tell you that
I hadn't been with anybody, even though I was drunk.
And a little bit hitting on you. But no matter how that
had worked out, I knew that I could trust you with that
information. Because I've always known that. And that
isn't about needing you, in the sense that I'm dependent
on you. That is about wanting you around because you
are the most trustworthy, wonderful, caring friend that
anyone could've ever asked for. And that's not… It's not
you needing to be my protector or my caregiver. That's
you being you."

And he realized something, as those words came out
of her mouth. She was right. She didn't need him. She
was hands down the strongest, most incredible woman—
person—that he knew. She had been through a lot, and
she had a sense of humor and a firebrand personality.
She was confident and capable. She had planned all her
finances out in order to get the loan for the hotel in the
first place, had even taken care of arranging all the logistics for the ghost sleepover.

She didn't need him.

He had told himself that she did for all these years.

But the truth of it was, he needed her.

He had told himself he had to protect her.

But it was himself he was protecting. All along.

And that was what every single movement that had happened since he had offered to spend the night with her at the hotel had been about. He had been looking for purchase, looking for roots, and of course, he had chosen to wrap them around her, because he didn't know what his life would look like without her.

She had become the thing that he leaned on.

He had fashioned her into a surrogate for every single thing that he missed. Everything he wanted and didn't have.

And he was… He couldn't give her what she wanted. He just couldn't do it.

Because he tried to think out that far ahead, and everything just went black. Because the idea of wanting anything, the idea of hoping for anything was something he was afraid to grab hold of.

"You should get dressed," he said, his voice scratchy.

"Why?"

"Because you should go home."

"This is going to be my home after we get married."

She was speaking with such a calm, firm voice, and he felt like an absolute dick for what he was about to say. But then, he felt that way about the entire situation. About everything. About the way that he had lied. To her. To himself. Because he had. He had found a way to convince himself that what he was doing was for her while he… Well he found a way to hold her close so that he could use her as a balm for his wound.

And at first it was all about taking care. Of somebody that he felt was vulnerable. Because he hadn't been able to take care of Sophia, had he? Not in a real way. Not in a meaningful way. She had died. So what had anything he'd done mattered? She had died, and that meant that he'd failed. And she just wasn't there. And there was a void where she should be. And he didn't know what he was, if he wasn't her older brother. Her friend.

And so he had become that for Cara, but that had gotten inconvenient when he'd started to become attracted to her, and for a while he'd been able to suppress it, because he was very, very good at suppressing emotion. Very good.

He had made a whole lifestyle out of it.

And that had worked for years, until she had looked him in the eye and told him that she was a virgin. And offered to let him be the one to change that. Yeah. It had all worked until that moment. And then… It had all gone to bright, burning hell. So he'd recast it. Recast her. Changing and shuffling the narrative into something, anything that allowed him to continue to run from the truth.

Because he really needed that. But she was there, calling him out, the way that she did. Because she was Cara Summers, and he was Jace Carson, and they were honest with each other.

To a point.

They had always lied about these things.

She had never told him that she wanted him, and he had never told her that he sometimes thought his life might fall apart if she wasn't in it.

Yeah, he went and traveled on the rodeo. He was away from her for large chunks of time sometimes, but she was always there. Waiting when he came back home. And it meant something. It mattered.

It was the reason he tried to live through those rides. That was just the truth of it. Knowing that she was there.

He had used her to give himself purpose.

He had used her as a conduit for all the spiritual things that he didn't allow himself to feel. Because she hoped enough for the both of them, was faithful enough for the both of them. Believed enough for the both of them. In the brightness and beauty of life, in a concept of miracles that he couldn't figure out how to hold in his hand, that she cradled in her palm effortlessly. The way she acted like her grandfather was simply a thought and a prayer away. The way she saw beauty in an old hotel, and potential in a half-empty Main Street.

What did he give to her, exactly?

And she said she loved him. And… And he was just broken.

But if he was going to do one thing, one good thing, it would be to stop this. To not continue to let his roots wrap around her, because all he would do is drag her down into the dirt, and she was meant for more than that.

She deserved more than that.

She hadn't chosen to be born to a mother that couldn't love her right. She hadn't chosen to have a father who wanted nothing to do with her. She didn't have to have a husband who was broken.

He'd wanted to keep her, because he was possessive. He wanted to keep her with him, to add security to his own life. And if he really wanted to do something for her, he needed to let her go. He needed to let her be free of him.

She only thought she was in love with him because of the sex. Because she had been a virgin. Because they'd been friends for so long.

"You should go home," he said again.

"Jace, you're scaring me."

"We can't get married, Cara. You want other things. Different things. Things I don't know how to give. And you're right. You're right. You don't need me. You stand on your own two feet just fine. I'm the one that's limping. I'm the one who's leaning on you. It's not right. I can't do it anymore, not now that I know."

"Jace, you idiot. Did it ever occur to you that I was fully aware of that?"

"What?"

"I know you. I know that there are things that are just really really tough."

"Why would you let me lean on you, if you don't need me?"

"I wouldn't fall onto the ground without you. How about that? But I have certainly leaned against you at many points over the years. You have been the single most important relationship in my life. Sorry, Grandpa. But it's been you, Jace. You taught me what I wanted from a friend. And then you taught me what to want from a lover. Those are huge things. But I've never been blind to the fact that you had cracks in your soul, Jace. Not ever. Because you went out of your way to befriend a sad, crying girl behind the middle school? Especially if he's cool and handsome and has all the friends he wants? You befriend the bird with the broken wing, because your wing is broken too. And neither of you can really fly. But together... We come pretty close."

"It's nice as a metaphor. But what it amounts to is me holding you down."

"I love you. What if I chose to be with you? What if I chose to be with you just because I wanted to be?"

"I'm telling you that I'm not going to be part of it. I'm not going to keep taking from you. Not when I can't give back."

"This is bullshit," she said. "You're just scared. You're scared, and you're too scared to admit that you're scared. I love you. I'm the one that admitted it. I'm the one that took the step. And you can't because…" Her eyes filled with tears, and suddenly she sucked in a sharp breath, like she had a realization in the moment between that last sentence and this coming one. "And you just can't hope, can you? You're afraid. You're afraid to hope that this could become the best that it could be, because you think it's easier to just imagine the worst. Or just imagine nothing. Because you hoped that she would get well, and she didn't."

He growled. "Forget it. Leave it alone."

"But that's it, isn't it? There is nothing that scares you more in this world than hope. Because you've hoped before. And it didn't go your way. It didn't go anyone's way. It devastated you. It devastated you, and you don't know what to do. Because you don't trust that it wouldn't just happen again."

"Don't psychoanalyze me. You don't know what it's like to have gone through what I have. You don't have any idea what it's like. And maybe it's not psychosis to refuse to believe in things that you can't see. Maybe I'm not the one that's crazy."

"Well. Even if I'm wrong, at least I can think of reasons to get out of bed in the morning. At night, when I get under the covers, I think ahead. And that's not a bad thing. I hope. Because what is life without hope? It's what you have. You can't reach out and take the love that is being offered to you, because you can't look ahead. Because you're afraid to want something that you can't…" She reached out and grabbed hold of him, placed her hands in his. "You want what you can hold in your hands. You're holding me. You're holding me. Can't you believe in me?"

No. He couldn't. Because he couldn't see the end of this. He couldn't see a way to fix this. Couldn't see a way to fix himself.

And he could not do that to her. He wouldn't.

"Go home."

And he did something he hadn't done in all the years since they'd met. He pulled away from her. He took a step back.

But she stood firm. She didn't get dressed like he'd ordered her to do. She didn't back away. She didn't even flinch. He could see deep anguish in her face, and he hated that he had put it there. But she didn't back down.

"All right. I will. But when you need somebody to talk to in the middle of the night, because everything is terrible, you call me. Because I'm your best friend. And you might be surprised to find out that I've been supporting you all these years, but I'm not."

"This changes things," he said. "I don't think that we can… I don't think that we can do this anymore."

"So wait a minute, you don't want to marry me, and you don't want to be my friend anymore?"

And that was when she faltered. When strong, beautiful Cara Summers looked like she might shatter. And he really stood there and marinated in his own sense of fear and anguish, because it had been a long time since he had felt anything like this. He thought that he was going to break. And he hadn't thought that there was any fragile thing left inside of him.

"I can't be. Because it would just be me hanging on to you when you need to be let go. It would be me keeping you in a place where you hope that something can be different when it can't be. You can't love me. Not anymore."

"You don't get to tell me what to do."

"I'm right. I'm just… I'm right about this, Cara."

"You're leaving me with nothing," she said, her voice frayed, wretched. "You're leaving me with nobody. You have your whole family, and what are you leaving me with?"

"Cara…"

"No. No. You don't get to do this. You don't get to try to make me feel bad for you. Or make me think that you're doing the right thing, that you're being all brave and self-sacrificing by doing this. You're just being a coward. You're ruining us. You are ruining the life that we could have. Because you're scared. And I will not let you turn it into anything else. I know you too well for that. That's the problem with breaking up with your best friend, Jace. I just see through it. Even if you can't." And then she did pick up her clothes. And she dressed, and she walked out of the house without a backward glance, and he felt like she had taken the entire world with her.

Butterflies and all.

Fourteen

She should have gone straight back to her house, but she didn't. Instead, she went to the hotel. She went to the hotel, because it just seemed like maybe it would be a little bit more comforting than being by herself. Though, she didn't think that anything could comfort her at this point.

As soon as she walked in, she was comforted by something. Maybe the presence of the raccoon. Maybe the presence of the orb. She didn't know. Or maybe it was just that… She could lie to herself here. She could remember when they had been here last, and they had been full of dreams, and he had stood there and asked her to marry him.

Like they could have a future. A future that looked so different than one she had ever imagined for herself. A future that looked bigger, brighter and better.

She had always been alone. She had always been the one that people just didn't love enough. And she knew that wasn't fair. Not to herself. She knew it wasn't fair to blame herself for this, not when Jace's fears about love were about him. They weren't about her. But it didn't mean they didn't brush up against all the tender places inside of her. That it didn't feel jagged and wrong. That it didn't make her feel lost and sad and all of fourteen years old again and somehow just not good enough. Just not enough.

Because if she was enough, couldn't she make him… Change?

Couldn't she make him see?

Couldn't she make him let go.

He doesn't want to let go. And if he doesn't want to let go, nothing can make him. Nobody can make him.

She knew that was true. Logically, she knew it was true. But nothing was logical about heartbreak.

She paused at the bottom of the stairs. Jace had broken her heart. She was literally living in her worst nightmare. She had fallen in love with him, and he had rejected her. And he hadn't just broken up with her… He had ended their friendship.

Of all the things she had ever worried about, she had never worried about that one thing. She had thought that it would be torture to be with him, and then have to watch him move on with other women, all the while at his side as his faithful companion.

She had never imagined that he would end the friendship completely.

She stood there. Waiting to fall to pieces. Waiting to fall apart.

And she didn't see any glowing lights, but suddenly,

she felt one. At the center of her chest, glowing within her soul. She waited to feel isolated, because Jace had been the only person that she'd ever had in her life long-term. The only one who was still here.

But she didn't feel alone. Because her grandfather was with her. And maybe something else was too. Some-one else.

Because whatever he thought, whatever he said, love didn't end when someone died, and neither did they. Ev-erything that they were to you was still there. And all the love that they had ever given you, and that you had ever given in return.

She knew that. It was why she was standing in this hotel. It was why she was here at all.

Her grandfather being gone didn't erase the love that he'd given her.

And Jace ending things didn't undo everything that they been.

She put her hand on her chest, and she felt like she might have a broken heart, but even within that… Even within it… She felt a rush of gratitude.

Because he couldn't undo all these years.

He couldn't take the love that he'd given her already and cut it out of her heart, take it out of her soul. Be-cause it was part of her. Woven into the very fabric of who she was.

This was like a death.

But like death… It wasn't really the end.

Because she loved him. And she had all the years before. She would have all the years after too. And she wished… She wished that it would look different. But it was the same as loving people who were gone, she supposed. She wished that it could look different too.

But it couldn't. And yes, it was much more within his control to make this something that was happy instead of sad and painful, but… But it simply was. It simply was what it was.

It was painful. But there was beauty in it too, and he couldn't take the beauty away.

It was part of who she was. And what she had to trust was that it was part of who he was too.

Enough that it would never really go away. Enough that he would never really be able to be rid of her.

Of course, that cut both ways. And she would never be able to get rid of him either.

But she didn't want to.

Even if it hurt, she didn't want to. And that was the difference between the woman she was now, and the girl that he had found crying by the creek. She had needed to be different. She had wanted to escape. Had wanted to fight and run away.

And the woman she was now didn't want to do any of those things. She was ready to stand firm and tall. He had said that he had tried to grow his roots around her, and he had dragged her down. But the reality was, her own roots went deep. She knew who she was. And it would take more than a storm to knock her over.

She knew who she was.

She was a woman who loved a man who wouldn't love her back.

And it hurt.

But she wouldn't falter or dissolve, or hide from the pain in drugs and in other meaningless relationships the way that her mother had done. Or just… Simply not show up the way her father had done.

And she wouldn't let it steal her hope, the way grief and pain had done to Jace.

And it wasn't because she was better. It was simply because… She had been given enough love in her life, that it sustained her now.

She walked up the stairs to the bedroom that she had shared with Jace. And she wasn't afraid of it. Wasn't afraid of seeing anything potentially spooky. Because there was nothing scary about it. She couldn't see the future. But there was nothing scary about that either.

Because she could believe that there would be something better.

She had to.

She had to.

Well he'd done it. He'd broken everything. He'd broken the world. Utterly and irrevocably. It was like he had reached up and hammered a nail into the sky and let it all shatter. Then it all rained down on him.

And that was more fanciful thinking than he ever allowed himself. Because he never allowed himself to… To hope.

She was right about that.

The other thing he had never allowed himself to truly believe was that he had the potential to be hurt more than he already had been. He thought that he had a clear-eyed view of life. And here he was, standing in the middle of a screwed up situation that he had created, feeling like he would never sort out the wreckage. Feeling like he would never be able to stand up straight again.

What had he done?

He had lost his sister. She had been the single most important person in his life. His best friend. And he had met Cara, and being with her, being near her had done something to finally soothe the ache inside of him. And now… He'd sent her away. He'd chosen to not have her. And he had…

It was him. It was his fault. He ruined it. He couldn't stand to sit here for another minute. He didn't sit. It wasn't the thing that he did. He was decisive.

And look where it got you.

He didn't look ahead because all he could see was blackness. Bleakness. Blank despair.

He walked out of the house, and he started to walk down the trail that went behind the place. The moon was full, so he could see just enough to walk without tripping over anything. The trail wound up the side of the mountain, through a thick copse of trees, where it all went pitch-black.

And this… This seemed right. It seemed fair. It seemed like a look at his life. A look at his future.

But he pressed on through, and when he came to the top of the mountain, he looked up and there were stars. Because, impossibly, the world was still turning, and everything was still up in the sky, and he hadn't shattered it at all. It just felt that way. Because it was him. Because it was his heart.

Dammit all.

And no matter how hard he had tried to make sure that it didn't… That it didn't want anything, not ever again… No matter how hard he tried, she had gotten in there. She was under his skin. She was in him, no matter how hard he had tried.

He sat down, right there on the mountainside, and looked out at the broad expanse of everything.

"She thinks that you're out there, Sophia," he said,

feeling like an idiot. But he had nothing. He had nothing to hope for, nothing to lose, nothing to gain. He might as well sit there and talk to the night sky. "But I just can't feel anything. Or I'm afraid to. I wanted to believe that there was nothing left to hope for so that I could never get hurt again, and here I am. I haven't hurt this bad since… Not since you. But I did it to myself. I did it to the person that I care about most in this world." He felt a stabbing sensation in his chest. "I love her. I am in love with her, and I sent her away, because I'm too afraid to claim that. Because I'm too afraid to want it."

He closed his eyes, and he waited for something. For inspiration to strike, a lightning bolt from heaven.

Yeah. Because you could ignore all that and say you didn't believe in it, and then just get a sign the minute that you asked.

It was dark, and so was his soul.

He lowered his head, keeping his eyes closed, and he waited. He waited there all night. Until the sun started to rise up over the view in front of him. And it was the strangest thing. Just as the golden rays of light began to touch the brush on the rocks all around him, the flowers, he saw them. Hundreds of them. Little white butterflies, rising up from every surface. All around.

And he felt…

Love. Like he never imagined before, like he never felt it before. Like everyone who had ever stood in the spot before him was still there, like Sophia wasn't gone.

"You tried to tell me," he said, looking all around. "But I'm a particular kind of dumbass, so you can't just send a few. I guess I needed a whole butterfly storm."

And he could see it, like he was looking straight past

that horizon. A life and the world all lit up with this kind of love. And he could see himself with Cara.

His Cara.

And once he could see that... Once he could believe it... In this thing that had felt intangible and impossible only a few hours before, he knew.

That he loved her.

And that life might not come with guarantees or certainty. That the world was a harsh and dangerous place.

But love was what made it worthwhile. Love was what endured.

Love didn't work all by itself. You needed faith to go along with it.

And that's what he'd been missing. The ability to believe, in this thing that was bigger than he was.

In this thing he couldn't control. It had been easier to do when she was beside him. Bright and perfect. But maybe he needed this moment, to try and see the light without taking hers.

Because he needed to bring back what he was taking. Needed to give equal to what he was getting.

And he was ready now.

He could only hope that she would still want him after how badly he had messed up.

But he'd loved her for a very long time. He could see that now. When he looked back and forward, and at the present moment, it all added up to love.

Maybe that was why he so obsessively didn't like to look at his life.

He'd been living a whole life.

But he was done lying. And he was done running.

Unless it was straight to her.

Fifteen

When she woke up the next morning and heard pounding downstairs, she was afraid that it was a raccoon. Or maybe a ghost.

She got out of bed, and when she moved the curtain, it disturbed a little white butterfly. She paused for a moment and looked at it, watched it flutter around the room, before the knocking became more insistent. And then she ran down the stairs, and she could see him through the window.

Jace.

She flung the door open. "How did you know that I would be here?"

"Well, it's not the first place I've been."

"It's really early," she said.

He took a step inside, and her heart began to throb painfully. "No. It's really late, actually."

"It's sunrise," she said.

"I just mean… I'm late with this. Everything I said last night was me running scared. But you knew that already. And I was… I was wrong. Everything I did to you was wrong. Everything I said to you was wrong. And everything you said to me was true. I was scared. More than scared, I've been paralyzed. When Sophia died, it was like my ability to hope that things would turn out okay was just… Killed along with her. But it's a bad tribute, if nothing else. I'm here. And I'm alive, and I've been acting like a part of me died. Except I had you. And you were that bright spot. And you know what, I didn't have to know very much as long as you were with me. It was only when I was forced to sit in the darkness of what my life looked like without you that I had to try and find the light for myself. That I had to try and see past the horizon line. And I can't see a future without you."

She sucked in a hard breath, and she waited.

"Because I love you," he said.

"Thank God."

"Yeah." She wrapped her arms around his neck and she just hugged him. Held him for a long moment. "I really love you too."

"Still? Even after… After everything?"

"Maybe especially after everything. Because this was a lot of work. I know it was. Because I know you."

"I have to tell you. I wanted a sign. Something. And you know that I was desperate if I was asking for signs. And this morning… There were all these white butterflies, everywhere. And I can't explain it."

She pulled back and looked at him, and she laughed. "I saw one this morning too."

"Cara Summers," he said, his voice rough. "I can't believe that I'm about to say this. But I think that this is meant to be."

Epilogue

They didn't end up rushing down the aisle. They took their time. Because Jace wasn't afraid, and he didn't need all those external things to prove to him that what they had wasn't going to evaporate, and because Cara decided that she wanted to get married at the hotel, so she wanted it finished before the event.

They'd gotten married in the newly landscaped back-yard, and had the reception both inside and outside.

The old restaurant and bar in the far wing of the hotel was beautifully renovated, and it was set up with free drinks for all of their guests.

And just behind the bar, on that top shelf, was Grand-pa's whiskey bottle.

Late in the evening, when the guests were all leaving, and it was Jace and Cara, sitting in the bar, her in her wedding dress, and him in his tux, she lifted a glass of whiskey up toward the bottle. "To Grandpa," she said.

"To Mitch," Jace agreed. "Thanks, old man. For everything."

She smiled. "You're even talking to him now."

"It just doesn't feel half so strange. Not anymore."

"Why do you think that is? Is it just because of the butterflies?"

He shook his head. "No. It's because of the love. Because that is a miracle, Cara, it really is. And once you believe in one miracle, it's not so hard to start believing in all of them."

She smiled. "I love you, Jace. You're my best friend."

"I love you too. And you know, you're definitely my best friend, but even better... You're my wife."

"I like that, husband."

"I think it's time to go upstairs," he said, tipping his glass back.

"You have a one-track mind."

"Yeah. I do. But you know what... After... After what I really want to do is dream about the future."

"I didn't think you did dreams."

"That was before."

"Before what?"

"Before you made my life the best dream of all."

* * * * *

A COWBOY KIND
OF THING

REESE RYAN

To Kim Matlock, whose quiet determination birthed this miniseries. And to K. Sterling – thank you for your continued support and generous spirit.

One

"What do you mean you aren't coming?"

Dionna Reed paced the floor of her hotel room at The Bellamy resort in Royal, Texas, where she'd arrived little more than an hour ago. She'd been expecting her best friend, actress Ariana Ramos, to arrive at the hotel any minute. Instead, her friend video called her to break the news that she wouldn't be coming to Royal after all.

"But this is *your* wedding, Ari. How can you *not* be here?" Dionna realized that her voice had risen higher than necessary. She didn't care. This was a full-out emergency.

"I've been dreaming about my wedding since I was five years old. Do you really think I'd prefer to be stuck here on set in Peru for another four weeks?" There was a slight tremble in Ari's voice, and instantly Dee felt guilty.

Yes, she'd sacrificed four days of her busy life to come to Royal—the hometown of Ari's fiancé, bestselling author Xavier Noble. But she was supposed to be there to lend moral support and her honest opinion as Ariana and her fiancé worked with their wedding planner to make arrangements for their nuptials.

Forget about yourself for a minute. Think of how devastating this must be for her.

"I'm sorry, Ari. I know how much you were looking forward to this." Dionna settled onto the brown leather sofa as she surveyed the luxury two-bedroom hotel suite her friend had probably laid out a small mint for. "What happened exactly?"

"We were four hours away from the film wrap-up party when the bomb dropped," Ari said, anger rising in her voice. "You know how I said my costar, Nicholas Rainey, gives me the creeps because of the way he's always looking at me when the camera isn't rolling... Well, apparently my spider-senses are on point. It seems Nick's eye isn't the only thing that has been roaming."

"Don't tell me..."

"Yes!" Ari hissed. "*Multiple* women have made harassment claims against the creep. Since the first woman filed a suit against him five days ago, at least ten other women have come forward—including his sister-in-law!"

"Oh no. Isn't his wife pregnant with their third or fourth kid right now?" Dionna asked.

"Their fifth!" Ari practically screeched.

"Wow. This dude is absolute trash," Dionna said. "But the studio has already wrapped up filming. What do they plan to do? Shelve the film and hope the fury dies down?"

"They're taking these claims seriously, and they should. Nick's agent and PR firm have already dropped him like a radioactive rock, and the studio is yanking him from the film. I support the decision one hundred percent. But that means we're going to have to reshoot *every freaking scene* that handsy jerk was in. And since he was the leading man, we're practically reshooting the entire film."

"I'm so sorry, Ari. And I'll do whatever I can to help. Should I call the wedding planner and try to get this rescheduled?" Dionna reached into her leather WANT Les Essentiels vertical tote bag and pulled out her planner.

"No! Don't!"

"Why not?" Dionna surveyed the current date. "This is supposed to be an exploratory trip to make decisions about your wedding. Seems pretty important for the bride to be here."

"We've already rescheduled twice. We can't afford to put this off any longer."

"But the wedding isn't until June," Dionna reminded her.

"And it's already the end of February. Not much lead time in the wedding industry. We've pushed this as far back as we can. I *cannot* cancel these meetings again. They must go on as planned," Ari insisted.

"Without the bride?" Dionna asked incredulously. "Is Xavier going to video call you to make every single decision?"

"About that…" Ari's expression reminded Dee of Lucille Ball's whenever she had to deliver bad news to her best friend, Ethel Mertz, on *I Love Lucy*.

"There's more bad news?"

"Ex won't be there either," Ari said sheepishly.

"Why? This is *his* hometown. *He's* the one who wanted to get married here instead of in LA." Dionna was still miffed that Ari had broken tradition and moved the wedding to the groom's hometown instead of hers.

But where they got married actually mattered to Ex, whereas Ari's only concern was that their wedding be spectacular. Ari considered moving the wedding a peace offering to Xavier's family who seemed less than thrilled about their son marrying into Hollywood. A small sacrifice for the man she adored.

It was sweet, sure. But it made planning the wedding complicated. Especially now.

"I know, sweetie," Ari cooed, employing the same voice she'd used to talk Dee into questionable decisions since the two of them had met and become best friends in middle school. "But the European book tour for *The Silence* is going really well. Xavier's publisher wants to extend the tour and they've lined up several talk show appearances."

"But this has been planned for weeks," Dee said.

"Which is why he'd intended to turn them down. But now that I'm not able to make the trip, we thought he might as well ride this wave while the book is hot. You know how fickle our industries can be, Dee. I need you there. No one knows me better than you. You always know exactly what I'm thinking before I've said a word. You know what I like and what I don't. You're the perfect stand-in for me. I even trust you to handle the tasting menu. If I need to make tweaks later, I can. But at least we'll get things started."

Dionna tapped the end of her fountain pen against her planner as she mulled over her friend's words.

"I *really* need your help on this, Dee," Ari said.

"There's no one else in the world I'd trust to do this. Not even Sasha," she said of her younger sister. "Pretty please. I'll even let you pick your own maid-of-honor dress."

That got Dionna's attention. She had been terrified her friend would put her in a sleeveless, backless dress that bared her navel.

"Deal," Dee said before Ari could change her mind.

"Thanks, Dee. You're the best friend a girl could ask for."

"Let's see if you still think that after the wedding. Because while I do know you like the back of my hand, I can't say the same for your fiancé."

Ari grinned a little too wide. "Don't worry, babe. Got that covered."

Dionna groaned, not liking the mischievous twinkle in her best friend's eyes.

"You're really backing out of this thing?" Tripp Noble asked his cousin Xavier as he pulled out of the driveway of The Noble Spur—the ranch Tripp's family owned and had run for four generations. "You're not getting cold feet about the wedding, are you? You can be straight with me."

Tripp and Ex had been thick as thieves as mischievous boys growing up on The Noble Spur together. But Ex had left Royal long ago. He'd dreamed of being a famous author—and he'd done just that. In fact, he'd become more successful than either of them could've dreamed.

Xavier had lived all over the country and currently called Los Angeles home. Yet, the two of them remained close. Still, it'd been a while since they'd seen each other in person. So Tripp had been looking forward to spending time with his cousin.

"No, I don't have cold feet. Are you kidding me? Ariana is the best thing that's ever happened to me. I can't wait to marry her," Ex said without hesitation.

"Then why are you *really* bailing on this trip home?"

"I told you why. My publisher wants to extend the tour." Ex sounded a little too defensive.

"And…"

They might've spent the past decade or so apart, but Tripp still knew his cousin well.

"All right, you've got me," Xavier sighed. "Everything I said about the tour is true. But Ari has already made such a *huge* sacrifice in moving the wedding to Royal. I don't want to screw this up. This wedding needs to be everything Ari has ever wanted and more."

"Well, who would know what she wants better than you?"

"I know a lot about Ari," Ex said. "But when it comes to this wedding stuff, I'm at a total loss. I cannot fuck this up. It's too important to her."

"Okay, so what's the plan? You rescheduling again?"

"Ari doesn't think we should. She wants to forge ahead and let Dionna handle the decision-making," Ex said.

"I realize they're close, but is Ariana really good with letting her bestie make decisions about her wedding?" Tripp asked.

He'd only met his cousin's future bride via video calls. But he couldn't imagine she'd want to be hands-off for something as important as her own wedding.

"Ari insists no one knows her better, and I'd have to agree."

"What about what *you* want?" Tripp asked. "I get that she's already conceded on the location. But you're telling me you don't want to have any other input into the ceremony? I mean, assuming this is going to be your only wedding—"

"Ha ha ha," Ex said drolly. "You're so un-fucking-funny."

"I'm just saying, if you're only planning to do this once, I'd think you'd want your stamp on things in at least some way," Tripp said.

"Glad you mentioned it. That's where you come in."

"Say what?" Tripp took his eyes off the road for a nanosecond and had to jam his foot on the brakes so he wouldn't hit a squirrel that darted across the street.

"Dionna is filling in for Ari, and I'd like you to fill in for me. You know me, Tripp. You know what I'd like, what I'd just roll with if it makes Ari happy, and what I'd hate."

"Dude. When it comes to the bachelor party, I got you. But what about me says *wedding planner*?"

"We've already hired a wedding planner, Rylee Meadows. She's flying into Royal this weekend." He could hear the grin in Xavier's voice. "All I'm asking is that you and Dionna work with her to ensure that this wedding has Ari's and my stamp on it. You know I wouldn't ask a favor this big if I didn't really need you."

Tripp sat in his truck, idling at a traffic light, and debated his cousin's request.

Of course, he was going to help Ex. They were blood and as close as brothers. So he'd do just about anything to help his cousin. Apparently even becoming a junior wedding planner.

Besides, hadn't he already been doing that the past

couple of months by tossing around ideas about when and where the couple would get married?

Ariana recognized how important family was to Ex. So she'd roped Tripp into the phone chats about their wedding, and it had been his teasing-not-teasing comment about his aunt and uncle, Xavier's parents, being none too happy about the wedding being in LA that had prompted Ari to move the wedding to Royal.

He honestly hadn't expected her to give up her dream wedding location in LA. But it was evident that she loved his cousin, and he respected that. So he wanted this wedding to be amazing for Ari and Ex because they both deserved it.

If Ari could make such a huge sacrifice for Xavier, it wouldn't kill him to dedicate a few days to the cause.

"Okay, I'm in. Just tell me what you need," Tripp conceded.

"We were supposed to take the girls to dinner tonight. Show them why Royal is such a great place. Dionna is already in town, and to be honest, she isn't on board with having the wedding in Royal. I'd appreciate anything you could do to change her mind."

In their video chats, Ari's best friend was pretty, quiet and very by the book. With her tortoiseshell eyeglasses and her hair always pulled up, she'd given him hot librarian vibes. By the third call, she'd gotten a little more comfortable with him and loosened up a little. The two of them couldn't be more different, but there was something about Dee that Tripp liked.

"So you want me to show Dee a good time? Consider it done."

"I don't like the sound of that," Ex said.

"You asked me to change her mind about Royal." Tripp laughed.

"Dude, do *not* fuck this up for me. Ariana means *everything* to me, and Dee and Ari are closer than sisters."

"C'mon, man. You're in there like swimwear," Tripp teased. "Seriously, Ari adores you. You're good."

"She won't if my playboy cousin hooks up with her best friend and breaks her heart. I've seen marriages crumble for a hell of a lot less. So excuse me if I don't want to risk finding out how forgiving she'd be about it," Xavier said in his serious voice.

Tripp was tempted to remind his cousin they were talking about a grown-ass woman in her midthirties, not some wide-eyed college coed. But Xavier didn't seem inclined to debate the point, so Tripp let it go. After all, it wasn't like he planned on hooking up with Dee.

"I promise to be on my best behavior. *There.* Feel better?" Tripp asked as he pulled into the lot of Corryna Lawson's flower shop, Royal Blooms.

"Actually, I do." Xavier heaved a sigh. "Seriously, thanks for doing this. I know wedding planning isn't exactly in your wheelhouse."

"Just remember, you owe me one. Now, I have shit to do, so I've gotta go. Hit me up when you get back from the tour."

"Will do." Xavier ended the call.

Tripp parked his truck in the lot of the flower shop and sighed. He honestly didn't have designs on Dionna. But the woman was as alluring as she was maddening. He'd be lying if he said the thought hadn't crossed his mind.

Two

"You want me to work with Tripp on your wedding," Dee repeated her best friend's sheepish request. "This just keeps getting better."

"Tripp knows Ex as well as you know me. You're the perfect partners for this. And if there's anything pressing, you can always contact one of us. We'll get back to you as soon as we can," Ariana said.

"Do we really need to involve Tripp? I mean… I'm sure Rylee and I can work things out on our own."

"What's wrong with Tripp?" Ari asked. "He's handsome. He's hot. He's got a sense of humor."

"Exactly!" Dionna said. "He strikes me as the pampered playboy-type who has had everything in life handed to him. The kind of guy who doesn't take anything seriously. You realize that's the worst possible personality type you could match me up with...on this project," she quickly clarified.

The last thing she wanted to do was give her friend ideas. Ari had already hinted more than once that the four of them should go on a double date.

"You're not being fair, Dee. Tripp is a rancher, and from what I understand, he works as hard as any of their ranch hands. And your opposing personalities are what make you a great planning match. You'll balance each other out. You'll make sure he's taking this seriously, and he'll help you loosen up a little. This is a celebration after all. I just want it to be the best, most lavish one that little town has ever seen."

"Great. No pressure then," Dionna groused.

"Nothing you can't handle," Ariana assured her. "Now, let's see what you're wearing to dinner."

"This *is* what I'm wearing to dinner." Dionna glanced down at her white button-down blouse, black pants and sensible shoes.

"Seriously?" Ari peered through the screen with concern.

"This isn't a date," Dionna reminded her best friend. "I'm meeting with the best man to iron out a few wedding details."

"It *is* a dinner date," Ariana objected after a suspiciously pregnant pause. "I have to run, but wear something fun tonight and try to relax. Or else you two will get off to a bad start."

Tripp Noble.

Just the thought of his handsome face, broad smile and those mesmerizing golden-brown eyes sent a shiver down her spine.

Do not fall for the trap, girl.

Yes, the man was handsome, funny and wealthy. But he could also be stubborn and incredibly frustrating, as he'd been on several of their video calls about the wedding over the past few months. One moment she'd fantasize about kissing Tripp's luscious lips. The next she'd want to wrap her hands around that thick neck of his and squeeze because he was so obstinate.

Sure, Tripp was attractive. Charming. Maybe even the slightest bit tempting. And he'd flirted with her a bit. But they were just too different. Besides, flirting was as second nature to a charismatic pretty boy like Tripp as breathing. It didn't mean he actually liked her.

Tripp had probably dated half the women who'd come through Royal. Dee had no intention of adding her name to that list.

She was thirty-five now. When she got involved again, it would be someone she could build a future with. Not another charmer who'd happily have the words *Eternal Bachelor* etched into his gravestone.

There was a knock at the door. "Delivery for Dionna Reed."

Dionna peeked through the peephole, trying to determine if the man outside her door was an actual hotel employee or a character in the opening scene of a murder mystery where she'd play the unwitting murder victim who'd been too stupid to live.

"Delivery from your bestie, Ari," the man said after knocking again.

Dionna undid the locks and opened the door cautiously. "I'm Dionna Reed."

"The instructions said you wouldn't open the door unless I said that last part," the man chuckled. "Guess your bestie knows you pretty well after all."

She frowned at the man. "You said you had a delivery?"

He straightened his expression and extended a box to her. She signed for it and tipped the man.

"What have you gotten me into this time, Ari?" Dee whispered to herself as she opened the gold box wrapped with a black-and-cream bow—the colors her best friend had chosen for her wedding.

Dionna pulled the garments from the box one at a time. Pretty, colorful skirts, blouses and dress pants. A textured, long-sleeved black minidress. A tangerine-colored one-shoulder midi dress. A pretty wrap mini-dress in a bold geometric print. A Mediterranean blue Kay Unger jumpsuit with a jacquard-print top and overlay skirt that went over midnight-blue crepe pants. And corresponding shoes and accessories for each outfit. All of it from Dee's very own closet.

Ari had been in Peru for weeks. When had her friend dug out the clothing Dee had purchased during their post-breakup retail therapy sessions and sent them to the hotel? She hadn't. It had to have been Ari's younger sister, Sasha.

She and Ari really needed to review when it was appropriate to use her emergency spare house key.

Her phone buzzed with a text message.

I see the package arrived. Your legs are amazing. I'd go with the black mini and lose the bun. Don't forget to send pics!

Ari Ramos didn't miss a single thing.

Dee sighed, then hung up each item of clothing.

After her two-year-long relationship had gone down in flames, she'd subconsciously adopted a black-and-white color scheme. The colors perfectly conveyed her constant mood: a combination of misery and hopefulness. But if her best friend had put this much effort into her look for this trip, maybe she should, too.

Hopefully, there were no more surprises in store for her tonight. She was nervous enough about meeting the frustrating yet intriguing Tripp Noble in the flesh.

Tripp parked his truck in front of The Bellamy and climbed out, clutching a glass vase overflowing with pink Asiatic lilies and pink, white and red roses. He handed his keys to the valet and made his way inside.

He and Dionna were supposed to meet at The Silver Saddle bar and tapas restaurant on the first floor of the luxury resort. But that was before he realized he'd be half an hour early, toting an oversized vase of flowers half as tall as he was.

It'd be awkward to sit at the tapas bar with that huge bouquet on the table between them. So he'd deliver it to her hotel suite and they could go down to the restaurant together. He retrieved his cell phone from his back pocket, scrolled to Ariana's last group text update and noted Dee's room number. He made his way onto the elevator and leaned against the wall, grateful for a moment alone.

The seconds he spent watching the elevator numbers climb felt like the first moments of stillness he'd had all week. He'd pushed through the series of daily and weekly tasks essential to keeping his family's ranch—The Noble Spur—running so he could clear his schedule to spend time with his cousin and his fiancée. But now he'd be spending that time with Dionna instead.

They had four days to meet with vendors on Xavier

and Ariana's behalf and get a good start on the decisions for their wedding, working with wedding planner Rylee Meadows.

After months of text messages and video chats, Tripp was still undecided about Dionna.

She was smart and savvy. But she was also a perfectionist who seemed determined to drain every ounce of fun out of the wedding planning process. She was also kind of a smart-ass. They often disagreed during their video chats. Dee had the kind of dry sense of humor Tripp had never really appreciated. Yet, he often found himself in a deep belly laugh about the conversations they'd had days or even weeks ago. There was just something about the woman that both got under his skin and made him wonder about the taste of hers.

Tripp shook the thought from his head, reminding himself of his promise to his cousin.

It wasn't as if he had some grand plan to ravish Dionna. Yes, they were friendly. And yes, there may have been some flirting on his part. But it had been more of a strategic move. An attempt to persuade her to agree with him. Not the precursor to some torrid affair. Still, the fact that Dionna was now off-limits made the idea of getting involved with her that much more tempting. In fact, he'd been slightly obsessed with the idea in the hours since he'd promised *not* to hook up with her. But that was just the rebel in him.

He'd get over it. They'd keep things friendly. And in a few days, Dee would be on her way. She'd go back to Hollywood where she belonged, and he'd go back to his life here in Royal. No harm, no foul.

So why was his pulse racing like a hormone-filled adolescent on his first date?

Tripp shut his eyes and released all the disquieting thoughts that had taken up residence in his head on the drive over. Then he knocked on Dee's hotel door.

Footsteps trailed to the door and there was a quiet pause as she likely checked the peephole. The door swung open.

"And what is this? The *I'm sorry for being a pushy nuisance* bouquet?"

Tripp shifted the flowers, which had inadvertently hidden his face. He studied her as she stood in the doorway with one hand propped on her generous hip.

Damn.

He knew Dionna was a beautiful woman. But he hadn't realized she was blessed with the kind of curves that sent his pulse into overdrive and made him a little weak at the knees. His mouth fell open, but his brain had temporarily forgotten how to make words.

"Tripp?" Dee's eyes widened with recognition. She pressed a hand to her cheek. "I'm sorry. I didn't realize it was you. When I looked through the peephole, all I saw was flowers. I thought it was another surprise delivery from Ariana to make up for not being here."

"Sorry to disappoint." Tripp shifted the vase. "Mind if I put these down?"

Dee stepped aside and gestured for Tripp to enter. "Those aren't for me, are they?" She studied the bouquet.

"You don't like them?" Tripp set the heavy crystal vase on the coffee table in the luxury hotel suite and rearranged a few of the stems that had gotten smushed on the journey.

"No. I mean, *yes*, I love the flowers. It's a beautiful arrangement. But this isn't a date, and no one has ever brought me flowers for a business dinner before."

Dee raised her hands to her face, as if to push her ever-present glasses up the bridge of her nose. Only, she wasn't wearing them. And for the first time, he really noticed how lovely her dark brown eyes were, highlighted by the drama of smoky, charcoal gray eye shadow and cat-eye eyeliner. Dee tugged her hair over one shoulder instead.

"Your hair..." Tripp said, before he could stop himself from thinking aloud, something his sister often admonished him about.

Just because you're thinking it, Tripp, doesn't mean you have to say it.

"What about it?" Dee ran her fingers through her sable-brown shoulder-length hair worn in loose twists rather than her signature sleek bun. "I had it up earlier. Maybe I should..."

"I like it. A lot," Tripp said. "I just haven't ever seen you without your glasses or with your hair down. You look *really* nice. Not that you don't normally," he added quickly.

Why am I blathering like an idiot?

"Thank you." Dee smoothed her palms down the fabric of the black minidress that molded to her curvy figure and showed off her thick brown thighs. Heat practically radiated off her cheeks as she flashed a lopsided smile. "But you didn't answer the question. Did you bring these for me?"

The way her eyes searched his filled his chest with an unsettling warmth.

"*Yes*, I brought them for you." Tripp shoved his hands into the pockets of his gray-and-black plaid pants. "But bringing them to you was actually Corryna Lawson's idea."

"Corryna?" Dionna's eyebrows scrunched as she rested her chin on her fist, the other arm folded across her body. "The name sounds familiar."

"She's the local florist I was telling you all about. The one you were convinced wouldn't cut it." Tripp tried to rein in a smirk. "The one I told you would be perfect for Ex and Ari's wedding."

"I see." Dee scrutinized the flower arrangement more critically as she turned the vase and rearranged a few of the stems. "While this is certainly a lovely arrangement, I'll need to see more before we commit to anything."

"Of course." Tripp tried his best not to break into a full victory grin as the two of them stood there. An awkward silence filled the space.

"Sorry about the way I answered the door," she said, finally. "It's made this weirder and more awkward than it should be." Dionna ran her fingers through her twists again and flashed a nervous smile. "It's good to finally meet you, Tripp."

She extended her hand in a handshake while he extended his arms for a hug. Then she opened her arms to give him a hug, but he'd extended his hand for a handshake. They both laughed nervously and ended up sharing an awkward hug.

What was it about this woman that made him revert to his floundering teenage self? Before he'd discovered the disarming power of the Noble family charm and his signature smile?

"It's good to finally meet you, too, Dionna." Tripp released her, quietly inhaling her subtle scent, like a field of wildflowers wafting on a calm spring breeze. "But I feel like we already know each other."

Dee folded her arms and raised one brow. "True.

You're the handsome town flirt who enjoys flying by the seat of his pants."

"And you're Ms. Do-It-by-the-Book, let's get all of our ducks in a row before we move forward." He said the last part in his best mock Dionna voice.

Dionna burst into laughter. A wide grin spread across her face, her dark eyes sparkling. She poked him in the ribs. "I do *not* sound like that, Austin Charles Noble the *third*." She stressed the suffix.

"Oh, we're going straight to my government name, huh?" He chuckled, then pointed a finger at her. "Don't make me regret telling you that."

Dionna shrugged and gave him an innocent "Who me?" smile before laughing again. A sound he was already obsessed with.

He'd loved her unique laugh from the first time he'd heard it in a video call. It'd been a notable contrast to her serious nature. But in person, the sound was so light and pure. He couldn't help smiling.

"So are we going to eat or not? Because the last thing I ate was that sad meal they served on the plane, and I'm starving." Dee pressed a hand to her belly.

"Absolutely!" Tripp gestured toward the door. "Whenever you're ready."

"Great. I just need to grab my wedding notebook and a few of the samples I brought that will give us a better sense of what Ari and Ex want for the wedding."

"Slow your roll, Dee." Tripp put a hand on her shoulder, pinning her in place. "You just arrived. I've had a really long day, and you probably have, too. How about if tonight we just relax, have a little fun, and get to know each other better? We can go all in with the wedding stuff when we meet with Rylee tomorrow."

Dee stared at him in silence as she worried her lower lip with her teeth. "Okay… But it's not—"

"A date," Tripp finished, trying not to be insulted by her insistence on it not being a date when she smelled like spring and looked good enough to eat. "I think we're both clear on that."

His mind was. His body… Not so much.

Three

Dionna reached for her oversized WANT Les Essentiels tote bag. But the size of the bag made the length of the dress seem much smaller by comparison. And she was already self-conscious about the amount of thigh showing.

Dee nibbled on her lower lip and glanced up at Tripp who was gazing at her with a look that fell somewhere between a bemused child and a voracious wolf. She sighed quietly.

What would Ariana do?

Dionna reached into her bag and grabbed the black Vavvoune Ursa wristlet wallet her best friend had given her for her birthday. She slipped her cell phone inside the zippered pouch, then slipped the strap over her wrist.

The restaurant was downstairs, so she wouldn't need a coat.

Dee raked her fingers through her hair, unaccustomed to her loose hair brushing her shoulders. "Ready."

Tripp opened the door and she stepped into the carpeted hallway. She'd requested a room far from the elevator because it would be quieter. Now she regretted that choice. Because it meant walking in awkward silence beside Tripp who was taller and even more handsome than he'd appeared in their video chats.

Plus, he smelled divine. A combination of citrus, ginger and clean laundry fresh out the dryer. She had the sudden urge to wrap herself up like a burrito in a blanket draped with that scent. She'd sleep like a baby, something she didn't often do.

At the end of the hallway, she veered toward the right. But Tripp hooked his large hand around her waist and steered her left.

"Elevator is this way," Tripp said in response to her startled look.

"I'm pretty sure it's this way." Dee jabbed a thumb in the opposite direction, trying to ignore the heat from his hand pressed to her side.

"Pretty sure it isn't." His light brown eyes sparked with mischief, though his expression was neutral. "Let's just say I'm familiar with the layout of the hotel."

Of course, he was *familiar* with the hotel. He'd probably been there with countless women.

"Then I'm sure you're right." Dee pulled out of his hold, inexplicably vexed by the idea of staying in a hotel where Tripp had visited other women.

This isn't a date. This isn't a date. This isn't...

They made another left at the end of a shorter hall and there was the elevator—just as Tripp had said.

To his credit, he barely gloated as he pushed the call button. She appreciated that.

They took the elevator to the main floor and went to one of the resort's two restaurants. The Silver Saddle was an elegant yet relaxed eatery with modern decor. There were leather and chrome chairs and dark wood tables. Leather booths in another section. And leather and chrome stools lined the bar.

Dionna surveyed the casually elegant space with its dim lighting and use of candles to make it feel warm and intimate. They were greeted by a beautiful woman with shiny red hair and a smattering of freckles over the bridge of her nose. Her smile was as big as Texas, and Dionna couldn't help relaxing a bit as she returned the woman's smile.

The woman showed them to their table, and Tripp pulled out her chair. Dee reminded herself that it wasn't a romantic gesture—simply a polite one, expected of Southern gentlemen.

"You seem to like the place." Tripp's warm gaze filled her body with heat and made her skin tingle.

Dionna's hands trembled slightly. The table for two suddenly seemed incredibly small. She needed a little space. Dee picked up her menu, creating a temporary wall between them.

"The decor is very nice," she acknowledged as she studied the appetizers on the menu. "But it's a restaurant, so… I'll hold judgment until I have my meal."

"Fair point." Tripp's chuckle vibrated through her chest, despite him being on the other side of the table.

Her stupid tummy fluttered, and her cheeks filled with warmth in response to the sound of his laugh, which she'd come to adore during their chats the past couple of months.

Not a date. Not a date.

"In the mood for anything in particular?" Tripp asked.

"Not really." She figured he was studying his own menu, so it'd be safe to lower hers. She was wrong. Those twinkling brown eyes met hers and his full sensual lips curved in a lopsided smile. "I…uh…" She cleared her throat, her cheeks blazing. "Is there something you'd recommend?"

The amusement in Tripp's eyes indicated that he recognized how nervous he made her.

He shifted his gaze to the menu. "If you like steak, they make a great T-bone. If you're in the mood for lighter fare, I'd recommend the prawns, the cod or one of their vegetarian dishes. But if you're feeling adventurous, and I hope you are—" he glanced up at her again with that sexy cockeyed smirk "—I'd say let's go for the paella. It's made with a combination of seafood and pork. Sounds like a lot, I know. And it takes about a half an hour for them to make it, but it's worth every minute. I promise." He winked.

And there was that fluttering again. This time accompanied by a warmth that made other places on her body tingle.

"Sure. The paella sounds good." She dropped her gaze from his, silently chastising herself for behaving like a besot tween when, in fact, she'd just turned thirty-five on her recent birthday. *Pull it together, girl.* She snapped her knees together and cleared her throat as she studied the appetizers again.

"Perfect." Tripp clapped his hands, and the sound startled her, bringing her attention back to his handsome face. "And since you said you were starving, I'm not gonna make you wait that long to eat. Let's order a few starters, huh? Fried calamari, Serrano ham croquettes and montaditos sound good?"

"Yes to the first two." Dee loved calamari and the ham croquettes sounded delicious. "What are montaditos?"

"Basically, little open-faced sandwiches made on the most amazing crusty bread with a variety of toppings. There are two of each kind, so you'll get to try them all."

"Sounds wonderful." She closed her menu and pushed it aside. "Add a glass of white wine and I'm in."

They placed their order with the server who promised to return with their drinks—a glass of cava wine for her and a pale ale for him.

"Our conversations have always been about Ari and Ex's wedding. So tonight, why don't you tell me a little about you?" Tripp leaned back in his seat and sipped his water.

"You want to know about *me*?" Dionna could sense the furrowing of her brows and made a point to relax them. She tucked a few of the loose twists behind her ear.

Tripp gazed at her expectantly.

"I grew up around the movie business. My father is a cinematographer and my mother is a set designer. I spent most of my career doing a variety of behind-the-scenes Hollywood jobs, which didn't make my parents very happy."

"Why not?" Tripp thanked the server who'd delivered their drinks.

"My father wanted me to become a lawyer. My mother hoped I would become a doctor. Neither of them wanted me to follow their career paths. Long hours, low-paid and nonpaying internships or apprenticeships in the business, which is pretty much exactly what I did." She laughed bitterly, but he didn't.

Instead, there was empathy in his eyes. This time, she felt the tiniest fluttering in her chest.

"I figured out pretty quickly that casting was what interested me most. So I interned and apprenticed for a variety of casting directors. Eventually, I got a job as an associate casting director for a tiny independent studio where I learned an awful lot but got paid very little. The rest you know." She shrugged, then sipped her glass of cava. "Ari hired me as a casting director when she started her own production company a couple years ago. End of story."

"And how long have you and Ari been friends?"

"More than twenty years." Dee smiled as she thought about that first meeting with her best friend. "Which makes me feel ancient."

They met in the bathroom of their middle school. Ari had knocked on the panel between them and whispered loudly, asking if Dee had a tampon she could borrow. Dee had slipped one beneath the stall. As they washed their hands at the sinks, Dee noticed a bright red stain on the back of Ari's white capris. She offered Ari her sweater to tie around her waist. But she wasn't about to reveal any of that to Tripp.

"That secretive smile tells me there's more to this." Tripp shook a finger. "So come on. Let's hear it."

Dee was mortified. As if he could see the images inside her head. Knowing Ari, she would have no reservations about telling Tripp the full story. But it definitely wasn't the kind of dinner conversation she wanted to have with the man.

"We met in middle school. I was the awkward, quiet, shy new girl, and she was super popular. Of course. She borrowed a couple of things from me. One of which was a sweater that got ruined, so she wanted to replace it." Dee shrugged. "First, I'm pretty sure I became her project. She was determined to make me over as one of the popular girls. Along the way, we became good friends and both realized I shouldn't have to become someone else to fit in. I should just be myself. When her popular girlfriends wouldn't accept that, she ditched them. We've been best friends ever since."

"I'm glad you came to that conclusion." Tripp sipped his beer. "The people who truly matter accept us for who we are. Anyone who can't... In my experience, you're usually better off without them."

"Agreed." Dee nodded, her ex coming to mind.

"By the way, you look *incredible* tonight." Tripp set his beer on the table and gave her the kind of smile that probably made women melt.

"Thanks. But remember when I said Ari sent me a surprise package? This dress was one of the things she sent. The clothing is mine," she added. "I just hadn't packed any of it. Ari insists I should loosen up and enjoy this trip. That means not wearing my typical business attire."

"Sounds like Ari is a devoted friend. I have no doubt she'll be just as supportive and loyal a partner to my cousin." Tripp held up his nearly empty beer bottle. "To Ariana and Xavier."

Dee clinked her glass against the bottle. "To Ariana and Xavier," she echoed.

As she sipped her wine, she couldn't help thinking that Tripp Noble was nothing like she'd expected him to be.

Tripp watched as Dee took her first bite of the warm crusty bread piled high with melted blue cheese, unspeakably good homemade tomato marmalade and microgreens.

"My God, that's good," Dee muttered around a bite of the montadito. "Where have you been all my life? I meant the montadito," she said abruptly, one hand covering her mouth when her eyes met his amused ones.

He reined in a smile, not wanting to embarrass her any more than she already seemed to be by the spontaneous statement.

"I'm glad you like it." He picked up the same variety she'd tried. It was one of his favorite variations. "Which one should we try next?"

Dee's dark brown eyes lit up. One corner of her mouth curved in a smile. He couldn't help wondering how those lips tasted and if she'd make the same soft moan if he kissed her good-night when he walked her back to her room.

Tripp shook the idea from his head.

Dee was adorable. Beautiful, without even trying. Glamorous when she did. Her all-business demeanor was nothing like the women he normally dated. Yet, something about her appealed to him. Tripp couldn't quite put a finger on what exactly it was about Dionna that he found fascinating.

"This one." She pointed to the montaditos piled with Manchego cheese, cured ham and sautéed spinach, onions and peppers.

"Let's do it."

They each grabbed one and took a bite. This time, he was pretty sure she purred. He felt the sound vibrating low in his gut and needed to shift in his seat.

"So far I'm impressed with the wine and the food," Dionna admitted. She spooned some of the fried calamari and a little of the accompanying sauce onto her small plate along with one of the ham croquettes.

"You almost sound disappointed." He added calamari and a croquette to his own small plate. "I told you Royal has some phenomenal eateries. Now do you believe me?"

"Total honesty?" Dee looked up from her plate, her brows furrowing.

"Please." He dipped a piece of the fried calamari into the sauce and popped it into his mouth.

Dionna's eyes studied his mouth for a moment. She sank her teeth into her lower lip and set her fork down. "I respect why Ariana changed the venue of her wedding. But I'm still a little resentful that you *guilted* her into moving it here to appease your aunt and uncle."

So he hadn't just imagined that Dionna had become snarkier in the video chats that followed Ariana's decision to change the wedding venue.

"Okay," he said simply.

His non-response seemed to irritate Dee even more. Her mouth tightened in an angry line as she poked an accusatory finger in his direction. "Do you have any idea how excited she was to have scored that cliffside castle for her wedding?"

"I can only imagine, and to be honest, I feel badly about that." Tripp finished his croquette and wiped his hands on a napkin. "I wanted to give Ariana a heads-up about how Ex's parents felt about a Hollywood wedding.

I never expected her to move the wedding here. Still, I'd be lying if I said I wasn't glad she did."

Dionna's nostrils flared slightly. "I understand that Xavier has a deep connection to this place. That it'll always be his hometown. But Ari has a family, too. And her family and friends are in LA."

"Which is where they're going to be living," Tripp noted. He signaled the server for another beer. "They'll get to see the people in LA all the time. Only seems fair that the wedding is here, with the folks who knew him first, since we don't get to see him often."

"This isn't just about Ari's friends and family," Dee said. "Xavier's life is in LA, too. He also has friends there."

"And in Chicago and in New York," Tripp said. "I understand all of that. But what *you* don't seem to understand is that while Ex might be gallivanting all over the globe now, his *roots*—" he pressed his hands to the table for emphasis "—are right here in Royal. This will *always* be home for him. And he means a lot to the people here who've been cheering him on every step of the way. The entire town is excited about this wedding... Not just Ex's family."

Dionna frowned as she nibbled on her calamari. But she was beginning to see his side of this; he was sure of it. She just needed a little more convincing.

"Ari might've agreed to a change of venue. But she still wants the big, beautiful, show-stopping wedding she's always dreamed of." Dee leaned across the table and lowered her voice. "Yes, this resort and restaurant are impressive. But I'm still not convinced your little town—cute though it may be—is capable of putting on an event of that caliber."

Tripp's hands balled into fists beneath the table. He was trying to be reasonable about this. But Royal was as much a part of his blood as Ex was, so Dee's remark stung.

No one got to talk shit about his family. Not even Ms. Thick-Hips-with-the-Pouty-Lips across the table.

"This *little town* is home to a crap ton of millionaires, quite a few billionaires, high-profile business owners and CEOs, and an entire town of hardworking folks who care about Ex and about each other. And for the record, it's not like we haven't hosted important events that were plenty grand before." Tripp gritted out the words.

He didn't normally get worked up about things like this, but Dee's insults of the town felt like an acid-dipped dagger to his heart.

"I'm sorry if I offended you, Tripp. That wasn't my intention." Dee wiped her hands on a napkin and dropped them to her lap. "I know that what's best for Ex is your priority, but mine is what's best for Ari. I believe that subconsciously her reason for sending me on this mission solo is because she needs my honest opinion about whether having the wedding here is viable. She's far too in love with Ex to be objective about it, so I have to be. I'm sorry if that upsets you." Her tone and expression had softened.

Tripp wanted to remind Dee she *wasn't* doing this solo. He was just as invested in ensuring the success of this wedding. After all, they'd moved it to Royal because of him .

"Look, you have my word that I...and everyone in this town...are going to do our damnedest to ensure this wedding is the stuff of Ariana Ramos's dreams.

Trust me. Whatever it is that Ari wants, we can make it happen."

"Got any cliffside castles here?" Dionna stabbed another piece of calamari.

Tripp wanted to kiss that self-satisfied smirk right off of Dee's face. He sucked in a deep breath and picked up his fork, too. "All I ask is that you keep an open mind about having the wedding here in Royal."

"For Ari's sake, I will. Of course."

They finished their appetizers, mostly in silence. Then their server delivered the steaming, fragrant paella pan and set it in the center of the table. The arrangement of the lobster tails, littleneck clams, jumbo shrimp and chorizo made for a beautiful presentation, placed atop the golden Spanish bomba rice with pops of green and red from sautéed onions, peppers, fire-roasted tomatoes and a sprinkling of parsley.

"My God." Dionna pressed a hand to her chest and Tripp's gaze followed. Her brown skin gleamed and shimmered in the light. "What a stunning presentation."

"Wait until you taste it." Tripp spooned some of the steaming paella onto each of their plates, practically inhaling the savory scent of saffron, chorizo and sofrito. He waited for her to take her first bite.

Dee dug carefully into the paella with her wooden spoon, being sure to get a little of the lobster and shrimp. He watched as she spooned it into her mouth and chewed.

"Mmm…" The sound of Dee's murmur vibrated low in his gut. "Tripp, this is fantastic. This might be my new favorite meal. I could eat it every single day for the rest of my life and never tire of it."

"Told you it was worth the wait." Tripp finally dug into his own plate. "The paella is my favorite, but everything on the menu is delicious. There's something for everyone, including vegan and gluten-free options."

"You sound like an advertisement," Dee said. "You own stock in this place?" She shoveled more of the paella into that pretty little smart-ass mouth of hers.

"I wish. But I am trying to sell you on the place. I think it would be a great place to hold the bachelor/bachelorette party." Tripp studied her reaction.

Dee chewed thoughtfully as she glanced around, surveying the place with new eyes. "It is a really attractive space. And I know that Ari and Ex both want the prewedding party to feel more intimate than the ceremony and reception will be. The location—at the hotel where most of the guests will be staying—also seems ideal."

She was making his case for him, so he didn't feel the need to interfere. He just nodded and continued eating.

"But as ideal as the place seems, it feels pretty lazy to pick the first place we've seen." Dee took another bite.

"It's the first place *you've* seen," he noted. "I know every spot in town from fine dining to the super casual diner and the occasional food truck."

"You eat out a lot then." She glanced at him momentarily before returning her attention to her meal.

"When I'm not bumming a meal off my sister and her husband," Tripp chuckled. "They live on the ranch next door and their cook is pretty incredible. Helene could easily start a restaurant of her own."

Dee looked at him with renewed interest. "Let's put The Silver Saddle at the top of the list. If we don't find a more suitable option, I'm all for recommending that we have the prewedding party here."

A small victory. He'd take it.

"Now. It's your turn. Tell me more about you. You said your sister and her husband live next door. Do you have other siblings?" Dee took a sip of her cava.

"No, it's just me and Tessa. Xavier and his family lived on a connected property when we were growing up. He and I were more like brothers. I was also close to my neighbor Ryan Bateman, who is now my brother-in-law. So our family felt bigger than it actually was."

"And what was it like growing up on a ranch?" Dee peered at him intently as she ate her paella.

"It's hard work but also a lot of fun." Tripp smiled, thinking of all the happy times he'd had growing up on the ranch with Tessa, Ryan and Xavier. "I have so many great memories of the four of us hanging out together. Riding horses, feeding and caring for the animals, bale jumping, riding tractors, you name it. Though to be honest, even back then, ranch life wasn't really Ex's thing. Pretty early on, he knew he wanted a life away from the ranch."

He missed those days when their lives were simpler. And he missed spending time with his cousin, whom he'd seen very little of the past several years. Xavier was always on a deadline or off on a globe-trotting adventure.

Tripp's parents had moved out of the main house and now lived in a small homestead on the property, which they considered their retirement villa. A not-so-subtle hint that they were ready to begin traveling full-time, leaving the responsibilities of the ranch to him and Tess. In fact, his mother, father, aunt and uncle were currently on a three-week-long vacation in Cuba.

And now that Tess and Ryan were married, she helped him over at Bateman Ranch, in addition to her administrative duties at The Noble Spur. So the bulk of the responsibility of running the family ranch now fell to him.

"Sounds like a really nice way to grow up." Dee's soft smile made her dark eyes—the color of maple syrup—twinkle. He'd momentarily forgotten what she'd said. He was too captivated by her warm gaze and the way the candle flickering on the table reflected in her eyes.

"It was," he said finally. "But I'm surprised to hear you say that, Ms. Hollywood."

"You don't know everything there is to know about me, Tripp Noble." Her playful smirk elicited laughter from him. "I was born in LA, true enough. But my parents were originally from North Carolina. My paternal grandparents had a dairy farm where I spent most summers. I loved spending time there."

"Really?"

"*Yes!* Why does that seem so impossible to you? I'm not high-maintenance like Ari and Sasha." Dee plucked a clam from the shell and popped it in her mouth.

"Sorry if I can't imagine you frolicking in the hay and milking cows," Tripp chuckled.

"Well, I *did*!" Dee insisted, her words accompanied by a laugh. "My grandparents had four dozen cows. They didn't have any of that fancy automated machinery you probably use. So I got damn good at milking them by hand," Dee said proudly. "Ari and Sasha could never understand why I preferred to spend my summers on a farm with my grandparents and their dog."

"Why did you?"

"My parents worked long hours in the movie industry, and I was a latchkey kid. We couldn't afford the pricey summer camps that Ari and Sasha went to, so if I stayed in LA for the summer, it meant spending a lot of time alone. But I had the best time with my grandparents on their farm." Her eyes lit up.

"I'd imagine your grandparents worked long days on the farm, too," he said.

"They did. But I got to work right alongside them. They were loving and attentive. Doting, yet firm. They'd tell the most entertaining stories about life on the farm. I adored them and the slower pace of life there. It was a welcome change from the pressures of life in LA." There was a hint of sadness behind her smile.

"What's your favorite memory from your summers on the farm?" Tripp asked.

Dionna's smile widened, and she set her spoon down on the edge of her plate. "My grandparents had the sweetest dog—a golden retriever mix named Doug. After I got done with my chores every day, I'd pack my backpack with a few snacks and a notebook. Then I'd take Doug and we'd go on little escapades, exploring the area. I'd sit and write my own adventures. Then we'd head back home before it got too dark."

"So you're a writer?" Tripp set his spoon down.

"No. I haven't written anything since college. Even then, I never considered writing as a career. It was just something I did for fun. To let off a little steam." Dee suddenly looked bashful. She resumed eating.

"Seems like it gave you a lot of joy." Tripp shoveled a little of the rice into his mouth. "What kind of stories did you write? Romance? Mystery?"

The grin returned to her face and her eyes lit up again. "Epic fantasy. You know, high-stakes heroic adventures set in magical worlds. But the heroes were diverse. Not just the side characters playing the Minotaurs and dragons, hidden beneath layers of makeup and prosthetics."

"That sounds amazing," Tripp said. "I'd definitely read that. You ever think about trying your hand at writing again?"

"No. Like I said, it was just something I did for fun." Dee shrugged. He couldn't tell whether she was lying to him or if she believed it herself. "Besides, there are authors like N. K. Jemisin and Tracy Deonn already doing that."

"Thanks for the recs," he said. "But that doesn't mean there isn't room for more."

"I'm perfectly content with my career choice." Dionna frowned. Tripp had evidently struck a nerve. "Besides, my life is busy enough. Speaking of which, we only have a few days to work together on this wedding, and we have a lot to do."

"You're right." Tripp nodded. "Once we're done with dinner, I'll show you the other restaurant on-site. See if you think Ari would prefer that option."

"Great." Dionna seemed relieved he'd dropped the subject.

At the end of the night, he'd insisted on paying for dinner. After several rounds of debate, Dee finally agreed, then thanked him.

Tripp showed her The Glass House, the other restaurant at The Bellamy. But she agreed it felt too formal and that The Silver Saddle would be better.

At the end of the night, he walked Dionna back to her room—though she'd insisted it wasn't necessary. But there was no way he was going to let anything happen to the maid of honor at his cousin's upcoming wedding on his watch.

"Thanks again, Tripp. I thoroughly enjoyed the meal." She turned to him once they'd arrived at her hotel room.

"And the company?" he teased.

The reluctant smile that spread across her face reminded Tripp how beautiful Dionna was.

"The company was great, too. I had a really good time."

"Me, too," he said. "I'll be here bright and early to take you to breakfast."

"You don't need to walk all the way up here. I can meet you in the lobby," Dionna said.

"You evidently haven't met my parents," Tripp said. "I'm thirty-four and they'd still probably ground me if they knew I hadn't walked my...dinner companion to her door. I'll meet you here in the morning."

She narrowed her gaze at him when he'd nearly called her his date. Not intentionally, of course. But if he was being honest, the awkwardness of the night had definitely given him first date vibes.

"We're scheduled to meet the wedding planner at nine," Tripp said.

"At the Texas Cattleman's Club." There was a hint of distaste in Dee's voice. As if the venue couldn't possibly be suitable for her best friend's glamorous wedding.

He chose to ignore it.

"So how about I pick you up at eight thirty?"

"I'll be ready." Dee unlocked the door.

"Perfect," Tripp said. "Oh, and Dee?"

"Yes?"

"It was nice getting to know you a little tonight."

"You too, Tripp." Dee's face lit up. She went inside, closing the door behind her.

Tripp felt the slightest bit of tension in his gut. Dee still wasn't convinced they could make her best friend's dream wedding happen here in Royal. But he had no doubt of it.

He needed to focus on how he'd prove that to Dionna and stop imagining how it would've felt to kiss her good-night.

Four

Dionna sat at a table at the Texas Cattleman's Club with Tripp and Rylee Meadows—the wedding planner Ariana had hired. The woman was stunning with sparkling blue eyes, shoulder-length blond hair and a curvy frame.

Rylee had met them at the Texas Cattleman's Club that morning. She greeted them with a warm smile. Yet, there was tension behind it. She was clearly just as shaken as Dionna by the sudden change of venue from Los Angeles—her home turf—to Royal, Texas. But she hid her disappointment well.

Dee only recognized it because it matched her own feelings about the change. Still, they'd both been pleasantly surprised that the outer building and its interior space were much more glamorous than the club's name had led them to expect. According to Tripp, the club had been renovated and modernized a few times over the years.

"Breakfast was wonderful, Tripp. Thank you." Rylee dabbed her mouth with a napkin. "But it's time we get down to business."

Rylee stood, collecting her portfolio filled with notes, inspiration photos, drawings, fabric samples and other items. "Can we see the space for the wedding now?" she asked Tripp.

"Absolutely." Tripp ate the last bite of his breakfast croissant, wiped his hands on his napkin and stood. He extended a hand to Dionna, who was still seated.

Dionna really didn't need any help getting out of her seat. But Tripp had been something of a surprise. Yes, he was full of confidence and swagger. But he was also thoughtful and kind.

Dee had expected Tripp to go on and on about himself at dinner. Maybe brag about his family's holdings and estate in Royal. But he hadn't. And she couldn't help admiring how vehemently he'd defended his little town and the people here. There was more to Austin Charles Noble the third than she'd anticipated, and she'd enjoyed her time with him last night.

Dionna gave Tripp her hand. Her palm tingled and sparks danced up her arm as he helped her from her seat. Dee pulled her hand from his, startled by the unexpected sensation.

"Thank you." Dee forced a smile to counter his look of concern. She gestured ahead of them. "Lead the way. We can't wait to see the space we're working with."

"I've seen photos online," Rylee said as they followed Tripp. "But photos don't always tell the complete story. The aesthetics don't come to me until I get a chance to stand in the space with the couple's inspiration photos and samples on hand."

"That makes sense." Dee nodded. She found it similar with casting. Sometimes an actor who seemed like they would be perfect for a part just wasn't a good fit once she got to meet and audition them in person. "But your portfolio is amazing. I can't wait to see what you come up with."

Dee put a hand on Rylee's arm, slowing her down as Tripp got farther ahead of them. She lowered her voice. "If you honestly don't believe this space can rise to Ariana's expectations, I need you to be completely honest with me about that."

"If that's the case, I will." Rylee offered Dee a reassuring smile. "But if this is where Xavier and Ariana want to get married, I *will* turn it into the glitzy wonderland she envisions for her wedding. I learned quite a few tricks about how to transform just about any space into whatever my client wants it to be whether that's formal elegance, rustic charm, bohemian, whimsical or gothic." Rylee grinned. "Or vintage Hollywood glamour, which is what Ariana and Xavier have asked for."

"Which would've been much easier to produce if we were actually *in* Hollywood," Dionna muttered beneath her breath.

"True," the other woman acknowledged. "But don't worry, Dee. I'm up to the challenge."

"So what do you think?" Tripp turned to them. "This is the space Ex and I were thinking would work best for the reception. When you're done here, I'll take you to the outdoor space that would be a good option for the ceremony."

"I think this will do quite nicely." Rylee's blue eyes

sparkled as she glanced around. "I see endless potential here. Give me a few minutes. I need to take photos
and measurements."

"Take all the time you need," Tripp told Rylee. Then
he approached Dee with a broad smile. "Not the dilap-
idated barn you expected, huh?" He nudged her with
his elbow.

"No," she admitted begrudgingly. "It isn't."

Tripp was two for two, and he seemed pretty pleased
with himself about it.

"Maybe I'm not so bad at this after all." His smug half
grin was both sexy and maddening. The man certainly
didn't lack confidence. Yet, he still managed to come
off as genuine and chivalrous. Maybe it was a cowboy
kind of thing.

Part of her wanted to elbow him in the gut. Part of her
wanted to kiss him. Neither seemed advisable.

"Don't get cocky, cowboy. There's still an awful lot
of wedding planning to be done. A viable space is a
good start, but if the related services can't be sourced locally..." She shrugged. "Having the wedding here might
not make sense. So I'd hold off on the self-congratula-
tory celebration for now."

"You're a tough cookie, Dee. But I happen to love a
good challenge."

"Just remember this little 'challenge' of yours is the
most important day of my best friend's and your cousin's life." She folded her arms and narrowed her gaze.

Tripp winked. "Yes, ma'am."

The man would probably be flirting with and trying
to charm the panties off his home health aide when he
was one hundred and lying on his deathbed. Seriously.

Weaponizing that natural charm and charisma of his came as naturally to the man as breathing.

Never trust a shitload of charm and a smile.

"Look, I know we're still getting to know each other." Tripp was suddenly standing closer, his voice low. His subtle citrus and ginger scent wrapped itself around her like a warm hug. "And from the outside looking in, it might seem like I'm not taking this seriously. But I understand the gravity of the situation. I just feel life is too short not to enjoy every possible moment."

With Tripp in such close proximity, she could feel the warmth radiating from his brown skin.

Dee took a step back. Just far enough out of his orbit to regain her senses. Breathing came easier and so did rational thought.

"As long as you take this wedding seriously, I don't care if you wear a clown suit and flip cartwheels down Main Street. I only care that we complete our tasked mission before I board my plane home."

Tripp laughed so hard it drew the attention of Rylee who was measuring the windows and a few of the club staff who were preparing the room for an event.

Dee crossed her arms, planning to continue her stern stance with Tripp, but she couldn't help laughing, too. That had often been the case when they'd chatted. She'd be all business and superfocused, and he'd find a way to make her laugh.

She could understand Tripp's appeal. From a completely objective perspective, of course.

"Okay. Enough playtime, mister." She poked a finger in his side, nearly jamming her knuckle on his hard abs.

Never trust six-pack abs and a smile. Never trust six-pack abs and a smile.

"The space is nicer than I'd expected. But I'm not as confident as Rylee over there that we can transform it into the Old Hollywood glamour Ari is set on for her wedding." Dionna scanned the space again. "It's lovely. But it lacks the character and charm the LA property possesses. I realize Rylee is very good at what she does. But you can't make a silk purse out of a sow's ear." She borrowed a pet phrase of her late grandmother's, then added, "No offense."

"None taken." Tripp stepped behind her and placed his hands on her shoulders. He leaned down, his voice low. "Now, close your eyes."

"But…" She turned toward him, but the light pressure of his large hands pinned her in place.

"This will only take a minute, Dee. And it'll be worth it. I promise." His breath warmed her skin, his lips nearly brushing her ear.

Dionna's tummy fluttered and her thighs clenched. Electricity danced along her skin, emanating from where his hands rested. She squeezed her eyes shut, as he'd requested. "Okay."

Tripp stood up straight again, his hands still resting on her shoulders.

"Imagine this space decked out in vintage Hollywood glamour. We can do long tables with cream tablecloths and fancy vintage gold chairs. Tall gold vintage-style candelabra centerpieces. Arrangements of balloons in black, cream and gold. They can put down a black-and-white harlequin tile floor to really give the space that vintage look. Hang gold chandeliers. That'll lean into the Golden Age of Hollywood theme. String up some fairy lights to give it an ethereal feel. And I know a guy who has a stable of vintage cars. Most, he'll barely allow anyone to breathe on," Tripp chuckled. "But a few he rents out for special occasions. Having the bride arrive in a vintage car and the couple exit in it would really help set the scene."

Dionna stood there with her eyes shut, as Tripp had instructed. She'd been prepared to bat down his ideas. But she could see every element he'd described in her mind clearly. A hint of excitement stirred in her belly.

She hated to admit it, but Tripp was right. If they could pull off what he'd described, they could transform the Texas Cattleman's Club into the Old Hollywood glamour Ariana wanted for her wedding.

"You know Ariana best, so what do you think?" The weight of Tripp's hands was gone from her shoulders, and she immediately missed the warmth radiating from his body and the heat it ignited in hers. "Do you think she'd like it?"

Dee turned to Tripp in amazement. He'd come off as a jokester during their video chats about the wedding. But he'd clearly been paying close attention to what Ariana wanted for this wedding.

"Ari will love it. All of it." Dee's voice was softer and more sentimental than she'd intended. "And I have to admit I'm pretty impressed."

"As am I," Rylee said, a wide smile on her face. She clutched the portfolio in her hand. "I'd swear you've been reading my notes."

Rylee looked as impressed with Tripp's vision as she was. "I'd already planned to suggest a lot of what you just said, but I hadn't considered the harlequin floor." Rylee rubbed her chin as she studied the floor. "That would definitely take the Old Hollywood glam to the next level. So would the chandeliers." She glanced up.

Tripp could barely contain his grin.

"I usually work with a few LA-and New York-based vendors to rent these kinds of assets. But that would add substantial time and cost to the project, particularly given the time frame." Rylee shook a finger in Tripp's direction. "But according to Xavier, you're the person to talk to when it comes to sourcing items locally. So if you have local connections for any of this, like your friend who rents out the vintage cars, I'd appreciate it if you'd share those contacts and set up an introduction."

"You've got it," Tripp said.

He was so proud of himself Dionna was surprised his puffed-up chest didn't pop the buttons off the denim shirt that highlighted his broad chest and the gun show he'd likely acquired from roping steer or whatever the hell ranchers did. The indigo shirt was a shade or two lighter than the dark washed jeans that hugged his impressive hindquarters.

Dee cringed inwardly.

Hindquarters? Pull it together, Dionna. He's a man, not a horse. And why are you looking at his behind anyway?

Never trust a guy with loads of charm, six-pack abs, a gun show, an impressive ass and a smile.

The list was getting hella long.

"Give me ten more minutes, then we can move to the outdoor space." Rylee was gone by the time Dee realized she was speaking to them.

Tripp regarded her with a lopsided grin.

Her nipples tightened and her belly fluttered. She squeezed her thighs together and cleared her throat, her face suddenly as hot as if she was standing in front of a furnace.

"What? I said I was impressed with your ideas." Dionna folded her arms over her chest, trying to remember if her bra was padded. "If you're expecting a cookie or applause—"

"The applause isn't necessary, but I will take that cookie. But only if it's homemade." Tripp unbuttoned his sleeves at the wrist and rolled them up, revealing a quick glimpse of tattoos on both his lower arms. "But what I'd prefer is that you have dinner with me tonight."

"Umm… Sure. Why not?" Her gaze lingered on the ink on his tawny-brown skin.

"Not the most enthusiastic acceptance of a dinner invitation I've ever had," Tripp chuckled. "But I'll take it."

"Sorry." Dee hadn't intended to stare, but she couldn't help trying to get a closer peek at Tripp's ink. "I didn't mean to sound…*not* enthusiastic. I was just a little preoccupied, I guess." She ran her fingers through her twists, worn loose again. Definitely not because Tripp had liked her hair down so much. But because, like Ari said, she was on vacation.

"You want a closer look?" Tripp asked.

"No." She shook her head, believing his response to be the adult version of "Take a picture already." It was a taunt often lobbed at her by the popular girls in high school when she'd stare at them with admiration.

"I don't mind." Tripp's gaze held hers as he extended both his arms so she could study the designs inked into his skin.

She should say no. Dionna realized that. But her hands and feet seemed to have a mind of their own. She stepped forward and reached out. "May I?"

"Of course."

Dee lightly traced the design etched into his brown

skin. Cattle horns protruded from either side of a capital letter *N*. A line underneath the *N* ended in what looked like a spur.

She glanced up at him. "Is this your personal logo?"

"It's the cattle brand for our ranch, The Noble Spur."

Dee moved to the other arm, studying the tattoo. It was a lovely illustration of a ranch surrounded by a split-rail fence. A bull grazed in the yard. A sign that read The Noble Spur hung from the archway over the entrance gate.

"So this is your family's ranch?" She glanced up at him again. Something in Tripp's intense gaze sent her stomach into somersaults. She swallowed hard and pulled her trembling hand from his arm. She stepped backward, nearly bumping into a passing employee.

"Careful!" Tripp pulled her to him, so she didn't crash into the server carrying a silver tray stacked high with glasses.

The near accident and being so close to Tripp, who felt and smelled amazing, made Dee's heart race and her hands shake.

"Thanks, Tripp."

"No problem." He released her. "And to answer your question… It isn't an exact spatial rendering of The Noble Spur. But it's a pretty solid representation of the house."

She studied his arm, fighting back the urge to trace his skin with her fingertips again. "It's stunning. The tattoo, I mean. I haven't seen the ranch."

Tripp's smile widened. "Consider this an open invitation. Come by anytime."

"Maybe next time." Dionna cleared her throat. "When I have more time and we don't have a wedding to plan."

"It's a date." Tripp's eyes danced with amusement when hers widened at his use of the word *date*. He'd probably used the word intentionally.

Dionna wouldn't give him the satisfaction of thinking he knew her that well. She swallowed her objection.

"Oh God! No, no, no."

Dionna and Tripp hurried toward Rylee Meadows whose hand was pressed to her open mouth as she stared at her phone.

"Rylee, what's wrong? Is there a problem with the venue?" Dionna asked.

"I wish it was something that simple." Rylee's skin blanched and her voice creaked. "That I could handle."

"So what is it?" Tripp asked.

"Are either of you familiar with Patrick 'Trick' MacArthur?" Rylee's voice was calm, but there was noticeable tension in her jaw when she uttered the man's name.

Tripp and Dionna shook their heads.

"Trick MacArthur is a juvenile, fame-seeking prankster who crashes high-profile weddings like this one. He makes his way into exclusive weddings and films himself pulling idiotic stunts for his audience of immature social media followers who find his brand of childish pranks hilarious." Rylee's distaste for the man seethed out of every pore, despite her placid tone.

"Okay, so the guy's an asshole," Tripp acknowledged. "From your reaction, I'm guessing you're concerned that he has his sights set on Ex and Ari's wedding. Why? Isn't there some bigger star remarrying his third or fourth wife for the second time?"

If the situation weren't so dire, Dee would've laughed.

"I deal with a lot of people in this business. And none of us wants his brand of publicity overshadowing our hard work," Rylee said. "I'm friendly with a server who works at a trendy restaurant in LA. Trick was there last night. The guy overheard him on the phone talking about Ariana and Xavier and saying that he'd learned through an exclusive source that the wedding was being moved to the groom's hometown of Royal, Texas."

"So he knows about Ari changing the location of the wedding. That doesn't mean that he plans to crash it." Dee hoped more than believed it to be true.

Rylee looked at her pointedly. "The last thing my source heard Trick say was, 'I've always wanted to go to Texas.'"

"Shit." Dee and Tripp uttered the word simultaneously.

"Do you have any idea how much Ari will freak out if some random upstages her at her own wedding?" Dionna was having heart palpitations just thinking about it.

"Trust me, I do." Rylee dragged a hand through her shoulder-length blond hair, and a puff of air escaped her cherry-red lips. "Having something like this happen at one of my weddings isn't a good look for me either."

"So what do we do?" Dee asked.

"I know what I plan to do if I catch his ass sniffing around this wedding." For the first time, Tripp looked genuinely distressed. "It's because of me they moved this wedding to Royal, and I promised Ari everything would be fine. I'm not going to let this guy ruin my cousin's wedding. Even if it means catching a case." Tripp struck his open palm with his fist.

"Calm down, cowboy." Dionna placed a hand on his tense arm. "The best man, who also happens to be the first cousin of the groom, getting arrested for assault isn't a good look either. Rylee is the expert here. I'm sure she'll come up with a more levelheaded solution."

"Like hiring a hit man," Rylee muttered under her breath, but they both heard her.

"Rylee! That's not helping," Dee said.

"I was joking. *Mostly.*" Rylee fluffed her bangs and sighed heavily. "Of course, I'll come up with a solution. One that doesn't involve bloodshed or anyone catching a case." The woman pointed a finger at Tripp whose chest expanded with each noisy breath. "I have no idea what that is just yet. But I promise you, I'll come up with something. So let's forget about Trick MacArthur for right now and focus on getting the plans for this wedding rolling. Tripp, if you're ready, I'd love to see the outdoor space you've been raving about."

Tripp didn't respond right away.

"Everything will be fine." Dee squeezed his arm. "And it's probably a good thing they moved the wedding here. It'll be easier to spot this guy and his entourage here in Royal than it would be in LA. This isn't your fault, Tripp. And I trust that Rylee will take care of it."

Tripp's eyes met hers. His expression softened, and the tension in his muscles eased. He nodded, his eyes filled with a mixture of gratitude and relief.

"The courtyard is through those doors." Tripp gestured toward a row of glass doors, and Rylee headed in that direction.

Before Dee could follow her, Tripp grasped her arm.

"Thank you for getting my head right on this." He kissed her cheek, then headed outside.

Dee stood there frozen. Her hand went involuntarily to the spot where Tripp's warm lips had quickly grazed her skin.

She sucked in a deep breath, then followed them out into the sunlight.

"Don't you dare fall for that cocky cowboy, Dionna Reed," she muttered to herself. But deep down, she knew that a tiny piece of her heart was already in a free fall.

Five

It'd already been a long day when Tripp parked at the restaurant.

He, Dionna and Rylee had spent a few hours at the Texas Cattleman's Club, where they also had lunch. Then they'd gone to visit florist Corryna Lawson at her shop, Royal Blooms. It had been Corryna's clever idea to create welcome bouquets for Dionna and Rylee. The women might've had reservations about entrusting a small local flower shop with the demands required by Ari and Ex's wedding spectacular. But such a personal preview of Corryna's work had undoubtedly swayed them.

And maybe he'd tipped Corryna's hand a bit by informing her of exactly what the bride envisioned for her wedding. So the sample options she'd created for them had blown Dionna and Rylee away. They were both on board and believed that Corryna was the ideal candidate to handle the floral arrangements for Ari and Ex's wedding festivities. They took photos to show Ari.

The celebrity photographer Ariana had hoped to book was doing a photo shoot for *Vogue Italia* the week of their wedding. Her second choice was doing a shoot for *Cosmo*. So Tripp had arranged a meeting with Seth Grayson, who was a local photographer. Both Rylee and Dionna were impressed with Seth's portfolio, but hesitant to engage a photographer who wasn't a well-known name in the industry.

Reluctantly, they agreed to recommend Seth to Ariana. But Dionna had essentially threatened his life if anything went wrong with the photos. Tripp was pretty sure Dee was only half joking.

While Rylee decided to walk around to get to know Royal, Tripp had dropped Dionna off at her hotel early that afternoon because she had a virtual casting meeting. He'd used the time to handle a few issues at the ranch, have a quick meeting with his sister about a potential vendor while entertaining his young niece and nephew, and grab a shower before picking Dionna up for dinner.

Tripp glanced over at Dionna again. He'd been sneaking glimpses of Dee the entire ride. He couldn't help himself. His eyes apparently had a mind of their own.

Dionna looked stunning again tonight. She wore a wrap minidress with buttons at the waist instead of a sash. The bold print in shades of green, hot pink, and blue looked good against Dionna's dark brown skin. The neckline of the dress revealed a hint of her full breasts. The strappy platform heels were sexy, yet practical. In other words: very, very Dionna.

The heels made Dionna's legs seem to go on for miles. His wayward brain couldn't help imagining how it would feel to have those long brown legs wrapped around his back.

"Are we waiting for someone?" Dionna glanced around.

"No. I..." Tripp loosened his collar and cleared his throat. "I just wanted to say that you look *really* beautiful tonight."

Dionna's glossy pink lips curved in a soft smile and her eyes twinkled. "Thank you. You look handsome tonight, too." She indicated his wool navy blazer, matching pants and white button-down shirt.

"Thanks." Tripp smoothed down his shirt. "I wanted to thank you again for keeping a level head when we learned about this wedding-crasher guy. And for helping me do the same."

Dionna's smile deepened. "Guess we make a good team after all."

"Yeah, I guess we do." Tripp nodded, unable to tear his gaze away from her full, kissable lips.

Dude, do not *fuck this up for me.*

Xavier's voice echoed in his head. Tripp tried to shake the vivid vision of him leaning in and kissing Dionna that had commandeered his brain.

Dee was a fiercely loyal friend. She was funny—mostly when she wasn't trying to be. And yes, she was beautiful. But she was also off-limits per the promise he'd made to Xavier. So he wouldn't be kissing Dionna Reed tonight or any other night.

"Tripp, are you okay?" Dee touched his wrist, and a spark of electricity danced along his skin, startling him. He withdrew his hand immediately.

Her eyes were filled with genuine concern as she studied his face.

"You must be exhausted after the day we had plus whatever you had to do at the ranch. Don't feel obligated to entertain me every night. I could've grabbed something at one of the restaurants at the hotel." Dionna's smile was warm, but he could see the disappointment in her eyes, hear it in her voice.

"It has been a long day," Tripp said. "But I'm fine. Just got a lot on my mind." He clapped his hands together. "I've been looking forward to tonight. I hope you're hungry because you're in for another treat."

Dionna's eyes lit up and her smile deepened. "I'm starving, actually."

"Perfect." Tripp jogged around to the passenger door and helped Dionna out of the truck. Her subtle wildflower scent tickled his nostrils, and his palm felt warm against hers.

Just two more days.

He could keep his mind together and his hands to himself for that long.

They entered the all-glass building and were seated in a more private area of the restaurant, which still offered a view of the open kitchen where the chef and his staff worked their magic.

"This is a beautiful restaurant." Dee studied the elegant furniture and contemporary lighting. "I wouldn't have expected anything like this here in Royal." She frowned immediately, her expression filled with apology. "I just meant that with the glass facade, contemporary furniture and open kitchen… It's more like something I'd expect to see in LA."

"Fair." Tripp nodded. "But that's one of the reasons I brought you here tonight. You've got a very stereotypical idea about what to expect from a small Texas town.

We're proud of our rich history of being ranchers and farmers. But there's much more to the town than that."

Dionna furrowed her brows, as if trying to decide how to phrase her response.

"You're overthinking it," Tripp said.

"I'm overthinking what?"

"Whatever you're attempting to say. So c'mon." Tripp gestured. "Out with it."

Dee sat taller and pulled back her shoulders.

"When you say there's so much more to the town... I'm thinking you mean compared to what the town was once like. I appreciate that," she said, when he nodded in response. "But most of the wedding guests reside in LA, New York, Atlanta, Chicago. Vibrant cities with lots for people to do. So they might not find the town quite as exciting as a longtime resident would."

Tripp tried not to look or sound as offended as he was. "You're right. We're not carbon copies of any of those places. Nor do we want to be. Royal is filled with people, places and experiences far different than anything those cities have to offer." He tapped the table with a finger for emphasis. "If you'd open your mind to seeing that...you'd realize it, too. So maybe stop acting as if we're asking the guests to slum it for the weekend."

"I never said..." Dee snapped her mouth shut when he glared at her. "Okay, I might've implied it," she admitted. "I'm not trying to hurt your feelings or insult Royal, Tripp. I'm here to ensure my friend gets the wedding of her dreams. She's trusting me to do this because she knows I'll be straightforward about my feelings...good or bad. So I'm gonna need you to put on your big-boy chaps and not be so precious about your beloved little town when all I'm doing is stating a fact."

"I'm not being *precious*." He totally was. "All I'm saying is that your uninformed *opinion* of Royal does not equate to facts." He leaned on the table, arms folded.

"Uninformed?" Dee practically spat the word.

Tripp enjoyed her reaction more than he should have. At least he had the decency not to laugh out loud. Though he had a good chuckle about it in his head.

"I do *not* make decisions based on uninformed opinions, Tripp Noble." Dee wagged a finger in his direction.

Tripp could only imagine how heated her cheeks were beneath her deep brown skin and perfectly applied makeup.

"I pride myself on doing thorough research, gathering available evidence, and then—*and only then*—making solid, educated, fully informed decisions." Dee folded her arms. The motion pushed up her breasts, dragging his attention to the shimmering skin and the hint of plump flesh revealed by the neckline of her dress.

He squeezed his eyes shut for a millisecond, reminding himself not to go there.

"Maybe that's the way you typically approach a situation. But you certainly haven't given Royal that same courtesy."

Before Dee could respond, two servers rolled out a cart with covered dishes on multiple shelves.

Dionna leaned across the table and whispered, "Why are they bringing us food? We haven't even placed our orders?"

"That's the other reason I brought you here. We could certainly have the wedding reception catered at the TCC as Rylee suggested. But I wanted to offer another option. I've asked Chef Colin Reynolds, the head chef here at Sheen, to prepare a sampling of possible offerings for a reception menu. If you're still hungry after the tasting menu, I'll buy you anything you want."

"So you didn't invite me to dinner just for my sparkling conversation, then?" Dee cocked her head and hiked a perfectly arched eyebrow.

Tripp chuckled and Dee dissolved into laughter, too. It eased the tension that'd been building between them.

"Why don't we call a temporary truce while we work our way through the delicious menu Chef Colin prepared for us? You can go right back to launching grenades at me and my beloved hometown when we're done."

"I'm *not* 'launching grenades.' I'm just trying to get this right for Ari. She's more than just my best friend. She's family, and she has *always* been there for me. So I won't let her down." Dee's tone was more solemn. "But I don't want to fight either. I'd much rather enjoy this lovely meal." She indicated the plates laid out in front of them.

"I'd like that, too." Tripp grinned. He turned to the server. "What do we have here, Delilah?"

Tripp could feel the heat of Dee's stare searing the side of his face. He chose not to acknowledge it. Instead, he remained focused on Delilah. If Delilah noticed Dee's reaction, her effervescent smile gave no indication of it.

"We have six options for hors d'oeuvres—prosciutto with freshly shaved parmesan and caviar with a smear of wasabi, an heirloom tomato caprese stack, shrimp cocktail shooters, mini buckets of tempura vegetables with a savory vegan mayo, delicious pork pot stickers and spicy lamb meatballs. The samples of red, white and sparkling wines are labeled. If you have any questions, just give me a call."

"You know I will." Tripp flashed the woman a smile. "Thanks, Delilah."

"Bon appétit!" Delilah bowed, her hands pressed together, then walked away.

Tripp surveyed the hors d'oeuvres laid out on the table. He rubbed his hands together. "I'm ready to dig in. You?"

Dee's expression was just short of a frown. She picked up the two small plates and handed him one without response. Then she carefully scooped one of each type of hors d'oeuvre onto her plate, and he did the same.

Dee spooned the caviar and prosciutto mixture into her mouth, and he did likewise. It would make it easier to compare notes if they sampled the items in the same order.

"It's good," Tripp said, feeling the need to fill the silence. "But I'm not a huge fan of caviar."

"Neither is Ari." Dee pulled her phone from her bag and typed out a few notes. "She tolerates it more than likes it. Pass."

"Agreed. What should we try next?"

"The heirloom tomato caprese stack?" Dee reached for it when Tripp nodded his agreement. They both murmured with delight as they bit into it. "Definitely a winner." Dee typed out notes on her phone again.

They tried the white wines next.

"I like the sauvignon blanc," Dee said.

"I prefer the Pinot Grigio," Tripp said simultaneously.

"I'm keeping a running list of items to consult the

bride and groom on when we chat tomorrow morning," she said. "I'll add this to it."

"We should take that call together," Tripp said. "Since you're here and we've been working on this together... It just makes sense, right?"

Dionna shrugged. "Sure. Why not?"

"Anyone ever tell you that you have a real gift for making a guy feel wanted?"

"Sorry. I thought you might be...otherwise occupied at that time of the morning."

"Our ranch hands handle the weekends for us unless there's some emergency." Tripp bit into a pot sticker.

"Actually, I figured you and Miss Hors D'Oeuvres over there would be tangled up somewhere together." Dee cringed, as if she hadn't meant to say the words aloud. She picked up a pot sticker. "Not that it's any of my business."

"What makes you think there's something going on with me and Lilah?" He genuinely wanted to know.

"Well, you just called her by a pet name," Dee said. "Then there was the way you said her name. *Delilah.*" She uttered the word in a deep breathy voice.

Tripp nearly choked on his pot sticker. "I did *not* sound like that."

"Whatever you say, boss." She pinned him with a self-satisfied smile. "Though it wasn't all on you. There was the way she looked at you when she said, 'If you need anything, I mean *anything* at all, just call me.' And then you were all, 'You know I will, sweetcakes.'" Dionna seemed to be enjoying herself imitating both his and Delilah's Texas accents and mannerisms.

Tripp broke into laughter and so did she. He ate the

last of his pot sticker. "You know that isn't what either of us said, right?"

"I might've taken a tiny bit of artistic license." Dee giggled, finishing her pot sticker, too. "But I think I got the general gist of the conversation. You two are a thing."

Damn. Was she that good or was his incognito game slipping?

"We don't have a thing." Tripp leaned in and lowered his voice. "We *had* one. Went out a few times a really long time ago. Chef isn't crazy about the staff dating customers, so we kept it on the low." He shrugged. "Lilah and I might not exactly be friends, but we are friendly. I make it a policy to end things on a pleasant note."

"Then I guess no one has ever broken your heart." The pain in Dee's voice made him want to reach across the table and squeeze her hand.

Tripp interlocked his hands on the table instead. His jaw tensed. "Actually, I have had my heart broken. It was devastating. That's why I made the conscious decision to take a more casual approach to dating and being up-front about that from the outset."

"Hmm…" Dee rested her chin in her palm as she studied him. "So you're *that* guy."

Tripp gave her a puzzled look. "Okay, I'll bite. What do you mean by *that guy*?"

"You're the 'I've been hurt before' serial dater who absolves himself of all the broken hearts he's left in his wake." Dee nibbled on another pot sticker.

"I never lead anyone on." Tripp tapped the table with his index finger. "I'm always up-front about my intentions."

"I get it. You enter each relationship with a label

slapped across your forehead that reads *Warning: Does not do serious relationships. Ever.* You figure that if they catch feelings for you… Well, that's their fault. Right?" She finished her pot sticker and wiped her hands on a napkin. "But we both know you're fully aware that your charm can be…*intoxicating* for the average woman. That pearly white smile and dynamic magnetism pretty much drown out that warning. So when you eventually walk away and leave her brokenhearted, you're all, 'Sorry, babe, but I tried to warn you I'm not a stick-around-for-ever kinda guy.'"

Tripp was irritated by her imitation of him this time. Mostly because it was a little too on-the-nose.

But he didn't need to justify his life choices with Ms. Dee "I-Know-Every-Damn-Thing" Reed. "No one I've dated thus far has complained. So maybe us Texans are a little more progressive than you think." He winked, determined to show her that he was unbothered by her armchair analysis of his romantic life.

"I honestly think you believe that. But if you had a candid conversation with those exes you're so friendly with, I wonder if they'd agree." Dee analyzed the plates in front of them. "Lamb meatballs?"

Tripp frowned, more irritated than angry. With himself more than Dee. Because for the first time, the slightest doubt crept into his mind about his dealings with his exes.

Were they really as okay with the ending of the relationship as they had seemed?

"Shrimp cocktail shooters," Tripp said gruffly, feeling the need to disagree with this woman who seemed dead set on killing his easygoing vibe.

Dee froze, her hand suspended above one of the meatballs. "Shrimp cocktail it is."

They both took a bite of the jumbo shrimp and tangy cocktail sauce.

"This is a winner," they said simultaneously, then laughed.

"If Ari was here, she'd say jinx." Dee smiled. She finished her other piece of shrimp, then typed out more notes. "Meatballs next?"

He nodded, plucked one of the lamb meatballs wrapped in a roasted sugar snap pea from his plate and took a bite. The savory meatball was juicy and delectable. Roasting brought out the sweetness in the pea.

"Delicious." Tripp discarded the toothpick and plucked the other meatball from his plate.

"They are really good." Dee shoved her plate toward him, indicating that he should take her other meatball.

"I thought you said you liked them?"

"I do. But we have a lot more food to try. I'm pacing myself," Dee said. "Plus...you know you want it," she teased.

He did. And he wasn't just thinking about that damn meatball.

The more this woman got under his skin, the more he wondered about the taste of her full lips.

He accepted the meatball and thanked her. Then they both tried the tempura vegetables and vegan mayo.

"I didn't think I'd like this." Tripp nibbled on the last veggie fry. "But these vegetable straws are really good. And that vegan mayo is the truth."

"Coming from a cattle rancher, that's high praise indeed." Dee typed out more notes. "And we definitely need vegan options."

"Five out of six are winners. Not bad, eh?" Tripp stacked their empty plates after Dee offered him the remainder of her fries. "I don't want to brag here…"

"You absolutely do," she countered with an eye roll.

"Maybe a little." He peered through his thumb and forefinger. "And since our local vendors have been blowing you away, I've been thinking… Why don't we make a point of choosing local vendors? It would be good PR for Ariana, Xavier, the town of Royal and the individual vendors. Plus, it would spread a lot of goodwill among the locals. Isn't that a huge part of the reason Ari moved the wedding here in the first place?"

"I don't know, Tripp," Dee said. "There's a bakery in LA that Ari has her heart set on. She has a makeup artist she works with regularly, and she's already engaged her stylist Keely Tucker, who is also a friend, to create her custom wedding dress. There's no way Ari will want to work with anyone else."

"The makeup artist and wedding dress designer… I get that. But transporting the cake from LA to Royal opens up the possibility of a slew of disasters. An unnecessary risk, given that we have a phenomenal bakery right here in town. I've seen them make some stunning wedding cakes. We could pop into the shop tomorrow. If I give her a call right now, I'm sure she could fit in a tasting for us tomorrow."

"Has anyone ever told you that you are incredibly persistent?"

"If that's code for pest…then yeah," Tripp chuckled. "Is that a yes?"

Dee heaved a quiet sigh, her eyes narrowing. "Fine. Yes."

Tripp made the call to his favorite local bakery, glad

Dee was amenable to the idea of going almost exclusively with local vendors. But he honestly wasn't sure if the sense of satisfaction he felt was because he was slowly winning the battle or because it meant he'd get to spend more time with Dionna.

Six

There had been a few tumultuous moments during the evening. But they'd sketched out a possible menu and agreed to recommend that Sheen cater the wedding reception. Ari and Ex could always make changes, but Dionna felt good about the solid options they planned to present to the couple. By the end of the evening, she could finally breathe a sigh of relief.

There were still a few important items to address during their group chat with Ariana and Xavier the next day. Then on Sunday, she'd order a car service to the Dallas/Fort Worth International Airport and take a direct flight back home to LA.

When she'd first learned that her best friend wouldn't be coming, she'd been counting down the hours until she could escape this town and board that plane home. But in spite of herself, she'd managed to enjoy her time here with Tripp. She'd gotten a kick out of needling him a bit. And it seemed that he had a knack for getting under her skin.

What she hadn't expected was just how palpable the attraction she felt to Tripp would be. It was like a living, breathing thing that seemed to take up space between them. She could feel it whenever those mesmerizing brown eyes of his flickered over her skin. Whenever he touched her wrist or pressed a hand to her back as he guided her through a restaurant or across the street.

Her skin felt as if it was on fire. Her nipples tightened. And there was the sweetest ache between her thighs.

She was much too old to have a rabid crush on the handsome cowboy who would probably be holding on to his international player's card until it was wedged out of his cold dead hands.

Not the kind of man she should be interested in. Besides, he lived in Texas and she lived in California. End of story.

Dee sighed. Why was she even thinking about this? The only thing going on between her and Tripp was the lustful thoughts happening inside her head.

"I forgot to ask what you're working on at the production company?" Tripp asked as they finished the evening with two espresso con panna.

"We're in the early stages of an ambitious project that's far different than anything we've done before. It's a Western about a Black cowboy in Texas who has to fight to keep his land."

"Sounds like the story of my family," Tripp said, his expression suddenly serious. "When my great-grandfather first acquired the land in the early nineteen hundreds, folks who owned property around here did just about everything they could to make him give up the title to his land."

Dee's chest ached from the pained look in Tripp's eyes. He didn't want to talk about this, and who could blame him?

"Ariana mentioned that Xavier's family…your family had a similar experience, but she didn't go into any of the details." Dee set down her coffee cup.

"Acceptance was a long process for my great-grandparents and grandparents. I guess that's where I get my stubbornness and occasional ornery streak." He attempted a small smile.

"Well, that stubborn streak has served you well. Your ancestors would be proud of everything your family has achieved," Dee said sincerely. "But I'm sorry for bringing it up. I should've realized that the topic might be upsetting."

Tripp placed his hand on her wrist. His gaze was warm. "It didn't upset me. Yes, the topic hits close to home. But it's an important story. One people need to know about. People need to know about the existence of Black farmers and ranchers—*then and now*. Their history has been buried. So I'm excited to see more projects like this happening. Where do you plan to film the movie?"

"There are a number of studios around LA or in the desert that—"

"Wait… You're making this movie about a Black cowboy in Texas, but you plan on filming it in Cali?" Tripp's expression shifted. He released her hand and shook his head. "Not gonna lie. That fucking sucks."

"I know, but it's easy and efficient. Central to all the

players." Dee sipped her espresso. "It's something that's done frequently in the industry."

Tripp looked sad.

"I feel like I accidentally told a wide-eyed little boy that Santa isn't real." Dee squeezed Tripp's wrist this time. Her tone was teasing, but she'd said the words with genuine empathy. "You look so disappointed right now."

"Good. Because I am. Damn green screen," he muttered the last words beneath his breath, and Dee couldn't help laughing.

"Sometimes it's just really amazing set design. Like the show *Friends*. It was set in New York but filmed on the Warner Brothers set in Burbank. *Casablanca* wasn't filmed in Morocco. It was filmed in Burbank, too. And *Scarface*—"

His eyes widened. "Don't tell me…"

"Most of the movie was filmed in California. Sorry." She shrugged, moving her half-finished espresso aside, already beginning to feel a little too wired. "But that's the magic of the movies. They can take us to outer space, to the future or to a city on the other side of the world and make it completely believable."

A soft smile curved one edge of Tripp's mouth, making him look even more delicious than he already did in his navy blazer that clung tightly to his impressive biceps.

"What?" Dee asked. "I'm geeking out about this, right?"

That picture-perfect smile of Tripp's expanded. "That's not what I was thinking."

"What were you thinking?" Dee leaned forward, her arms folded on the table.

She was afraid she might not like his answer. Still, she couldn't stop herself from asking.

"Honestly? I was thinking about how beautiful you are. More so when your eyes light up like that and you're practically glowing from within because you're bursting with excitement." Tripp drank more of his espresso. "It's incredibly cute."

Incredibly cute? Like a puppy? Just what every woman wants to be called.

Then again, he'd also called her beautiful.

"Thank you." Dionna ignored the heat rising in her cheeks. "And I'm totally at ease with the fact that I can be an unabashed geek when it comes to what happens behind the scenes in the film industry. Casting, set design, costume design, mixing, editing, you name it. I was a goner the first time my parents took me on set when I was about eight. There's been no turning back ever since."

"It's great that you're in an industry that you're so passionate about." Tripp switched to drinking his water with lemon. "I envy that."

"You're not passionate about ranching?" Dee asked.

"Ranching is in my blood. The thing I was born to do." He gave a half shrug. "I enjoy life on the ranch, and I'm honored to continue my family's legacy."

"But?" Dee propped her chin on her fist and studied his face.

Tripp sucked in a deep breath. "Sometimes I do wonder what my life would've been if I hadn't been born into a role, you know?" He folded his hands on the table, mere inches from her fingertips.

Dee fought back the urge to reach out and squeeze

his hand. "It's never too late to do something different with your life, if that's what you really want, Tripp."

"Xavier opted out of ranch life over a decade ago. My sister married the rancher next door four years ago, and she has two young children. That makes me the heir apparent by default. There's no way, after everything my grandparents and great-grandparents went through to hold on to this ranch, that I'd let it go to someone else. And if I don't carry on the family tradition, that's *exactly* what would happen."

There was a mingling of pride with a hint of sadness in his eyes. Her heart ached for him. Maybe he did enjoy being a rancher. But in some ways, it seemed he felt as if his life was not his own.

"That's a heavy burden to bear," Dee said.

"Maybe. But what I do matters. I have a good life. Wonderful family. Great friends. The freedom to expand my interests would've been nice," Tripp acknowledged. "But I'd never want to call any place but Royal home. I love it here."

"It must be an amazing feeling to be so rooted in a place and to know without a doubt that's where you belong," Dee said.

"You live in LA and love being part of the film industry." Tripp looked puzzled. "I'd think that you'd be in heaven."

"I do love the industry and stepping behind the magic mirror of filmmaking. But I don't love the traffic and the hustle and bustle of life in LA." It pained her to say it, but it was true. LA living was the price she paid for doing work she loved.

"So if you could be in the film industry but live anywhere you wanted, where would that be?" Tripp leaned forward, his chin resting on his open palm.

Dionna smiled. "I'd live on a little farm like the one my grandparents owned."

"What happened to your grandparents' farm?"

Dee frowned, her heart breaking at the thought. She cleared her throat and sighed. "My grandparents were really proud people. So when Grandad got ill, he didn't want us to know how serious it was. Nor did he want us to know his treatments and hospitalizations were draining them financially. They got a second mortgage on the farm. Then they sold it. By the time we knew any of this, it was too late. They'd already sold the place for a cut-rate price and my grandfather only had a few months to live." She dragged a finger beneath her eyes, trying her best not to ruin her makeup.

Who knew I'd need waterproof mascara tonight?

"I'm sorry that happened to your grandparents, Dee." Tripp handed her the handkerchief in his pocket. It was white with a navy, purple and black abstract design.

"I can't. My makeup will ruin it," she objected.

"It's okay." He shoved it in her direction again. "Plenty more where that came from."

Dee thanked him and accepted the hankie. She dabbed at the corners of her eyes.

"Remember when I said my parents didn't want me to follow them into the film industry? The last thing my gram said to me before she died was, 'It's your life, sweetie. Not your parents. Follow *your* dreams. They'll get over it.'"

"Did your parents get over it?" Tripp asked.

"They were furious. They said I was wasting my gifts in an industry that would never truly appreciate them."

Dionna winced, recalling the conversation she'd had with her parents. "My dad didn't speak to me for a year. They weren't used to me going against them. I spent my entire childhood trying to be their perfect little girl. I know my parents love me. But sometimes it felt like being exactly who they wanted me to be was the only way I could get them to show me that they did. To say that they were…" The words caught in Dionna's throat and her eyes burned with tears.

"Proud of you?" Tripp squeezed her hand.

Dee nodded, dabbing beneath her eyes with the hankie.

Why had she allowed herself to get worked up about this again? It was ancient history. This had happened seventeen years ago. Still, her heart felt as raw as if it'd happened yesterday.

Dionna tugged her hand from Tripp's and forced a smile. "Sorry. I'm *really* tired. Is it okay if we call it a night?"

"Of course." Tripp stuffed several bills into the black leather folder, then shoved a copy of the bill in his shirt pocket. He stood, holding his hand out to her. "Shall we?"

Dee slipped her hand in his. They waved goodbye to Delilah and to Chef Colin who'd come to their table to introduce himself to Dee when the entrées had been brought out to the table. Then they walked to Tripp's truck in a silence that felt…comfortable.

On the way to the hotel, Tripp made small talk. Recapping some of their favorite foods and wines. Making her laugh by reminding her of some of the funny moments they'd shared over the course of the day. By the time he pulled his truck into the parking lot of The Bellamy, she didn't object to him walking her to her room. Because if she was being honest, she wasn't ready to say good night.

They got off the elevator on the third floor and made the trek to her room, still chatting about the films she knew of that had been filmed someplace other than where the story was set. Finally, they reached her door.

"Thank you, Tripp. I have to admit that this wedding planning experience has been a lot more fun than I expected. You've really come through with the vendors so far. Are you sure this isn't your side hustle?" Dee teased. "Because you're really good at it. Even when you're dealing with a tough customer."

"I've always enjoyed finding ways to connect the right people." He shoved his hands in his pockets. "If I could figure out how to make it a side hustle, I would." He grinned. "But I wouldn't call you a tough customer. You're a dedicated friend. One Ari is damn lucky to have." Tripp winked.

Dionna's tummy fluttered. A wave of warmth made its way down her spine, and her pulse raced. She waved her small bag, which contained her room key, in front of the lock and it clicked. Dee pushed the door open and stepped inside. She glanced at the refrigerator, where she had a bottle of wine chilling that she'd purchased earlier in the day.

Tripp seemed as reluctant as she was to say their goodbyes. The seconds of silence ticking by felt like minutes.

"Thank you again, Tripp. For everything." Dee dropped her bag on the table near the door. "Would you like to join me for a nightcap or maybe some really overpriced chocolate from the minibar?" She laughed nervously, the words rushing from her lips before she could stop herself.

What are you thinking?

She needed to create distance between herself and the ridiculously handsome cowboy she'd become far too fond of. Not scheming ways to spend more time with him.

Tripp opened his mouth, and Dee was sure he was going to say yes. But he dragged a hand down his handsome face and released a quiet sigh. His smile was polite, not the genuine one he'd flashed her moments earlier.

"I wish I could, Dionna. But like I said, it's been a really long day. I need to handle a few things early tomorrow before I meet you here for that chat with Ariana and Xavier at ten. I should call it a night."

Or you could just spend the night here.

For a moment, Dee wasn't sure whether she'd said the words aloud or if she'd only said them in her head. When Tripp didn't react, she breathed a sigh of relief.

"I thought the ranch hands handled weekends."

Why couldn't she keep her mouth shut?

Tripp was trying to turn her down politely, and she'd just made it awkward.

"Typically. But some things I prefer to handle myself."

They stood in silence for a few painfully awkward moments.

"Well, good night then," Dee said finally.

She moved to shut the door, but Tripp leaned and dropped a kiss on her cheek. His beard abraded her skin.

"Night, Dee," he said. When he stepped back, his eyes locked with hers for a moment before his hungry gaze dropped to her lips.

Suddenly, her skin felt as if it was on fire. And there was a steady pulse between her thighs.

"See you in the morning." Tripp turned and strode back toward the elevator.

Her heart thudding in her chest, Dee's hand went to the spot where Tripp's lips had touched her skin.

Maybe it was a good thing Tripp had turned down her invitation. Clearly, that irresistible charm of his was starting to work on her, too.

Seven

The next morning, Tripp stepped off the elevator and made his way to Dionna's hotel room. At this point, he was beginning to wear a path in the carpeting.

Tripp sighed, trying to cleanse his brain of the thoughts that had kept him awake staring at the ceiling until the wee hours of the morning.

Dionna Reed was living rent-free in his brain, and he wasn't even sure why. They were complete opposites. She was all buttoned-up and straitlaced with her to-do lists, research and endless note-taking. While he was more of a go-with-your-gut kind of guy.

And yes, they'd had a few laughs and managed to enjoy each other's company. But there had been more than a few moments when they'd rubbed each other the wrong way.

So why couldn't he stop thinking about her?

His brain had insisted on replaying Dionna's bright smile and contagious laugh. And her sweet, subtle spring scent seemed to linger in his senses long after he'd showered before bed.

The teasing lilt of Dee's voice had drowned out the urgency of Xavier's when he'd made Tripp promise not to get involved with her.

Every time he'd touched her—even in the smallest, most insignificant ways, like guiding her through the restaurant door—he'd gotten a little thrill. Like when he was a kid and would tread as close as possible to the lines his parents had told him not to cross.

He stood in front of her door at twenty to ten, took a deep breath and knocked.

Dee opened the door wearing a white terry cloth robe. She tightened the belt at her waist, then smoothed back her twists piled atop her head.

"Sorry, but you're early and I'm running late." She opened the door to let him in and gestured toward the sofa. "I went to the gym this morning and there was a wait for a treadmill. Time got away from me."

"It's my fault. Like you said, I'm early. I thought you might want to go over a few things before we chat with Ari and Ex." Tripp shoved his hands in his pockets and tried really hard not to think about whether or not Dee was naked beneath that robe.

The way she was clutching at the fabric shielding her chest with one hand and the fabric covering her thighs with the other, he was betting she was.

"Talking beforehand would've been a terrific idea… had I known in advance." Dee hiked one eyebrow, and her nostrils flared.

"Should've suggested it last night. Sorry. Just pretend

I'm not here." Tripp headed for the sofa. "This'll give me a chance to address the emails I didn't get to yesterday."

"I was about to step into the shower. In fact, I left it running." Dee nodded over her shoulder toward one of the two bedrooms in the suite. He could hear the faint sound of water running. "Have a seat. Help yourself to anything in the minifridge. And I ordered breakfast, so could you let them in if they come while I'm in the shower?"

"Sure thing." His eyes were drawn to the flashes of smooth brown skin revealed when she released the robe to rummage through her purse.

"Here." Dionna extended several bills.

"What's this for?" Tripp didn't reach for it.

"For the tip," Dionna said.

"Don't worry. I've got—"

"Ari paid for my room and travel, and you've paid for *everything else* since I arrived. I think I can afford to tip."

"I don't mind." Tripp dug his hands deeper in his pockets.

"Take the money, *Austin*." Dee shook the bills.

Shit. She'd gone government name on him again.

"Fine." Tripp raised his hands in surrender, then accepted the cash.

"Great." Dionna tossed the word over her shoulder as she hurried off, that damn robe swishing behind her.

Tripp tossed the bills on the table and sank onto the leather sofa. "Stubborn, recalcitrant woman," he muttered under his breath.

It was a phrase his grandfather and father often used about their better halves. The phrase was almost always accompanied by a head scratch and a reluctant chuckle or grin.

After thirty-four years of life, Tripp was beginning to understand.

How could Dee be so damn exasperating, yet also so incredibly appealing?

Maybe he was a masochist who enjoyed banging his head against a wall. Or maybe…

Tripp shook his head. Dionna Reed answering the door wearing nothing beneath her robe was the very last thing his overactive imagination needed.

One more day, then Dee is heading back to LA.

Tripp should've been relieved. Once Dee was gone, he could stop gallivanting around town playing the role of Royal's one-man convention and visitors bureau slash weekend wedding planner. Then he could return his focus to running the ranch. Only, the more time he spent with Dee, the less excited he was about her leaving.

Ten minutes later, Dee emerged from the bedroom in a cream off-shoulder sweater, slim black pants that highlighted her delicious curves and a pair of black riding boots. Half of her hair was pulled back by a fancy gold barrette. The loose twists dusted her shoulders. And for the first time since she'd arrived, Dee was wearing her glasses. These were dark brown accented by gold rhinestones and gold trim. Jimmy Choo was emblazoned along her temples.

On a one-to-ten scale of hot librarian vibes, Dee was dishing up a solid twenty.

"Dee." Tripp stood, unable to tear his gaze away from her. He rubbed the back of his neck where flames licked at his skin. "You look…*fantastic*. The glasses—"

"The pressure in the shower is a little *too* good." She

shrugged. "I accidentally sprayed myself in the face and blasted one of my contacts down the drain."

Tripp tried his best not to laugh, but when Dionna did, he couldn't help joining in.

"Well, I'm sorry you nearly lost an eye while showering." Tripp almost managed to keep a straight face. "But I was going to say, I've never seen you in those glasses before, but they look really good on you."

Honestly, he couldn't imagine there was much that wouldn't look good on Dee. But the hot brainiac look she was serving up in spades was something he hadn't known he needed in his life.

"Thanks." Dee pushed her glasses up the bridge of her nose, her mouth curved in a bashful smile.

His heart pounded, the knocking sound in his chest echoing in his ears. Could Dee hear it, too?

"Tripp?" Dee waved a hand in front of his face. "Ari and Ex will be calling soon. I need to grab my planner and notebook. Could you get the door? That's probably room service." Dee gestured toward the door: the source of the *actual* knocking.

He wasn't sure if he should be relieved because the knocking was real and not coming from his chest…like some lovestruck animated character. Or if he should be alarmed that he'd zoned out for a minute…like a lovestruck animated character.

Either way, he needed to get it together. *Now.*

Dionna retrieved her planner and notebook, her stomach still fluttering from Tripp's compliment.

Girl, you really *need to get out more.*

Her best friend's plea echoed in Dionna's head. "Dee,

don't take this the wrong way, sweetie, but you need to get a life."

She had a life. A damned good one. A job she loved. A few good friends. Her parents were still alive, which she was grateful for, even if they drove her crazy. And a tiny overpriced apartment in LA that she could actually afford.

What more could a woman want?

"Ready to eat?" Tripp's deep, sexy voice snapped her out of her temporary daze.

That was what more this woman could want. A man who was charming, funny, incredibly sexy and who looked at her like she was his last meal.

Dee clutched the planner and notebook against her chest to hide the swell of her nipples against her Angora sweater. She swallowed hard, her throat dry as she ambled over to the dining table where Tripp had rolled the service cart bearing their breakfast.

"I wasn't sure what you'd want, so I ordered everything." Dionna lifted the silver domes to reveal bacon and sausage, pancakes and waffles, scrambled eggs and eggs over easy, plus a variety of juices.

"Perfect." Tripp rubbed his hands together, his light brown eyes gleaming in the Saturday midmorning sun. "Ready to dig in?"

"First, I was thinking we should move our seats closer together, opposite the window." Dionna gestured toward the light streaming in and warming her face. At least, she assumed that was the reason her face suddenly felt so hot. "To get the best lighting for our call," she clarified when Tripp gave her an amused look.

"Yes, ma'am." Tripp shrugged, sliding his chair over, opposite the window she'd set up her iPad in front of.

"According to Ari, perfect lighting is the first rule of film. Especially for those of us with darker skin."

"Your skin always looks radiant in those video calls." Tripp reached for the metal handle of the glass syrup dispenser. "So I'll take your word for it. Syrup?"

Tripp held the dispenser aloft, and with the sunlight shining through the glass container, the liquid inside was nearly the same soft brown as Tripp's eyes.

"Please," she said.

Tripp poured syrup on her waffles until she'd indicated it was enough, then poured some on his pancakes. Since she was still standing there, her brain apparently short-circuiting with Tripp in such close proximity, he moved her chair beside his and gestured for her to have a seat.

She thanked him and did just that.

They ate in companionable silence except for the occasional commentary on how good the food was. And though this was now the fifth consecutive meal she'd eaten with Tripp, something about the two of them sitting so close together felt more...*intimate*.

A shiver rippled up Dionna's spine, and she dropped her fork. The metal clanged against her plate, bounced onto her pants, then onto the carpeted floor, splattering syrup along the way.

She moved to retrieve the wayward utensil, but Tripp squeezed her arm.

"I've got you." His luminous grin made her feel all kinds of awkward and apparently rendered her speechless.

Tripp retrieved the fork, carried it to the small bar sink, then opened the drawer that contained a full set of silverware. Dee tried not to think about why Tripp knew *exactly* where to find a fork in her hotel suite.

Let's just say I'm familiar with the layout of the hotel.

"Thank you." She flashed an awkward smile and accepted the new fork. "I'm not usually this clumsy, I swear." Dee shoved a fork full of the fluffy Belgian waffles in her mouth.

Tripp handed her a damp dishcloth so she could wipe the syrup off her pants while he stooped to clean the splash of syrup off the carpet using a soapy paper towel.

Dionna's blood seemed to heat to a simmer as Tripp kneeled on the floor beside her.

Imagine him kneeling like that, but in front of you.

Dionna cringed. Her best friend's dirty mind and wicked sense of humor had rubbed off on her more than she realized. She shook the thought from her head, muttered her thanks again, then wondered aloud why Ari's call was already ten minutes late.

"Sounds like things are pretty wild for both of them right now." Tripp discarded the paper towel, washed and dried his hands, then joined her at the table again. "I wouldn't be surprised if they needed to reschedule."

"I hope not," Dee muttered. "The longer it takes us to hammer out the details of this wedding—"

"The more time you'll be forced to spend with me?" There was a teasing lilt in Tripp's tone and a half-hearted smile. But there was disappointment or maybe hurt in his eyes.

Dionna felt like the Wicked Witch of LA.

"That isn't what I was going to say," Dee said truthfully. "And the past couple of days have actually been..."

"Surprisingly fun?" This time Tripp's smile felt more genuine.

An involuntary smile spread across Dionna's face. She nodded. "Yes. Exactly that."

"Good. Because I've enjoyed hanging out with you, too." Tripp nudged her shoulder playfully.

Heat filled his brown eyes. When his gaze dropped to her mouth, it felt as if she'd forgotten how to breathe. But this time she managed to hang on to her fork.

Her phone and iPad rang simultaneously. Dee sucked in a much-needed breath and accepted the call.

"We were beginning to think you two had forgotten about us. Don't y'all know people got shit to do around here." Tripp's wide smile and playful Texas twang belied the irritation conveyed by his words.

Ariana and Xavier laughed, both of them looking and sounding guilty.

"Sorry, you two." Ari was practically glowing. "But we didn't think you'd want to hear us gushing for fifteen minutes about how much we love and miss each other."

"Aww…" Dee pressed a hand to her chest.

"Eww," Tripp said. "Good call."

"Hater," Xavier chuckled.

"You two certainly look…cozy." Ari pursed her lips and batted her eyelashes. "Are you two at the breakfast stage of the relationship already?"

Ari giggled, endlessly amused, and Tripp shook his head, but grinned. Dee gasped, suddenly unable to speak. The only other person who seemed as disturbed by the implication of Ari's words was Xavier.

It looked like he'd sucked a whole lemon as his eyes narrowed at the screen in a message that seemed meant for Tripp.

"Relax, bro. Don't pop a blood vessel. Dee and I figured that taking the call together would allow us to immediately game-plan a few things afterward," Tripp said in an easy voice as he plucked the remaining piece of bacon from his plate and popped it into his mouth.

"Exactly." Dee nodded, finally finding her voice. "So if everyone would refer to the agenda I emailed you."

Ari and Tripp both groaned.

"I see that you've been introduced to my incredibly organized best friend's love of spreadsheets and 'meeting'—" Ari used air quotes "—agendas."

"For which we're grateful." Xavier smiled. "We realize what an imposition this is for both of you, and we really appreciate you taking time out of your busy schedules to help us out."

This was exactly why Xavier had won her over. He was a genuinely good, kind and thoughtful guy. And so, it seemed, was his cousin.

"Okay, then," Dee said. "Here's what we're thinking…"

Eight

Tripp couldn't help smiling as he watched Dee gesticulate about the pros and cons of each option they were recommending. The woman was determined and focused whether she was discussing wedding venues or her favorite television show.

Normally, he'd considered anyone that impassioned about mundane matters to be a little too high-strung for his laid-back demeanor. But there was something about Dionna. She had a gift for getting others excited about things that might've seemed unimportant. And for making the most basic tasks seem fun and a bit exciting.

He wouldn't have believed it possible, but he was actually enjoying this whole wedding planning adventure with Dee. Not once had he felt the need to trot out the countless excuses he'd prepared in the event he felt the need to dip. And since he was as stubborn as she was, he was determined to make Dionna see how special Royal was.

"I love this point about intentionally selecting local vendors," Ex said. "Brilliant idea, Dee. This will generate excellent PR for the town and for us. And it'll create a lot of goodwill among the locals—including those who might be hesitant about the media circus this wedding is going to bring to their doorstep."

"Actually…that was all Tripp." Dionna gestured to him. "Honestly? I was against it initially. And while I realize there will need to be a couple of exceptions, now I can't help but agree. Utilizing local vendors is a good PR, logistic and financial move."

Tripp turned to Dee and winked, using the eye facing away from the camera. A secret gesture between just the two of them.

Dee took a sip of her ice water.

"You don't like the idea?" Dionna studied the worried look on her best friend's face.

"I do…*in theory*," Ari said carefully. "As long as Keely Tucker making my dress is one of those exceptions."

"Of course, I already told Tripp you'd want to work with Keely and your regular makeup artist, Lisette." Dee nodded. "Any other concerns?"

"You're sure this Seth Grayson is a top-rate photographer?" Ari's voice was filled with hesitation. "If he screws up our wedding photos… We'll never get the magic of that day back."

"Seth is a consummate professional and his work is always outstanding," Tripp assured the nervous bride-to-be.

"I was really impressed with Seth's portfolio. You'll

find the link to it in the email. And you know I would never have cosigned this recommendation if I hadn't been blown away by his work." Dee offered her friend a reassuring smile. "Just wait until you see it."

"All right." Ari nodded, looking more at ease. "You know how much I value your opinion, Dee."

"I'll try not to take that personally." Tripp smirked.

"You know what I mean." Ari waved his comment off. "By the way, Mr. Connections, you wouldn't happen to have an award-winning makeup artist up your sleeve, would you? Because Lisette is expecting a baby around the same date as our wedding."

"Don't worry. I've got you," Tripp said.

"Don't tell me, you've got a personal makeup artist up your sleeve, too?" Ari marveled.

"Milan Valez is a makeup artist here in town. She works at the luxury spa PURE, and she does exceptional work. Her specialty is giving her clients a flawless finish without looking too made-up."

"You know an awful lot about makeup, cowboy," Dee noted.

"Milan did this incredible makeover for my sister when Tessa was the lone bachelorette in a charity auction at the Texas Cattleman's Club about five years ago. She's been booked solid ever since. So if you're interested, we'd better inquire about her availability right away," Tripp said. "Here. I'll drop her website link in the group text chat."

A moment later, everyone's phones dinged. There was silence as Dee and Ariana clicked on the link and scrolled to Milan's online portfolio.

"Milan does amazing work," Dee noted after scrolling through several photos.

"Have you seen the before and after photos? This woman is a freaking miracle worker." Ari looked up at the screen. "Tripp, please try to book Milan as soon as possible."

"Will do."

"After the wedding, we can have your publicist draw up a nice fluff piece about the wedding, naming all of the local vendors used." Dionna scanned her planner and notebook. "Unless anyone has something else, I think that covers everything."

"Actually, there is one other point I wanted to address," Tripp said. "When you'd planned to have the wedding in LA, you'd mentioned hosting a weeklong celebration with a variety of guest activities. Did you change your mind about that?"

"My plans were location-specific," Ari said as diplomatically as possible. "A visit to Disneyland, a film studio tour, whale watching, an evening cruise, a bonfire at the beach." She ticked the items off on her fingers.

"The events themselves would need to change, sure. But we can still have a week of prewedding festivities right here in Royal," Tripp said.

"That could be a lot of fun," Xavier agreed.

"This is the first I'm hearing about this." Dee peered at Tripp with one brow raised. A look that indicated they'd be having a *serious* talk after the call. "We haven't discussed any options, so I certainly can't weigh in on any recommendations. And I'm leaving tomorrow. There's no way I'll have time to help create and vet a weeklong agenda of guest activities."

Dee's in-control demeanor had shifted. She was flustered.

"Sorry, Dee." Tripp turned toward her, one hand

pressed to her low back. "I didn't mean to throw you off. I just thought of this last night. That's why I came a few minutes early. I was hoping we could talk about it beforehand. But when I got here you were about to hop into the shower. I kind of forgot."

"Wait! You were there when Dee showered this morning?" Ari looked excited. "I need to hear more about this."

Dee flashed him a look that screamed *You had to say that right now?* Then she turned to the screen. "Tripp arrived earlier than we agreed. He sat in the living room and waited while I showered. Honestly, Ari, it's no big deal." Dee snapped her fingers. "Let's stay focused."

"Right. I need to leave for a speaking engagement in about forty minutes." Ex glanced down at the expensive watch on his wrist.

When Xavier looked up again, his expression contained a clear admonition: *Remember your promise, man. Do* not *fuck this up for me.*

Had the girls noticed Ex's warning look? If so, neither of them remarked on it.

"Tell us what you're thinking, Tripp," Ex continued.

"Most of the guests will be big city folks. So let's expose them to some fun things they wouldn't normally get to do," Tripp said.

"Like horseback riding or visiting a working ranch." Ex rubbed his chin and nodded. "I like it. What about you, babe?"

"I've kind of always wanted to visit a dude ranch and go horseback riding," Ari said excitedly.

"Ari, really?" Dee cocked her head. "I've never once heard you say you wanted to visit a dude ranch." Dionna folded her arms and stared at her friend incredulously.

"You didn't even want to go bike riding a few weeks ago because you were afraid you'd break a nail."

"I know. But this sounds cool. Besides, I'm sure they have a nail salon there somewhere, right?" Ari giggled.

"Absolutely." Tripp had expected more pushback from Ariana.

"Won't you be sore after a day of dude ranching?" Dionna glared at Tripp. "Whatever that entails."

"Which is why we'll follow it up with a relaxing day of massages and pampering at PURE Spa here in town." A small smirk crept across Tripp's mouth when Dee's glare intensified.

"Brilliant idea, Tripp. I love it!" Ariana clapped excitedly. "But are there any other options for people who might not want to do something as vigorous as horseback riding or visiting a dude ranch?"

"Maybe a pottery or mosaic class at this really amazing antique shop in town, Priceless. And maybe Chef Colin or one of the other chefs in town might consider doing a cooking demo or something. And since you wanted a bonfire, we could end the week with an old-fashioned hayride and end the night with a bonfire party."

"Would there be line dancing involved?" Ari asked hopefully.

Tripp chuckled, glad the bride was on board. "You know it."

"This sounds amazing, babe," Ari said to Ex. "It would be a unique experience for our guests and a way to make our wedding stand out. What do you think?"

Xavier grinned. "I think we should do it."

"Great!" Ari said. "Sorry, Tripp. I hate to add more to your plate here. But would you mind working with

Rylee to arrange the events?" Ariana held her hands together in prayer with pleading eyes.

"I'll get started on it as soon as possible."

"I'm thrilled that you're good with all of this." Dee's deep frown contradicted her words. "But there's no way I can fit all of this in before my plane takes off tomorrow."

"Which brings me to my second idea," Tripp said carefully. "I think Dee should stay a few more days. Maybe a week."

"What?" Dee turned to him, her eyes widening.

"That would give us time to figure all this out without being rushed," Tripp continued.

"I don't own my own ranch, mister," Dee reminded him. "I have a job to go back to."

"And as your employer," Ari said with a smile. "I would be totally okay with you working remotely for the next week or so. You don't have any big meetings at the office, right?"

"Well, no—"

"And we're still in the early stages of developing the cowboy story, right?" Ari continued.

"Well, yes—"

"Then this trip can add some insight to the project. Think of it as a research trip." Ari shrugged innocently.

Tripp could feel the tension rolling off Dee's shoulders.

Her eyes drifted closed for a micromoment. When she spoke again, she was as calm and logical as ever. "Ariana, this room costs a small fortune. Do we really need to pay for another week?"

"Which brings me to my third idea." Tripp focused on Ari's side of the screen and ignored the growing look of concern on Xavier's face. "Dee could stay in Tessa's old suite at the ranch. Got plenty of space, and it's just me rambling around that big old house now."

"I don't think Dee wants to—" Ex was saying.

"What a fantastic idea, Tripp," Ari said.

Dee turned to him. "You're suggesting I move in with you?"

"I'm inviting you to be my *guest* at The Noble Spur," Tripp clarified. "The suite is like your own apartment, so you'll have plenty of private space. It even has an office."

"From what I've heard, it's a pretty big place," Ari said. "And with Tripp being out on the ranch during the day, it sounds like you'll have the place mostly to yourself, right?"

"Yes, ma'am." Tripp gave Dionna a reserved smile. "I can have the place prepped and ready for you by the time you check out tomorrow morning. So what do you say?"

Dee was still frowning. Her gaze shifted from his to Ari's.

Tripp refused to look at his cousin's side of the screen. And when his phone alerted him to a text message, he already knew it would be from Xavier. He discreetly set the phone on the table facedown without looking at the message.

"C'mon, Dee, it'll be fun. Besides, I told you there's a lot more to this town than you think. This will give me the chance to allay your concerns. What do you say?"

"Dee's not really the outdoors type. She's more board games and badminton," Ex interjected. "We shouldn't push her to do something outside of her comfort zone."

Dee's attention jerked to the screen. She folded her arms. "You're saying I'm a soft city girl who couldn't possibly handle life on a ranch for a week?"

"Uh-oh." Ari's expression made Tripp snort. "You're on your own with this one, partner."

"Of course not." Ex backpedaled. "I'm simply saying ranch life isn't your thing, and there's nothing wrong with that."

"I'm not asking Dee to come milk all our cows," Tripp said.

Xavier looked like he wanted to strangle him through the screen. "My point is you shouldn't make her feel obligated to—"

"I happen to be really good at milking cows."

"Xavier is right," Ari chimed in finally, casually filing a nail. "If Dee doesn't want to stay at Tripp's ranch, I can just put her up in the hotel for another week. I'm sure the room isn't that expensive."

"*Fine.* I'll do it," Dee said to Ari's side of the screen. She turned toward Tripp. "Okay, cowboy. You've got one week to convince me that Royal can be the Mecca of fun."

Tripp extended a hand and grinned. "You're on."

She slapped her palm against his a little too hard.

Tripp held back a chuckle. Maybe he was out of his skull. But it mattered to him what Dee thought of him and this little town. By the end of the week, he'd have Dionna Reed singing Royal's praises and wishing she could vacation here.

That's what this was about. Not about the fact that he looked forward to spending seven more days with her. Nope, that had nothing to do with this at all.

Nine

Dionna finished her call with one of the talent agents she often worked with, then sent what she hoped was her final email of the day. She shut her laptop, then glanced out of the window over the writing desk in what was once Tripp's sister Tessa's suite at The Noble Spur.

She couldn't help smiling.

The rolling plains, open fields and tree-lined creek were surprisingly beautiful and serene. For the first time in a really long time, it felt as if she could finally breathe—despite the flurry of calls and emails she'd waded through the past two days.

To be honest, after she'd gotten over the initial awkwardness of being in Tripp's home with his suite just down the hall from hers, being here had been...*nice*.

She'd forgotten how peaceful it was to be in a place where people didn't live on top of one another. Where she wasn't forced to battle grueling traffic daily. Dionna walked into the attached bedroom and out onto the small balcony. It was late February. Yet, the temperatures were in the midsixties, and beneath the glare of the sun it felt even warmer.

Dee closed her eyes and soaked in the sun's rays. She took a deep breath. The air was pure and exhilarating. And except for the occasional conversation that drifted her way when a few of the ranch hands passed by, it was quiet. She could hear herself think, a luxury she hadn't been afforded in so long.

"Afternoon, Miss Dee." Roy Jensen, one of the ranch hands, removed his hat and wiped the sweat from his brow with his sleeve before settling his lovingly worn Stetson back onto his head. "Mighty pretty day, ain't it?"

"Please call me Dee." Her smile widened as she glanced around. "And it certainly is."

They chatted briefly, then the older man was on his way. Roy reminded Dee of her grandfather back when she'd spent summers on their farm. Roy Jensen and every other person she'd encountered in Royal seemed so warm and *genuine*.

Tripp had introduced her to several of the locals when they ate lunch at The Royal Diner earlier in the day. It was a quaint little 1950s throwback-style diner with chrome stools, red faux-leather booths and a black-and-white checkerboard floor. Something about just stepping into the place had made her instantly giddy.

Her grandmother always said she was an old soul born in the wrong era. Maybe Grandma Elaine was right.

Because despite all the unexpected modern touches, in some ways being here in Royal felt like stepping back in time to a simpler, quieter life. A life she hadn't realized that she'd missed. Not that she'd ever considered moving out to her grandparents' farm full-time. But those wondrous summers she'd spent with them were cathartic and refreshing. They prepared her for another school year and the stress of being the oddball teenage girl living in LA and attending classes with the *cool kids*. She'd been a square peg that hadn't even attempted to fit into the round holes her fellow students happily occupied.

At the diner, unlike in LA, no one tried to pitch her a script to pass on to her famous bestie Ariana. They were more impressed that Ariana seemed like a sweet girl and that she and Xavier always looked so happy whenever they were on the red carpet. And they all seemed to appreciate Ari's gesture of moving the wedding to her fiancé's hometown. It made them even more endearing.

Dionna was beginning to see why Tripp loved Royal so much.

She stepped back inside and closed the sliding glass door. She was startled by the doorbell. As far as she knew, Tripp was still out on the ranch surveying some of their unused land. Land that had originally been allotted to Xavier's family.

And since Tripp's part-time housekeeper had left about an hour ago, leaving a savory beef stew simmering in the Crock-Pot, Dee was the only one in the house.

It felt odd answering Tripp's door when he wasn't there. But when the bell rang again, she made her way down the stairs.

"Yes?" She smiled at the tall, lanky young man.

"Delivery," the boy said. "Should I sit it down inside? The box is kind of heavy."

"Sure. I guess." Dee permitted him to set the box just

inside the door. "Tripp isn't here right now, but I can sign for it, if you need me to."

The boy's eyes finally met hers. "These aren't for Tripp. You're—" he studied the small black pad "—Dionna Reed, right?" When she nodded, he extended the pad. "Great. Sign here."

Dee thanked him, then closed the door. She hoisted the heavy box up to her room.

"I swear to God, if Ari sent me lingerie, I'm going to strangle her," Dee muttered under her breath.

Her best friend had been teasing her endlessly about her and Tripp making a good couple. She'd been particularly sensitive to Ari's gentle ribbing because the more she'd gotten to know Tripp, the more she actually *did* like him. Not that anything was going to happen between them.

Tripp had been a perfect gentleman. And as much as she hated to admit it, a small part of her was disappointed by that.

Aside from their meals together and their wedding planning field trips, Tripp had given Dee her space. During the day, she had the house to herself mostly.

Does Tripp ever get lonely in this big old house all alone?

Given how well he knew the layout of The Bellamy and its suites, the answer was probably no.

Still, she couldn't help thinking back to when she'd first arrived.

"Aren't all ranchers supposed to have a dog?" Dee had teased. "A Saint Bernard isn't going to come rushing out and tackle me, is it?"

Tripp's features had pinched. He'd shoved his hands in his pockets. "My last dog, Ace… We lost him about a year ago." He'd shrugged. "I was more broken up about it than my niece." He'd tapped a hand on his chest. "Don't think I have the capacity to go through that again just yet."

If she hadn't already been into the guy, that moment would've made her fall for him instantly.

Dee grabbed some scissors from the desk and opened the box.

The clothes inside weren't hers this time. But she doubted they were from Ari either. Definitely not her friend's style.

The prices had been removed, but the sales tags indicated that everything in the box had come from The Rancher's Daughter, one of the shops Tripp had taken her to the previous day prior to dining at a restaurant called The Eatery.

She examined the contents of the box. Saddle-brown canvas work pants with loads of pockets. A pair of boot-cut jeans with a star stitched on the back pocket, that had fit her body like a glove when she'd tried them on in the store. Distressed ankle-length jeans frayed at the hem that she'd admired on the rack. Button-down plaid rodeo shirts in a variety of color combinations. The gorgeous cowboy boots she'd tried on.

Dionna lifted a tall, studded brown boot from the box, inhaling the scent of the leather and admiring the turquoise-colored sole. She ran her fingers over the gorgeous stitching: a mythological firebird embroidered with tan thread.

The boots were stunning and surprisingly comfortable. Like they'd been made for her. But they were also expensive. And since they didn't exactly mesh with her white shirt and black pants LA wardrobe, she'd left them in the store.

So why were they here now?

Dee reached for the card at the bottom of the box, which bore her name. She flipped it over.

Gear up for our ride tomorrow. No more excuses.

The card was signed by Tripp.

He bought me clothing?

For the past two days, he'd asked her to go riding with him. She'd begged off, saying she hadn't brought appropriate clothing. Maybe next time.

Well, Mr. Problem Solver had apparently solved her little problem. But she couldn't believe he'd shelled out the amount of money he had just to get her to go horseback riding with him. And she certainly couldn't accept such an expensive gift. She would thank him and then politely return everything.

Dee held up the jeans that had made her ass look incredible.

Maybe I'll keep these... But I'll pay for them myself.

She picked up the boot again and looked at it longingly. Maybe she wasn't going to go home with them. But would it hurt if she tried them on again? Then again, to get the full effect, she should probably try on the entire outfit. She'd snap a couple of mirror selfies to send to Ari. Then she'd pack everything up and send it back to The Rancher's Daughter along with her apologies for the misunderstanding.

Still, she couldn't help being moved by how generous Tripp had been.

Tripp stepped out of a hot shower, his muscles already starting to ache. It had been a long time since he'd helped bale hay and mend fences, but a couple of his ranch hands had fallen ill, and they'd been shorthanded that day. He'd rediscovered a few muscles he'd apparently been missing in his weekly workouts. Experience told him the following day would be much worse.

Tripp shrugged on a pair of his favorite broken-in jeans, tugged on a black T-shirt and headed down the hall to check on Dee. The entire house smelled of savory beef stew, and he was starving. Hopefully, Dee was ready to eat, too.

The door was partially open, but Tripp knocked anyway, startling Dee. She was modeling the clothing he'd had sent over from Morgan Grandin's shop, The Rancher's Daughter.

"Tripp!" Dee whipped around. "What are you, part cat? I didn't realize you were home."

The look on her face reminded him of when Tessa had gotten busted wearing half of their mother's makeup when she was about five. He reined in a grin.

"I got here about a half an hour ago. It was a tough day. I needed a long hot shower." Tripp leaned against the door, taking her in. Dee was wearing those jeans that looked like they'd been tailored to her body with its mesmerizing curves, one of the rodeo shirts and the boots she'd fallen in love with at the store. He rubbed his chin and nodded approvingly. "You look amazing in that outfit, and it fits perfectly."

"You really think so?" She faced the mirror again, giving him a prize view of her...*assets*.

Don't even think about it.

He repeated the words in his head, but Dee was all he'd been able to think about for the past week. More so since he'd had the genius idea to invite her to stay at The Noble Spur.

"Sweetheart, I have eyes," he said. The term of endearment had slipped out without thought.

Dee seemed surprised by it but didn't object. Her gaze met his, reflected in the mirror. She cleared her throat and turned to face him. "Thank you for this incredibly thoughtful gift, Tripp." She gestured toward the open box sitting on the trunk at the foot of the bed. "But I can't accept it."

"Why not?" Tripp kept his voice neutral. "I've gifted you things before."

"This isn't a bouquet of flowers or lunch at the diner, Tripp. It's an entire freaking wardrobe." She glanced down at the clothing she was wearing, seemingly frustrated that he didn't seem to understand the difference between the two.

He did. Didn't mean he wouldn't downplay it anyway.

"You needed some ranch gear. It's a few pairs of pants and a few shirts. Not a big deal," Tripp said.

"Yes, but everything here was pretty pricey. Those boots alone cost nearly six hundred dollars." She extended her leg, showing off the vibrant turquoise sole of her boot. When he didn't respond, she crossed the room and stood a few feet in front of him, her soft spring scent filling his nostrils. "This was really thoughtful of you, Tripp. But—"

"Honestly, Dee, it's fine. I've blown money on things far more frivolous. If it helps, don't think of this as a gift. Think of it as me being a selfish bastard dead set on getting what I want."

"Which is…"

You. Right here. Right now.

He willed the voice inside his head that was way too fucking honest to shut up.

"For you to go horseback riding with me," he finally managed. "It'll be fun."

"Tripp…"

"That's why you stayed another week, right? To get a feel for the prewedding events I'm proposing. So we can make a decision on them before you leave next Sunday."

Why did those last words catch in his throat?

He couldn't keep Dee here with him forever. But it had been nice having company in the house again. And he'd enjoyed the time they'd spent together exploring Royal as they helped plan the wedding and shared meals all over town.

He hadn't realized how much he'd missed the company. Maybe this wasn't about Dee at all. Maybe he'd become a hermit and he just needed to get back out there again, date, and be social.

Tripp studied Dee's face as she debated her response.

You're full of it, and you know it.

This was definitely about Dionna. He wasn't lonely for just any company. He enjoyed *her* company.

"Yes, that's why I stayed," Dee said finally, shaking Tripp from his thoughts. "But I could rent a car and drive to a big-box store in Dallas. I'm pretty sure the horses won't mind if I'm not wearing designer gear and a pair of six-hundred-dollar boots." The slow smile that spread across her face made her dark eyes twinkle and tugged at something in his chest.

"I don't know." Tripp shrugged, taking a couple steps closer, leaving a foot of space between them. "Deuce and Nick Fury have *pretty* discriminating tastes."

Dionna dissolved into laughter. The joyous sound filled the room and made his heart dance.

When their laughter had died down, Tripp placed a hand on Dee's shoulder. "Seriously, Dee, you look amazing, and I want you to have this stuff. I'm a bachelor with zero responsibilities and very few vices other than spoiling my niece and nephew. So let me do this."

Dee cocked her head. "On one condition."

He'd never found it quite so difficult to gift a woman with anything before. "Name it."

"Tell me why it's so important for you to convince me of how great Royal is?"

Tripp dropped his hand from her shoulder. There was an intensity in Dee's eyes. Telling her anything other than the truth wasn't an option. If there was one thing he'd learned about Dionna Reed, it was that the woman was a walking, talking bullshit detector.

He scrubbed a hand down his face and sighed. "Because maybe I care what you think."

"Hmm." Dee sized him up. "The way Xavier tells it, you're this badass rebel who doesn't care what anyone thinks."

"And that's true." He shrugged. *Mostly.*

Dee inched closer. "Then why do you care what I think of Royal or you, Tripp?"

The room felt hot and a little claustrophobic. He searched his brain for anything he could tell her. Anything other than the truth. He came up empty.

"Because your opinion matters to me, Dee. So what you think of the place that made me who I am and that I call home matters to me, too."

"Why?" Dee's voice was barely more than a whisper.

There was a hunger in her gaze that he knew well. One he'd promised himself he wouldn't give into.

"Because I like you, Dionna. A lot." The words scraped at Tripp's throat like tiny shards of glass. Yet, he felt a sense of relief once he'd finally uttered them.

"What if I said I like you, too, Tripp?"

Tripp's gaze dropped to her full lips. His brain was suddenly overwhelmed with imagining the taste and feel of those lush lips.

Dee's chest rose and fell with shallow breaths as she awaited his response.

He tried to summon his cousin's plea for him not to mess things up for him. But Ex's voice was tinny and distant. Imperceptible over the sound of his own heart thundering in his chest.

Tripp closed the space between them, his lips crashing into Dee's. One arm slid around her waist, tugging her body against his. The other hand cradled her cheek, angling Dee's head as his lips glided over hers.

Warmth filled his chest and trailed down his spine. And when Dee wrapped her arms around his waist, as if she desperately needed the contact between them, he thought he might combust from the sensation of his growing length pressed hard into her belly.

Dee slid her hands beneath his T-shirt. She traced the damp skin on his back with her fingertips, then lightly grazed it with her short nails.

Dee's lips parted, and Tripp nibbled on her lush lower lip, evoking a soft gasp. He glided his tongue between her lips, swallowing the soft murmurs that made him increasingly hard. Hungrier for the taste of her mouth. The taste of her skin. Desperate to know what sounds she would make when he slid inside her. Or when he drove her over the edge. When she fell apart beneath him.

Tripp tightened his arm around Dee's waist. He pressed his other hand to her back as he ravaged her mouth—sweet and warm. Tasting of chocolate and mint. In that moment, there was nothing he wanted more than to strip every single piece of clothing from her body and taste the soft brown skin that had teased him from the moment he'd laid eyes on Dee in that little black mini-dress the day she'd first arrived in Royal.

Suddenly, Dee pulled back. Her chest heaving as her teeth sank into her lower lip. Her eyes searched his.

Tripp swallowed hard, still holding on to Dee as they both caught their breath. When she didn't speak, he opened his mouth to apologize. To tell her he hadn't intended to kiss her. Even as he realized he wasn't sorry at all that he had.

"Dee, I—"

Dionna grasped the hem of his T-shirt, and he helped her tug it over his head. She tossed it onto the floor.

Tripp's heart pounded against his rib cage as she dipped her head and pressed a kiss to his chest. Then another and another. When she gazed up at him again, he could clearly see the desire that was likely reflected in his own eyes.

Every ounce of control he'd been wearing like a suit of armor for the past few days had been weakened by that look in her eyes. It'd crumbled and turned to dust at his feet.

Tripp kissed Dee as if hers was the last kiss he'd ever need. His hands fumbled with the snaps on her shirt, ripping them open. He tugged the garment off and dropped it into the box it came from. He unclasped her bra and slid it from her arms, taking a moment to appreciate the full round breasts he'd been imagining for the past week. He grazed the dark brown peaks with his calloused thumb, eager for a taste.

He palmed Dee's deliciously curvy ass and lifted her. She hooked her legs around his back as he carried her to the bed a few yards away. He deposited her there, and together they tugged off the jeans that fit her like a second skin.

"Shit," Tripp muttered. "I need to grab a condom." *Or three.* "Don't move. I'll be right back."

A smile spread across Dee's gorgeous face. She nodded.

Tripp sprinted to his end of the hall and grabbed a strip of condoms from his nightstand before hurrying back.

Dee was beneath the covers smiling. She'd let her hair down, her dark brown twists spread across the pillow. And the last garment she'd been wearing—a lacy pair of black underwear—had been discarded onto the floor.

Tripp quickly shed his remaining clothing and sheathed himself before climbing beneath the covers. He reveled in the sensation of her soft bare skin gliding against his as he kissed her. And he loved the way the hardened brown peaks poked at his chest, and the thrill of his painfully hard dick nestled between their bellies.

He loved the soft murmurs that emanated from her throat as their kiss heated up. Especially when he rolled off of Dee and glided his hand up her leg.

"Oh God, Tripp," Dee murmured against his lips when his fingers reached the warm, wet space between her thighs.

He couldn't help thinking that he'd do just about anything to hear her utter those words again in that breathy tone that made him so hard he ached with the need to be inside her.

Tripp watched her expression, eyes shuttered, as he slipped two fingers inside her and grazed her clit with his thumb. He wasn't even inside her yet, and already he was addicted to every little sound she made. And the way she whispered his name desperately again and again.

He covered one of her stiffened nipples with his mouth, sucking it and teasing it with his tongue. Grazing it gently with his teeth. Loving how her pleasure continued to spiral beneath his touch. He moved to the other nipple, then trailed kisses down her body, his fingers still working as he slipped yet another inside of her.

When he sucked her clit into his mouth, she cursed and lifted her hips, silently begging for more. He loved the salty sweet taste of her. The way she whimpered his name as her legs and belly stiffened and her body shuddered around his fingers.

Tripp pressed soft kisses to her quivering flesh. Then he kissed his way back up her belly before kissing her neck and jaw as her breathing slowed.

Dee sucked in a deep breath, then opened her eyes. She smiled at him almost shyly.

He couldn't remember the last time someone had looked at him that way. Or made him feel as possessive as he felt about her now. Like he couldn't bear the thought of her gifting that incredible smile to anyone else. Because he wanted it all for himself.

Tripp swallowed hard. Tried not to think about the implications of that statement. Or all of the reasons he shouldn't feel so deeply for a woman who'd be gone in a few days and lived thousands of miles away.

Instead, he gripped his hardened length, pumping it a few times before pressing it against her slick entrance. He closed his eyes, reveling in her soft whimpers and the way her nails grazed his back as he inched inside her until he was fully seated.

Was she just as titillated by the muffled groans that escaped his throat as her body swallowed his?

Dee wrapped her legs around him, her bare heels pressing into the small of his back, as he moved inside her. He circled his hips, his pelvis grounding against the bundle of nerves. Evoking increasingly intense murmurs of pleasure every time he made contact with it again.

Tripp's arms trembled slightly, supporting most of his weight as he increased his speed and intensity. Until Dee's back arched and she practically screamed his name. A few more thrusts of his hips, and he let the pulsing of her body pull him over the edge.

He tumbled onto his back and heaved a sigh, his chest rising and falling. Tripp wrapped his arms around Dionna and cradled her to his chest. Their heavy breathing, nearly in sync, were the only sounds in the room.

Tripp pushed a few of the long twists off her face and kissed her forehead. Inhaled the coconut and vanilla scent of her hair that he'd come to crave.

"That was…amazing, Dee." Tripp glided his hand up and down her back, loving the feel of her soft bare skin.

"It was, wasn't it?" Dionna flashed him her shy smile again, one hand pressed to his chest. She snuggled against him and sighed contentedly, like there was no place in the world she'd rather be. After a few more minutes of silence, she said, "Xavier made you promise not to make a move on me, didn't he?"

Tripp wasn't surprised she'd deduced as much. Not after the evil eye Ex had given him during their video chat.

"He did, and I probably deserve to get my ass kicked for this," Tripp admitted. "But the only thing I regret is having made the promise in the first place."

Dee looked up at him and smiled, like it was exactly what she needed to hear.

Tripp kissed her, then excused himself for a trip to the bathroom. Then he slipped back into bed. He'd never considered himself a cuddler. But lying in bed with Dee's cheek pressed to his chest and her arms wrapped around him... He couldn't deny that it felt *nice*. He'd gladly fall asleep to the sound of her breathing as he held her in his arms.

"Hello! Tripp, we're here!" a familiar voice called.

Shit.

Tripp glanced at the Asorock watch on his wrist with its leather band and rose-gold case. Time had gotten away from him.

Dionna lifted onto one arm, her brows scrunching as she pulled the sheet up around her. "Is that your parents?"

"My sister. I forgot that Tess invited herself and her family over for dinner tonight. Their cook is on vacation, and Marguerite's beef stew is one of Tess's favorite meals."

"This is her old room. She isn't coming up here, is she?" Dionna glanced toward the partially open door.

"Not if I cut her off first." Tripp pressed a quick kiss to Dee's lips. He climbed out of bed, shrugged on his boxers and jeans, then called down to his sister. "Hey, Tess. Can you set up the table? Dee and I both took naps before dinner. I'll wake her and then we'll both be down shortly."

There was a long pregnant pause. "Sure. No problem."

He could tell his sister wasn't buying his story. But no need to alarm Dee. She'd put on her underwear and was searching the floor on her hands and knees, presumably for her bra.

"What a spectacular view."

"What?" Dee glanced up at him, looking irritated.

"No need to panic. I'll stall them with my sparkling conversation." He retrieved her bra from beneath the bed, then helped her up. He kissed her again. "Besides, we're unattached adults. We can do whatever the hell we want."

"We're adults who'd prefer to keep this to ourselves," she reminded him, her eyes pleading.

"Got it." Tripp nodded. But if he knew his sister, keeping this a secret was a ship that had already sailed.

Ten

Dionna stood in her underwear staring at the jeans, shirt and cowboy boots she'd hastily discarded. Her hands shook as she debated whether or not to put them back on.

Dee shrugged on the jeans, one of her own shirts and a pair of socks. Then she stuffed her feet into the slippers Tripp had loaned her and went to the bathroom to pin her wild, just-tumbled-out-of-bed hair back up into a sensible bun. The kind of hairdo that said, "I *wasn't* upstairs screwing your brother just now… *Really.*"

She wiped off her smeared tinted lip gloss so she could reapply it. Once she was satisfied she didn't look like she'd just gotten done banging the woman's brother, she placed her hand on the doorknob of the now closed door. She froze in place, her hands still shaking.

Dee was a terrible liar. Tessa would know something was up the moment she laid eyes on her.

"We are so busted." Dee leaned her head against the door.

Her cell phone rang, and she retrieved it from the desk. Molly Hawthorne, the talent agent, was calling her back.

Something work-related. This, she could handle.

"Hey, Molly. What's up?"

Nothing happening here. Really!

"Sweetie, are you okay? You sound like you just ran up a flight of stairs?" Molly said.

"I was working out." Not a lie...*exactly*. That was certainly the best workout she'd gotten in a long time. "But I'm sure you didn't call to discuss my exercise routine. What's going on?"

"Marcus Maybury is *definitely* interested in this role of a badass Black cowboy fighting to hold on to his land!" Molly squealed. "But you know how Marcus is. He's all about authenticity. He wants to know if a consultant will be on set to ensure that the movie comes off as being completely credible. And he isn't interested in making some green screen Western. He'll only consider the project if you're filming on an actual ranch—not on some studio lot."

"I see." Dionna rolled her eyes, hoping her tone didn't reflect her earnest feelings about Marcus's request. "Well, we certainly appreciate how dedicated he is to his craft."

Marcus's star was steadily rising in Hollywood. And he'd be the biggest star that Ariana's fledgling studio had snagged thus far. Her best friend had been adamant that they should do whatever it took to book Marcus for this movie—their most ambitious film to date. But filming on-site, God knows where, and hiring a consultant? Who was this guy to dictate such terms?

Would he be throwing his limited weight around if they had been a larger studio? Or one headed up by a male actor instead?

Dee tried to push aside her personal objections. Her job was to execute Ari's wishes for the project. And what Ari wanted was to secure Marcus Maybury for the lead role in this movie.

"We're certainly willing to entertain both requests," Dee said as she stared out onto Tripp's property.

"Excellent, because he's deciding between this project and two others." Molly switched from hard-nosed negotiator to Valley Girl cheerleader in three seconds flat. "He'll want to know where you'll be filming. What should I tell him?"

"Uhh…" Dionna hadn't expected to have to come up with an answer right away—before she got the chance to speak to Ari about it. If she didn't come up with a satisfactory answer, Marcus would walk.

"Well?" Molly's tone indicated that she had the feeling Dee was bullshitting.

Suddenly, the answer was right in front of her. Dee stood tall, her gaze sweeping the rolling plains she'd been admiring the past few days. "I'm scouting a possible site right now. It's a gorgeous sprawling ranch in Royal, Texas, that happens to be owned by fourth-generation Black ranchers."

"Talk about authentic," Molly said, almost reverently. "So I assume the owners will be your consultants—to ensure the movie feels authentic."

"That's what we're hoping." Dee palmed her fore-head and cringed.

What on earth was I thinking?

"Fantastic! If you can nail down this location and the consultant, I can pretty much assure you Marcus will be on board with the project. We both feel this could be that breakout role he's been searching for. Get back to me as soon as you can, doll."

Dee paced the floor, her head throbbing.

Now all she had to do was convince the man she'd just slept with to agree to it. Before she'd even had a chance to process what had happened between them.

Tripp had undoubtedly expected their little tryst to be a no-strings-attached encounter. But now she needed to ask him to let them film on his property for several weeks.

It sounded like the kind of request that would make an unattached playboy like Tripp Noble panic, thinking she wanted something more. She just needed to assure him that she didn't. Even if, in her heart, she already knew she did.

"Hey, sis." Tripp hugged his sister, then kissed the forehead of his six-month-old nephew, Dylan, perched on her hip. The infant offered him a gurgle and a gummy grin of recognition. "Sorry, we were short-handed today. I had to be a lot more hands-on than I'm used to. Needed a hot shower and a quick nap. Time got away from me."

"And was your houseguest baling hay, too? Is that why she also needed a *nap*?" His sister didn't do the dreaded air quotes, but the way she'd said *nap* said it well enough.

"My guess? She's had a pretty taxing day, too."

"I see." Tess switched Dylan—a rather solid infant—to her other hip. "But that doesn't really explain *this*—" Tess motioned around her mouth "—now does it?"

Tessa produced a tissue from her pocket.

Shit. Dionna had been wearing a colored lip gloss.

"Is this thing clean?" Tripp raised an eyebrow.

"Of course!" Tessa popped his arm. "And I assume we'll talk about this later."

Tripp wiped his mouth without committing to anything. He stuffed the tissue in his pocket and turned toward his brother-in-law and young niece who'd entered through the door off the kitchen.

"What's up, Ryan?" Tripp slapped palms with his brother-in-law. Then he swept his three-year-old niece off her feet and tossed her in the air.

Tiana squealed with delight.

"Be careful, you two," Tessa pleaded.

"Hey, Tee! How is Uncle Tripp's favorite niece in the whole wide world?" Tripp tickled the little girl's belly.

She giggled, wriggling in his arms.

"Daddy took me to say hello to Deuce and Nick Fury," Tiana declared, once she finally got her giggles under control.

"You did?" His niece loved horses. "Well, that was nice of you. Did you take them a treat?"

"Mmm-hmm." The little girl nodded vigorously. "Daddy let me give them apples."

"One thing I know about Deuce and Nick is that they love a woman bearing gifts. So good job." Tripp kissed the little girl's cheek, then set her on her feet. He gently tugged one of her braids, accented with colorful beads. "Ready for dinner?"

"I'm famished." Tiana pressed the back of her hand to her head dramatically.

"Famished?" Tripp eyed his sister. "Have you been reading her the dictionary at bedtime?"

Ryan slipped an arm around Tessa's waist, both of them laughing.

"Blame our mother for that one and for the dramatics," Tess said. "Tee picked it up from some old black-and-white movie she was watching with Mom before they left for their trip to Cuba with Xavier's parents."

"Figures," Tripp chuckled. Their mother, once an aspiring actress who yearned to be cast in cowboy movies, had ended up marrying one instead. Tripp squeezed the little girl's shoulder. "All right, Little Miss Famished. We'll be eating soon. So you'd better go wash your hands."

Tiana didn't need to be told twice. She took off toward the first-floor powder room as fast as her legs would carry her.

"We can't start dinner without the guest of honor." Tessa handed Dylan to Ryan. "Should I go check on her?"

"No, nosy." Tripp raised an eyebrow.

"Sorry to have kept you waiting. I had to take an important call." Dee made her way down the stairs. "You must be Tripp's sister, Tessa. I'm Dionna Reed, a friend of Ariana and Xavier's. It's a pleasure to finally meet you." Dee extended a hand.

"It's a pleasure to finally meet you, too." Tess bypassed Dee's hand and wrapped her up in a hug. "I feel like I already know you. Tripp has told me so much about you."

"Same." Dee seemed pleasantly surprised by the hug.

Tessa introduced Dionna to her husband and their children. They chatted about the wedding and some of the shops and eateries Dionna had visited around town while she helped Tess prepare everyone's plates.

By the time they settled around the dinner table, Dee seemed more relaxed, the tension melting from her shoulders.

He liked having Dionna here. She got along well with his family. His niece and nephew gravitated toward her, and Dee was incredibly patient with them.

Tripp tried to play it cool. But he often caught himself sneaking glances at her. Touching her whenever he could manufacture a plausible reason to do so, even if it was something as simple as leaning his leg against hers beneath the dinner table.

They played a few games after dinner and ended the night with a round of spades and ice cream sandwiches made from Dee's homemade chocolate chip cookies and filled with Neapolitan ice cream—Tessa's favorite.

"It's been a lovely evening." Dionna stood after she and Tripp beat Tessa and Ryan handily in a game of spades. "But there are a few emails I need to send before I head to bed. It was such a pleasure meeting your lovely family, Tess and Ryan. I hope I get to see you all again before I leave."

"The pleasure was all ours." Tessa stood, with Dylan on her hip, and wrapped Dee in a one-arm hug. "And if my brother doesn't keep you hidden away here at the house… He never did like to share—" Tess added in a mock whisper. "Then we'll definitely see you again before you leave."

"Looking forward to it." Dee's smile was so sweet and genuine. He couldn't help smiling, too. "Tripp, don't worry about the dishes. I'll clean up as soon as I've sent my emails."

"Absolutely not," Tess insisted. "You're a guest."

Tripp tipped his chin toward the stairs. "Like Tess said, we've got it."

Dee waved good-night, then headed upstairs.

"I should get the kids home, give them baths and get them to bed." Ryan stood.

"But I'm not sleepy, Daddy." Tee yawned. "I want to help Mommy and Uncle Tripp clean up."

"Next time, pudding." Ryan squatted and kissed his daughter's cheek. "Tonight, I need your help giving your baby brother a bath. Think you can help your old man out?"

"Yes, Daddy." Tiana gave her father a sleepy smile. She kissed her mother and Tripp good-night.

Tripp and Tessa carried the dessert dishes into the kitchen, and Tess began rinsing them.

Tripp pulled out the dishwasher rack and loaded the dishes as his sister handed them to him. "All right, Tess. What is it that you want to talk about?"

"It should be pretty obvious what we need to talk about."

"I'm a grown-ass, bill-paying adult," he reminded her. "We don't *need* to talk about anything."

"True. But let's just say we will anyway. Not because you owe me an explanation. Because I care about you and Xavier, and I really like Dee. I don't want to see anyone get hurt." Tessa kept rinsing dishes and handing them to him.

"What makes you think I'll hurt Dee?" Tripp's jaw

tensed. "You're my sister. You should know me better than that."

Tessa turned off the water and faced him. "I do know you, Tripp. I realize you wouldn't intentionally hurt anyone. That doesn't mean that you don't leave people hurt in your wake. Face it, big brother, you're a lovable guy. So maybe it's easy for you to walk away. That isn't necessarily so for the other party."

Tripp frowned. "Are we talking about anyone in particular?"

"It doesn't matter." Tessa sounded sad. "The point is just because you don't mean to hurt someone, it doesn't mean they won't end up hurt. And in this case, there's a lot at stake. Isn't that why you promised Ex you wouldn't—"

"Ex called you about this?"

"You stopped answering his calls."

Touché.

"Okay, I shouldn't have done that," he admitted.

"Nor should you have made him a promise you had no intention of keeping," Tess scolded.

"The way Ryan did when he promised he'd never lay a hand on my little sister?" Tripp glared at her.

"That was different." Tess glared right back. "First, you two had no right making such an agreement on my behalf. Second, yes, you and Ryan were close friends, but he and I had an established friendship." Tessa ticked off each point on her fingers.

"Same on both counts."

Tessa rolled her eyes. "Ryan and I have been friends since we were kids. It isn't the same, Tripp."

"Maybe we haven't known each other as long. But

we have been steadily building a friendship over the past few months... Before she came to town," he reminded her.

"Ryan and I were willing to take the risk because we truly cared for each other. We could imagine having a life together. The risk was worth the reward." Tess's frustration showed in the creases between her brows. "Can you say the same?"

"Maybe." The word flew out of Tripp's mouth before he could stop it. It shocked them both into silence. He leaned against the old butcher-block countertop and shrugged. "I don't know."

"You've *never* said that before about *anyone*." Tessa was still stunned.

"I know."

"Wow." Tessa leaned against the countertop, too. "But you've really only known each other for like a week," Tessa noted. "Or have you been crushing this hard on her all along and just tried to be chill about it?"

"I'm a little old for crushes." He folded his arms and crossed one ankle over the other. "But was I into her since before she arrived here? I guess. More than I realized, apparently."

Tessa's brows furrowed in thought. He could tell she was thinking hard about what to say.

"Have you considered maybe the reason it feels safe to fall for Dionna is because (a) she's not anything like the women you typically go for and (b) the relationship feels...impossible."

"I think that her not being my usual type is, surprisingly, what I like most about her." Tripp smiled fondly, then turned to his sister and frowned. "Wait... Why do you think the relationship feels impossible? I'd think that you and Mom would be thrilled that I'm considering getting serious about someone."

"I've never pressured you about settling down. I trust that when you find the right person, you will."

"How do you know Dee isn't that person?" Tripp asked.

"You live in Royal and run this ranch. Your life is tied to this land and to this town. Dee is a Hollywood casting director. Therefore, her life is tied to LA. Surely, this isn't news to you." Tess laid a gentle hand on his arm and sighed. "I really do like Dee. I'd love it if she was The One. But I just don't see how you two could ever make that work without one of you giving up a huge part of who you are. Do you?"

Tripp rubbed his chin and sighed.

He didn't have a response to that. And maybe Tess was right. Maybe feeling this way about Dee felt safe because there were so many obstacles to overcome.

"You're right. Our lives and livelihoods are tied to specific geographic locations thousands of miles apart." He met Tess's gaze. "But I do feel something for her."

Tess slipped her arm through his and leaned her head on his shoulder. "I wish I had some brilliant solution."

"Me too." The words caused a deep ache in Tripp's chest.

Tessa turned to face him. "You know, if you ever decide that running the ranch isn't what you want, I'd understand."

"Thanks, sis." He gestured to the tattoo on her arm. The same Noble Spur brand in the same place on her forearm as his. Something they'd done together a few weeks before Tessa got married. "But this place is in my blood, same as yours. It'll always be home."

The fact was, Dee would be walking out of his life soon and he had no alternative to offer her. It was a reality he wasn't prepared to accept.

Eleven

Dee paced her room at The Noble Spur, her heart racing and her head spinning. She'd had to set what had happened between her and Tripp aside while they had dinner with his sister and brother-in-law and pretended that nothing had happened between them. But it had. And she hadn't been able to stop thinking about it and about Tripp.

She'd left the dinner table more than an hour earlier. And she'd watched Ryan walk the kids back over to their place next door—Bateman Ranch. When she'd ventured out of her suite, she could hear Tripp's and Tessa's voices downstairs. She couldn't hear what they were saying, but she couldn't help thinking that she was the subject of the conversation.

They'd insisted that they were just friends. But so many times during the evening, she could feel the heat of Tripp's stare warming her skin. She'd been grateful that her dark brown skin tone camouflaged the flush of her skin whenever he'd placed a hand on her back or grazed her knee with his beneath the table.

Her skin had run hot, and a zap of electricity ran along the surface and shot down her spine. She'd barely been able to look at him without reliving the moments they'd shared in this room. Even now, she could practically feel his soft lips caressing her skin. His calloused fingers exploring her body and taking her to heights she hadn't known.

Dionna stood in the mostly dark room, lit only by the lamp on the desk, as she stared out of the balcony window.

What have you done, Dionna Reed?

She ran her fingers through her twists and sighed. The moments between them had been absolute magic. Everything she could've hoped for and more. But she'd also screwed things up, hadn't she?

Because Tripp Noble was clearly not the kind of man you got serious about. She'd gone into this well aware of that. Still, she couldn't stop herself. And she hadn't wanted to. But what she was feeling for him right now... This was about more than Tripp being charming and amazing in bed.

They'd gotten to know each other a little through their online interactions. At first, it had been easy to dismiss her growing feelings for Tripp as a silly crush. But the time they'd spent together the past few days had shown her a different side of Tripp. Made her believe that there was so much more to him than the charming jokester he showed to the world. And she felt such a deep attraction to the man. The thought of walking away in a few days and pretending none of this had ever happened made her heart ache for whatever might have been.

It was silly. She realized that. But it was also how she truly felt. And her pouting about it would only ruin the mood and cast a shadow over the wedding and any of the remaining planning they had to do. Not to mention how awkward it would make things if Tripp did agree to allow Ari's studio to film their next project here on his ranch.

She wouldn't do that to Ari and Xavier. Which meant she needed to get it together and be okay with the fact that whatever happened between her and Tripp during her stay here was a one-off best forgotten the moment she boarded that plane for home.

There was a knock at her door. Dee straightened her spine and regretted the fact that she hadn't packed any lingerie. She was wearing an old nightshirt that read Do Not Disturb.

"Come in," she said.

Tripp opened the door, and even in the limited light from the hallway, the man was more handsome than ever. "Hey."

"Hey." Dee clenched her thighs together, slightly embarrassed by how much she wanted this man right now. She folded her arms over her chest, trying to hide the Pavlovian beading of her nipples in response to the gruff, sexy tenor of Tripp's voice. "Your sister and her family... They're really nice. You're lucky they live right next door."

"Yeah, I guess I am." Tripp shoved his hands in his pockets and made his way to the center of the room. "They really like you, too, by the way."

"I'm glad." Dee held her ground, resisting the urge to

walk closer. "It was a fun night. I haven't played Taboo in ages."

"My sister loves that game." Tripp was making his way closer. "She plays it every chance she gets. She knows they have the advantage because they've known each other since the beginning of time."

"I can be pretty competitive," Dionna said, looking up at Tripp who now stood in front of her. "The fact that they have that kind of history is the only reason I didn't feel quite so bad about them kicking our ass in that game. But we made up for it when we took it to them in—"

Before she could finish, Tripp had looped his arms around her waist and covered her mouth with his. The kiss had taken her by surprise, but her eyes drifted closed and her hands clutched at the back of his black T-shirt.

His tongue teased the seam of her lips, and she willingly parted them, eager for another taste of his mouth. Tripp's hands glided down her back and over her bottom. This time he lifted her onto the desk as he continued their kiss.

Dee's hands drifted beneath the black fabric, her hands gliding up his back as she pressed her fingertips to his skin, pulling him toward her. Did he have any idea how desperate she was for his touch? How much she needed to feel him inside of her again?

Tripp yanked up the hem of her nightshirt, and she lifted her arms to allow him to tug it over her head. He dropped the fabric onto the floor and stood still a moment, as if mesmerized by the sight of her topless, seated on what was once his sister's desk.

"God, Dee, you are so fucking beautiful." His words

sounded almost reverent as he grazed her bare skin with the back of his hand.

Her entire body warmed, and her pulse raced. Dee tried not to squirm as Tripp kissed his way across her chest and up the other shoulder. She cleared her throat and tried to regain her focus. "I think we should talk."

Tripp froze for a moment. She could feel his back stiffen beneath her fingertips. "Okay. So let's talk."

"I... I... Um... I realize that you're... That you don't..." She was babbling like an idiot. With every fluttery, sensual kiss Tripp pressed to her bare skin, the harder it became to think. To breathe. Yet, she wanted more. But first, she needed to ensure there wouldn't be any hard feelings on either side.

Dionna swallowed hard and tried again. "I know you don't do serious relationships, Tripp." He stopped kissing her neck, and his eyes met hers. "So I just wanted you to know I'm not expecting anything to come of this. In fact, I went into it knowing there wouldn't."

Tripp dropped his gaze momentarily, and she could swear she saw him frown. Finally, he met her gaze again. "And you'd be okay with that? With this being just a vacation fling?"

Now she winced. Because it hurt her to think that this was just sex for Tripp when for her it felt like the beginning of so much more. Still, she nodded.

"Of course." Dee forced a quiet laugh, despite the deep ache in her chest. "You live in Royal. I live in LA. What else would this possibly be?"

Tripp pulled back a moment and stared at her, his expression unreadable. "That's good to know," he said finally. "And since the clock is ticking on this thing, I think we should make the most of every day that we have left together, don't you?"

"Yes," she practically whispered the word. She could feel her eyebrows furrowing even as she forced a smile. "I guess we should."

There was something devilish in Tripp's smirk and in the flare of his nostrils. But when he dropped to his knees on the carpeted floor, she didn't have time to consider what was behind his expression.

"What are you—"

Before she could finish the question, Tripp had his large hands on her waist, gliding her panties down her hips and onto the floor. He set her on the edge of the desk, and before she could react, his mouth was on her, his tongue lashing at her already sensitive flesh.

Dee leaned back, her hands gripping the back of the desk, involuntary whimpers escaping her mouth as he licked and sucked her with increasing intensity. And the way he stared at her, practically daring her to look away. Her entire body trembled with an intensifying pleasure that felt overwhelming and yet like not enough all at the same time.

Her legs dangled awkwardly, and she tried to hold them open, giving his broad shoulders space. But then Tripp placed one leg and then the other over his shoulders. His smirk deepened as he dived two fingers inside of her and curved them.

"Tripp, oh my God!" she'd practically shouted in response to the incredible sensation of his fingers moving inside her and his mouth on her clit. Dee's belly tensed, her back arched and her head lolled back. Her biceps ached and trembled with the additional effort required just to stay upright. "Oh my God, yes. Yes, yes, yes."

Dee panted, her heart racing, as she shattered into pieces. Her inner walls pulsed, gripping his fingers.

Tripp pressed a kiss to her sex. Then down her inner thigh. Behind her knee. He watched with satisfaction as her chest heaved and she slowly came down from the intense high he'd given her.

He let her legs down and slowly rose to his bare feet—something she'd never found sexy on a man before. Tripp dragged the back of his hand across his lips and chin, gleaming with evidence of her pleasure. He flashed her the most wickedly delicious half smile. The kind of smile that indicated this was only the beginning of what he had in store for her.

Dionna swallowed hard, her chest still heaving. Her skin felt warm all over.

Tripp leaned in, his whiskered chin grazing her shoulder as his lips brushed her ear. "You taste so fucking good."

How exactly did one respond to such a compliment?

She wanted to make a joke about it being the peach sangria sugar body scrub she'd just used in the shower. But the shiver that rippled down her spine impeded her ability to be quirky or clever.

"Turn around." Tripp's voice had deepened. Its lower register apparently also reaching down deep in her soul and strumming the parts of her body his clever mouth had just brought to orgasm.

"Wh-what?" Dee felt like she was in a haze, her mind too foggy to even comprehend basic instructions.

Tripp didn't repeat himself. Instead, he tugged her to her feet and turned her around, pressing her palms to the desk.

"Seriously, I'm all for fun and games. But if you're

thinking of doing a strip search... I'm out." She'd finally found her voice and at least a hint of her ability to be a smart-ass. A natural reaction whenever she felt nervous.

And this Tripp—the infinitely sexy man who growled orders into her ear and glared at her with the intensity of a lion who hadn't eaten meat in a month—made her incredibly nervous.

Tripp chuckled, the low sound vibrating through her back, pressed to his stomach. He tweaked a beaded nipple as he leaned over and kissed her neck. "You got jokes. Cute."

Dionna could hear the crinkle of the foil packet as he tore it open and the sound of his zipper as he tugged it down and sheathed himself. Tripp pressed one hand to her hip and the other pressed to her back as he bent her over the desk. Then both his hands were gone for a moment, just before he pressed himself inside her in a motion so quick that it took her by surprise, despite the fact that she'd been anticipating it. Craving it even.

"Oh my God," she muttered at the delicious sensation of being filled by Tripp. Seriously, why did he feel even bigger than he had just a few hours before? She couldn't help her soft whimper—her cheek pressed to her spiral planner on the desk.

She didn't care. If she had marks on her skin from the items on the desk, it would be well worth every moment of pleasure this man was giving her. And she wanted to give him the same. When she tensed her inner muscles, Tripp responded with a low growl of his own.

He took a deep breath and retreated, leaving just the head inside of her. He leaned over and whispered, "I wouldn't do that just yet, sweetheart. Not if you want this to last."

She did. In fact, a part of Dee wanted this moment to last forever. Another part of her wondered just how much more she could take.

"Please," she whimpered, a little angry with herself for begging for it. For him.

"Please what?" Tripp trailed a finger down one bare ass cheek.

"Fuck me. Please. Now."

She'd never said those words to anyone before. But even without him saying it expressly, she already knew that was exactly what he wanted to hear.

Dionna could hear the smirk in Tripp's voice.

"As you wish."

The glide felt so delicious as he pressed inside of her. Like a desperate itch that she couldn't reach, and someone had finally scratched. She pressed her lips together, determined not to moan, whimper or otherwise embarrass herself because the sensation of Tripp inside her felt better than words could say.

And as he started his continuous motion, his hand pressed to her low back, her murmurs grew louder. After a while, she didn't care. She just wanted more of him as she pressed her hips back to meet his thrusts.

Then Tripp lifted her leg, pressing her knee onto the desk. The hand that was on her hip glided down her stomach and flicked her clit, already sensitive and aching for more of his touch. Her pleasure spiraled, her head feeling lighter, until he drove her over the edge, his name on her lips until her throat felt hoarse.

Tripp groaned, the sound deeper than before, as the pulsing of her sex seemed to pull him over the edge, too. He leaned on his hands, now pressed to the desk on either side of her as they both tried to catch their breath.

Finally, he dropped a soft kiss on her shoulder blade and patted her hip.

"Let me take care of this and I'll be right back."

Dee nodded, not capable of coherent speech. Once the bathroom door closed and she could hear the water running in the sink, she took a few more breaths before finally hoisting herself upright again, though she still leaned most of her weight on the desk. Her legs felt like noodles.

She sighed, glancing over at the bed, which felt like it was miles away. Well, at least if she tumbled to the floor, unable to make it across the room on what felt like newborn giraffe legs, the floor was covered in a thick plush carpeting that felt like heaven beneath her feet.

Dionna retrieved the silky pink underwear Tripp had discarded earlier. Then instead of grabbing her nightshirt, which she couldn't seem to find, she tugged the black T-shirt that smelled of citrus and sandalwood—just like Tripp—over her head. She didn't even care that it was inside out. Then she climbed into the bed and drifted off to sleep.

Tripp washed his hands, then dragged his fingers through his hair. His jaw and shoulders still tense. He stared at his reflection in the mirror, unsure who he was more upset with—Dee or himself.

He was pissed at himself because after more than a decade of living his best, relationship-free life, he'd finally met someone who made him reconsider the position. Made him want to step out of his safety zone. He was agitated with Dee because before he could share his revelation with her, she'd declared that she wasn't interested.

Tripp scratched at his chin—overdue for a shave—and glared at his reflection. Had he really been that off about Dee? About what she wanted?

Then again, maybe his sister was right. Maybe the only reason he'd even considered a relationship with Dee was because it felt impossible. So maybe it wasn't really what he wanted either.

Tripp heaved a sigh and slipped off his unzipped jeans, setting them on top of the clothes hamper. He'd deal with all of the confusing thoughts running through his head like a herd of cattle in search of water tomorrow. Right now, he just wanted to sleep.

He stepped out of the bathroom in his boxer briefs and bare feet, in search of the T-shirt he'd shed earlier. It was no longer on the floor. When he glanced over at the bed, Dee was cuddled under the comforter, a hint of his black T-shirt peeking above it.

His frown softened. There was something sweet and tender about the fact that she'd donned his T-shirt before crawling into bed. As he walked closer, Dee was breathing softly and down for the count. Tripp chuckled to himself and made a mental note to tease her the next day about how he'd laid her ass to sleep.

He stood beside the bed for a moment. Dee was already asleep, so he could return to his own bed. After all, it's what he would normally do. But he couldn't resist the surprising desire to crawl into bed with Dee. To wake up to her the following morning.

Tripp turned off the desk light, then slipped beneath the covers. Dee, who was lying on her side, facing away from him, scooted back against him. Tripp turned over onto his side and wrapped his arm around her stomach, tugging her closer, so he was the big spoon to her little spoon. He pressed his nose to her hair, inhaling the delicious scent of coconut and vanilla.

"Thought you were asleep." He pressed a kiss to her ear.

"I'm a light sleeper." Her face was still buried in the pillow. "I thought you would leave."

"It's my house. It'd be kind of weird if I left." He couldn't help fucking with her.

She elbowed him in the side, and he laughed. Dionna turned in his arms so she was facing him. She gently cradled his cheek. "That's not what I meant, and you know it. I figured you would go back to your own room." She searched his eyes in the mostly dark room, lit only by a sliver of moonlight coming through the sheer curtains that shielded the balcony doors. Dee dragged her thumb across his lower lip. "Didn't take you for a cuddler."

"I'm not usually." Tripp shrugged, liking the feel of Dionna's soft hands on his rough skin. "Why? Would you like me to leave?"

"No. Don't go." Her response was instant, without a moment's hesitation. She pressed a kiss to his lips. "I like having you here."

It felt as though Dee's words had reached into his chest and squeezed his heart. He swallowed roughly and nodded. "I like having you here, too."

Her eyes glinted as she smiled, caressing his cheek.

Tripp pressed a kiss to her palm. "Good night, Dionna."

"Good night, Tripp." She turned over, wiggling so her ass was snuggled against him. Then she laid her arm on top of his arm, draped over her waist. A few moments later, Dee had fallen back to sleep again.

There was nothing Tripp wanted more than to join

her in la-la land. But instead, he lay awake racking his brain for the answer to Dee's earlier question.

You live in Royal. I live in LA. What else would this possibly be?

Because despite what either of them had said, he couldn't help feeling that whatever was going on between him and Dionna was meant to be much more than a fling.

Twelve

Twelve

Dionna stood in the horse stable at The Noble Spur and stroked the silky black mane of Deuce, the majestic Arabian horse she'd been riding the past few days.

Dee had reluctantly agreed to go horseback riding with Tripp the day after they'd first slept together. She'd been terrified, but Tripp had been so patient and encouraging. And Deuce seemed to sense her fear. Yet, he'd been gentle and docile. She'd fallen in love with riding.

Tripp had made time to take Dionna riding every afternoon since she loved it so much. She adored the time they spent together riding on the Nobles' vast property. In fact, she loved every single minute she got to spend with Tripp.

The passionate nights they'd spent together. Falling asleep in each other's arms after sharing stories about their lives and their families. Starting each day together making and eating breakfast. Planning Ari and Ex's prewedding festivities over lunch. Exploring the ranch on horseback in the afternoons. Then venturing into Royal each evening after he'd finished his day on the ranch and she'd finished hers working remotely.

Last evening, they'd taken a mosaic class together at the antique shop in town called Priceless, housed in a big red barn. It was another activity Dee hadn't thought she'd enjoy, but it'd been fun. More so because they'd done it together.

Since the night they'd first made love, Tripp had spent every night in her bed or she in his. But she hadn't gotten around to asking Tripp about filming on his land. Or about the other idea she had that he would probably consider even crazier.

Dee sighed heavily, thinking of the call she'd had earlier with Molly. Marcus was waiting on an answer, and he wasn't known for being a patient man. She'd already run the idea past Ari, and she'd loved it. Now she just needed to get up the nerve to ask Tripp.

She nuzzled Deuce's snout, then handed the gentle yet majestic animal a well-deserved apple. She patted his head. "You're such a sweet boy."

"I'm glad you two are getting along so well." Tripp grinned as he led his reddish-brown quarter horse, Nick Fury, to his stall and closed the gate.

Tripp tossed Nick an apple, then glanced around to ensure no one else was around. He slipped his arms around her waist and gave her a kiss that made her skin warm and her pulse race. Tripp leaned his forehead against hers. "Is it weird that I'm suddenly a little jealous of my horse?"

"Trust me, I'd prefer to be riding you." Dee cradled his whiskered cheek and kissed him again.

Reluctantly, she pulled out of his arms. Partly because she didn't want one of the ranch hands to catch them making out in the barn—which had come close to happening twice before. But also because she needed to put on her business hat. Something that would be hard to do when she was cradled against Tripp's solid chest and other hard parts.

"Tripp, there's something I need to talk to you about."

"Okay." His expression became more serious. He shoved his hands in his pockets. "Does Ari not like the plans we've come up with so far?" He shifted his hat enough to wipe sweat from his forehead with the back of his sleeve.

"Ari will probably end up revamping the reception menu. But that's not what I want to talk to you about. This isn't related to the wedding. It's a business proposal."

"All right." Tripp's face took on that unreadable expression again.

"I... Uh... That Western about the Black cowboy we're filming... Well, we're trying to land Marcus Maybury for the lead role, and we're this close to signing him, but we've run into a small problem."

Tripp folded his arms, his legs planted wide. "Let me guess, he wants more money."

"They always want more money." Dee waved a hand. "That I can handle. It's just that Marcus believes this story could possibly put us in the running for Cannes and some of the other big film festivals. Ari and I believe that, too. Which means, this could be the breakout role

Marcus has been waiting on, and the breakout film that would launch this studio to the next level."

"But…" He eyed her cautiously.

"But Marcus is a method actor and he is all about authenticity. So he won't accept the role if we film at a studio in Cali. To come on board, he's insisting that we actually film the movie in Texas, where the story is set." Dee kept her voice steady, despite the sound of her heart pounding in her ears.

"Good for him." Tripp nodded, seemingly impressed. "Enough with all of these sad green screen films."

"Which brings me to my proposal." Dionna stood taller, her shoulders back as her eyes met his. "That unused land you all have been deciding what to do with… What if we filmed the movie there?" She forced a big smile and held her breath.

"You want to film *here*?" Tripp asked incredulously. "On The Noble Spur?"

"Yes. And like I said, this is a business proposal—not a favor. So we'd pay you for the use of your land."

"Hmm…" Tripp rubbed his chin thoughtfully, his gaze elsewhere. "That would mean the place would be overrun with your film crew and you'd be filming at all hours of the day." He seemed to be talking more to himself than to her.

"We're not a major studio, so we operate with no more crew than is necessary to get the job done," she assured him. "As for the hours, since Ari is an actor, too, she's sensitive to keeping the cast and crew on set too long. Besides, the area of land we're talking about is quite a distance from your place. So filming shouldn't disrupt business here on the ranch."

"Dee, I need you to lose the bright, shiny, happy sales

pitch for a minute and just talk to me. Not like I'm some random vendor." Tripp leveled his gaze with hers. He stepped closer and lowered his voice. "Talk to me like I'm the man who knows how every inch of your skin tastes. The man whose name you call until your voice goes hoarse."

Dee sank her teeth into her lower lip, her skin raging with fire and the space between her thighs damp and wanting. She nodded. "Okay."

"Is this going to turn into a shit show? Create a circus that'll piss off all my neighbors? Will there be any damage to the land or danger to my animals?" he asked.

"No, of course not." Dionna placed a gentle hand on his arm. "I know how much you love this ranch and this town. I'd never do anything to jeopardize either of them."

"Then why the whole sales shtick?" Tripp raised a brow.

"Because I didn't want to make it seem like I was using our *relationship* to pressure you to agree to this." Dionna leaned into him, her hands pressed to his chest as she gazed up at him. "I'd love to film here, but only if that's something you'd want, too."

Tripp sucked in a deep breath and nodded. "All right."

"As in all right, you'll do it?"

"As in all right, I'm considering it. As long as we can come to terms on a price."

"Of course. Thank you, Tripp." She resisted the desire to squeal with joy. "But there is one more thing I need to ask."

His raised eyebrow made it clear that she was pushing it. But she asked anyway.

"In the spirit of authenticity, Marcus also insists that we have a consultant on the set. You know, someone who will ensure that everything we're doing is accurate and credible. Someone like...*you*."

"Me?" Tripp jabbed a thumb to his chest and took a step back. "C'mon, Dee, you can't be serious. I'm a rancher. Not a Hollywood movie consultant."

"We don't need you to be Hollywood. In fact, that's the very opposite of what we need you to be." She grabbed his hand as he started to pull away. "All we need is for you to be your charming, knowledgeable, well-connected self. Nothing more, nothing less."

"It would take time away from my work here on the ranch."

"I know. But the fee will cover hiring a few new ranch hands and maybe promoting someone like Roy to take on a bigger role. And you still have Tess to help with the office stuff. She was just saying the other night that she was ready to take on a bigger role with the ranch again now that they have a nanny." Dionna tried not to sound too eager. "Besides, you said that you love the ranch, but a part of you wanted to do something else. Maybe this is that something. You could make a career out of this."

"I have a career." He glanced around the barn, then rubbed his chin. "But maybe it could be a fun side hustle."

"Even better." Dee smiled. "But I need to know as soon as possible. And I know you said your mom wanted to be an actress. So if it'll sweeten the pot, I'm sure we could get your parents in the film as extras. It might not be a speaking role, but it'd definitely give them bragging rights."

"That means we'd see a lot more of each other, right?"

Dee nodded, her belly fluttering.

"All right. We can move forward on one condition."

Tripp slipped her arm through his, and they headed back toward the house.

"Name it." Dee tried to stay focused on the issue at hand rather than the warmth and electricity that crawled down her spine in response to his touch and being so close to him.

"Seems to me you would need to stay another week or so to give us time to sort out the contract, decide on exactly where we should film, maybe where to source supplies… Things like that."

Dee could barely contain her grin. "Funny. Ari mentioned the same thing this morning. I have meetings in LA and New York coming up. But Ari suggested that for now—just while we work all of this out—maybe I could make Royal my home base. If that's okay with—"

Tripp pulled her into his arms and kissed her, setting her entire body on fire and making her wish they were inside the house and away from prying eyes right now.

Dee finally forced herself to pull free. She glanced around, hoping they hadn't given one of the ranch hands—or worse, his sister, Tess—an unexpected peep show.

"I take that as a *yes*." Dee smiled.

"You can take that as a *hell yes*." Tripp leaned in to kiss her again.

She gave his shoulder a gentle shove. "Calm down, tiger. Someone, like your sister, might see us."

He dropped a quick kiss on her lips anyway. "I don't care."

Dionna sucked in a deep breath, her smile waning because she did care. She felt slightly irritated that Tripp was suddenly trying to change their agreement and a hint of guilt because she still wanted to keep their relationship a secret.

Yes, this arrangement would extend their little liaison. She was as grateful for that as he was. But it didn't change the fact that Tripp's life was here in Royal and hers was in LA. At some point, they'd have to come to terms with that hard, cold reality and this relationship would be doomed.

"I care." Her voice was soft, steeped with apology. "We both know what this is… What it has to be." Dee touched his cheek, her heart breaking at the disappointment she saw behind his eyes. "So there's no point in worrying Xavier and getting Ari's hopes up unnecessarily. If your decision is predicated on…"

"It isn't," Tripp sighed, then offered her a cursory smile. He extended a hand. "As long as we can come to terms, we have a deal."

"Really?" Forgetting herself for a moment, Dionna jumped into his arms and hugged him.

Tripp laughed when she stepped back and cleared her throat, glancing around again.

"Thank you, Tripp. I promise to do everything in my power to ensure that this is the best possible experience for you," Dee said.

Tripp cradled her cheek. His warm gaze reflected a deep affection that made her belly flutter. "Trust me, sweetheart, it already is."

Thirteen

Tripp stepped out of the shower, dried himself off and wrapped a towel around his waist. He wiped the condensation from the bathroom mirror, pulled out his razor and carefully trimmed his beard.

It still felt odd that Ari's company wanted to film on his land and asked him to serve as a consultant on the film. The first request didn't bother him as long as the film crew didn't damage his property, disrupt his business or piss off his neighbors. The second request had given him pause.

Yes, he knew ranch life inside and out. And he was well versed on the history of Black cowboys in Texas and in other parts of the country. Both his parents and grandparents had ensured that he and his sister knew their history and never, *ever* forgot it. They didn't have the luxury of pretending the past hadn't happened just because it was unpleasant. He knew all too well that atrocities forgotten were destined to be repeated.

Still, being a Black rancher in the present didn't necessarily make him the best person to consult on a film about Black cowboys in the past. But he'd read the script. Ari and Dionna and that pretty boy actor, Marcus Maybury, were right. This was an important story. One that deserved to be told authentically rather than being swept under the rug—where so much of the history of Black cowboys in this country had been relegated.

Maybe he'd initially agreed to sign on to the project as a way to keep Dionna here—in Royal, in his home and in his bed. But it was about more than that now. He believed in the project. So he'd do whatever he could to ensure the story was told authentically. Still, he was glad Dee had promised to support him in this new role in any way she could. Her promise had been comforting. Much like the woman herself.

Tripp rinsed the razor and put it away. He leaned against the doorframe, watching Dionna asleep in his bed. His mouth curved in an involuntary smile. Something he'd been doing often since Dionna had come into his life.

Not that he wasn't happy before. But since he and Dee had connected, his life felt…*different*. Being with Dee brought him a surprising sense of contentment. As much as he loved being with Dionna physically, he'd been just as content in the quiet moments they shared. Settling on the sofa to watch a movie they'd both seen before. Playing a hand of gin rummy. Or riding Deuce and Nick Fury on one of The Noble Spur's trails. And he loved that Dee seemed to truly enjoy spending time with his sister and her family. That despite being an LA girl her entire life, she fit into his life here in Royal so well.

Tripp sighed quietly, then made his way to his closet to get dressed. A few more minutes, then he'd wake Dee.

Keely Tucker, who was creating Ariana's bridal gown, had arrived in town. Tripp had promised Ex and Ariana that he'd help Keely source her materials and accessories in Royal, keeping with the bride and groom's determination to work with local vendors. There was a mixer at the Texas Cattleman's Club that evening. It was the perfect way to introduce Keely to as many vendors as possible in a single night. But he'd much prefer to spend the evening at home with Dionna.

They'd had an early dinner, made love, and had both fallen asleep. They would probably have slept through the night if he hadn't obligated himself to attend the mixer tonight. He'd keep his word, show up to the event and connect Keely with local shop owners. But once he fulfilled his obligation, he'd be right back at The Noble Spur, lying beside Dee.

Tripp treasured every moment he and Dionna got to spend together. Perhaps because they were on borrowed time. Soon Dee would pack her bags and return to LA for good. Whenever he thought of her leaving, a knot tightened in his gut.

He didn't want Dee to go, and he couldn't help thinking that she didn't want to leave either. Not just because of him. Dionna seemed happier and more relaxed in Royal. As if a burdensome weight had been lifted from her shoulders.

Tripp sat on the edge of his bed and traced a finger down Dee's arm a few times until she gradually awakened. Her dark brown eyes fluttered open.

"Hey." Her bashful smile did something to him. *Every. Damn. Time.*

"Hey, sweetheart." He threaded their fingers and kissed the back of her hand. "I hated to wake you, but the event kicks off in about an hour. I know you hate having to rush."

Dee stretched and yawned, wiping the sleep from her eyes. She'd spent the past few days flying all over the country. Dee had flown to meetings in LA and Chicago. She'd flown to New York to meet with Marcus Maybury, who was officially on board for the film. Then she'd returned to Royal earlier that day. It was no wonder she'd fallen asleep the moment her head had finally hit the pillow.

"What time is it?" she asked through a yawn.

"Quarter to seven, and the party kicks off at eight."

Dee released his hand and buried her face in the pillow. "I need at least another hour of sleep to feel human. You go ahead to the party. If I'm up to it, I'll join you later."

"Of course. I understand how exhausted you must be." Tripp tried not to sound disappointed. "I'm only going myself to make sure Keely connects with the vendors she'll need to work with."

"Oh gosh!" Dee sat up. "I completely forgot. I'll hop in the shower and get dressed."

"No, get some sleep, babe." He braced her hip, holding her in place. "I've got this. If you're up for it later, give me a call and I'll come back for you. If not, no problem. Stay in bed, get some sleep, and I'll be back as soon as I can. All right?"

"You're sure you don't mind?" Dee kissed him, then cradled his jaw.

"I'll be fine." Tripp stroked her cheek. "Now go back to sleep. I'll see you in a bit."

He grabbed his shoes and jacket, turned off the light and closed the door behind him. He hadn't left the house and already he was counting the moments until he'd be holding Dee in his arms again.

Dionna had slept another hour, then got up, showered and got dressed. It seemed silly to ask Tripp to come back to pick her up. So she used her rideshare app to request a ride to the Texas Cattleman's Club instead. She entered the club, as a friend of Tripp's, then made her way to the bar, hoping that the bartender could make a decent mojito.

She sipped her drink and sighed with contentment. Then she dropped a generous tip in the glass jar on the counter. Dionna perched on a stool with her back to the bar as she studied the room. Eventually, she'd find Tripp. But for now, sit there and take the temperature of the room before she ventured into the crowd.

Dee had enjoyed every experience in Royal. Meeting locals. Going out to eat. But this was the biggest event she'd attended there thus far. And she was always more comfortable taking a big event like this slow. Hanging out on the edges like a wallflower until she got comfortable enough to wade into the crowd of unfamiliar faces with its requisite small talk with strangers and mindless chitchat.

She wasn't antisocial. She was just very introverted. She liked people as much as the next person. But she needed quiet time before and after such an outing to recharge her batteries. Otherwise, she'd be cranky and completely drained.

"Milan!"

Dionna's head snapped toward the sound of the voice for two reasons. First, because she hadn't gotten a chance to meet Milan in person yet, though Ari had already booked her as the makeup artist for the wedding. Second, because she recognized the voice that had called her.

It was Tripp's.

Dee took another sip from her glass as she watched Tripp open his arms to a gorgeous Afro-Latina woman whose hair was light brown with blond streaks running through it and with flawless makeup.

The woman kissed his cheek, and they shared an intimate embrace that fired up heat in Dee's cheeks and gave her a sense of unease.

Tripp was friendly and harmlessly flirtatious. She realized that. And despite the time they'd spent together, she certainly had no claim on him. Still, she couldn't help the knot tightening in her gut and the ache in her chest. The gaze between them as he continued to hold her hand felt much more intimate than a friendship.

Two women perched on the empty barstools beside her and ordered their drinks. The blonde elbowed her friend—a redhead—in the side and nodded across the room.

"Looks like things are heating up again between Tripp Noble and his ex," the blonde said, as if it was the most delicious piece of gossip.

"Which one?" the redhead asked with a bitter laugh.

"Milan Valez, the makeup artist from PURE. They're right over there." The blonde pointed impatiently.

"Ahh…" The redhead sipped the cosmo the bartender handed her. "I was so sure she was the one who would finally get our eternal bachelor to settle down."

"So did she." The blonde chuckled, then muttered, "Welcome to the club, honey."

"Amen." The two women clinked their glasses together and giggled. "Now c'mon. This is a mixer, so we should be mixing it up. Grab your drink and let's go. Got my sights set on a handsome rancher at two o'clock."

The women laughed and then they were gone.

Dee sucked in a deep breath. Her face was hot and her eyes stung with tears, and she wasn't even sure why.

She and Tripp had never talked about being exclusive. In fact, she was the one who'd been adamant about keeping their relationship a secret. So what right did she have to be jealous, even if Milan Valez was his ex?

That was what the logical part of her brain insisted. But her heart felt…betrayed.

Dee glanced over to where Tripp and Milan were still engaged in an intimate conversation. He leaned down closer to the woman who was at least a head shorter than him. Presumably to be heard over the din of music and conversation. Yet, she couldn't help thinking of all the times he'd leaned in like that to whisper something intimate and adorable to her. Or to nuzzle her neck.

I was so sure she was the one who would finally get our eternal bachelor to settle down.

So did she. Welcome to the club, honey.

The women's derisive words and laughter rang in her ears.

Dee's neck and cheeks burned. She wasn't sure who she felt sorrier for—Milan, who'd evidently believed that what was happening between her and Tripp was real or herself. Because despite what she'd been telling herself, there was apparently a small part of her that had been holding on to that same hope.

Dionna jumped down from the stool, inadvertently tipping over her half-full mojito glass. "I'm such a klutz. I'm so sorry."

"Happens all the time." The tall handsome bartender retrieved her glass and mopped up the mess before she could grab a handful of napkins to do it herself. The man leaned in and lowered his voice. "Don't let the sour grapes get to you." He winked. "I'll get you another drink."

"No, you don't have to—" Dee raised a hand to object, but he was already gone. She didn't want another drink. All she wanted was to call a rideshare and get the hell out of there. Pretend she'd never even been there. Then retreat to her room and claim a headache or the flu. Maybe mono.

"Dionna, I thought that was you." A big smile spread across Tessa's face as she and Ryan approached the bar hand in hand.

God, the two of them were beyond adorable. And Tess had been so sweet to her. She wouldn't just bolt on Tripp's sister. No matter how badly she wanted to get out of there.

"Hey, Tess, Ryan. How are you?" Dionna flashed her widest smile as she accepted hugs from the couple. "You two look great."

"So do you." Tess held her at arm's length and studied her Mediterranean blue Kay Unger jumpsuit with the overlay skirt over midnight blue crepe pants and nude heels. "This jumpsuit is absolutely gorgeous."

Dee thanked Tess and flashed her an awkward smile. She accepted her drink from the bartender and dropped another tip in his jar. The guy was working overtime to keep her afloat tonight.

When she'd gotten dressed in this outfit earlier, all she could think of was what Tripp would think of it and how long it would take him to get her out of it. Now the memory made her want to start bawling like an infant who'd been served spinach when what she'd wanted was sweet potatoes.

"Dee, honey, are you okay?" Tessa looked concerned.

Ryan took the hint, said he was going over to say hello to someone, kissed his wife's cheek and promised to catch up with them later.

"Yes. Sure. Of course," Dee babbled, her smile feeling strange and plastic. She'd never been good at faking her feelings. Whatever was in her head and her heart was automatically plastered over her face. "I just got here actually. And I'm not really feeling so well."

"I'm so sorry to hear that, sweetie. Where's Tripp?" Tessa's gaze swept the place. "If he can't take you home, I will."

Home.

Dee hadn't really thought about it before, but so many times Tripp had said "Let's go home" or "When we get back home" to her. As if his home was her home, too. But it wasn't. She was an interloper staying on his family's estate. Any thoughts of The Noble Spur being her home was an indulgence in a schoolgirl fantasy that would never, *ever* come true.

And dammit. Now Tess was blurry as Dee's eyes clouded with tears. Had her new friend noticed?

"That isn't necessary, really. I took a car service here tonight. Tripp doesn't even know I'm here. There's no need to bother him with—"

"Is that why you're so upset?" There was a mixture of pity and fury in Tessa's voice as she stared at her brother standing across the room. Tripp's hand rested low on Milan's back, and he seemed to be introducing her to Ariana's stylist Keely Tucker, who'd been engaged to create Ari's custom bridal gown.

"No, of course not. Why would I be upset about that?" Dee could feel her face shifting into a frown, even as she attempted to ratchet up her unnatural smile.

God, I must look like some bizarre serial killer right now.

"Sweetie, I know what you both are saying, but I can see what's really going on with you two." Tessa's words felt more like a warm hug than chastisement. "I realize as Tripp's sister my words might not mean very much to you right now, but I'm confident this isn't what you think this is."

It felt like a load of bricks were piled on Dee's chest and she could barely breathe. "I should go. It was good seeing you again, Tess. Have a great time tonight."

Dionna hugged Tess, chugged the last of her drink and made her way toward the coat check to claim her coat. She headed outside, not caring that she hadn't called the rideshare service yet and there might not even be one available on this chilly March night.

She'd walk all the way back to The Noble Spur in her four-inch heels if she had to.

Dee sniffled as the cold air assaulted her nostrils and wetness stained her cheeks. She pulled the coat around her tightly and dug her phone out of her coat pocket.

"Dionna!"

Dee didn't answer. Instead, she cringed and turned her back to the source of the sound as she quickly dabbed at her damp eyes and wet cheeks with her knuckle.

"Dee, what's going on? What are you doing out here?

It's freezing tonight." Tripp stood in front of her without a coat, his arms folded over his chest as he shivered.

"Nothing's wrong. I just…" She gazed at the darkened fields just over his shoulder. "I shouldn't have come. I'd like to go back ho—" She stopped herself. "I'd like to go back to the ranch. I think I'm just going to go to my room and crash for the night. Maybe even for the weekend."

Tripp lifted her chin, forcing her gaze to meet his. "You've been crying."

It wasn't a question, so she didn't bother denying it.

She pulled out of his grip and sniffled again, wrapping her arms around herself. "Like you said, it's cold out. I think I'm coming down with something."

"You were supposed to call me. I would've come for you."

"Is that so you'd have a heads-up before I showed up and surprised you while you were flirting with half the women in the room?" Dee squeezed her eyes shut, hating herself for saying exactly what she was thinking.

"What are you talking about?" Tripp grasped her shoulders. "You're the one who's insisting that we keep this a secret. I wanted to tell Ari and Ex. Hell, I would've told anyone who wanted to listen by now. I've kept my mouth shut because it's what *you* wanted." His jaw clenched and his eyes flashed in the darkness. "So what the hell has gotten into you tonight? Tess said you looked upset. Is this about me talking to Milan and Keely? I never took you for the jealous type, Dee."

She hated that he sounded monumentally disappointed in her when it was her who had every right to be disappointed in him.

"You never mentioned that Milan Valez was more than just the makeup artist who made over your sister for the bachelor auction. And you certainly never mentioned that she was your freaking ex," she whispered loudly, pointing an accusatory finger at him.

Tripp sucked in a deep breath and released it, visible in the night air. "I didn't," he acknowledged. "At the time, you and I weren't involved. It was strictly a business decision. So I made the conscious decision *not* to bring up our history because I didn't want her to be selected or dismissed based on our past connection. I wanted Ari to choose Milan based on her own merits because I know Mimi well enough to know that's what she would want."

So now it was *Mimi*?

"Okay, *Mimi* would've wanted to stand on her own two feet. I get it." She really did.

Dee hadn't ever used her friendship with Ari or her family to get a job in the past. An opportunity… Yes. But she'd wanted them to choose her because she was damn good at what she did. Not because of whose names were in her high school yearbook.

"But once we were…" Dionna glanced around the dark parking lot.

"Involved?" Tripp glared at her, his patience clearly wearing thin.

"Why didn't you mention your relationship with her then?" she asked.

Tripp toned down the self-righteous glare and sighed. He rubbed at his forehead. "I've already hurt her enough, even if it wasn't intentional. I couldn't let her lose out on a career-making opportunity because of me. I wouldn't have been able to forgive myself for that."

"So you didn't trust me enough to tell me the truth? Even though you were sleeping with me. Is that really what you take me for? Some vindictive woman who has it in for everyone her man has ever slept with in the past?"

"Like you didn't trust me enough to find out if there was anything actually happening between me and Milan? You just jumped to the conclusion that I'm some cheating dickhead who'd leave you home in bed and then come hook up with my ex?"

The hurt in his voice came across more loudly than the anger. She cringed, her chest uneasy with guilt.

Dee inhaled deeply and folded her arms. "If you'd seen things from my vantage point, you would've thought the same thing."

"No, I wouldn't have, Dee. Because I know you… Or at least, I thought I did. And I already know that the woman I adore would never do anything to hurt me intentionally. So I would've given you the benefit of the doubt."

Dee stood there, staring at him. What he'd said was sweet and warm, and it made her feel foolish. But hadn't her ex been good at saying all the right things and making her feel guilty when they both knew he was the culpable one?

Her mouth fell open, but she didn't know what to say. The chill in the air seeped through her bones. She shivered, wrapping her arms around herself.

Tripp sighed. And though she was wearing a coat and he was only wearing a blazer, he stripped it off and settled the jacket that smelled like him on her shoulders.

"If you want to go back to the ranch… Fine. I'll take you there myself. Just give me a minute. I'd promised to take Keely back to her hotel. I need to ask my friend Jay to see her home instead. Just, please step inside while you wait. It's freezing out here. You're gonna get sick." Tripp placed a hand on her back. The other gestured toward the club.

Dee nodded.

They took a few steps toward the door, but suddenly Tripp froze. He turned to her. "No, you need to come back inside. We won't stay, if you don't want to. But Milan is looking forward to meeting you tonight because I couldn't shut up about you, and Keely is looking forward to seeing a familiar face. So hate me if you want to for absolutely fucking nothing. That's fine. But the last thing either of us want is to insult two of the key creatives Ariana is relying on for her big day."

"Are you *telling me* I have to go back in there?" Dionna folded her arms and glared right back at Tripp.

"Fuck it," he whispered beneath his breath. "*Yes*, Dionna Reed, I'm *telling* you that you need to stop acting like a spoiled, immature, jealous brat. To come inside and introduce yourself to these two *very* professional women who we *need* for this wedding. And, *yes*, I expect you to behave like the classy professional woman you've always been. Now, whether you choose to do it or not, that's up to you. But it seems your only other alternative is to stand out here freezing your ass off while you're waiting for a rideshare that may or may not come." He extended his elbow. "So what's it going to be?"

Dee huffed, her breath fogging the air around her. She slipped her arm through his and allowed him to lead her back inside.

Tripp slipped his blazer back on and checked Dee's coat again. Then he escorted her inside the main space.

"There you two are. You must be Dionna." The

woman she recognized as Milan stood behind them at the bar with Keely Tucker flanking her.

"Yes." Dee turned around and flashed the woman a smile as bright as the morning sun and extended her hand. "And you must be…"

Before she could finish speaking, Milan had pulled Dee into a hug.

"Sorry." The woman finally released her. "I'm Milan Valez. Thanks to you both I'll be doing the makeup at the wedding of Ariana Ramos, whom I absolutely adore. I honestly can't thank you enough. I've always made a big deal about wanting to do this on my own and not needing help. I'm glad Tripp didn't listen to me this time."

The woman's excited grin lit up the entire room and melted Dionna's heart. She felt awful for assuming bad motives of this woman and of Tripp.

"It was your flawless work that got you this job, Milan." Dionna took the woman's hand in both of hers, her smile genuine this time. "Tripp just made sure Ari got to see what you were capable of. The rest was all you."

Milan's cheeks flushed and her eyes were shiny with tears of gratitude. She hugged Tripp, and then she hugged Dee again.

"You couldn't possibly know how much that means to me." Milan laughed, wiping at her eyes. "But thank you just the same. And thank you, Tripp, for introducing me to Keely. She's already recommended me for a few other high-profile events."

"That's fantastic," Dee and Tripp said simultaneously. They glanced at each other momentarily before returning their attention to Keely.

Dee exchanged hugs with Keely, Ariana's stylist and friend, whom it was always good to see.

"I hear you've been here in town working your magic, as always," Keely said.

"It's nothing, really. And I haven't done it alone. Tripp has been amazing. He's remarkably resourceful."

"True, but don't be so modest, Dionna." Milan waved a hand. "I've heard so much about you. You're a hit around town. And Tripp here hasn't been able to stop gushing about you all night."

Dee swallowed hard, her throat dry as she glanced over at Tripp. She felt like a complete ass for thinking the worst of him. He'd come here and done *exactly* what he'd promised to do. And he'd gone out of his way to make her look good, too.

He slipped his arm around her waist and smiled broadly. "Every word of it is true."

Tripp's words were kind and the gesture of pulling her closer was warm. But she could feel the tension in his arm, in his voice and in the heat radiating off of him. But he was too much of a gentleman to say all of the things he was probably thinking about her right now.

She'd screwed up. *Immensely.*

Dee wished she could take back the things she'd said. But it was too late. And things would never be the same.

Fourteen

Tripp climbed into his truck, clicked his seat belt and pulled out onto the street.

After their argument in the parking lot, he and Dee had stayed at the club another couple of hours. And while they'd been personable, friendly and full of smiles for everyone else, the tension still lingered between them.

He'd been glad when his sister told him Dionna was there at the club but stunned when she'd informed him that she seemed to be upset and that she was leaving. And he'd been more than a little pissed that Dee had essentially accused him of trying to hook up with his ex when the two of them were…

Tripp frowned and gripped the wheel tighter. To be honest, he wasn't quite sure what the two of them were.

Saying they were *lovers* felt ridiculous. Dee didn't want anyone else to know about them, so he certainly couldn't call her his girlfriend. And whatever the hell this was, it was certainly more than a hookup.

Tripp dragged a hand down his face and turned onto the road that led toward the ranch, glad his friend Jay Chatman had offered to take Keely back to her hotel. He and Dee had been able to keep up the pretense that nothing was wrong during the event. But the moment they'd exited the Texas Cattleman's Club, an uncomfortable silence descended over them. They'd been in the truck driving for at least five minutes and neither of them had said a word. He was about to speak when Dee turned to him suddenly.

"Tripp, I'm sorry I was so awful earlier. I'm not usually a jealous…ass." She sighed heavily and swept her twists over one shoulder. "I honestly don't know what came over me tonight. I had no right, nor did you give me any reason, to behave the way I did. I'm truly sorry."

Tripp could feel the heat of her stare as she waited for him to say something. Anything. But he wouldn't let her off that easy. Not after she'd thought him capable of casually leaving her in bed and then…what? Hooking up with someone else?

No, they hadn't ever talked about exclusivity. In fact, they hadn't really discussed the relationship at all beyond the fact that they needed to keep it under wraps. Her choice, not his. Still, he thought it was understood that he was with Dee and no one else.

"I didn't have the right to behave that way because you never committed to any obligation between us, and I never asked you to. You gave me no reason to be jealous because…because you were doing exactly what you'd promised you would. And the sweet things you said about me to Mimi and Keely… The way I behaved this evening… I don't deserve them…" Her words trailed off as he stared at the road ahead without reply. "You can stop me anytime," she added with a bitter laugh.

"I will." Tripp gripped the wheel tightly. "When I actually disagree with anything you've said."

"Ouch." Dee faced forward in her seat again and settled her hands on her lap. "I certainly deserved that, didn't I?"

"You certainly did," he said without hesitation. After a few moments of heavy silence, he said, "God, Dee, I am absolutely furious with you right now. I realize that we haven't known each other as long as you and Ari. But I guess I thought you knew me well enough to know I'm not the kind of guy who pulls this kind of juvenile shit. If I'd wanted to be with someone else, I would've been. I'm with you because I want to be with you and just you. And the only reason that isn't common knowledge around here is because keeping it a secret was what you wanted—"

"I know. You're right. And I do know you better than that, Tripp."

"Then what was that scene outside the club tonight about? That wasn't you, Dee. At least, I didn't think it was. But hell, maybe I was wrong."

"No, you weren't. I honestly didn't even recognize myself tonight." Dee turned toward the window.

"Then what the hell happened tonight? You know why I was there."

"I know. But the moment I saw you with Milan and these two women sat down beside me and they were saying that it looked like you and your ex were getting back together…" She heaved a quiet sigh. "I lost it."

"Why?" He needed to know why she'd acted so out of character tonight.

"Seeing you two tonight took me back to what happened a year ago when I discovered that the man I was in love with was in love with someone else." Dee huffed quietly.

"And you had no idea?"

"Honestly? I'd been blind to all of the little signs that there was someone else because I didn't *want* it to be true. But my blind belief in him didn't make me some loyal, ride-or-die chick. It just made me naive and stupid. I promised myself I'd never, ever let someone gaslight me like that again."

Silence filled the cabin of the truck, neither of them speaking. He pulled into the long drive of The Noble Spur and parked his truck, then turned to her.

"I'm sorry about what your ex did to you, Dee. I really am." Tripp settled a hand on her arm. "But I'm *not* him. I would *never* treat you or anyone else that way. If it was over, I'd have the guts to tell you so. Don't make me pay for his fuckup. Got enough of my own to make amends for."

"You're right. I'm sorry for doubting you and for ruining our night."

"Yeah? Well, I'm sorry you did, too." Tripp hopped out of the truck, walked around it and opened the passenger door, helping Dee down.

Dionna looked stunned. But his bruised ego and battered feelings wouldn't permit him to give her a pass. Not yet.

He closed the passenger door, and they walked toward the house. "By the way, I didn't get to tell you how incredible you look tonight."

"Thanks," she practically whispered as she followed him into the kitchen. She hung by the door, as if she suddenly felt out of place in the space she'd called home for most of her time in Royal. "If you'd prefer that I take my things and check into The Bellamy, I'd understand."

"For God's sake, Dee. I'm not tossing you out. I'm pissed and disappointed and maybe a little hurt because I would never have presumed the worst of you." Tripp rubbed his forehead and winced, his temples throbbing. "I'm gonna turn in early. I promised to help Jay with a small project out at his place tomorrow morning. I'll be gone before breakfast, but I should be home in time for dinner." He dropped a hurried kiss on her forehead. "Good night."

Tripp walked away, then halted at the bottom of the stairs. "Apology accepted."

He trotted up the steps, stripped out of his clothing and got ready for bed. But he couldn't go to sleep because his bed felt colder, emptier and a hell of a lot lonelier without Dionna Reed in it.

After several nights of the best sleep of her life in Tripp's arms, Dee awakened frazzled and exhausted.

She'd spent the entire night tossing and turning. Seeing the hurt and disappointment in Tripp's eyes over and over again. Hearing the pain in his voice. And she'd felt exactly like the ass she'd been to him.

Tripp had begrudgingly accepted her apology. But he hadn't said he'd forgiven her or that he'd been willing to put the incident behind them. She couldn't blame him. Every awful word she'd said to him had been burned into her brain and played over and over on a loop.

If she couldn't forgive herself, why should he?

Their tryst had been fun while it'd lasted. But she'd proven to be more trouble than she was worth.

He'd probably wanted to toss her out on her ass last night but had refrained from doing so for Ex and Ari's sake. Hadn't this been Xavier's concern all along? That if the two of them got involved, things would spin out of control and then cause excruciating tension that would ruin their wedding?

Ex had been right. They'd been playing with fire.

Dee's phone rang and she quickly picked it up, hoping it was Tripp calling to check in, as he often did throughout the day while working on the ranch.

It wasn't; it was Ari.

"Hey." Dee tried to muster a smile. "How are you, hon?"

"What's wrong?" Ariana's voice was fraught with alarm. "Did something happen with the wedding plans?"

"No. Everything is fine with the wedding plans." Dee sank onto the desk chair in her suite.

"Then this is about you and Tripp," Ari said matter-of-factly. "What happened? Did you two have a fight?"

Dee's face was hot. Despite Ari's teasing about her and Tripp, she hadn't told her friend what had happened between them. Yet, she instinctively seemed to know. And Dee was too hurt and exhausted to deny the truth about them anymore.

Dionna's eyes burned as tears spilled down her cheeks. "This was a mistake… I shouldn't have come to Tripp's ranch. And I should never have…" She sniffled, unable to say the words. "I should leave."

"Did Tripp do something to make you uncomfortable?" Ariana asked.

"No, it's nothing like that. I'm the one who screwed

up and now…" Dee pressed a hand to her mouth to muffle her quiet sob. "I let what happened with my ex get in my head, and I was awful to Tripp when he's been nothing but sweet. What I said… I think it really hurt him."

"Did you apologize?"

"Of course!"

"Did Tripp ask you to leave?" Ariana asked.

"He's too much of a gentleman for that," Dee said with a sad smile. "He wouldn't, even if he wanted me to."

"People make mistakes, Dee. And couples have arguments. That doesn't mean—"

"We aren't a couple, and we never will be. In a few days, I'm returning home and he'll be…here." Dee dragged a hand across her face, glad she hadn't bothered to put on any makeup. "Maybe it's better if we just cut the cord now. Maybe it's cleaner this way. Less painful."

"It doesn't sound less painful for either of you," Ari noted.

Dee smoothed her hair back and sighed. "I tried to convince myself I could have this little meaningless fling and then just walk away. I didn't expect to feel so…*connected*, you know?"

"To Tripp?"

"And to Royal," Dee confessed. "I never imagined that I'd actually enjoy being here. That this was a place I could see myself living."

"Wow." Ariana's declaration was followed by a few moments of silence between them. "I guess neither of us saw that coming."

"No, I guess we didn't. Which is why getting involved with Tripp was a mistake."

"Dee, you don't actually believe that, and you know it," Ari said. Suddenly, there were sounds around her, like she was in a public space. "You're both just hurt, and the relationship feels untenable, so maybe you're both trying to retreat as a way to protect your hearts."

"What did Tripp do?" Xavier's voice was in the background.

"Nothing, sweetie. Your cousin has been a perfect gentleman, just like he promised. Settle down." Ari's response was followed by the sound of a kiss.

"Did Xavier join you on the set in Peru?" Dee asked.

"Actually, he just met me at JFK. We'll be boarding our flight to Dallas in a couple of hours. So sit tight and don't do anything until I get there. Everything is going to be fine, honey. I promise."

"Okay." Dee sucked in a deep breath and nodded. "Do you want me to pick you two up at the airport?"

"No, we're going to rent a car. And we're staying with Ex's parents. They'll be back from their trip to Cuba later tonight. And Tripp's sister is throwing an impromptu party for us tomorrow," Ari said. "I guess Tripp didn't tell you."

"No, he didn't." Dee's shoulders sagged and her stomach knotted. "Clearly, Tripp hasn't forgiven me. I honestly can't blame him for that."

"Dee, sweetie, you don't always have to be perfect, you know. None of us are. And I will love you to the moon and back…no matter what. Whether you're in LA, Paris or right there in Royal. I will always be your biggest fan, and I will always support whatever it is you want to do. You know that, right?"

"Same," Dee said. "Now don't miss your plane. I'll see you when you get here."

Dionna ended the call and sighed softly, unsure of how her final days in Royal would turn out. But regardless of how things ended between her and Tripp, she hoped they could walk away as friends. Because she'd much rather have Tripp as a friend than to not have him in her life at all.

Fifteen

Tripp leaned against the doorway of the great room at his sister and Ryan's place, Bateman Ranch, with an ice-cold bottle of beer in his hand. As soon as Tripp had alerted Tessa that Ex and Ari would be popping into town for a few days, his sister had hastily planned this little afternoon party of around fifty people.

The sun had set, and the crowd had thinned out. Tripp's parents had returned from their three-week trip to Cuba. His mother had spent most of the party catching up on lost time with her beloved grandchildren and playing twenty questions with Dionna, under the guise of getting to know her. Which made him wonder *exactly* what Tess had told their mother about him and Dee.

His dad had given him a knowing look and chuckled.

But an hour ago, his parents had taken the kids back to their little ranch house to spend the night with Grandma and Grandpa. Tessa and Ryan looked like they'd won the lottery and probably couldn't wait until everyone left so they could get some adult time in without the kids.

Tripp was glad that Ariana seemed to get on well with his aunt and uncle, who both really seemed to appreciate her moving the wedding to Royal. And even though he and Dee hadn't spoken much since the night of the mixer, he was glad to see how well she got along with his family. Especially his mother who'd given him what he could only describe as a nod of approval just before she and his dad had practically kidnapped his niece and nephew.

Tripp bumped fists with his friend Jay Chatman as Jay headed out. He was surprised by the sudden voice behind him.

"I like her. A lot," Audra Covington said.

He didn't need to ask whom she was referring to. He'd been staring at Dee again and now Audra was, too.

Audra was a celebrity-status jewelry designer who'd made Royal her part-time home, along with her husband, Darius Taylor-Pratt, who was the owner of a quickly growing athletic clothing company, Thr3d, and an heir to the fortune left by late billionaire Buckley Blackwood. Something Darius hadn't known most of his life. Tripp, Tessa and Ryan had befriended Audra when she'd come to town to work on a commission by another one of the Blackwood heirs. They'd first met while working together on a volunteer landscaping project at the Texas Cattleman's Club.

"Dee? Yeah, she's great. She and Ariana go way back to middle school," Tripp said.

"You know what I mean." Audra propped a hand on her hip, which only accentuated her pregnant belly.

"No, I don't." Tripp finished the last of his beer and feigned innocence.

"Look, I know you didn't ask for my advice, and if you don't want it, feel free to tell me to shut the hell up." Audra repeated the same words Tripp had uttered to her three years earlier.

Tripp couldn't help chuckling. He tossed the empty bottle in a nearby recycling bin, then turned to Audra, his arms folded. "Okay, Mama Bear. Shoot. Let's hear these words of wisdom you have for me."

"Be honest with her and with yourself. Whatever you're feeling, just…feel it. Don't pretend the feelings aren't there. Wade through them, rather than trying to find a way around them. That'll only get you stuck in the quicksand. If you don't tackle your emotions head-on, they'll sabotage any future relationships you have," Audra said.

Tripp shook his head and chuckled. He rubbed his bearded chin. "You realize you pretty much said *verbatim* what I told you when you and Darius were at your little crossroads three years ago?"

"I do." Audra grinned proudly as she stretched her back and rubbed her belly. "What you said that day was a turning point for me in my relationship with Darius. If it hadn't been for your unsolicited advice, who knows? Dare and I might never have come to terms with our feelings for each other. Your advice was life-changing for me, Tripp. That's why I never forgot it. Seems you could use a little of your own advice where Dionna is concerned."

Tripp leaned against the doorway again and frowned. He shoved one hand in his pocket. "The situation is different with me and Dee. I'm here and she lives in LA."

"Did you forget why Darius and I have two homes and split our time between Royal and LA?" Audra laughed. She caught her husband's gaze as he stood on the other side of the room chatting with Ryan. Darius winked at her and she blew a kiss at him.

Tripp wasn't jealous of their relationship at all. *Really.*

"I didn't forget," Tripp said. "And I'm glad you two were able to make it work. But it was different with you. You and Darius had been in a relationship before. You were simply rekindling the feelings you already had for each other."

"Don't downplay your intuition when it comes to Dee. If you think there's something special between you two, don't be afraid to tell her so."

Tripp glanced up at Dee again. He rubbed the back of his neck. "Thanks, Audra. That honestly does help."

"I'm rooting for you both." Audra grinned, then handed him her empty bottle of sparkling water. "Now I'm headed to the restroom again because our child really seems to enjoy bouncing on my bladder."

Tripp laughed then chucked the bottle into the recycling bin. Maybe Audra was right. He and Dionna weren't twentysomethings who were still discovering themselves. They both knew what they wanted in life. Maybe they both knew *who* they wanted, too.

But he couldn't just up and leave the ranch for months at a time the way Darius and Audra were able to. It wouldn't be fair to put such a burden on Tessa who already had her hands full raising a family. But it wouldn't be fair of him to expect Dee to be the only one to make sacrifices so they could be together either.

He'd looked at the situation a dozen different ways, and it just felt hopeless.

Right person. Wrong situation.

"Hey, Tripp." Ari stood beside him. "I wanted to thank you again for everything you've done for Xavier and me. But most of all, I want to thank you for taking such good care of my best friend. She adores you, you know."

"I feel the same way about her," Tripp admitted. He'd been hurt and angry because he cared for Dee so much. That hadn't changed.

"Then don't let a stupid argument ruin the time you have left together." Ari's expression was the most serious he'd ever seen it.

"That's the thing." Tripp's brows furrowed. "No matter what, in a few days she'll be boarding that plane back to Hollywood. Then what?"

Ari slipped her arm through his and smiled as they both glanced over at Dee who was talking to Xavier and his parents. "That, Tripp Noble, is up to the two of you."

Tripp turned to her, confused. "Dee is your right hand at the studio."

"And in case the two of you haven't noticed, she's been running things from here just fine. In fact, she hasn't skipped a beat. When she's needed to travel, she has." Ari grinned. "Don't make this more complicated than it needs to be."

"And you'd go for that? If she wanted to make Royal her base of operations long-term?"

"Would it be the most ideal situation? No," Ari admitted. "But Dionna is first and foremost my best friend. I want her to be happy. And it seems to me that she's been pretty happy here in Royal with you." Ari squeezed his shoulder, then returned to the sofa where she snuggled up beside Xavier.

Nope. He wasn't jealous of their relationship either. Or at least that's the story his brain was trying to sell his heart. But it seemed neither of them were buying it.

Who was he kidding? The time he'd spent with Dionna made him see that was exactly what he wanted. He'd watched Dee with Dylan and Tiana, and he couldn't help wondering what *their* kids might look like.

Tripp's mind was running at a million miles an hour with all the things he wanted to say to Dee. But first, there was something he needed to do.

Dionna returned to The Noble Spur with a bag filled with leftovers from the party. She carefully removed each dish Tessa had packed for her and Tripp from the cloth bag and stored it in the refrigerator.

Tripp had suddenly left the party, asking Ex if he wouldn't mind dropping Dee at the ranch. He'd barely spoken to her since *accepting* her apology. And since Ari and Ex's unexpected visit, they'd been busy showing the couple the plans for the wedding or game planning with Rylee Meadows about how they should handle the infamous wedding crasher, Patrick MacArthur, who'd apparently set his sights on disrupting Ariana and Xavier's wedding.

Headlights flashed through the kitchen window, indicating Tripp had returned to the ranch. Dionna's first instinct was to turn out the kitchen lights and hurry up the stairs to her suite. To continue giving Tripp the space he seemed to need. But in a few more days, she'd be leaving.

Dee couldn't help thinking about her conversation with Ari. About people making mistakes and couples having arguments. Maybe what she and Tripp had was destined to be short-lived. That didn't negate how momentous their time together had been... For her, at least. So she'd never forgive herself if she didn't do everything in her power to ensure they both had fond memories of the time they'd spent together.

Tripp stepped into the kitchen and closed the door behind him. He seemed surprised to see her there.

"Hey." He shoved a hand in his pocket and leaned against the counter. "I figured you and Ariana would be out somewhere painting the town. She was a little—"

"High-strung tonight?" Dionna smiled, wrapping her arms around herself. "Yeah, she was. She's so happy to be off set and to be with Xavier again and—"

"And her best friend." A small smile lit his eyes. "She obviously missed you. I thought she was going to squeeze you to death when she first saw you."

"It was a distinct possibility." Dee's eyes stung with unshed tears despite her smile, and her stomach was tied in knots. She swallowed hard and took a few steps toward Tripp, her heart racing. "Tripp, about the other night... I am really, *really* sorry. I wish I could go back and—"

"I know." Tripp took a few steps forward. "Me too."

"You don't have any reason to apologize." She inched closer still, her eyes locked with his.

"Given what you've been through and what you saw... I understand why you were upset." He gathered a few of her loose twists, running his fingers through them. "I overreacted. I sort of flashed back to a past relationship of my own."

"I've missed you so much." Dee wrapped her arms around him, fisting the back of his shirt. Her voice trembled slightly.

"It was just two days, and the entire time, you were right down the hall. But…" Tripp cradled her face. "It felt like so much longer. What am I gonna do when you're two thousand miles away?" His voice grew quiet, and he sighed.

"That's what I've been asking myself these past few days," Dee whispered. She blinked back tears. "But I don't want to think about that anymore. I just want us to have the most amazing time together for the next few—"

Suddenly, Tripp's mouth was on hers. His tongue parted her lips and glided along hers. She was overwhelmed with a deep sense of joy, thankful they'd made up and that he was kissing her again. Setting her skin on fire and causing a steady pulsing between her thighs from his kiss and touch alone.

Her eyes brimmed with fat tears that spilled down her cheeks.

Tripp kissed her tear-stained cheek. Then he slipped the off-shoulder sweater over her head and dropped it on the floor. He unbuttoned her jeans, slid them down her hips and carried her to the sofa. Then he pulled the large cashmere throw over them and lay atop her. Dionna tugged his Henley shirt and the T-shirt he wore beneath it over his head. She dropped them to the floor. When she reached for the button of Tripp's pants, he stopped her.

"The condoms are upstairs," he practically growled between kisses to her neck and bare shoulder. "I'm not feeling the strongest sense of control right now. So maybe we'd better play it safe and—"

"Keep the python in its cage?" Dee pressed a hand to the clearly visible outline of his erection pressed against the fabric of his pants.

Tripp shuddered visibly, and in that moment, she'd felt incredibly powerful.

"Something like that." Tripp grinned. "Besides, I'm not gonna need a condom for what I have in mind."

Tripp's brown eyes twinkled, and before Dee could speak, his head had disappeared beneath the cashmere throw. He spread her legs wide, to accommodate the width of his shoulders, and tugged aside the soaked fabric shielding her sex.

Dee gripped his shoulders, moaning with pleasure at the delicious sensation of his tongue against her most sensitive flesh. Lips pressed together, Dee tried to hold back all of the involuntary sounds of satisfaction trying to escape her throat. It was a lost cause.

Her head lolled back against the pillow, and her eyes wrenched shut as her soft murmurs became more vocal, followed by a few choice curse words, and perhaps some begging. And when Tripp had pushed his fingers inside her, stroking the space that always drove her wild with desire, and sucked on her sensitive clit, she'd fallen apart. Her fingers in his hair and his name on her tongue, she shattered, her chest heaving and her eyes clouding with tears.

She wanted to savor this moment between them, and every other moment they'd get to share over the next few days. But all she could think about was that this was one of the last times she'd be with him, and it broke her heart.

Tripp pressed a kiss to her damp cheek. "You okay, sweetheart?"

She nodded, wiping at her wet eyes and probably making an absolute mess of her makeup. But at this point, she didn't care.

Since they'd been housemates, Tripp had seen her in

various states of undress, with and without her makeup. Her hair a mess. Her sleeping in her bonnet. And it had never once changed the way he'd looked at her. The only thing he hadn't witnessed was her on her knees. Something she honestly hadn't ever been very fond of. But for him… She wanted to give him this. For Tripp to understand how deeply she felt for him, even if she couldn't make herself say the words.

"Ready to go upstairs?" he asked.

Dee shook her head. She squirmed from beneath him and stood. "I want you sitting right here."

When she sank to her knees, he seemed surprised.

Tripp tipped her chin. "You know that's not why I do that, right? That I get off on it as much as you do?"

Dee nodded, but she unfastened and unzipped his pants just the same. Then she looked up at him and smiled. "And this is something I really want to do for you."

Tripp's chest heaved as he watched Dee grip the base of his length and take him inside her mouth until she gagged a little before backing off a bit. He groaned at the intense pleasure of her warm mouth gliding up and down his already painfully erect dick.

She started off slow and tentative. But with each murmur of pleasure and each curse he uttered, she seemed to gain more confidence. To relish the power she had over him.

Tripp lightly gathered her hair, which had fallen forward, in his fist, not wanting to miss a moment of his length gliding in and out of that pretty little mouth. The erotic scene escalated the incredible sensation crawling up his spine, making his head feel lighter with each breath he took.

He fought the urge to move his hips. He was already so close, and he wanted to make this unexpected moment between them last as long as he possibly could.

But when Dee added the twisting of her hand as her mouth glided up and down his dick, he was at his breaking point.

"Fuck, Dee. If you don't stop now, I'm gonna…"

A wicked glint lit Dee's dark eyes as she intensified her efforts. She understood his warning, but she had no intention of backing off. She sucked harder and faster, her jaws hollowing and her hands working him until he'd lost complete control, his body emptying into hers.

Tripp collapsed against the sofa, his chest heaving and his pulse racing as he pulled Dionna into his arms, settling her onto his lap. He kissed her shoulder, her neck, her jaw. Then he pressed his mouth to hers.

"I love you, Dionna Reed." He whispered the words into her ear before pressing another kiss there. But instead of his declaration making her happy, she buried her face in his neck, her warm tears wetting his skin.

Dee hadn't responded in-kind to his spontaneous utterance. And maybe he didn't have the right to expect her to after their short time together. Still, she obviously felt something for him, too.

That would have to be enough for now.

Tripp lay in his bed in his darkened room, with Dee's cheek pressed to his bare chest. He'd come to love holding Dee in his arms like this after they'd made love. He cherished the comfort of her warm, soft body molded to his. The way her dark hair spread out over his chest.

The soft sighs she made in her sleep. The tickle of her warm breath skittering across his skin.

But tonight, his brain couldn't stop reminding him that every moment with Dee would be one of their last.

It'd never bothered him before. Every relationship had an expiration date. Like a gallon of milk or a block of cheese. He'd been grateful for the memories, edified by the lessons and ready to move on. But the thought of moving on from Dee… It felt like someone had carved a hole in his chest and was pulling his heart out.

He didn't want to move on from Dionna. He wanted her in his life. Wanted to keep waking up to her each morning and falling asleep with her in his arms each night.

This didn't feel like the end. It felt like the beginning of his future. A future that revolved around Dionna Reed. He was devastated by the thought of losing her.

Tripp glided a hand up and down the soft skin of Dee's bare back. He kissed the top of her head.

"Mmm…" She pressed a kiss to his chest. "You hungry? Your sister loaded us up with leftovers."

"I'm good." He tucked her head beneath his chin. "The only thing I'm hungry for is you."

Dee giggled and kissed his chest again, her hand planted dangerously low on his belly.

"After we just made up for those two days apart and a lot more?" she teased, sitting up in bed and pulling the sheet up to cover her bare breasts. "I'd think you'd be exhausted by now."

He was. But that hadn't abated his desire for her in the least. He was already partially erect and thinking of positions they had yet to try. "I'll catch up on my sleep once you're gone."

Dee frowned and her shoulders tensed. "I should get ready for bed."

She climbed out of bed, then dipped into the bathroom. When she returned, she was wearing one of his T-shirts emblazoned with The Noble Spur brand, and her hair was neatly secured beneath her bonnet. She nuzzled her face into his shoulder and settled in to go to sleep.

"Dee, have you considered *not* returning to LA?" Could she hear the erratic thumping of his heart as he finally managed to ask the question that'd been brewing in his head since his conversation with Ariana.

The muscles of her back tensed beneath his fingertips, and she didn't speak right away. He knew Dee well enough to know she was measuring her response. Trying not to say the first thing that popped into her head.

"Of course, I've thought about it," Dee said finally. "But we both know that isn't an option, Tripp. My life is there and yours is here."

The aching silence between them lingered, as if time itself had slowed.

"What if you could keep working from here...like you've been doing? And then traveling whenever it's required?" he asked.

"Ari would never go for that." Dee lifted onto one elbow, her gaze searching his in the dim bedroom light filtering through the curtains.

"But what if she would? Would you consider it?" He stroked her cheek.

Dee swallowed hard. The pained expression in her eyes provided her answer before she opened her mouth. "Tripp, what's happened between us has been incredible. We've fallen so hard and so fast that...it scares me."

"Why?" He sat up, too. The question came out sounding too desperate, and he did his best to reel it back, not wanting to pressure her. "I mean… I honestly haven't felt like this about anyone else. I can't imagine not holding you every night. Not making breakfast with you in the morning. And I'm pretty sure Deuce believes he's your horse now instead of mine." He swallowed hard and took her hand in his. "Am I really the only one who feels like this is just the beginning of something special?"

"No," Dee whispered. "I feel that, too. Every day. But what if we're wrong? What if this feels so amazing because it's new? Because other than my screwup the other night, this hasn't really been tested?"

"Then we'll work it out. Just like we did tonight." Tripp squeezed her hand.

"What if we can't? Leaving LA where my family and friends are… Maybe changing my career… It's a big ask, Tripp. It's thrilling, but also terrifying. I want to stay, believe me. But… I can't. I'm sorry." She sniffled.

Tripp winced, his head spinning and his chest aching. "It's okay, baby. I understand."

He pulled Dee into his arms, and she settled against his chest again. He kissed her temple, then propped one arm behind his head as he stared at the ceiling in his darkened room.

He'd made his big ask, and Dee had turned him down. Tripp was disappointed, but he understood her reluctance when she was the only one making a sacrifice.

But he had one more card left to play.

Sixteen

Dee zipped the last of her luggage closed and handed it to Roy Jensen, who had been patiently waiting for her while she stalled in packing the last of her things.

She and Tripp had spent nearly every moment possible together over the past few days. And when they'd gone to dinner at The Royal Diner, The Eatery or The Silver Saddle, they'd held hands and he'd kissed her. And she hadn't cared who'd seen them together.

They'd spent time with Tripp's family and the new friends she'd made in town, and she'd never felt more at ease. Every day it got harder, knowing she'd have to board her plane today.

So she'd been surprised to wake up and discover Tripp gone. He'd yet to return to the ranch, though he'd known she'd be leaving soon. She'd been stalling, hoping he'd come back in time to say goodbye. But maybe avoiding a painful goodbye was best.

Wouldn't she prefer to remember all the wonderful moments they'd shared instead of making her last memory of Tripp her blubbering like a lovelorn fool?

"Ready, Miss Dee?" Roy asked for the fourth or fifth time. "I hate to rush you, but I've got to make a quick stop before we hit the road."

"Of course. Thank you for being so patient, Roy. We'd better go."

"Yes, ma'am." Roy placed his Stetson back on his head and gathered up the last of her luggage.

As she rode in the truck with Roy, Dee was determined not to cry again. She'd shed enough tears, and it hadn't changed anything. She was still leaving Royal, and she was brokenhearted over it. As devastated as she was about walking away from Tripp, it pained her to leave behind the town of Royal that had truly begun to feel like home these past few weeks. And the people whom she'd come to regard as friends and family. But she couldn't help feeling as if she was betraying her own friends and family by thinking that way.

Roy pulled into the parking lot of the Texas Cattleman's Club and parked. "Sorry, ma'am. This won't take long. Promise. We'll still be able to get you to your flight in plenty of time."

"All right." Dee nodded, glancing out of the window as Roy climbed out the other side of the truck. She was stunned when the passenger door opened, and Tripp extended a hand to her. "Tripp, what are you doing here?"

"You didn't think I'd actually let you leave town without saying goodbye, did you?"

Dee forced a smile and shook her head. She gave Tripp her hand and he led her inside.

"You'll have plenty of time to catch that plane," Tripp said. "But I have something to show you."

They walked into the club and entered the space where Ariana and Xavier's reception would be held.

Dee stopped, both of her hands pressed to her mouth as she glanced around. The dimly lit space was decked out in fairy lights and candles.

"It's beautiful, Tripp." Dionna glanced around the room before turning back to him and cradling his stubbled cheek. "This was incredibly sweet of you. Thank you."

He looped his arms around her waist and tugged her closer. "I have a proposition, Dionna Reed... Stay with me."

"What?" She met his gaze. "Tripp, you know I can't—"

"Before you answer, there's someone you should talk to." Tripp pulled out his phone and handed it to her.

"Hello?" Dee's eyes didn't leave Tripp's.

"Hi, sweetie." It was Ariana. "I just need you to know that I appreciate what an amazing friend you are. That you've always been there to look after me. That's why there is nothing more important to me than seeing you happy. And there in Royal, with the man you love, you are the happiest I've ever seen you, Dee. So if you want to return to LA, do it because it's what you want. Not because you're worried about me or the company."

Dionna turned her back to Tripp as tears streaked down her face. "I appreciate what you're doing, but I love my work."

"Good. Because I love working with you. But,

sweetie, we're in the age of technology. You've been working from Royal for the past few weeks and everything here is just fine. Yes, we'd have to rearrange the duties here a bit. Maybe bring on another staff member. But it would be worth it. So make your choice based on what you want, Dee. We'll work everything else out. Now, I think there's someone waiting for an answer from you. Either way, know that you have my full support. Love you."

"Love you, too." Dee ended the call and handed the phone back to Tripp. She wiped tears from her eyes with the back of her fingers. "You really want me to stay, huh?" She laughed nervously.

"I really, *really* do," he said. "And I realize it isn't fair for you to be the only one to make sacrifices in the relationship. So I've made a few arrangements."

"Like?" She studied his handsome face.

"The fee I'm being paid for the film… I'm using it to pay up your apartment lease for the next year. So if you ever decide this isn't what you want…you can always go back home. You already know your job will still be there."

"Tripp, that's very generous. But I can't ask you to do that."

"And you didn't. I need to show you I'm just as invested in this relationship as you are, Dionna." Tripp said. "I obviously can't transport the ranch, but I'd like to be able to travel with you sometimes. So I've given Roy a well-deserved promotion. He'll be taking on more responsibilities at the ranch, so the additional burden doesn't fall on Tess."

"Why are you willing to do all this for me, Tripp?" She leaned in closer, her hands pressed to his chest.

Tripp's eyes shone in the dim club as he wrapped his arms around her. "Because I am madly, deeply in love with you, Dionna Reed. You're beautiful inside and out. You're brilliant and funny, mostly when you're not trying," he chuckled. "You're truly special and you challenge me in all the right ways. With you, every day I feel like I'm becoming a better man. And I don't want to lose that. I don't want to lose you. Say you'll stay. *Please*."

Tears filled Dee's eyes and her heart felt so full it might burst. "I'd like to see you get rid of me now, Austin Charles Noble the third. Because I love you, and there's no place on earth I'd rather be than right here with you."

Tripp hugged her tight, lifting her from her feet momentarily before returning her to the turquoise-colored soles of her cowboy boot–clad feet. Yet, it felt as if she was floating. She honestly couldn't ever remember being happier.

Tripp pressed his lips to hers and kissed her, reminding her of the moments they'd shared and how much she adored him. But when they pulled out of their kiss and opened their eyes, the room was pitch-black, except for the flickering candles on the table.

"What happened?" she asked.

"It's not just the club. Looks like we got ourselves a town-wide blackout." She recognized Roy Jensen's voice. "That means we might run into traffic. So if we're still headed to the airport, I reckon we better head on out."

Tripp looked at Dee and she grinned.

"No, sir. I'm not going anywhere. I plan to stay right here."

"Yes, ma'am." Roy seemed pleased. "Then I'll return

your bags to the ranch and I guess I'll see you two there later." He turned and left.

"I hope you don't take this blackout as a sign of bad luck." Tripp nuzzled her neck, his beard tickling her skin.

"We don't need luck," Dee said. "We have love."

Tripp stared at the gorgeous woman who'd blown in like a tornado across the rolling plains of Texas and had stolen his heart. He kissed her again. "Yes, indeed, we do."

* * * * *

COMING SOON!

We really hope you enjoyed reading this book.
If you're looking for more romance, be sure to
head to the shops when new books are
available on

Thursday 2nd
February

To see which titles are coming soon, please visit

millsandboon.co.uk/nextmonth

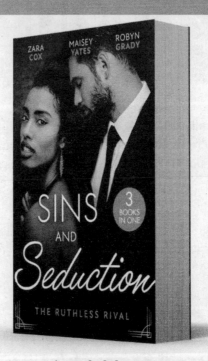

MILLS & BOON

THE HEART OF ROMANCE

A ROMANCE FOR EVERY READER

MODERN

Prepare to be swept off your feet by sophisticated, sexy and seductive heroes, in some of the world's most glamourous and romanti locations, where power and passion collide.

HISTORICAL

Escape with historical heroes from time gone by. Whether your passion for wicked Regency Rakes, muscled Vikings or rugged Highlanders, aw the romance of the past.

MEDICAL

Set your pulse racing with dedicated, delectable doctors in the high-pre sure world of medicine, where emotions run high and passion, comfort love are the best medicine.

True Love

Celebrate true love with tender stories of heartfelt romance, from the rush of falling in love to the joy a new baby can bring, and a focus on t emotional heart of a relationship.

Desire

Indulge in secrets and scandal, intense drama and plenty of sizzling hot action with powerful and passionate heroes who have it all: wealth, stat good looks…everything but the right woman.

HEROES

Experience all the excitement of a gripping thriller, with an intense ro mance at its heart. Resourceful, true-to-life women and strong, fearless face danger and desire - a killer combination!

To see which titles are coming soon, please visit

millsandboon.co.uk/nextmonth

LET'S TALK

Romance

For exclusive extracts, competitions
and special offers, find us online: